CW00552004

SEMIOTEXT(E) NATIVE AGENTS SERIES

Originally published as Guillaume Dustan *Oeuvres 1*, © P.O.L, 2013.
Dans ma chambre © Editions P.O.L, 1996
Je sors ce soir © Editions P.O.L, 1997
Plus fort que moi © Editions P.O.L, 1998

This book © 2021 Semiotext(e)
Published by Semiotext(e)
PO BOX 629, South Pasadena, CA 91031
www.semiotexte.com

Special thanks to: Hedi El Kholti, Christine Pichini, Noura Wedell, Brad Rumph, Bruce Hainley and Juliana Halpert.

Cover: Louis Monier: Guillaume Dustan, Paris, March 20, 2000.
Design: Hedi El Kholti

ISBN: 978-1-63590-142-9
Distributed by The MIT Press, Cambridge, Mass. and London, England
Printed in the United States of America

The Works of
GUILLAUME DUSTAN

Volume 1

NOVELS

In My Room
I'm Going Out Tonight
Stronger Than Me

Edited by **Thomas Clerc**
Translated by **Daniel Maroun**

semiotext(e)

CONTENTS

Introduction by Thomas Clerc   9

In My Room   33
Introduction by Thomas Clerc   35

I'm Going Out Tonight   149
Introduction by Thomas Clerc   151

Stronger Than Me   247
Introduction by Thomas Clerc   249

Notes   377

"I'll never get old"
— Guillaume Dustan, *I'm Going Out Tonight*

Introduction by Thomas Clerc

The short life of Guillaume Dustan (1965–2005) did not stop him from leaving his mark on contemporary French literature. That said, his collection of works remains rather unknown because of misunderstandings that surround each work, and in particular these days, a devaluation in reading the actual text versus its reputation or what we might have heard about it. Andy Warhol, whom Dustan wildly admired (and who was the subject of one of his novels), had, as we know, coined the perhaps excessively mimetic phrase, "In the future, everyone will be world-famous for 15 minutes," which meant, of course, eternal anonymity. It is my sincere hope that Guillaume Dustan's works will betray his master's voice.

The scandalous reputation that surrounded Dustan, which he himself constructed rather recklessly, concealed the essence of his work, either by assigning him the label of pure provocateur, or drowning him in a media maelstrom that, as he admitted, he liked participating in. But if the name Guillaume Dustan deserves to live on within the larger collective memory of French literature at a major turning point in the twentieth century, it is because the strength and richness of his works do not allow themselves to be defined either by his sadly short life or by their apparent concession to the themes of his time.

Militant homosexual, self-proclaimed hedonist, fervent supporter of drug use, champion of nightlife, political pornographer, fanatic autobiographer, free-spirited continuator of the May '68 spirit, and supporter of a social project infinitely more ambitious than the Green Party program, Guillaume Dustan, dead at thirty-nine, was one of the very rare bearers of utopia in the very controlled world of turn-of-the-century French literature overcome, like the rest of society, by a wave of nihilism, melancholic cynicism, and ridicule linked to what can only be called a negative version of postmodernism. Seen from this angle, Dustan was a notable exception whose philosophical vitalism was curiously even more snubbed by critics in that he proposed an alternative path to the collective depression. If it is true that he deserves to be studied as the exception of this time period, it is because he did not highlight the sad atmosphere of nihilism: his way of blending the rawest form of self writing with a radical, political undertaking obliterated the prejudice which held that autobiography, formerly criticized by Marxist theory, was a narcissistic, petty-bourgeois genre disconnected from the world. For somewhat superficial reasons, self writing was denigrated due to its self-centeredness. This completely missed the stakes of its generalized use from the '70s onward, which many considered a reactionary regression that refused societal transformation. If self writing as a genre, improperly renamed "autofiction," is the sign of a withdrawal into the self, then how is it that all of the writers who practiced the form were, without exception, at the heart of violent polemics?[1]

Reading Dustan's texts requires that we interpret them in a way that is completely opposed to such accusations of narcissism, but such an interpretation demands that readers change their esthetic and ideological criteria in order to appreciate their impact. They are thus contemporary literature, in the Modernist sense of the term, largely renewing ideas and concepts, and disrupting literary expectations in at least two ways: first, by refusing the separation between the self and the world for which critics admonish the genre (as if fiction was liberating in and of itself, and as if writing about oneself was an apolitical act), and secondly, by proposing another way to think about life, one that is totally foreign to the French tradition dominated by humanist intellectualism, with its narrative rules unique to a structured world that maintains its ivory tower with suicidal constancy.

For Dustan, literature, like politics, took shape through the body as much as through lifestyle: blending an American, or more specifically a Californian approach with the politics of a Nietzschean view on existence, his works could not but be misunderstood by a literary world that had little experience thinking outside of strict separations between forms and ideas, *a fortiori* when they were expressed disrespectfully. The disapproval of autobiography was all the more pronounced because the genre had become political in the truest sense of the term by associating intimacy with a strong critique of the established order.

Arguing that Dustan is a new type of intellectual is risky: current French ideology reserves such a title for fancy philosophers. But Dustan wasn't just anybody, as his *curriculum vitae* shows (and which he would transform into a true literary genre in *The Divine Genius*): laureate of the Concours Général, awarded a degree in political science, graduate of the National School of Administration, tribunal judge, and, *last but not least*, essayist and writer. Dustan received a liberal bourgeois education, one largely capable of helping someone decide to be a rebel against the established order. Of course, his first three books are void of intellectual references—there are almost no philosophical names but instead music bands and well-known underground figures. But how could one not notice this was on purpose, not cunning as much as a program? Dustan wanted to highlight what was mistrusted by Western logocentric culture. Like a night-club DJ, Dustan became one of the apostles of Western hedonism even if it meant destroying the essential fact, something David Vrydaghs noted in an article on the author: "No one ever said that Dustan was an intellectual."[2] May this collected works repair this boorish error due to French intellectual snobbery (that is, unless it's more a matter of their unsophisticated narrow-mindedness).

The third issue that interfered with Dustan's reception as a writer was that he belonged to the homosexual world. The strategy of French literary circles was to reduce him to an internal troublemaker in that restricted field, as if homosexuals could only be interested in gay problems. The entire history of ideas demonstrates the contrary: if there is any social progress, it's due to marginal groups. Progress is made indirectly from the moment their struggles concern society as a whole. But these groups must fight for a cause that extends beyond themselves, and one that, instead of being reduced to an issue unique to their class, is beneficial to the community. Dustan's literary activism was entirely motivated by this belief. His biggest success was being able to produce a universal literature from an ultra-minority position within an already marginal group. His action confirmed Pierre Bourdieu's position on the importance of "rendering universal the benefits of the particular," but at the cost of a very particular place within the gay community.[3]

Entering the Scene

William Baranès died Monday, October 3rd, 2005, of a pulmonary embolism. Known as Guillaume Dustan, he had made his entrance onto the literary scene in 1996 with *In My Room*, the first of eight novels he would publish in eight years, an oeuvre to which one must also add the enormous amount of unpublished work whose publication will comprise the third and final volume of his *Complete Works*. Written in small bursts, likely unequal in both quantity and quality but still exemplifying a strong energy and emotional investment that was not only linked to his youth but also linked to the urgency of his fight against death and the need to speak out, Guillaume Dustan's surprising stylistic diversity speaks in his favor. His first three novels reveal a neo-clinical writing style molded by a constant tenderness piercing the raw and cruel vacuity of his sex scenes. His second era is full of political and lustful outbursts, an autobiographical writing style that freely accepts its zany creativity. His third and final epoch, that some might call an ebb, takes up a sort of classicism specific to the moralist tradition whose presence one could barely foresee in his first novels. Although his works are imperfect according to an aesthetics of measure, they are unquestionably alive. These three phases of writing were not at all formal "exercises in style" destined to satisfy the author's skill or the reader's sophistication. Dustan had always been an anti-formalist, vilifying an inherited literature of modernist principles on auto-referentiality. He was, on the other hand, a true experimenter with form, which, in and of itself, should define him as a writer. All of Dustan's works are therefore the condensed fruit of a rapid evolution, remarkable for their aesthetic dimension.

This first volume is made up of his first three novels published by P.O.L.: *In my Room, I'm Going Out Tonight,* and *Stronger Than Me.* The stylistic coherence is clear and easily inferred from simple titles that immediately establish their mark. In this trilogy, which could be considered "explicit" akin to song lyrics or film, the world of homosexual sex and of illicit nightlife pleasures is exhibited without any warnings. Far from being anecdotal, this collection inscribes itself in a true literary tradition at the same time as it asks fundamental questions of contemporary subjectivity. Yet the critical reception of Dustan's works did not meet his own ambitions. Rejected by critics, ignored by universities, Dustan's reception occurred essentially through the media.[4] Likewise, the relative silence in which queer studies holds him to this day, more interested as it is in endless questions of gender and strategic battles for representation, can be explained in at least two ways. First, by the esthetic superiority of his novels over those of his predecessors or contemporaries. Second, more objectively, by the fact that Dustan came a little before the explosion of the French reception of queer theory, which he would incidentally comment upon later, favorably, in his last novels. But in 1996, Dustan was first and foremost a man who was looking for salvation in writing, a young author concerned about blasting apart traditional narrative frameworks and representations of homosexual life.

Questions of Sex

The fundamental question of (homo)sexual identity rests at the heart of Dustan's work—it holds together the entire first trilogy and nourishes the second. It was logical that he started by writing that which most preoccupied him. The controversial and disturbing characteristics of his first novels are due to this tacit point, which Dustan would only abandon partially and progressively, that homosexuality is a specific identity. This proclamation may indeed bring a smile, but without it, we might not be able to understand Dustan. Before it founds a culture (which Dustan will show in his political trilogy), this identity is of a sexual nature. This is where all the misunderstandings begin.

My hypothesis is as follows: if it's true that Dustan was hardly or poorly received, it is first because he reaffirms homosexuality as an identity, something which queer studies, inspired by Deleuzian and Foucauldian thought, tried so hard to deconstruct after the start of the twenty-first century. In other words, theorists of queer studies believed that Dustan had remained tied to topics that they wrongly deemed outdated. Refuting the terms "homosexual" and "heterosexual" has become an obsessive line of argument for disciples of Foucault, who incessantly repeat that these are recent historical constructions (the word "homosexual" dates back to 1869) belonging to a medical discourse whose aim was to monitor homosexuals in order to better punish them. Without going too far into a discussion that is beyond the scope of this preface, it is important to note that a term doesn't get discredited by the context of its production. There's an insistence on the sexual nature of identity within the term "homosexual" that isn't necessarily the sign of an essentialist recruitment and doesn't betray medical or psychiatric connotations. In other words, the word also contains a vitalist affirmation of sexual identity which is exactly what is at play in Dustan's first works. During an interview with Michel Foucault, the director

Werner Schroeter admitted to Foucault, "If there's one thing that I've never suffered from in my life, it's my homosexuality."[5] This is the image of Dustan that we'd like to transmit, rather than enter into a systematic logic of distrust of identities because they would be too restricting.

Of course, there is definitely something exclusionary in the notion of identity especially for those who don't belong to said group. This is the constant argument made by humanists, for whom identities risk privileging communitarianism, a threat to collectivity as a whole, because it valorizes the notion of identity, which generates dissent at the heart of collective life. Yet despite the fact that this false universalist argument was critiqued less abstractly by modern deconstructionists (Derrida, Barthes, Lacan, Foucault) and by scholars of gay and lesbian studies to whom our author is undoubtedly indebted, for Dustan, the sexual dimension of homosexuality is something that must be valorized and represented. It would be cutting corners to deliver a sophisticated reflection about post-identity while refuting the necessity of a precise exposure of physical pleasures. Deconstructing identity presupposes that we have one: it was impossible for Dustan to even attempt this when the world then, and now, is still constructed upon an undeniable homophobia.[6]

In other words, Dustan is "gay" but he is also, first and foremost, a "fag." For indeed, considering homosexuality outside the framework of sex, as a pure abstraction, removes its truly subversive side. That few heterosexuals enjoy reading Dustan and are understandably reluctant to do so because of the representation of gay sexuality, and that Roland Barthes didn't like Surrealism because of its homophobic and gynophilic elements, is proof that exposing the body necessarily poses the problem of reader address. The major risk of desexualizing homosexuality is to open it up to being considered complete folklore, something perfectly tolerated by a liberal society. For Dustan, sexual representation, especially the *hardcore* kind, shares a bond with the work of Sade and Bataille not for the underlying system they share, but because of the liberating potential of the rawness of their depiction. It's blunt, therefore it's true it could be said of all successful autobiography. Although Dustan wasn't censored, he ran the risk of being censored by taste, which is equally dangerous. As he often did, he summarized the problem of defining oneself in definitive terms: "I liked *fag* better. *Gay* was a bit too clean, too Gringo. It wasn't hard enough. When *queer* came on the scene, I really started getting pissed. It took ten years to build an identity, and then I had to change everything."[7]

Condemning the identity-based dimension of sexuality is one of the reflexes of contemporary orthodoxy, shared and constructed by the majority of the literary and theoretical scene. It's not that we believe Dustan was an essentialist, but rather that, in order to construct his own identity, he had to pass through a phase of affirmation, strategic essentialism of sexual differences if you will. Before deconstructing sexual identity, one must first construct oneself. That is to say, accept oneself fully. To do this, he had to find a form of expression for this identity and to leave behind former literary models. In other words, move from a question about sex to a question about gender/genre.[8]

Questions about Gender/Genre

It just so happens that both are intimately linked. Dustan's system of sexuality as principle could not find a better expression than in autobiography because that is in essence the literary genre in which questions of identity can play out. However, by tying a scandalous image of homosexuality to a polemical understanding of writing the self, Dustan faced both literary and theoretical obstacles.

The usage of the term "novel" regarding the first three works is, in fact, problematic. Only editorial norms could justify its use, norms which come into play all the more strongly for a first book published by an unknown writer under a pseudonym.[9] For *In My Room* is not a novel; neither are the others works. Unless one considers the "novel" not as a specific literary genre but rather as something that has become a synonym for "literature," the result of an historical evolution that led to the dismantling of literary genres, Guillaume Dustan's works are fundamentally anti-novelistic. This is one of the things that makes him "modern" and carves a place out for him in the larger continuum of French literature of the 1990s and 2000s, a time known for self writing. He touches upon this later in *The Divine Genius* when he writes, "The novelist is inherently reactionary (as opposed to the auto(hagio)biographer, who is always looking to get better)." It can't get much clearer than that. Dustan belongs to a long line of anti-fictionists in French literature, the avant-garde.[10]

As nitpicky as some may find it, the debate around genre is crucial to grasping what Guillaume Dustan brought to the literary world of his time as well to understanding the necessity for truth that was at the center of his project: describing his life as directly as possible, practically *live*. This was the only way for him to ward off death, with which he had begun to cross swords since he discovered his seropositivity, and which he had indirectly started in his first work. Of course, he was not the first to use literature in this cathartic manner; the entirety of Dustan's works is part of a larger corpus of AIDS literature that belongs to a specific historical moment, and is close to first-person documentary. But whereas fiction protects its author by means of a narrator dissociated from its author's own experience, autobiography renders its subject vulnerable to all sorts of risks, something whose theorization goes back to the 1930s in the preface of Michel Leiris's *Manhood*. But the choice of autobiography was, above all things, the sign of a strong acknowledgment of the esthetic stakes of Dustan's era, characterized by a "post-Freudian, post-May '68 context of linguistic emancipation and freedom of mores."[11] Understanding Dustan from the sole angle of his writing narratives of illness would therefore be reductive, if not a complete misrepresentation. For what came out of his work, which can neither be summed up as characteristic of the novel nor of the literature of testimony, was an extraordinary vitality held up by a unique writing style and a totalizing project that became clearer after his fourth book, *Nicolas Pages*. Dustan was undoubtedly the heir of a French autobiographical tradition, but he renewed it through direct exposure.

Dustan Face to Face with Gay Literature

Dustan found the appropriate literary form for such direct exposure: it's what makes him unavoidable for those who want to study this moment in literature, largely because Dustan killed bad *gay* literature—the kind that had never found the proper means of representation. Of course, there are interesting texts from this time, but they are few and far between, examples such as *Cargo Vie* by Pascal de Duve, or *Corps à corps* by Alain-Emmanuel Dreuilhe, which Dustan mentioned.[12] But these texts fell under a sort of pathetic isolation that was foreign to the birth of a true *gay* context of which Dustan was one of the main actors, whether his naysayers like it or not. Incapable of escaping the *deploratio* associated with AIDS, these accounts were, in the best of circumstances, a sort of psychological self-analysis, for example the emotional *This Wild Darkness: The Story of My Death* by Harold Brodkey, or the more debatable *Savage Nights* by Cyril Collard, a realist novel full of complacency.[13] Dustan's literary angle, which was both direct and phenomenological, changed everything. In contrast to this, we can measure the obsolescence of Gilles Barbedette who continued to believe in the infinite potential of fiction, which of course has its own value,[14] but remained an old way of writing about a new phenomenon. Thus, the literature of the mid-'90s found itself revived by a young unknown whose story has not been including in any overarching study of this time.[15]

There is often a delay between literature and theory: whereas the proclamation of homosexual identity appeared a given for North American critics and their French counterparts, there was no literary representation in 1996 that painted a strong picture of it. Besides a few aficionados, who really had read Renaud Camus, one of Dustan's inspirations, before the scandal that gained him popularity and discredit at the same time?[16] Only Hervé Guibert had attained mainstream popularity, but for our author, his vision of homosexuality remained imperfect as it called for a certain form of compassion indexed on AIDS and showcased a predilection for betrayal of which we have hardly seen a satisfying reading thus far. Guibert presented a vision of homosexuality that was in all likelihood not homosexual enough and certainly not "*gay*," (by which I mean subversive and political) which explains his notoriety. Or, in other words, according to Philippe Mangeot as quoted in Frédéric Martel's history of homosexuality, "I joined Act Up to fight against Hervé Guibert."[17] Dustan would go on to radicalize the author of *To the Friend Who Didn't Save My Life* by politicizing him; he became his successor but with an infinitely more explosive style. Whereas Guibert would associate a form of writing whose quality was based on its classicism to an acceptable image of homosexuality, in particular regarding AIDS presented as an unjust tragedy, Dustan's reception was problematic. Adopting an esthetic closer to Dennis Cooper or Bret Easton Ellis's, authors who were not widely accepted in France, Dustan was downgraded as a writer. He was seen first of all as a provocateur (of course he was guilty of contributing to this persona in his media appearances), but, and this is one of the reasons for this collected works—it's impossible to mask the literary quality of his writing or the motives of a struggle that extended beyond himself. The radical nature of Dustan's style, inherited from a literary and political history, made all the difference between him and others.

A Liberating Endeavor

For Dustan, the idea that homosexuality was well-accepted was intolerable. He therefore refused a discrete conception of it. He first had to represent his condition as he was living it, an unembellished sexual celebration, both joyful and grim but through which Dustan constituted himself as a subject. This first trilogy is the story of a liberation from the heterosexual, puritan, and normative world from which Dustan had already broken as a man, but not yet as a writer, and makes us witness to his birth. The most important characteristic of his work is this form of simplicity or brutalism that puts expenditure at the forefront. It was an almost Bataille-like position where the worshipping of pleasure was mixed with a sort of confidence in his own destiny that was the other side of an identity threatened but also constituted by AIDS. Although Dustan didn't shrug off the question of his illness (the word "AIDS" is nonetheless quite rare in the first three texts), it was diverted into a paradoxical power of life. As thorny as it might appear, the fact of knowing he was ill drove Dustan towards a literary birth, the urgency to write having been freed by the threat of death.[18]

By not tying the question of homosexuality to AIDS but rather to sex, which was the opposite of what his great predecessor Hervé Guibert had done, Dustan occupied an ambiguous position regarding the communitarian-like *doxa* according to which homosexuality couldn't be dissociated from AIDS and responsibility would be the watchword. It was the very representation of homosexuality that was at stake with Dustan's vitalism in entering literature in such an intensely subjective manner. Such intensity was able to open his work to a readership for whom it hadn't been destined. But for all that, this hedonistic vision was in no way a denial of the actual reality of AIDS in the years 1996–2000, a time marked by a strong resurgence of the disease. However, and this was *the* deciding factor, one could not enter literature through the sole question of sufferance, guilt, and death. Although this was of course present in his work to the point of functioning as a kind of negative, Dustan refused to reduce homosexuality to this *ethos*, and therefore put up a smokescreen. In opposition to the arguments that look to minimize the homosexual act to the benefit of homosexual culture, Dustan, from the very start, incarnated an ambivalent position within the homosexual world, revealing niche internal quarrels that he would exacerbate through certain positionings that eventually exiled him from his own community.[19]

Dustan was a troublemaker working to undo certainties. Even though he acted in some ways to further ideas inspired by Foucault in terms of *gay* culture, in no way can can they be compared on the double question of literature and sexuality. This contradictory situation regarding intellectual expectations is without a doubt the most fascinating aspect of what Guillaume Dustan brings to literature.

Foucault or Not Foucault?

Dustan's position concerning the choice of autobiography is clear, since it relies on a necessity which is the criteria for its literary value. What is not clear is its intellectual expectations. Let us try to untangle this delicate situation. Through a brilliant paradox, in his *History of Sexuality* Michel Foucault showed that with the paradigm shift that occurred with modernity, far from being repressed by Western society, sex had become the center of its discourse: "Man has become a confessing animal."[20] Foucault suggested abandoning what he called a repressive hypothesis that consisted of thinking of sex as the object of a major taboo, in favor of considering it a verbal incitement. "An imperative was established: Not only will you confess to acts contravening the law, but you will seek to transform your desire, your every desire, into discourse."[21] The birth of the autobiographical genre, dating from the end of the eighteenth century, stems from the will to knowledge.

But if self-expression replaced a literature of imagination, we can sense that Foucault perceived this as a threat. This point has rarely been discussed even though it is of paramount importance.[22] Indeed, writing the self can only be understood from a Foucauldian perspective as a trap destined to lead the producer of such a discourse to link sex and truth, and therefore, to fall victim to a subjection that is favorable to power all the while giving the subject the illusion of existence. According to Foucault, far from telling us to suppress sex, the modern Western world enjoins us to talk about it—a subtle way that power has found to control sex through the production of inexhaustible and sophisticated discourses such as law, psychoanalysis, or medicine. Literature couldn't escape this movement of interiorization that stemmed from Christian notions of confession, influencing autobiographical production in a judicial manner: "Evil had to be confessed in the first person."[23] However, the entirety of Foucault's conception stemmed from a mistrust regarding the idea that subjects could liberate themselves by narrating their sexuality, the reason for which the author of *The Order of Things* would continue to valorize other, impersonal forms of literature. Very suspicious of the notion of the subject, the early Foucault was marked by a structuralist heritage. Profoundly influenced by Maurice Blanchot, for whom "I" was always "he," in the first half of his career Foucault chose authors who were considered marginal, such as Hölderlin or Raymond Roussel, because he was interested in the entwined nature of literature and madness. He would later evolve, accepting examples of self writing as long as they were anonymous or authors who were considered to be outside of the literary establishment.[24] He would become increasingly disinterested in literature the more he studied power.

Self Writing, Sex Writing

With the sexualist motif that was passionately his own, Dustan ran up against the Foucaldian *doxa* according to which the overly simplistic repressive hypothesis would be better forgotten. Indeed, Dustan never stopped reaffirming what he felt to be the intrinsically repressive dimension of modern Western society: the repression of the body, of sex, and of homosexuality. Dustan's political struggle was to contest repression in action; his literary struggle was to disintegrate its justification. From the point of view of society, suppression is inevitable (Freud proved it), but Dustan, an engaged writer, looked to limit its effects at the risk of a clear naivety (as his adversaries would say), but also more tragically at the risk of his own life. Of course, Foucault did not say that repression didn't exist in society, but that the dialogue surrounding sex was itself the actual political tool of subjectivation, a term to be understood in two contradictory ways, as the production of subjects and their domination. In this respect, Dustanian literature threw off the Foucaldian paradigm. For Dustan not only believed in the possibility of beating back repression (maybe this was one of his deep motivations for writing) but also that autobiography was the best literary way to do this—another point of difference from Foucault, according to whom self writing was doubly problematic.

Firstly because of its confessional mechanism. For Foucault, confession was an ensnaring genre because it repeated the coercion that subjects thought they were escaping. The discursive framework would contradict the eventual affirmation of homosexual subjects, as if, by designating themselves as such, they gave society a public guarantee of their identity and eventually, of their domestication. The exteriorization of interiority that defines autobiography would therefore be the procedure by which power pretended to liberate the subject from the very situation it had itself constituted. Secondly, modernist thought had completely discredited the triple alliance of Truth-Subject-Author that the autobiographical genre presupposed. However, one can't understand the 1980s without acknowledging that this triple prohibition had had its day. Although Dustan was an heir of the 1960s in terms of counterculture (and affirmed the heritage of May '68), it is impossible to connect him to structuralist modernism and/or Marxism which considered that they had eliminated the genre of self writing as pure illusion, a petty-bourgeois myth, or a reactionary counter-movement. For a man born in 1965, anti-subjectivist principles had become such injunctions that their favorite zealots, Barthes or Foucault, would go on to question them during the second part of their lives by initiating a paradoxical "return of the subject."[25] Dustan, like Guibert, was influenced by Barthes and Foucault, but contrary to their disciples, he understood that the best way to transmit their principles was to betray them: the direct exposure of the autobiography incarnated this betrayal.

The literary and cultural context that surrounded our young author would make this double grievance obsolete. For Dustan, like many in my generation, the structuralist framework hadn't been operational for some time and self writing as a genre would be the historical literary form to bury it. The success of self writing was, among other things, an internal reaction to a literary field governed by the outdated tyranny of the hypothetical "death of the author." This theoretical reversal occurred in the 1980s. The thesis of the ensnaring nature of autobiography obliterated the specificity of literary discourse and silenced the decisive consequence of auto-biography; the power of autobiography is measured in light of its capacity to produce a self, to create a self-image that is allergic to Power. Through its desire for freedom and its effects on the reader, it draws its esthetic and political strength from its own constraints. Perhaps all autobiographical texts moved by this necessity to speak are destined to fail, but where, in literature, do we situate failure?

Literature or Philosophy

The question of whether autobiography is fiction, a lie, or a dis-cursive trap is perhaps acceptable on a theoretical level, but literature is superior to philosophy because the practice of writing questions the certainties of thinkers who, as we have seen, themselves shifted their views on the issue.[26] In other words, as long as it hasn't been experienced, self writing seems to be a naïve theory, a conceptual trap whose limits structuralism assumed it had shown. From the very moment one seriously engages in it (and it's clear that writing was far from a simple game for Dustan) things change completely. Reason being that the effect produced on the reader, if writers were truly engaged in their practice, shattered the intellectual constructions of critical thinkers whom Dustan admired like any good child of the 1960s but who had provoked reservations among Dustan's generation because of their pronounced intellectualism.

One of the numerous reasons neo-modernists misunderstood (or ignored) Dustan was his passion for transparency, which they found suspicious because it supposed that the subject was too much in agreement with itself. This direct expression of the self seemed to have been condemned by the philosophical tradition of deconstruction. But what is true for philosophy isn't always true for literature: "truth" in literature is impossible because of its intrinsic subjectivity which, by means of a crafty flick of the switch, makes it necessary and touching in the second degree. The unconscious of Philosophy is Rhetoric; the unconscious of Literature is Truth. This truth effect gives Dustanian discourse its unique, distinct tone by throwing us into the center of a world he knew so well, but also because of the authentic expression of the one who guides us through it. To condemn Dustan in the name of anti-auto-biographical ideology is to purposefully skip over the reasons behind this discourse, its context, and the means by which Dustan enacted them in his work. A philosophical approach to literary texts often collides with the same theoretical obstacles because it immediately invalidates the idea of speaking about oneself and considers it an illusion, even more so if the notions of truth and sex are intertwined.

Reclaiming one's homosexuality might very well be considered "outdated," according to the analyses that consider homosexual and heterosexual identities to be discursive creations that are more cumbersome than liberating, however, at the individual level, that is to say at the literary level, for Dustan, a young, thirty-year-old writer, there was no other option than his liberating autoscopic experience. Today, we know that queer theory seeks to create unattributable identities— gender identities more so than sexual ones. But when Dustan arrived on the literary scene during the 1990s, these sophisticated nuances were largely unknown. But mostly, they don't stand up against Dustan's creative urgency. It was unthinkable that Dustan not pledge allegiance to both identity and truth—even if it meant criticizing and outgrowing them later.

It was therefore because Dustan experienced the stigmatization of homosexuality in his flesh that he had no choice but to express it in an outrageous manner. Seeing in his (homo)sexual preference the key to his ego, he felt the need to produce an offensive discourse against a society he considered to be normative. Faced with this salutary self-affirmation, speculations about the legitimacy of Foucault's repressive hypothesis do not seem to hold much weight, to say the least. The history of modern homosexuality is one of repression/liberation; autobiography was understood as the "art for those who aren't artists."[27] Today, it is easy to use the normalization of homosexuality (and of "autofiction") to put Dustan aside. One of the most astounding recorders of his time, he was also ahead of it. He was "modern" in the Baudelairian sense, a man who did not scorn fashion or the ephemeral since they expressed the truth of a period. Dustan was always searching for ways to go beyond it through the perpetual questioning of the self.

Yes to Power and Sex[28]

The crystal-like dimension of his work united two indissociable necessities: to expose a nonconsensual image of homosexuality and to invent a form of writing that would be its most direct expression. Exposing sex, which should not be interpreted as a way of surveilling the body but as an affirmation of its supremacy, was the first step of a political esthetic. Generally speaking, through the potential inherent in desire, but this theme, already rehashed by straight people, wouldn't hold without its homosexual component. Dustan described homosexual sexuality as immediately accessible, a well-known *topos* that no one had ever so ferociously shown. There is clearly something fascinating about direct access to pleasure that justifies either an empathetic reading or one of rejection. Dustan was a sexual anarchist: by putting forth this image of masculine homosexuality, he exposed himself to contrasting reactions. On one hand, the fairly widespread moralizing approach condemning the orgiastic dimension of his works understood through the psychoanalytic lens of drive theory ultimately leading to death. On the other, the concern about the social effect of such a depiction. In 1981, Foucault had already curiously claimed that "one of the concessions one makes to others is not to present homosexuality as anything but a kind of immediate pleasure."[29] According to Foucault, who had already turned his back on Sade and rejected the notion of desire,[30] this comes down to creating a "tidy image [of homosexuality] that lost all its potential worrisome parts."[31] Yet Dustan's first trilogy was the opposite of both of these critiques. Not only did he maintain the subversion that was specific to sexuality, but he also showed that the liberal sexual regime existed in direct opposition to the puritan and family-oriented social structures that were at the heart of what he would call, after Monique Wittig, "the political system of heterosexuality."[32] Negative reactions against Dustan were just as frequent from heterosexuals, who considered his debauchery alienating and felt that it negated the other, as they were from homosexuals, flabbergasted at the caricature that Dustan drew of their milieu. For them, Dustan favored homophobia by depicting the homosexual world as "decadent."

We believe that Dustan's work is neither decadent (that is a reactionary *topos*) nor tidy (this goes without saying). On the contrary, it belongs to an anti-illusionist esthetic tradition passed down from Rousseau as well as to a libertine-utopian tradition that is more linked to Herbert Marcuse and Wilhelm Reich than to Foucault and is contemporary with the rise of a global youth culture. This is why the puritan hypothesis seems much more solid, in its constancy, than its repression or negation. Dustan's sexual expenditure reveals an initial condemnation of both sexuality and homosexuality. He would be very clear about this later as his work became more discursive, blaming his education and especially the authoritative role of the father in society. But here, we would risk going too far if we considered the paternal dogma as no longer functional in society. On the contrary, the law of the father gave shape to Dustan's sensitivity and to the extremely violent revolt of *I Accuse the Law*, the great unpublished work that became *LXiR*.

We cannot truly understand Dustan's attempt to destroy puritanism if we do not refer it back to Foucault's own denial of it.[33] We truly miss the point of Dustan's literary project if we do not see the emergence of a new conservatism that coincided with the moment he began to write, that of a "reactionary Left" which had renounced the principles of May '68, and had adopted a "moral" position which shifted it to the right.[34] Contesting French neo-puritanism could only occur violently given the degree of repression Dustan attributed to it. Obviously, a reader who is unconvinced by the idea of a regressive Left will judge Dustan's work as useless provocations, the very product of what it builds on. But in this case, we would need to toss out all contemporary literature and its desire for exhibitionism, from Christine Angot to Virginie Despentes, from Catherine Millet to Annie Ernaux. Instead of this sacrificial solution, we prefer to think that exhibiting sex in this way, rather than a trend, corresponds to the need of a specific historical period that was encapsulated quite well by De Certeau's phrase "capture of speech."[35] Dustanian self writing blends both de Certeau's speech capture and bodily exhibition with a crafted immediacy that is accessible to all. This form of writing would be presented explicitly in his next trilogy. As for pornography (used here in the neutral sense of the word), expressed via autobiography rather than fiction as it was in his earlier books (a game changer), it does not offer a refined erotism destined to titillate the reader but rather a model of protest which involves the subject itself. Dustan's work is thus inseparable from the exploding intellectual fields of gay and lesbian studies but also porn studies[36] and cultural studies, in short, from intellectual innovation that he helped bring to France.

Another Culture

If the first survival action put into play by Dustan was to fanatically proclaim his identity, running the risk of finding himself labelled a "ghetto writer" and marginalized by his own excess, the richness of his position nonetheless resides in its ambivalence. For indeed, the sexualist side of his identity was coupled with a cultural one. Foucault's philosophy becomes useful once again to explain the creative side of Dustan's work, a progressive call to overcome the notion of sex. As we will see, the second collection of Dustan's works would update this position, which is more cultural than identity-based. Furthermore, one cannot but be struck in these first three books by the intensities that guarantee Dustan's status beyond that of the scandalous homosexual. By linking his awareness of his own difference to the pleasures of a moment, he succeeded in creating both a political and cultural dimension that went beyond measly entertainment.

Indeed, music in its popular forms (techno, house, disco, trance), drugs, sex, dancing, bodybuilding or sadomasochism weren't just simple themes for him. They were primarily ways of expanding his own being and that he shared with an ever-growing community that was not exclusively homosexual, and that eventually became global. The "I" quickly becomes a "we," proof that the singular and the plural are not as distant as we might believe. For Dustan, such openly accepted and glorified practices seemed the most efficient way to contest the puritanical order he wanted to topple and which he believed had planted its roots during the 1980s in France. Dustan was the only French author to have viewed hedonistic practices as a way to promote a new, entirely democratic world founded on pleasure, open to all, and practiced by a global youth in which he saw a non-violent avant-garde. This was where the shift in meaning from sexual identity to gay culture occurred; indeed, the latter probably derives from the former but is not restricted to it. We can thus better understand how Dustan placed himself in the wake of liberal and anarchist principle of pleasure. His strength was not only the fact that he described and conceptualized it (thus making him both an artist *and* a critic), but moreover, that he did it in a way that appeared the most universal to him, in a pop-culture-style autobiography.[37]

All of the elements of the Dustanian counterculture were weapons in his battle against the old order (which repressed them) but were also tools to build a freer world. Obviously opposed to the right-wing conservatism that was entrenched in France, Dustan had no illusions about the traditional Left, which he would critique more and more aggressively, feeling that it had betrayed the principles of liberty that had enabled its rise to power in 1981. What was interesting in the new culture extolled by Dustan was that it got rid of the Left/Right paradigm, replacing it with the paradigm of progressive vs. conservative that was essentially linked to sociocultural issues. Dustan refused the distinction between legitimate and illegitimate cultures, which he believed characterized the elitism that he felt was so harmful in supposedly democratic societies. Dustan's sexual self-assertion was also a sort of allegory of mass culture. His accessible yet scandalous work was a program meant for the educated middle-class against which Dustan had spoken quite harshly, especially when it claimed to be socialist. Thus, it was the enormous question of literary postmodernism and of political liberalism that was posed by an author who was not simply "attentive" to the demands of a generation that no longer recognized itself in established representations but by a young man who belonged to it. There will be traces of this question in the prefaces to each of the novels in this collection, and it will be developed more fully in the next collected works.

There is an evolution in Dustan's literary orbit, a rushed evolution that draws its beauty from that very precipitateness and includes within its ten-year span the recent history of the homosexual movement with its greatest contradictions. Dustan's prized anarchy takes on two forms: the Dionysian glory of the endangered body, and the creation of a redeeming figure of an anti-intellectual intellectual. Only a starkly rational or moralizing approach can ignore the subversive aspect of this unsettling and questionable yet highly exhilarating work. Reducing Dustan to simple polemics cannot stop readers from enjoying an oeuvre that glorifies life much more than it excoriates it.

After Guibert, Dustan had to create a new homosexual *ethos* close to Pasolini's "rabbia analitica"[38] but one that was equal parts pop and postmodern, refusing the nostalgic tendencies of the Left and adhering to the original idea of a subversion specific to mass culture. What brings these three works together, sex (*In My Room*), club music (*I'm Going Out Tonight*), and drugs (*Stronger Than Me*), is the manifesto of a youth that is an "inferiority," to borrow from Witold Gombrowicz. To express it through a literary genre that all of Western history considered until recently to be an "inferior" genre was certainly a stroke of genius.

Thomas Clerc would like to thank Liza Rynkowska, Sophie Baranès, Philippe Joanny, and Tim Madesclaire.

In My Room

A Novel

Introduction by Thomas Clerc

Published in 1996 when he was thirty-one years old, *In My Room*, Guillaume Dustan's first book, is rough: in this way it truly is a "first book," sketching out Dustan's fiery and desperate existence. The book is something of a "descent into hell" with its nearly single-minded focus on sex. The often unbearable representation Dustan gives of it explains the suspicion that surrounded him. Guillaume Dustan would have loved being a popular writer; his radicality prevented that. If there is something "pop" in his work, it's a pop culture that did not forgo negativity. Andy Warhol painted flowers, but they were chrysanthemums.

Hitting Hard

Writing style is primary in establishing an author's identity: Dustan's rested upon a shocking stylistic tension between a minimal syntax and an informal vocabulary. His style was both trashy and cold. The direct exposure of sex scenes, the continuous narration in the first-person present, the obsession with mundane details, the high-rate of unsafe sexual encounters, and the verbal and physical violence resembled the photographic worlds of Nan Goldin or Robert Mapplethorpe with a mix of trance and house music as a soundtrack. Dustan's language was in perfect harmony with what he wrote: truncated words, Anglicisms, hipster speech and/or slang, nouns phrases, repetitions, cleft sentences borrowed from oral speech, and usage of implicit references that excluded the uninformed reader. This collection of traits, hardly concerned with pleasing, provocatively built an off-putting novel that would never have brought Dustan into the mainstream. But

this act of cutting himself off from the traditional readership—
the straight, intellectual, bourgeois establishment—was much
more than a pose. His implicit refusal of literary codes and
traditional norms of behavior was coupled with a manifesto on
the behavioral practices of his milieu.

There is something about Dustan's writing, however, that
resists the simple classification of trashy literature, which implies
a certain complacency, the use of stereotypes, and a lack of humor,
all of which Dustan carefully avoids. Indeed, trashy literature aims
at pleasing the expectations of its reader with the intent to shock.
Yet Dustan, probably because he was interested in the question of
evil, never played smug. All of his literature was literal; beyond the
disgust some passages may evoke, this is precisely what gives it its
undeniable power, even, dare we say, its morality. This moral
sincerity, which is comprised of not being "not duped," is one of
the two ethical forms of literary modernity, the other being, on
the contrary, the ironically postmodern play of clichés and pop
cultural references. In the first case, autobiography; in the other
case, self writing. Dustan was never kitsch. If he would later
affirm an esthetic closer to camp or queer, these were not the
stakes of the first three books collected here.

Inscribed in its time, nearly bordering on the ephemeral but
overcoming it by its mastery of a perceptible form, Dustan's
deliberate flat writing style is the inheritor of a literary history.
Stemming from a Modernist degree zero of writing as well as
subjective speech, it exposes the brutal surface of things. The
unbridled voice of the underground is superimposed upon an
Albert Camus-like "white writing," whose influence on Bret Easton Ellis has hardly ever been noticed. Indeed, Ellis is the major
reference for Dustan. Continuing the avant-garde tradition of
pushing the limits in terms of representation, in an autobiographical framework, Dustan creates a formal *mimesis* of a porn
film with the following unwritten rule: no chitchat just action.
And indeed, narrative logic cedes the way to visual dynamics.

His ultra-focused descriptions reduce sex to an intense series of acts and gestures that are empty of all sensuality. Structured in short chapters similar to Polaroids, *In My Room* manifests an esthetic intelligence that consists of keeping it short. Extremism thus meets its limit. The first trilogy oscillates between hardcore and minimalism, a minimalism that does not need any transcendence to justify its existence and implies no emotional loss, while on the contrary reinforcing its own *pathos* through its distancing.

This first book performs a mixture of hot and cold: Dustan's writing style is neo-clinical. Behind this literalist coldness, one can continuously observe a sensitivity bloom. Perhaps Dustan's limit will have been his inability to remain completely cold, which was the reason for his admiration for Warhol. For language itself acts: the informal nature of the words, the irony distilled here and there, and the demonstrative dimension of the sexual scenes all betray a constant presence that provides a unique tonality to this trilogy, something between a phenomenological approach and a dark romanticism.

A Room of One's Own

Dustan defines a space that is perhaps the only benchmark for his disorganized existence: the bedroom. There is something touching in the desire for protection that the title demands, as if this intimate space, that of sex—that is, the most precious and intense form of identity—is first and foremost a pushing away of the world. Of course, the bedroom is a social space, but it is first a personal space: "In my room, I am free,"[1] noted Dustan in one of the columns he wrote for the magazine *e.m@le*, as if he couldn't possibly be free in the streets. However, the bedroom isn't "the closet," that metaphor used to designate both the real or mental hovel where homosexuality must hide under the yoke of repressive social laws.[2] Opening up his room to the reader, whom he transforms into a voyeur, Dustan designs a space that is both private and public (its twin is the nightclub): paradoxical interiority, defined by a place more than an awareness. Dustan's autobiographic undertaking is experienced less in psychology and more in action. The "I" that appears in *In My Room*, which is closer to an amateur porn video than to a "home sweet home," rejects intimacy, opting instead for the rawness of sexual representation. For that matter, the term "representation" is imperfect, and we prefer the term "action," as if Dustan were emptying sex of its human dimension in order to substitute the immediacy of its pure presence. Governed by scopophilia, *In My Room* is subject to an analysis according to which the sexual act is not shared between two people, but rather in the presence of a third person, the reader-voyeur who is essential to autobiography. According to Bénédicte Boisseron, "the virtual, exterior eye allows both subjects to exteriorize themselves and to stimulate their desire with the idea of someone viewing their copulation from the outside."[3] Pornography belongs to the realm of thought, both as image and idea, but one must know how to give it shape. In order for this "thought from the outside" to be effective it paradoxically needed to be grafted onto a constant "I" that never let go of the reader—something Dustan maintains from the very start through the use of "my" in his title.

The bedroom is no more a secretive place than autobiography is the realm of intimacy. Rather, it is where the opposition between public and private is abolished. How can we not compare the bedroom of pleasures with the one that makes writing possible, according to Virginia Woolf?[4] The most personal space is thus the one that is depersonalized by sex.

Dustan the Pornographer

Sex, depicted in an extremely raw fashion in this first opus (something to which Dustan will return in his third book under the form of sadomasochism), is immediately affirmed. The role of sex in Dustan's existence and in the development of his sensibility is crucial—he had an obvious sexual passion that he threw, without any hesitation, right into the reader's face. And yet Dustan wasn't a cynic in the trivial sense of the word since his provocations had another aim than themselves. Since "sex is the main focus"[5] it is out of the question to create an "erotic" version of it, in the tradition of a certain bourgeois—and heterosexual—fictionality destined to seduce the reader. For Dustan, describing his sex life is not an exercise dictated by considerations heterogenous to his work.

Sexuality is one of the foremost pleasures of life and constitutes a reason to live, or in Dustan's case—to survive. Consequently, it must be faithfully recorded: here autobiography is in the service of a "sexual truth" that is affirmed and carefully depicted. This sexual expenditure goes hand in hand with a certain age in life, youth, the true "golden years" for Dustan who, let's not forget, lived and wrote during a very short period of time, barely a decade. Dustan would go on to reverse the ageism he was accused of,[6] shifting a negative value into a positive one, by means of a rhetorical strategy well known to avant-gardists and oppressed minorities and about which he would later theorize. Discovered and practiced by a subject who rejected the straitjacket of Western, Judeo-Christian, puritan social and familial constraints, the porn film also had a political side to it. The sex described here was not abstract but was instead the sexual life of a man determined to render a minority excessively visible. There was no need to be militant, all that was required was to show what was being hidden, according to a logic of transparency that remains controversial, depending on whether it fights power, or becomes its accomplice.[7] Regardless of that undecidable debate, it nonetheless remains that this logic is at the very core of the autobiographic esthetic and of the criterion of the pleasure (or the rejection) it provokes.

This baring all was additionally aimed at describing a milieu, his own, that of the hedonistic homosexual night owl who represented an active portion of the gay population in the 1990s. From this perspective, the sociological import of Dustan's literature is undeniable. For those who want to understand a milieu as coded as that of the gay world, there is no better introduction than this first trilogy. The debates around autofiction masked the work of documenting a micro-milieu described by its own actors, a milieu that had never been the object of any deep study, with the exception of a precursor, Renaud Camus. Far from the polemics that poisoned the reception of Camus' *Journal*, we mustn't forget the debt that Dustan owed this important author. *Tricks*, published in 1978 with Hachette/P.O.L., is a masterpiece, and Dustan's great intellectual honesty (he was very generous towards those who influenced him: he named them directly) also consisted of knowing who his predecessors were. *Tricks* is a list of 85 short accounts of Camus's sexual encounters written in diary-like fashion. So what separates *Tricks* from the first trilogy? Other than a more structured writing: simply twenty-five years. *Tricks* came onto the scene during the 1970s, before AIDS, during a sort of happy time that seems unreal to us now, a time that Mathieu Lindon captured in his book *Learning What Love Means*. Dustan wanted to create his own mimetic code, less correct than the Camusian narrator's (we could also cite other, more discrete sources like Pierre Guyotat or Tony Duvert).

When Marguerite Duras wrote, "I would rank porn above commercial cinema,"[8] she highlighted an ethical quality that is unique to the genre, one that emphasizes its incapacity to lie about what it has to offer. But for all that, pornographic art entails a totality that restricts its interest to genre literature. There is no break in porn (aside from intermediary scenes, which are, themselves, metaphorically pornographic through the ideas they have of reality), which makes its reception more delicate. Burdened by a purely performative aim, the pornographic genre is either poorly written or excessively well-written. It's because style is actually the locus of the obscene, which is not to be found the representations that it accompanies. Dustan is a true writer for he measured up to this demanding experience, one which opened a new horizon for the uncultured, with an additional pedagogical aim.

Although physical, porn is no less metaphysical by implication. Theorized as an area of research in its own right—"porn studies" gave an intellectual legitimacy to something previously delegitimized[9]—porn has left its mark on contemporary literature. It's tempting to offer the following paradox: Dustan brought gay literature out of its ghetto thanks to pornography, that universe that extends beyond the sole question of sexual identity to reveal the contemporary subject. "The true song of the pornographic is that it reveals the essential, the unspeakable essential, the essential as unspeakable: pornography is maddening."[10] This quote from Georges Molinié underlines the importance of the pornographic as an ethical and esthetic regime that refuses to ennoble the human, but also one that no longer cultivates the transgressive religion of the forbidden. The pornographic neuters both the moralist credo that make it a symptom of modern inanity, as well as the anti-literary stance that laments the role of the exhibitionist. In a recent essay, Laurent de Sutter shows how there is a "tautology of sex"[11] that only refers back to itself. This is a possible definition of pornography, which has two opponents. The first, eroticism, in so much as it embellishes sex with a chatty intentionality; the other, puritanism, in that it tags sexuality as something "outside" the norm so as to diminish its value. At the intersection of subjectivity and de-subjectivation, Dustan's oeuvre is neither chatty nor puritan; through porn it aims at an *intense Neutral*.[12]

Sex and Terror

Although essential, sexuality is no less indissociable from its counterpart, death, which here carried the name of AIDS. For Dustan, sex was certainly an antidote to his death drive, but it was continually interrupted by it. There was no excessive idealism here, as one can well imagine, and the ambiguity of the text was only the stronger for it; as, far from separating Eros from Thanatos, it blended them inextricably until they bordered on the unbearable. Dustan's vitalism, which is undeniable in his discourse, therefore ran up against a certain limit in this defense of a pleasure that was not devoid of the enormous weight of the guilt that it claimed to fight. An "innocent" reading of Dustan is not possible: we must see in this orgy a ferocious battle pitting the fanatical desire to escape guilt with the Western impossibility of detaching from it. In his magnificent essay, *Sex and Terror* (which Dustan highly regarded), Pascal Quignard suggests that "pleasure is puritan."[13]

The Dustanian text was an excessively affirmative declaration of life threatened by death. The radicalness of Dustan's writing was inevitable; it is as if he knew that he had to "liberate" himself from a destiny burdened by the disease. From this point of view, the turnaround between the end of the second to last chapter, "Then I'll be so disgusted with myself that it will finally be time to kill myself," and the escape abroad in the last chapter stand for the movement of a book oriented towards an exit or salvation. It's not easy to forgo Judeo-Christian morality, and as we know, its complete negation is only the opposite of its presence. Experimenting with the extreme created a disturbing ambiguity, awareness of which was raised by the author when he wrote, "I wonder if it's sinister or if it's good."[14] Beyond its terrible reality, unsafe sex became a metaphor for a literature haunted by evil. The voluntary direct exposure of his text, at times quite scary, (take Chapter 9 for example, where Dustan gets his testicles pierced) is a sort of manifesto about the harshness of those years. AIDS was still destructive and strategies to combat it required the letting up of behaviors that Dustan did not hide: "everybody's HIV-positive now,"[15] he has a character say. Now is not the time to reopen the debate on this topic; Dustan would lead the charge in the following trilogy, with his disputable and disputed defense of unsafe sex. But the gnawing problem was already present in these pages, similar to porn films where actors don't wear condoms. Real practices must be shown; it is not up to literature to hide the contradictions of reality. Dustan did not cheat us: we can critique the underlying reasons that motivated his actions, but not the representation that he gave of them.

In My Room has the outrage of beginnings, those which bring to life Baudelaire's quote, "One must enter the literary scene with a thunderclap." Dear reader, abandon all hope: the despair this text leans up against, written in a purposefully impoverished style, heralds a rise in power. From the outset, an *auteur* carved out his space in the dark room of sex, death, and writing.

To Philippe and Philippe

PART I

1. Good Intentions

I left Quentin the bedroom. I moved into the little room at the back of the apartment so I wouldn't hear them fucking. A few days later, a week maybe, I thought it was getting to be too much of a downer. I demanded to get my room back. Of course Quentin immediately decided to move himself and Nico into the living room, which meant I would have to bang on the wall to get them to quiet down the nights I had to go to work the next day. As a bonus, I was able to hear Quentin say he was going to kick my ass and Nico replying Sweetie, calm down.

I was living day to day, not knowing where I was going. It wasn't unpleasant. I am always bored shitless whenever there's nothing going on. This is probably why I was still living with Quentin even though we were no longer together. His most recent idea consisted of entering my room without warning. The first time I was lying on my bed, jerking off, smoking a joint. The door opened. He came in. He said, Did you happen to see my mom's datebook by chance? She thinks she left it here. I didn't answer the question. I said Please knock before coming in. He said I knocked. I said I didn't hear anything. He started asking about the dumb planner again. I said Quentin, get the fuck out, now. He looked stunned. And then he left. It took me another ten minutes before I was able to jerk off properly.

The second time he knocked. Just as I screamed NO! he came into the room. This time I was literally getting railed on the edge of the bed. I said Get out! Instead, he looked at me all confused. I was furious. I told the other guy Don't stop, he'll leave, he's just doing this to fuck with me. I focused on the sex. Quentin watched us doing it. After a while, he left without saying a word.

After that, I decided I wouldn't let myself get pushed around anymore. I started yelling systematically every time he got shitty with me. I yelled about the cans of food he didn't replace, the disgusting bathroom, and about the messages he never gave me. I insulted him regularly. Quentin would say nothing. I savored my vengeance. I liked yelling at him with impunity. My good friend Alessandro was living in the little bedroom so that put me at ease. I thought that in the presence of a third party, Quentin wouldn't dare do anything seriously stupid, he liked his comfortable life too much to risk it for prison. And then one day, I was feeling pretty good and I started talking to him like we did before. I talked about what I did the night before with some super hot guy. When I was done, he looked at me and said You like that pretty little mug of yours, don't you? Well, you won't be so proud of it when I throw acid all over it. This shook me up a little. I asked Alessandro if he wanted to share a place with me. I didn't want to live alone. He said OK. As soon as I told Quentin I was going to move out, he started threatening me again. I asked Alessandro to start bringing his girlfriend to the apartment. And then it got to be so unlivable that I ended up moving into Terrier's shitty studio all the way up in the 18th arrondissement.

Terrier and I were having better and better sex. I had a feeling my presence was doing him some good. I was the first person he told he was HIV-positive. He found out he was positive the first time he went to get tested, he was only twenty—just seven years ago. Ever since he told me, he no longer has these nightmares where someone nails down the coffin lid over him while he pushes against it hard but it never budges and then suddenly he wakes up. I had also given him a makeover. I made him cut his bangs that hid his face and cut his nails that he kept long. It made him a lot better-looking. Maybe even a little less shy.

I didn't want to move out of my neighborhood. I found another apartment about three blocks away. It was perfect timing. I was a little bothered by the thought that I would still be running into Quentin, but it was a part of the neighborhood where he'd hardly ever go and we didn't have the same schedule. I left him all the appliances and the furniture we'd bought together. I had money anyhow. I bought everything again at Darty one morning as soon as they opened with Terrier. A new life was beginning.

2. The Meeting

It was hell with Terrier. He'd get drunk. He'd make a scene at bars as soon as he saw me looking at someone else. I realized he wasn't going to change quickly enough. I told him that I would only see him during the week and that I needed the weekends for myself. I went out alone. The first night, I fucked a guy who was nothing special. The second night, I went to the Keller,[1] I got fucked a little first by two guys in the *backroom*, then I went back to the bar to drink a beer, I felt better, I was a bit paranoid about my look, I was worried my light-brown cowboy boots looked too tacky with my black leather 501s. Fortunately the top half looked great: bare chest, black leather vest.

Right in front of me, I saw this guy leaning back against the bar. It was his face that kept my attention. He looked very normal, not at all the type of guy to play the pervy, tough leather look. Plus he was cute and had a nice body, was short and clearly older than me. He looked at me indifferently. It was then that I ran into Serge. We'd fucked six years ago when I had just met Quentin (and at Quentin's no less, who was away on vacation at that time). I asked him Do you know that one? He said For one night, it's very nice. And he is *very* well-hung. This bothered me because I thought now that he had seen me talking to Serge, he knew that I knew he had a big one. It was going to be a lot more difficult to hit on him now.

I found a spot next to him at the bar, I stood there without looking at him. I waited a little not wanting to appear so obvious. Actually, he was with another guy, a tall blond dressed all in leather, kind of cute, who laughed the whole time. And then after a while, they weren't talking any more. The guy next to me looked straight ahead and then a little to his right. I took advantage of the situation by saying Hey. And then I said nothing so I could play hard to get. He said Hi back. I said My name is Guillaume. He said I'm Stéphane. I said The guy you're with, is he your man? He said No, he's just a friend. I asked Is he a good fuck? He said Yes, why? Do you want me to introduce you to him? I said Uh yeah. He said Éric let me introduce Guillaume. I don't remember what I said to keep this conversation going. And then this big ugly leather guy came up to the group and what was cool is that he started to hit on me saying he wanted to take photos of me. I gave him my number and told him that I was always up for narcissistic activities, then I was rather negative regarding all that was "art," I told him I didn't give a shit about art. This snobbish asshole asked So what are you into then? I'm into the fuck of the century I said, looking at Stéphane. It worked. I still had to struggle a bit but I ended up bringing him home.

Serge was right in a way. The first time was nice, in a rabid dog kind of way. I liked what I was seeing in the mirror when he was fucking me from the front. I thought we looked good together. His super big cock hurt a little but I felt the potential. I decided to keep him. Instead of letting him leave I asked him if he was hungry. The fridge was full since I had gone shopping earlier that day. We ate in the kitchen.

I told him that I thought he was super cute. He tensed up, but not like he was used to that type of compliment, but because he thought I was making fun of him. I told him Just because you have one eye smaller than the other, and one is green and the other blue, and one eyelid is higher than the other, that won't keep me from thinking you're super cute if I think you're super cute. This surprised him. He calmed down a little. I told myself I liked him. I gave him my number. I waited for him to call me.

3. Country

I didn't have to wait long. We talked. After a while I said You
know, I was pissed that you saw me talking to Serge about you
the other night because I thought you knew I knew you had a big
dick and I thought that you must have found that tacky to hit on
you for that reason. He said it's true that guys are only interested
in him for his dick.

So I proposed that we have a lunch date instead of fucking.
He showed up a little late, visibly upset, dressed pretty bad. I
had picked a chic place to impress him. Lunch went well. I
was not bored. We decided to meet up again to fuck at my
place because his boyfriend was at his place. That next date, I
jerked our dicks off together, mine was seven inches, hard, his
nine. I had to stop myself from being hypnotised by it. I
wanted there to only be two dicks, no difference between
them, each one loving the other's as much as his own, no
more no less. I also learned a little about his life and his relationship with Jean-Marc that was headed down the drain.
They have been together for the past ten years but less and less
for the past five, and for the past two haven't slept together. He's
at his lover's house right now. Stéphane said He told me he is
in love with him.

We see each other a third, a fourth, and a fifth time. Each time
he fucks me. But we also talk. We go on walks. We're starting to
get to know each other. I ask him to talk to me about his life with
Jean-Marc, he tells me what I was expecting, that he spends his
time running errands, cooking, doing the dishes and waiting for

Jean-Marc to fuck him. I tell him he shouldn't let himself be treated like that.

We start seeing each other regularly. One night each weekend plus one evening during the week. Stéphane tells me that he doesn't feel like he is betraying Jean-Marc because Jean-Marc also has something on the side. But this bothers me. I demand three nights a week. We end up seeing each other every weekend except when they host a dinner at their place. The second thing that starts to bother me is that I am not allowed to fuck him because of an agreement he and Jean-Marc have. Each of them can fuck whomever they want, but can't get fucked. I point out to Stéphane that, according to what he'd said, this isn't as fair as it sounds because Jean-Marc doesn't like getting fucked. I tell him that I can't go on much longer like this.

He asks Jean-Marc for permission. Jean-Marc doesn't give it, but he says that he knows he will do it anyway. I invest. I take Stéphane out to the country for a weekend, to an ugly chateau hotel full of salesmen. Stéphane is a little uptight, he claims he isn't used to this. I tell myself he's just hung up on his social status, but it'll pass.

It's sunny in the suite. We take a bath in the hot tub, I brought some seaweed bath salts that I saved from my last thalassotherapy. Champagne and weed for when we wake. I gently rub the head of my dick against his hole. I fuck him later, after the pool or the countryside walk, I don't remember anymore. I squeeze my thighs, standing at the edge of the bed. I'm a little soft because his ass is super tight, I hate that, but whatever, it's a start. I'm very careful not to hurt him. He comes without touching himself. He tells me it's the third time in his life. I wonder how many times has that happened to me, it's true that it isn't a common thing.

We come home Sunday night. Stéphane brings me back to my place before he goes home to his and Jean-Marc's. It's eight o'clock, a bit early for the Palace. I lie on the bed. I smoke a joint, listening to music. I think about what Quentin asked me on the phone two days ago. Do you still want me? I said Yes. And then I told him I can't live with him. But tonight, I tell myself that I'm really going to be able to stop loving him because there really is someone else. I cry from happiness, I think that I will truly be able to love him, that what I'm listening to is true, *I wanna make you mine, I'll love you till the end of time,* and it's such a relief. I tell myself that it's been a while since I've cried. I feel like calling Stéphane right now and telling him he must choose between Jean-Marc and me. He has to decide right now and if he's not here in an hour I'll never see him again. And then I tell myself that wouldn't be so smart. I know very well he's going to leave him anyway. It's only a matter of time. But it gives me a weird feeling all the same. I've only been single for two months. Not even really. And then all of a sudden I get super paranoid, it's probably the hash, when I hear the tick-tock of the clock at the end of the song by D:ream, it doesn't give me the same feeling as it did the first time I noticed it when Stéphane and I were chilling after fucking. This time I tell myself it's the countdown to my end. I'm scared. I cry. And then I calm myself down and I manage to make it to the bathroom clinging to the walls I'm completely gone and I'm still listening to D:Ream while I take a shower to try to come down from my high.

4. My Lovers

It's been forever since I've danced. Stéphane doesn't like it much since he doesn't know how to, but since it makes him happy to make me happy, he's cool with it. We can't go to the Queen² because I don't want to run into Terrier, but tonight there's this thing at the Bataclan, so after a few beers at a bar we head out. At the Bataclan, the music is rather average and since the place isn't packed, the atmosphere is pretty cold, the people are a bit pretentious because it's a special evening and at any rate there are too many straight people. In short, after about an hour, when the gin-get starts to wear off, the Queen became inevitable.

I am no more than four inches from Stéphane's face when Terrier sees me. I'm asking him if he found a third while I was on the toilet. He smiles and tells me that he hasn't had time yet. Terrier looks pale. He passes by me without saying a word. I catch up to him in the bathroom. I tell him Hey, I thought I recognized you. He's completely trashed. He says But who are you? You know perfectly well who I am, I told him. Yeah, so what are you doing here? Can't you leave me the fuck alone? he says. I say I have every right to be here, shit. I'm not going to hide out at home just because you go out. And then he starts crying. You didn't even recognize me… I wasn't even thinking about you… and then I saw you, and your hairy body…

I don't know what to do so I split. I grab Stéphane along the way and drag him across the crowd. There's some space past the bar. I dance. It's Tony D. Bart. Quentin had Nico bring it back from London for me last December, three or four months ago, around the time I met Terrier. I'm dancing like a crazy man, I toss my head in all directions, I feel my cheeks throb, I'm having trouble keeping my balance, but then people back away around me giving me some space to dance. When I stop, there's this frustrated guy who shoves me in the back. The others, gorgeous and high, great muscles and wearing classy shirts all smile back at me. I am out of breath, I look at Stéphane, I start dancing but chiller now. I lift my head. Terrier is about ten feet away. Apparently he has been following us. I tell Stéphane Come on, we're heading upstairs. We head upstairs. We smoke a cigarette while watching the dance floor below. The music is good. I've got a good buzz going from the gin-get and the joint. I dance by the security barrier. I rub up against Stéphane's ass. It makes me hard. We kiss.

When I open my eyes, Terrier is still there at the end of the walk-way. He doesn't even pretend not to be staring at us. I say Fuck this let's go. On the way up the stairs and out I see at least five cute guys I could do. But who gives a shit I tell myself. I've already fucked a thousand guys in my life. The one I'm going home with is in the top four, so it's all good.

And then outside, Terrier shows up completely drunk. He is shirtless, just wearing a white tank top, black jeans, his pale slightly too-thin shoulders shine in the night. He looks super hot to me. It's freezing-cold out. I'm coming home with you two, he says. No, you're fucking delirious I say. Yeah, Yeah, it's gonna be great, he replies. I love his hoarse voice. It's not going to be great because you're not coming, I say. Oh really, and how are you going to stop me? He says. Watch, I say. I grab him by the shoulder. I turn him around towards the entrance. Now, go back in there! He breaks free. He starts walking towards the Étoile. I follow him. He starts running. I run. He speeds up. I'm starting to get excited. I finally catch up to him on the next block. OK that's enough, leave us alone I say. He laughs at me. We head back down the Champs-Élysées, now empty. I pull him by the wrist. You're hurting me, he says. I don't care I say.

Now there's a line to get in to the club. I drag him through the crowd to the door. Shame on me, he keeps saying. The bouncer asks Sandrine, the girl at the door You know these guys? She knows him, I say, and he's going to catch a cold. I let him get dragged into the club. I think everything is going to be OK especially considering the comment he made before leaving, disappearing into the mist, the persuasive house music: Maybe just one last drink. I go back to find Stéphane, totally sober. I say That totally killed my buzz. He says I can see that. He's been waiting for me sitting on the hood of a car, super cute in his little green bomber jacket. I say Wanna go to the Transfert?[3]

We finally decide not to bring anybody home and fuck, just the two of us. We go home. Four a.m., MC Solaar on the radio, we enter the tunnel under Place de la Concorde, the Quai du Louvre, the Black taxi driver and his North African buddy are chatting. I tell Stéphane it's all good, it was just a lot for me, that's all. Terrier stopped dead in his tracks on the way to the bathroom. It was the first time he saw me with his replacement. No one planned it.

Five a.m. Stéphane is on top of me. I have both ankles on his shoulders. He's ready to enter me. I say I don't want you to fuck me. He says Oh yeah? I say I want you to make love to me. He says OK. The first fifteen minutes are perfection, my dick is out of its mind, hard without me touching it, I spread my legs to the max and take in all nine inches. After a while it gets so good that it reminds me of Quentin, the way he fucks me so deep. I am rock hard. We come at almost the exact same time. He tells me after we finish that he is beginning to understand what fucking is all about. I tell him that out of the thousands of men I've fucked, there are maybe four or five, OK a dozen really, who know how to do what he just did to me. There is also Chad Douglas, but it's only on VHS. In fact, he's listed in the credits of one of the ones I bought two days ago. *Remote Control.* I just hope he isn't dead in real life.

5. Sex

Robert cuts my nape while shaving me with a new blade. So I tell him Do me a favor, and put some of this on it, then wait about a half-hour, cool? He says Thirty? That's how long you have to wait for HIV-1 according to the label on the antiseptic, for other diseases it's shorter. I say Yeah. He says Shouldn't I just throw out the razor? I say Yeah. Robert likes me, he bought me coffee the last time I was around and today he asked if I wanted a Marlboro. Handsome, straight, cowboy look, big belt, faded 501 jeans, with a lock of hair on his forehead. I see him leaning over the banister looking at me from above while I am almost at the bottom.

After this incident, I was so uncomfortable that I went somewhere else for a month. When I came back, he was there. What's up? he asked me. Not much, I said. He did this thing that I didn't know, a slow wink.

We leave Robert's salon. Stéphane walks behind me as usual. We go across the street to buy me a new bomber jacket and a pair of chaps. For years I've been dreaming about owning some chaps. I'm feeling invincible. My hair is very short, I have on my black leather 501s, German leather boots, a blue trucker sweater, the collar of my shirt adds just a splash of color. I've been going to the gym for seven years, I have a small belly, just a little one, but it would go away in two weeks if I worked on my abs. The only thing is my calves, they're a little on the small side.

Saturday, around six, Stéphane came back from running an errand, he fucked me, it was nice, but I don't remember anything. We had dinner, Allessandro made us pasta with asparagus, then he left for Beaubourg, supposedly, but in reality he was going to see his girlfriend. We do another line of coke, and smoke a joint. Stéphane is constipated. It pisses me off, I think he is still scared of getting fucked. I say that, but it's true he has made progress, he told me that before, he used to only open up when he was high on poppers. I send him off to go shit and wash his ass. During this time, I take off my jeans, and put my boots back on, then my awesome leather chaps. When he comes back, the latex chaps are laid out on the bed, with the right size Rangers and matching socks. I help him get dressed, then I help him get into position: knees on the bed, ass in the air. I have trouble getting hard at first, seeing as there was really no foreplay. I look at his ass, I put some more lube on. That finally turns me on. I enter him, not super hard, he's really tight but I get him to open up a little using my riding crop. I grab the belt of his chaps with my left hand, and use my right hand to gently whip his ass, his thighs, and his lower back, I get harder inside of him, he pushes back against me, I turn around and see something world class in the mirror, I like what I see, it reassures me, it flatters me. I pound him for a while, and then I get sick of the position, we climb up the bed, then back down to the edge, then I pull out, I tell him to face me, I've gone a little limp, I enter him again, I get hard inside the condom. In the end, he comes.

It's already two a.m. I don't feel like going out. We are hungry. I open a can of tripe, I make some instant rice, two individual packets. There's some leftover Sancerre in the fridge. The tripe doesn't have much flavor because of the coke. I put on Soft Cell. I bought two old albums I didn't know except for their amazing hit song, *Numbers*. *Who's the person that you woke up next to today?* Marc Almond asks me. I roll a joint and then I light it and then I turn off the stereo with the stereo remote and then I turn on the TV with the TV remote because I haven't figured out how to get them both to work with the universal remote I bought last week, and I flip through the channels and I pass the joint to Stéphane.

I want to play Microbots, *Cosmic Evolution*, it's a really great cut from the DJ Brainwasher mix, but the CD refuses to work. I'm looking for something repetitive but not cold to listen to while I get fucked with a dildo. It's five a.m., Stéphane is getting tired, he falls asleep but tells me it's OK, I wake him up so he can fuck me with my dildo. I get out another mix, Guerilla in Dub, the sixth track will do the trick if the title means anything: *Intoxication*. It's actually pretty good. The bass is muffled and cool. From time to time there are actually some lyrics, a voice whispering Funky marijuana. I don't even notice the words until I switched to my third dildo, the big black one. We started with the day-glow ultra-soft pink one I bought at Pleasure Chest in West Hollywood two years ago when I went to the U.S. between two hospital stays. It's perfect for easing open an ass. Then another, thicker pink one, the Kong (9 ½ x 7 inches). We move on to the big black double-headed one bought in Berlin that is seven and a half inches around. I take it half-way. Off to the side is the enormous pink one, eight and a half inches thick. I usually never use this one because I can only take it fully when I am completely wasted. But tonight, with the quarter tab of acid, the coke I did, and all the joints I've been smoking, I'll be able to take it, and I know that an incredible feeling awaits me, every bit as mind-blowing as a parachute jump or a deep-sea dive. I like strong sensations.

Stéphane covers it with lube, the black one is still in me because I don't want to leave my ass empty too long, I have a hard time staying hard if there's nothing in me when my ass is already very dilated. Stéphane adds more lube to the big pink one, I want it dripping, if not, I feel it going in. Here we go. It pops in, first the head, as fat as a fist, pushes past my asshole, then the three ribbed bulges one after another glides in. The morons who designed this thing must have thought they were clever putting those on the back, I guess they thought that made it look prettier. Wait that hurts. It doesn't feel good, I say, take it out, take it out, take it out! Thirty-second break before trying again. OK now, it goes in but it's still pretty big, it hurts just a little, even after taking a huge hit of poppers. I wonder what I can do to get hard again, then I have an idea. I tell Stéphane, Put your hand around it so I can feel how big it is, that'll turn me on. Obviously it worked well feeling just how much this enormous thing was stretching my bitch ass. I'm raging hard. I'm really turned on. OK now, fuck me with it. He does. I realize just how deep he's got it in me, I've never had it so deep. After twenty seconds of hard fucking, I feel like I'm about to come. Pull it out quick, quick, quick! He pulls it out fast. I explode. I think about Quentin because he is the one who taught me to pull your dildo out before coming. That way you don't damage your sphincters. If you leave the dildo in, the muscles smash up against the latex and can't close back while you ejaculate. I check. As usual, no blood, which has been the case for about a year now. That I learned all by myself. With this type of play, you shouldn't force it if it hurts or you will bust a blood vessel and wind up with a bleeding asshole, that isn't fun at all.

The next day is Sunday, we wake up too late to go shopping so we end up doing nothing. I roll a joint after breakfast, we watch some TV and then I start to get bored and decide to go down on him. I blow him for a little, and then I get up and go wash my asshole in the bathroom, I don't really explain myself because he can hear the noises, it takes me a while, and when I come back, I'm not as turned on so I roll another joint, we smoke it while watching some TV and then I go back down on him and when he gets real hard I lie on my back and spread my legs and he gets on top and goes in deep with a perfect understanding of my insides, my dick is rock-hard without me touching it, for twenty minutes I think, I fondle him, I play with his nipples, I push my throbbing cock up against his belly, he does this trick that I absolutely love doing too where he rolls his belly against my balls while fucking me. So much stimulation of sensitive spots. He tells me he wants to come, I say OK, a fuck from behind and off we go. From the back the penetration is deeper and also it makes it easier for me to jerk off. I turn around, forty-five seconds of fumbling and then we're good, he settles in, I wrap myself around his waist, my heavy package throbbing, I jerk and he pounds me hard, I come before him, after I can't keep going, he has to stop. I am a little worried that he didn't come in my ass but he is happy anyway, he tells me it's wild how his cock feels in someone's ass. I say, I know but I'm totally wrecked, it's the first time I've managed to let him pound me so deep with his super hard tool. I'm too worn out to help him come right now. I tell him he'll come when I fuck him in a little while, OK?

And that's what happens an hour later. I've pulled myself together, we've been watching TV, I start fondling him, I'm getting hard, balls hanging low. Great erection, relentless, absolute. He doesn't know if his ass is dirty. He goes to the toilet and then the bathroom. It takes a long time. When he comes back, I've gone limp. I spend a minute in his mouth to take care of that first. I slip on a condom. I place him on his back, a pillow under his head. I slide two fingers in him like butter. I start to go at it. Shit. He's so tight, impossible to get in. I try again. Nothing. I go limp. He looks freaked out. I say All right, we're going to take our time. I sit my ass down on the bed and rub the head of my dick against his ass for a little while, he relaxes, I slide in very carefully. It's OK. And then I fuck him like I never have before. It lasts a long time, the way I like it. I see in his eyes he's beginning to take me seriously. I take him from the front, holding him first by the ankles. Then I grab his ass. Then the middle of his thighs. Then behind his knees. Then around the neck. I pull out to put on some lube. I dive back in. In the end, he explodes. I pull out, I rip the condom off, I jerk off looking at his ass, I think about the straight porn video I have called *Juicy Anus*, the tagline on the cover is Any gaping asshole will be showered in beautiful strands of jizz. Too bad we can't do that for real. I'm coming. I get back up. Boom. It's the fifth time we've fucked this weekend.

It's eleven. We go to dinner, nearby in the ghetto, totally wasted. The waiters are nice. A girl comes in from the Privilège, it was the anniversary of Tea Dance this Sunday. We're the last to leave the restaurant. It's cold outside. We decide to sleep together, three nights in a row for the first time, it's good.

6. America

I jacked off while watching Eric Manchester do what he does best, things I know how to do. He's no Chad Douglas, but he loves his dick just as much. I go brush my teeth, my nightly routine consists of: AZT, teeth, warts. I'll jerk off again, I hope, after I finish this. I see myself in the mirror, I find myself handsome. A low-angle shot, then I choose other angles, I change my expression, I look concerned, I tell myself my conception of beauty has changed. Before, I only paid attention to the physique. The guy could have looked stupid or tormented but still handsome. Now, I tell myself that beauty is in the expression. This is why I'm having so much success these days. I have that same expression I had when I was fifteen, when I was away on vacation in Los Angeles at the L.s and people in restaurants would serve me alcohol because I was French even though it wasn't allowed for anyone under eighteen. Whatever I would do with the L.s was great, like drinking chilled California white wine out of a cranberry juice bottle, from a cooler at the beach, the waves of the Pacific crashing in front of us. The smell of eucalyptus is very strong as we head downhill to the beach. We're styling, in a white Jaguar that was in Le Mans in 1964. Julie L. takes me to dinner in Tijuana. We both order Sideways and a steak with garlic and onions. The beautiful Mexican ladies go to dinner in red or black evening gowns, the men in black suits. I have on a jacket Papa gave me that was too tight for him, and a short-sleeve blue oxford shirt with mother-of-pearl buttons that looks very good on me because of my tan. I have on OP corduroy shorts, cream color, and navy blue Dockside boat shoes. It's cool. A Mexican sitting on the ground asks *Is he her son or her lover?* as we pass by on the sidewalk of Tijuana's main street, around five or six p.m., in the middle of July. My father refuses to let me spend the following year with the L.s even though I could have gone to the French high school that was right next door.

It's been four years now that I've been thinking I'll die next year. I think I still look handsome. I'm listening to Depeche Mode, *In Your Room*—higher love adrenaline mix. François Kevorkian's mix is really awesome.

I think about Quentin and me in LA two years ago. Right when we get there, I tell the L.s that the trip has been cut short, I am only allowed two weeks, the time it takes for my platelets to drop back under twenty thousand, after that, there's a serious risk of internal hemorrhaging and the only way to get them back up is by IV drip and you can't do that here because it would cost too much. The L.s leave us after two days, they have to go. As soon as we're by ourselves we start fighting again, as usual. He says terrible things to me, as usual, but nothing so bad that we actually kill each other. I leave to go grocery shopping at the supermarket, I calm down in the car. In any case, it was unavoidable. At the supermarket, since it's late, I find myself almost alone in the canned goods and boxed goods aisle. I buy everything you need to be happy. The lettuce looks like cabbage. There isn't any real cheese, only cream cheese with chives, for salmon. I spend time choosing wine, red and white. Pinot Noir. Chardonnay. From what valley? I read about the regions on the back of the bottle. I go home. It's already the middle of the night. I park on the flower beds. I have all the groceries in my hands when he appears at the entrance to the kitchen. He isn't like he usually is. I realize he isn't going to punish me.

I don't know why he agreed to making all of this possible for me. The guys emerge from the dense fog that night on Santa Monica

Blvd, West Hollywood, two by two, all dressed the same: tight t-shirts, skinny jeans cut into shorts, thick white socks rolled down, and work boots. We dance to En Vogue, everybody knows the lyrics, the bars opened the walls and windows on to the street, like a warehouse. Everyone knows how to dance. We go find a back street to smoke a joint. I have a hard time breathing because of the humidity, but it's nice, me and him forever, that night in West Hollywood.

Probe. Spike. The Arena. Every night a different place at the end of the world. We go shopping. At Pleasure Chest, some butch lesbians are ordering chains while I peruse the mountain of dildos on display. This is where I discover the soft day-glow pink dildo. I buy two because there aren't any in France. (Actually there was one a few months ago, old and dirty at Yanko[4] in Les Halles. I guess nobody wanted to buy it because of its color, too surreal). Miles and miles of desert highway to get to the beach. We go to the gym in West Hollywood. The cruising is half-assed in the hot tub under the greenery, like at the start of a porn movie. We fuck hardly no one, except one or two guys we meet at the cowboy bar in Silverlake. I fuck Quentin everyday—unheard of for us. We drink Coors in front of the TV and eat sushi I found at the supermarket down the hill. I drove really fast to get there. I am happy.

Stéphane told Jean-Marc that he was leaving him. Jean-Marc kicked him out of the apartment. I offered to let him stay at my place rather than have him look for a studio. The whole time I was telling myself this was a mistake. But I wasn't brave enough to tell him it would be better if he got his own place, we just started dating, I couldn't see myself doing that to him. I knew he had never lived alone and he was scared to. I told myself that if we didn't live together I would inevitably dump him, whereas if we did live together maybe I would love him like I was supposed to. I told myself I no longer knew what love was. I didn't want to be on my own. I didn't want to have to go out searching for someone any more. Stéphane would eventually acquire the qualities he was lacking, and I would love him.

7. Our Youth Is Flying By

Saturday afternoon. We are naked in bed. The telephone rings. It's Nico. I say Hi, how are you? Not too happy about the fact that he's about to talk my ear off about his love problems. He says Not good. Quentin almost killed me last night. He bashed my face in with his boots, kicked me all over, I've got bruises everywhere. And how do you feel now? I ask. Uh, I hurt all over, I can't walk, he answers. You want me to bring you something to eat, I say? He says Yeah, that'd be great and could you buy some yogurt, I can't open my mouth that much. OK, I'm on my way, I say. It was Nico, I tell Stéphane. Quentin almost killed him. You want to come? Sure, he says.

It's true, he was really messed up. I make some tea; he eats some yogurt with bananas. Well, I say, I thought you two weren't seeing each other any more. He says, Actually, I promised myself that I wouldn't see him anymore after I tried to kill myself ten days ago. I'd been drinking a lot. I told myself, You've got a hundred T4s left, Quentin doesn't love you, why bother anymore? I swallowed everything in the medicine cabinet and then a friend called two hours later, I told him, I'm not doing so well, I took ten packs of Y and Z and I drank a bottle of scotch. He took me to the Saint-Louis hospital, they pumped my stomach. Do you know what Quentin said? He said That just proves what a stupid little shit you are. That's when I left him. Of course after that he tried everything to get me back. He came over Wednesday afternoon to bring me my things. He had gotten his hair cut, he even did a tanning session, he put on his fancy shirt, the one you gave him with orange and purple squares. As if by accident, he had no underwear under his sweatpants. He'd forgotten to wear them, supposedly, and he wouldn't stop touching his dick. Before he left I told him if you feel like fucking, give me a call. Of course the next day, Hello? I feel like fucking you. We saw each other Thursday night, hugs and kisses, we didn't fuck but it was great. He told me he wasn't sleeping around right now, but his answering machine was full of messages from guys saying I'm calling back like you said. We saw each other again the next day. Quentin wanted to go dancing at the Queen. I wanted to fuck. He had taken ecstasy before I got there, there wasn't any left for me, he said, You see baby, I just took some E, I want to dance, I'll be back home around five and I'll really feel like fucking then, yes, yes, just stay here and relax. I stayed. Around five, Quentin comes home with some dark-haired guy with ears that stick out. They grab a drink in the living room, they start talking rugby (the guy plays rugby). So you'll be around next week? Can I have your number? When should I call? I caught up with him in the kitchen. I told him Quentin, enough of this, for three months you've been acting this way, are you fucking kidding me? He told me Nico you're pissing me off. Can't you see I am not going to fuck this guy right now? I slapped him across the face. He said, As soon as this guy leaves you're going to pay for that. And as soon as the guy left, he jumped me. Five-eleven, one hundred and ninety pounds versus five-two, one hundred and twenty pounds. He threw me against the wall, the shelves fell on top of me, he kicked me in the face and stomped me in the ribs with his boots. Stop! You're going to kill me. Then he stopped, he started crying, Baby I love you, come on let's go to bed, I want to fuck you. I told him No. So he said, Aha! I guess I haven't beat you up enough. I'm going to beat your face in. I love you. You won't get out of here alive. I felt like I was going to pass out but this drove me mad, I kicked him in the balls with my knees, I got free, I threw him down on the bed, I grabbed my jacket, he got back up, he grabbed me, I punched him in the face so I could escape. I was bleeding everywhere. I went straight to the emergency room.

I leave Quentin a message telling him I'll smash his face in if I ever see him again but that I am going to restrain myself. Actually, it's only because I am too scared that he will kill me.

The next day I run into Cédric. I tell him things aren't going so well, Quentin almost killed his lover kicking him with his Doc Martens Friday night. We grab a drink, I tell him the story. We catch up, he's very chatty, boasting like the formerly ugly. (Once, Quentin and I were over at his place and there was this picture of him on the cover of a German porn magazine lying around.) He tells me that he's doing better than last week, that they thought he had cytomegalovirus, that he goes through a lot of psychosomatic stuff, that he went out on an audition to host a getting-back-into-shape show, that he never stops fucking, that he has a new lover. I asked about him and it turns out I know the guy. I went to cut some wood at his place in the countryside with Quentin a year ago. Quentin had sex with him. Cédric tells me his new boyfriend loves getting fucked by him but he hasn't fisted him yet. I ask him if it's with or without a condom. He says You know, nobody uses condoms anymore, not even the Americans, everybody's HIV-positive now, I don't know anyone who is negative (me neither, come to think of it, apart from Quentin. His last test was six months ago I believe), and you know me, I go right ahead and swallow come. I said Yeah that's true, come is good, I want to eat plenty of it, fucking is really good when you can do everything. Cédric is really surprised that I found a guy so quickly. I told him I even had two and that it's because I'm so kind and that guys get attached to me. But when something is not right with them, I replace them. I don't try to make it work. He talks to me about this editor friend of his for my diary who published a book by this masochist chick. It sold 10,000 copies;

she just died in a car accident with her master, how awful. We exchange our new contact info. Then we kiss each other on the lips right in front of the cops.

Two days later Stéphane and I grab a drink at Quetzal.[5] We run into Marc, Peter's former eternal benefactor and former lover of Quentin and me. We chitchat. He ditches us to go say hi to some people at the back of the bar, but then he comes back. Are you and Quentin on bad terms? he asks. I'm not speaking to him anymore, I say, I'm not seeing him either but other than that, no, why? Because he's here, he says. Indeed, he is. Ten feet away, with Éric our former housekeeper. He's wearing the blue bomber jacket I gave him, an old white t-shirt and some dirty blue sweatpants. He is pretty scruffy, he still has two blackeyes from his fight with Nico. He looks hunched over, small, wrinkled to me. From the side Éric says something apparently funny in his ear. I say, I think I'm gonna split immediately. We leave.

The next day I feel depressed as soon as I wake up. The weather is gorgeous. It's Saturday. On top of that I have work to do. I feel like calling him and saying Save yourself. He looked so much like an old lost baby. I tell Stéphane, Quentin's right, I do want to kill him. Maybe I'll want to kill you too one of these days. That way the last thing you'll see before you die is me. I love you. I kill you. And then I start to tear up. I console myself; with Stéphane, you get over things quickly. I listen to Jam & Spoon, *Tripomatic Fairytales*, something my friend Christophe recommended. The last time I saw him was at the pool at Les Halles. When I asked him how he was doing, he said Not so well. I asked, Why? He said, My test came back positive about a month ago, I don't know how it happened. I wanted to hug him, but couldn't because we were in public. Instead, I'd stroke him discreetly when we met up at the end of the lanes.

8. Possession

I penetrate him from the front, it's not bad. He's a little tense and is unaware that I want him to play with my nipples because my dick isn't that hard, I can't feel his ass but whatever it's not too bad, at least his asshole isn't shut or super tense. I grab him from behind his knees, I lock his arms down so he can't move anymore. I fuck him gently but thrust deep.

I fuck him exactly like Quentin used to fuck me. First I grab him. I take him in my arms and I hold him softly but strongly. From the front, there are a lot of possibilities. From the back there are too, but fewer. With his ankles on my shoulders, I put my wrists around his neck or around his hips to fuck him from the front. I hold him by the ankles, spread his legs: his legs are tucked in against himself, his feet are against my belly or against my ribs. If I grab him from behind his knees, I'm able to fuck him deep, arms extended and all of the weight is in my lower body, it's the best. I can also hold him by his lower back or lift the lower part of his body slightly in the air or by his ankles with his legs crossed like a frog, or else straight out and together against my chest. I can also hold him by wrapping my arms around his thighs or his legs. These positions are the best, the stablest, for mastering penetration, plus, by changing up the positions, I can feel different parts of a dick and ass each time, sometimes the underside of my dick and the bottom of the asshole, others the top side, even right down the middle, a bit from above, or from below... Then there's the arch of the back. That's to make them feel your cock as much as possible. The more I arch my back, the broader and deeper the penetration is for the guy.

It relaxes him. Then there is the thrust. At the very end, don't forget to start to push harder and harder from the hips to open him up wider and wider. Hold back from pounding him hard right away knowing that later on you'll be able to pound him for a lot longer and in an ass that is a lot more moist, arousing a lot more gratitude. I'm able to fuck him deep for the first time, he lasts a pretty long time before he comes and I finally get to play with his relaxed asshole, so relaxed that it makes a slurp, slurp, slurp sound and I'm covered in sweat and after, my thighs hurt. Like Quentin with me back in the day.

The next day I woke up before him, around one o'clock. I puked up all my dinner from the night before. I cleaned up the toilet in the bathroom and then went back to bed. He woke up because of the noise. I asked him to fix me a bowl of hot milk and honey. As soon as I had finished it, I ran to the toilet and puked again. It was a wave of white and green because of the bile. I told myself I shouldn't have drank any milk. Around an hour later I had a glass of water, it went down OK and after I ate two spoonfuls of rice. I immediately puked it all up on the plate and the bed. I fell asleep. When I woke up, I had shit the bed. The doctor from SOS Médecins[6] gave me a letter for a week's sick leave.

9. No Comment

It's a beautiful day. Stéphane comes by to pick me up after work. We head home in his car. I don't feel like fucking. This morning I told him I'd rape him when we got home. I said that to make myself do it and to make his day. But actually, I am sick of fucking him. I watch the passing scenery. I decide to put a hood on him. That way at least I'm sure to get hard.

I grab the leather one because it's more S&M and because I am mad at him. I blindfold him. A good idea apparently. It makes him hard. He gives his ass up gladly, I can see he's really obsessed with his man cunt. I fuck him for a little over an hour. This put me in a better mood so the next day I decide to start it all over again. This time I am not pissed at him any more so I put the black latex hood on him. I think latex is more mysterious, more intimate. He opens up slowly, milli- meter by millimeter, like an apricot. For the first time I pay careful attention not to hurt him in any way. I chew on the hood. I spit on it and lick it clean with big and long strokes from my tongue all the while screwing him. He moans softly. He grabs my nipples. He's the same way I was when I discovered my asshole with Quentin five years ago. I fuck him for an hour and a half.

I fuck him until I realize that once again I don't feel like coming. Right then I wish I were dead. I start to go faster to get it over with. When he comes, I pull out of his ass and rip the condom off and I think of squirting on his hole and smearing it all over to really let death sink in, penetrate him and I start to jerk off and then my cock swells up and takes over and since I'm close to coming, I'm not thinking anymore and then I explode in a geyser and it's like in a really good porn movie and right after that I start thinking again.

10. Try

It's a beautiful day. I go outside and grab breakfast on the terrace of the Bon Pêcheur.[7] Ten a.m. The neighborhood is still empty at this hour. Very calm. I head back home, running some errands along the way. I call Stéphane at work. He picks up. He says Hey I'm in a meeting now, can I call you back? I said No need, I'm just calling to let you know that when you come home tonight, I'll have a dildo up my ass and a hood on, so all you'll have to do is cuff me before you ravage me. He says OK, that's perfect, in a professional tone of voice. I ask What time do you think you'll be home? He says Around eight.

At ten past eight he rings the bell. I open the door. He looks real aroused. I turn around. I cross my wrists and let him handcuff me to the big leash hanging off my back. Click. I start getting hard. He comes in, closes the door behind him, I'm already on my knees in front of his package, I open my mouth wide but it's difficult because of the leather hood, he unzips his pants as fast as he can, takes out his semi-hard dick. I take advantage of this and swallow it down whole, all the way to the pubis. I suckle. He gets larger fast. I have to back off but I go right back down on him and since I am really aroused I manage to swallow all of it until the head of his dick is behind the glottis, I massage his dick like that with the back of my throat breathing through my nose as I can, slobbering everywhere.

For five whole minutes I've been sucking him off but I'm starting to lose steam. I start sucking less enthusiastically, sucking up and down the side of his shaft, sucking only on the head. Not too long because he grabs the top of my hood and shoves my face back down his shaft. This turns me again at once. After a while he pulls my head away. He looks down at me. You little slut! Then he spits on me. Wow! I'm so happy that things are starting to get hot again so I do something I don't usually do because I think it's dirty but now I want to show who's who tonight. I drop down and start licking his boots. At the same time, I spread my knees and arch my back completely to offer up my ass. I know it's hot to look at: hairy except the crack which is shaved clean, my balls and the tip of the day-glo pink dildo poking out from the center of my ass, held in place by the thin strap of my leather jockstrap. Further up, he can see my hands cuffed to the leash that's hanging down my back, even further up the leather dog collar around my neck, the leather hood laced up tightly in the back. I didn't put on my chaps though so I would seem more vulnerable, but I have my Rangers and thick brown polyester socks looking a little trashy rolled down over the boots.

He smacks my ass. When this gets to be a little too much I come back up and I start sucking on his balls and cock. He stops me, pushes me back down to the floor, he's a bit rough but who cares, this is no time to complain, he grabs me by the neck and pulls me toward the bedroom. I make my way as I can, half on my knees, half crawling. He takes the opportunity to smack my ass really hard. Once we get into the bedroom, he grabs me by the shoulders and throws me on the bed, I get into position with my chest at the bottom of the bed, still kneeling with my ass in the air, no, that isn't what he wants, he makes me climb up the bed, I try a new position, my Rangers spread wide in the air, I lower my ass so that it isn't too high for his dick, he goes for a condom, puts it on and smacks my ass two, three times, he moves my thong off my crack, the dildo starts to come out on its own, he pushes it all the way back in, once, twice, then he pulls it out, he throws it on the bed, he rams me with his big dick and he fucks me like a queen.

We never do it again. I think it would be pointless to make him repeat exactly the same thing so I wait for him to suggest it. He doesn't.

11. Back from Vacation

I grab the mail. Quentin wrote me. I read Part one of our story is over. Part two has not yet begun. I regret that I made you suffer. I long to hear your voice, to talk to you calmly, in a garden. I show the letter to Stéphane. Stéphane says It could be from Jean-Marc. I think Not a chance.

I'm furious. I unpack our bags, I load the washing machine, I throw out the rotten food in the fridge; I'm not hungry. I have a hard time falling asleep despite the two beers I got at the QG[8] and the joint I smoked. The neighbor's guests leave around three a.m. Car doors slam, diesel starts up. The front door shakes, screeches, and creaks. I rush to the window, I feel like mowing them down with a machine gun like in *Taxi Driver*. I go over what I am going to say in my phone call to the building manager tomorrow. First version, second version, third version.

I don't go to work the next day. Stéphane finally comes home from work. I order him down on all fours to suck me while I finish rolling a joint. I spread my legs real wide so I can look at my dick. I am naked wearing nothing but my sneakers and tube socks hiked all the way up. I tell him to go shove a butt plug up his ass and to put on some nipple clamps. I handcuff him. They're leather and there is one for each wrist. They are more bracelets than handcuffs really, they don't hurt, you can wear them for hours. Then I put a black leather dog collar on him. I lock each handcuff to the rings that are on each side of the collar for that purpose. I connect each handcuff to the thighs with some rope, then attach them to the nipple clamps. Now, his smallest movement will strangle and pinch him a little, just enough for it to seem like two hands squeezing, not enough to hurt. Pain is not the aim of the game.

I fuck him from behind, gently whipping him. I say, Open your ass up wide now. He opens his ass wide. Then I say, Now close it. He closes it. It's real nice. From the back, his hands are cuffed behind his neck and his hard-on has been raging for a good fifteen minutes without him touching himself at all. I undo one of his cuffs so he can pull on my balls. He's not allowed to jack off, of course. I tie him back up.

I push him onto the bed to fuck him on his back. And then I start to get really bored. So I put a pillow over his head. I push down on it. This turns me on. Him too by the way. He perks his ass up. I push down harder. An orgasm starts rising. I push down harder and harder and then I have to stop because it's getting too risky. I feel the orgasm going away and I know that there's nothing I can do to get it back so I change positions and I fuck him hard to help him come and he comes and I pull out and jerk off and after I lie down next to him without touching him. I close my eyes. After a while, he asks me what's wrong. I tell him I want to kill everyone in the world, smash all my toys, stay all alone in the blood and scream until I die. He says that would make a nice scene in a movie.

12. Consultation

I explain to my female doctor that my T4s have gone back up. They were down the last time I saw her, but I was over-tired, I'd just moved, and I'd left the man I'd been with for the last five years, he was threatening to throw acid on my face. I tell her The problem is that I am bored with the new one, he doesn't fascinate me, the other one was crazy and I loved him, It's always the less crazy of the two who's crazy about the crazier one, and the crazier one is only crazy about himself it seems. She tells me that we can't escape it, that's just how it is, either you're sensible and settle down with a normal person and get bored, or, you stay with the crazy one who wants to throw acid on your face and have fun. That's just how it is. I tell her that I was depressed about it for four years, but now that I've matured, maybe things could work out with Quentin. I read in a magazine this weekend that what works with pathological seducers is someone who is extremely reassuring and knows how to play their game, with a touch of perversity, if possible. She asks me Where is he now, did he leave town? I tell her He lives three blocks away.

She gives me the usual, concerned check-up. My doctor has round blue eyes, a round, outlined mouth and a round head with brown hair. She's young but knows her stuff. She asks what's new and about my job. I talk to her about my book. She asks What is it about? I laugh and tell her the subject of my book is the same as Modern Mesclun's,[9] in the comic *Agrippine*. Have you read *Agrippine*? They are in a café and he's talking to her about his projects, among which is his erotic autobiography set to Gregorian rap music. I tell her that my book is also an erotic autobiography set to Gregorian rap music since when I write, I listen to Depeche Mode.

I tell her that Quentin wrote to me. I tell her that I replied to his letter on the back of the final cut-off notice for electricity I got because his electricity is still in my name. I wrote I don't know how to answer just now. Guillaume. My doctor shrewdly observes that this doesn't mean no.

13. Compulsion

I go to Marks & Spencer by the Opéra. I first explore the food section entirely, then I go upstairs to menswear where I browse through the underwear and after, the sale section. I curb my impulse to buy stuff that isn't useful or something I couldn't carry. I do however buy two pairs of tight-fitting blue long johns for winter and then four pairs of semi-black socks, ten francs a pair, mostly cotton—two with designs and two without, and then I find a great dark grey wool winter sports jacket for Stéphane marked way down. I go back downstairs to the food section and I buy some coleslaw and some inexpensive white Australian wine that looks simple and good, some fresh spinach in a microwavable bag, some fresh mini cocktail sausages ready to be fried up (two packs of six different kinds), and a party tray with carrot and nut salad, bean salad, and more coleslaw, and then some aged Cheddar cheese and some whole-wheat muffins, some stir-fry vegetables (soybean, carrots, and mushrooms), some smoked Canadian bacon and some baked beans in tomato sauce. I get the real kind, not the spicy Boston baked beans but the basic English ones you eat in the morning with eggs and toast.

Marks & Spencer is fascinating. There's nothing left for you to do. Everything's been prepared, the egg and watercress sandwiches, the chicken tikka meatballs, the Irish salmon brochettes, the shrimp cocktail, the coleslaw, the vegetables washed, cut, and ready to sauté, the pork paté, the cheese cubes. The store's only shortcoming is the desserts. Even the cakes look average. I guess it's a generational thing. This store's customers are surely more into bean sprouts and cherry tomato salad than mince pie and pudding. I go home like an idiot with all my shopping bags on the métro. Pretty soon there will be a Marks & Spencer at Hôtel de Ville. That will be nice.

Once I get home I put away the fresh food in the fridge and then I put on a pair of the long johns and I smoke a joint and I jerk off and then I fall asleep. I wake up when I hear Stéphane turn his key in the door. I tell him to go to the front room to try on his new jacket before he gets his clothes off. The jacket looks good on him, I knew it would, it's the same cut as the blue one and the green one that both look so good on him. He won't be able to say that I don't take care of him.

14. Living in the Ghetto

On Sunday night at La Loco[10] I ran into Tom. He told me his ex died. It's only on the way home that I thought about inviting him to dinner that next evening with two of Stéphane's friends. I left a message on his machine when I got back from shopping. He called back to say he could come. At dinner Stéphane found out a guy he knew from ASMF[11] is dead. It freaked him out but he didn't talk to me about it until the next day.

The guests went home. I was horny, we drank five bottles for the five of us. I said to Stéphane I want to fuck you in a sling at the sex club. He washed his ass before we left. I took some condoms and Xylocaine. I was already depressed. We got there. I fucked him in a sling in one of the private rooms, the chains had two extra links that went clink clink clink, and the sling was a bit too high, I had to get on my tiptoes to get in deep. My dick got soft, then hard, then soft, then hard. It went on like this for a good half an hour. I said All right, let's finish up at home, it's more comfortable. I didn't say anything on the drive home. We went back upstairs. I rolled a joint in silence. We started again. I was going limp. I wound up saying a bunch of terrible things to him. You're not sexy, there are no surprises with you, you don't know how to play with my nipples, I'm bored in your ass, sorry but I am depressed right now, I'd rather you fuck me or else I'll fuck you without a condom. He said Fuck me without a condom. Instantly my dick got hard. I thought Well I don't have any precum oozing out and surely I can avoid squirting in his ass. I dive back in. Five minutes later of course I was ready to come whereas with a condom on I usually never do it keeps me at a distance. I said I'm ready to come. He said Go ahead. I said I think we'd better wait for the results of your test. He'd never been tested. He had persuaded himself that he already had HIV anyway. I pushed him to go get tested. I say We'll do this later. I pull out and blow my load all over his little bitch ass.

The next week, his test results come back negative. I tell myself I did the right thing not coming in his ass. And then I feel alone. Disappointed. And then alone.

15. People Are Still Having Sex

I live in a wonderful world where everyone has slept with everyone. A map to this world can be found in the community magazines I read assiduously. Bars. Clubs. Restaurants. Saunas. Minitels.[12] Party spots. Cruising spots. And all the addresses, telephone numbers, and names that go with them. In this world, every man has fucked at least five hundred other men, though mostly the same guys. The guys who go out. But these networks don't cross over exactly. There are guys more into bars. More into clubs. More into clubs with bars. More into saunas. More into parties. More into cruising on the Minitel. More into dark hair. More into blonds. More into muscles. More into rough sex. More into vanilla sex. Take your pick. You've got a lot to pick from and nobody's looking to start a family. We're single or a couple, not more, in this world except when for a more or less short period, there's a sex slave in the house. I find all that invention great. I have a friend who put his two hands around his boyfriend's hands inside the ass of some guy who's well known in the community, who also has both his nipples and his cock pierced; he's got some impressive equipment that he shares to everyone's enjoyment.

Like me with what I've got at home, in my little bedroom closet, on five shelves. On the top there's the bulky stuff: two pairs of chaps, one in leather, one in latex, a shower douche and its hose, plus an enormous cone-shaped dildo for sitting on. Under that shelf there are dildos and butt plugs arranged by size on two shelves: two fat butt plugs and four small ones, four double-headed dildos, eight ordinary ones. Under that shelf, the lighter items hanging on nails: five different pairs of nipple clamps, some clothespins, a parachute ball stretcher, a dog collar, two hoods, one in leather, one in latex, six cock rings, steel or leather, regular or with built-in ball stretcher, two dick sheaths, a regular one in adjustable leather and one with spiked tips pointing in, that one's a little medieval, a riding crop, a martinet, a black and a red bandana for gagging or tying up, a funnel tube gag that directs piss right into the throat, a ball gag, the ball is inflatable, nipple clamps mounted on an extendable leather Y that can be linked to a cock ring so that the crotch can pull the nipples, a metal ball-stretcher, not too heavy, about half a pound and one inch wide (you place it between the balls and the cock or like a normal cock ring), two pairs of leather handcuffs, a leather collar with handcuffs that may be worn around the back or the front, depending on which side it's placed. Finally, at the very bottom, there's more bulky items: an adjustable iron bar with leather-tipped handcuffs, a leather harness, two pairs of Rangers, my German boots.

I've been buying these things for years. A lot of them. I've chucked out plenty of stuff I'd bought without a clue, dildos that were too hard or too crooked, cock rings that were too tight, clamps that were too strong. I've only kept this stuff. The bare essentials. I have, within arm's reach, everything I need. Alcohol. Hash. Acid. E. Coke. Weed. Poppers. Sex Magazines. Porn tapes. A Polaroid camera.

Certain things are more useful than others. I love them all. They are like parts of me. I decide where they stay, maintaining my hold over them. But it's also their duty to serve the body. Hood collar gag nipple clamps handcuffs dildos cock ring cock choker parachute ball stretcher handcuffs. Head mouth neck tits wrists arms ass groin cock balls ankles legs. All is mobilized. Ready to maximize the effects of the dick in the mouth or in the ass, the strokes of the crop on the ass the legs the back the shoulder the arms the hands the feet the balls the cock. It never hurts when it's done right. I'm no sadist. Only a bit of a megalomaniac. It leaves no marks. At any rate, whatever I do, whatever I use, was previously tried out on me. That way, everything goes as planned. Even the big dildos come out without a drop of blood, even the ones that are fatter than a fist and can make it past the second sphincter. I've become very conscious of my body, of its exterior, of its interior, because of this, I think. I train. My nipples, my ass, my ejaculations, my performances.

I wonder if it's sinister or if it's good. I think about what Jeanne Moreau says to her niece in an American movie where she's old and extravagant. No, she tells her. I don't think you're stupid. I think you've lost hope. You should do nothing. Absolutely nothing. Until hope returns. Like she's sure it always returns. Maybe she's right. I tried last night. Instead of cruising on the Minitel or going out for a drink at a bar I typically go to, I waited. After a few minutes, hope really did return. It returned in my left leg, I felt it. A muscular appeasement. All the fags I know work out. If not, they swim. Almost all of them are HIV-positive. It's crazy how they are still alive. They still go out. They still fuck. Plenty of them get stuff like meningitis, diarrhea, a case of shingles or KS lesions or pneumocystis. But then they're fine. Just a little skinnier, some of them. The ones that get a CMV or some other crazy stuff haven't been seen around for a while. They aren't talked about. That said, none of my close friends have died. I only know of four guys that I've fucked who are dead. I suspect others. Not a lot. People don't die a lot apparently. They say that AIDS is evolving towards a thing like diabetes. As long as the healthcare system can support it, we will be treated for whatever comes up. There's not much to worry about.

It's been a few years now since I entered this world. I spend most of my time here. I myself would prefer to go to London on vacation rather than discover Budapest. Budapest, that's for later. We feel good in the ghetto. There are a lot of people. More people all the time. Fags who start fucking all the time no longer go into the normal world as often as before. Apart from their job and seeing their family, everything can be done without leaving the ghetto. Sports, shopping, movies, eating out, vacations. There aren't ghettos everywhere. There's the center of Paris. There's London, Amsterdam, Berlin, New York, San Francisco, Los Angeles, Sydney. In the summer there's Ibiza, Sitges, Fire Island, Mykonos, Majorca. Sex is the main focus. Everything revolves around it: the clothes, the short hair, the nice body, the sex toys, the drugs you take, the alcohol you drink, the stuff you read, the stuff you eat, you can't be too stuffed when you go out or else you won't be able to fuck. You'll rarely go home alone as long as you're persistent, and not too depressed. If you don't tell yourself that you've already had all the guys worth having in there. Or all the ones you know you can get. But often you can get the ones you thought you couldn't. That's progress.

Last night Stéphane was recovering from the weekend, I couldn't sleep as usual especially when I'm not over-exhausted. I wondered if I would live alone or move back in with him in three months. I gave my notice, I couldn't stand the apartment anymore. There's this plan of mine to have an apartment with a balcony that I could never afford on my own. I began sorting out my sex magazines, tearing out the pages that I thought were a turn-on. I made a tableau on the living-room floor with them. Twenty square feet of pictures of dicks, a few asses too, but mainly cocks, hard ones for the most part, very pretty ones. It wasn't bad. When I got through, I sat down on the sofa and I jerked off looking at them while drinking a Heineken and sniffing poppers. Afterwards, around three in the morning, I got into bed. I live in a world where plenty of things I thought impossible are possible.

PART II

1. The Handsome Serge

We met him at the Queen pretty late, at an hour when there's practically no one left but the hardcore ones. Slightly bald. 6'1", a hundred and seventy-five pounds. His body, a knockout. White, evenly-spaced teeth in a perpetual smile. Sufficiently young. Nice face. Visibly smashed on some high quality stuff. First we caught each other's eyes. Then I was dancing, holding on to Stéphane trying to turn him on. He came closer. We were putting on a show on the dance floor, making it seem like we were fucking each other. That made him swell up. I could feel that there was some volume. I peeled Stéphane off. We said one or two things to each other through the blare of the music. I sent Stéphane to go get us some drinks. To the other guy I said Man I really want to blow you. He said No problem. He led me off to the bathroom. I said to myself Cool, he knows what he wants. I followed him without resisting. The bathroom was packed, a giant line just to get in. I said OK, now what? He dragged me over to a blind spot by the entrance. He turned his back to the dance floor. I got down on my knees. He whipped out his super beautiful cock. I took it in my mouth and sucked on it while jerking off for about five minutes. It was hot. Then I said Look my boyfriend is waiting for us, we have to get back, OK? He said OK. Stéphane was waiting at the bar with the drinks, super chill as always.

We all agree pretty quickly about what to do next. First, we stop by his place to do this new American drug I haven't heard of that's supposed to be great for fucking, and after we go home because we have toys at our place and he doesn't at his. By now,

I am fairly convinced that this is going to be a hassle because of this last detail but he is so gorgeous that I can't imagine for a single second turning down the possibility of having him.

His apartment is great. Loft style. TV and speakers in the bathroom. Classy furniture. An envelope addressed to him from a TV network lies on the American kitchen counter. He puts some trance music on, loud. The sound system is the best. We snort some drugs. Within ten minutes we are completely fucked up. We should film this. We take off our clothes. He is sublime. Great dick, very thick and long, big balls with lots of skin. I suck him. I lick his balls. He smacks my back, my ass. He plays macho man. I like it. He's like You're a real slut, you, a real one. You're making me hard. I check. He's exaggerating. I'm sure he's not going to fuck me but oh well. In the bathroom there was an old, unopened box of Prophyltex condoms and Prophyltex are much too small for a cock like his, if he was using condoms on someone with any frequency he'd have Manix large. What's equally weird is the pair of classy women's heels on his bedroom floor by the mirror. But it's the only trace of woman in the whole space. Maybe he's bi, the pretentious prick. He looks me in the eye. I do the same. We smile. He tells me Don't give me that look or I'll marry you. I say It's not my fault, that's just how it is. He's like Wow wow wow! clapping his hands while I paddle the cutie-pie's ass with my hands to make the ambiance a bit sexier. Turns out this cutie-pie is too stoned and passes out on the parquet with his leather pants down to his ankles. I like this Serge, that's for sure, it's like being in love. The problem is that of course he's not fucking me. Just a couple pumps of his cock, no condom, just like that, in his kitchen, the windows open, after he snapped the antenna of his cordless phone trying to insert it up my ass. Clearly this guy isn't used to fucking. It's true you can't do everything in life. He tells me several times how sorry he is that he's too high. I tell him It's no big deal.

He falls asleep on the sofa while I am sucking his dick. The stereo is playing opera music now, this must be what he usually listens to. I am alone. I go into his bedroom, scope out a few books: workout plan for the perfect body and how to train it under the table by the bed, VHS tapes under the TV in front of the bed, no porn or else they're well hidden, a dresser full of briefs, boxers, socks, scarves. Everything is perfect. The briefs are perfect. The boxers are perfect. The socks are perfect. I try on a pair of blue briefs, not bad, then a jockstrap, I had almost the same one, not good, then an old pair of Nikos underwear with a super hot cut that look great on me. I put it in my jacket, then I search for a container to put the drugs in. I find an empty film container on his desk. I collect my little gift. I eat a slice of whole grain bread. There's nothing else in the fridge. The opera's still playing. I wake Stéphane up. You all right? He's OK. I leave a note for the beautiful Serge, with our telephone number. Beautiful out. I put on my sunglasses. The streets are already coming back to life. We go home. Stéphane drives. We park. Pain au chocolat. Croissants. The baker's son is still our fan. It's good to be home. So we smoke a joint. And I fuck Stéphane.

He calls around seven, eight in the evening. Hi, it's Sergio. That's what I called him in my note. He's going to dinner, but we can meet up later. He's weird. He says I'll call again at midnight. All right, that's normal, with three it's always a little more complicated. But for once, there's someone who interests me. Who impresses me. The bastard. I'm sure he's not even going to call back.

He calls again, but at one thirty. It's not looking good. He apologizes. I cut him off. He still isn't done with dinner, can we meet at Folie's at three, no better make it three thirty? I say OK. I hang up. I tell Stéphane Look for real, I want this fuck so bad just this one time. I've got to go. Stéphane says that it's not a problem.

2. Meeting Up

I'm at Folies Pigalle.[13] There's a very beautiful girl in a hot pink, super tight tee shirt with Babie written in silver. She's a great dancer. She's just as flashy as a fag or a Black. It's three a.m. I took a quarter hit of acid, three lines of coke, smoked two joints and drank a beer at home before going out. High, but not too high. I chat with the cab driver. At the door of Folies, there's a guy Quentin and I had a threesome with ages ago. He says Hi, are you with somebody? I get super paranoid. I don't understand what he means. I tell him No I'm by myself, can you let me in? He looks at me a little surprised, but he's got to see I'm stoned. Once I'm in, I tell myself Obviously he's not going to turn away somebody he knows. And I think Wow, it's cool, I know the bouncer at Folies. This sort of stuff impresses me. I know it's dumb. Then there's a Chinese guy at the entrance, one of the promoters, really really tall and thin who makes provocative t-shirts as a side gig. I ran into him at a fashion show my friend Georges took me to. He has to bend over, almost in half, just to give me a weak kiss. Hi! I buy myself a beer. I smoke. I dance.

I don't know a soul here tonight. No friend, no past hook-up, nobody I've ever exchanged more than two words with before. This stresses me out a little. Plus, the acid is strong. It gives me these pains in my back and it pulls on my cheeks and I'm speeding and from time to time I'm a little short of breath and get hot flashes. I calm myself down by telling myself it's always like this on acid. It has its positives though, the light and the colors are ten times more real than in real life. Since I'm having a good trip, I can't think about anything unpleasant for more than two seconds. My only real preoccupation is what I'm feeling and the absolute necessity to move so I can unload the truly excessive energy that it gives me.

Only three a.m. I decided to arrive at two thirty to make sure I wouldn't miss him. I get off on acting like a teenage girl. The music is good, the sound is better than before, so I dance. When I take acid, dancing relaxes my back. First I warm up, then when I'm really hot, I get up on the stage, I take off my t-shirt, I dance bare-chested, in jeans, my suspenders trailing down my thighs on top of my Rangers. It's best to have on big shoes when you have a tendency to stumble around.

And then the music gets worse, too hardcore. I get down. I am dripping with sweat. I go to the bathroom to freshen up. Long pink corridor. There are some *Beur* girls turning some *Beur* guys on. One of the chicks claims she can piss like a guy, in the urinal. I wasn't able to pee, so I took a step back so she could show us. She comes up, unzips, but then she chickens out. They shoot the shit a bit aggressively, but that's how *Beurs* cruise. I go empty my bladder in a closed stall that just opened up. I tell myself they shouldn't have let them in; the *Beurs* kinda mess with the vibe.

I think the evening is a huge success. There are only *beautiful people* who dance so well and everybody looks spellbound, totally trashed or else completely new to the club scene, maybe even both. No one to hit on. Too trendy. Whatever, the acid makes it OK. I'm not that crazy about acid, I think it's too strong, but still, you have to admit, it perks you up. As soon as the music isn't such hardcore trance, I go back and dance all out. The DJ is really great, he mixes deep disco, shake-that-ass, extreme trance to the point where it is almost too much, we start to lose interest, and BOOM it's on again. The guys scream out in pain when the DJ cuts the beats in the middle of a mix. I take a break. Stairway. Gallery. Bar. I'm covered in sweat, a little rough for this place, they don't serve me right away, but it's OK, the gin-get is substantial.

Ten to four and he never came. I leave alone. I walk around the Place Pigalle. I'm raging. When I get to the Transfert the doorman smiles at me. Stéphane is there, with his big gentle eyes and slutty low-cut tank top that shows off his nipples. We make out and then I say You doing OK sweetie? He says No, I was getting a little bored. This place is mayhem. The Transfert's anniversary celebration. Nothing is worse than a party at an S & M bar. Cake is being passed around on paper plates. Nobody wants any, but to be polite the guys closest to the bar force themselves. The bartender throws a tantrum No cake boys? Well let me remind you there are plenty of people out there who would want some.

I head around the back to the backroom and suck on this random skinhead's dick who was hanging out naked by the big trough everyone uses for pissing, but what he really wants is for me to piss on him but I don't want to piss. I split. I snag a couple kisses, a couple guys play with my nipples. I do the same to them. The guy in front of me sticks two fingers in my ass. I pull up my pants. I turn around. I know the guy in front of me but I haven't ever been with him yet. He goes out a lot but I don't think he fucks a lot of people. He looks at my cock, I stroke it a little in front of him for fun. After that I chitchat with this tiny skinhead who looks like a mouse. He's super sweet. I tell him You make me want to do bad things. He's like I do?, full of hope. But I am not really convinced, he doesn't seem slutty enough. He feels the same, and we leave it at that. I head back to Stéphane at the bar. We get champagne squirted all over our face. This is beginning to bother me. We decide to leave.

I'm wiped out in the car. Stéphane tells me five or six times that he wants sex. I don't answer. At home when we get undressed, the carpet around the bed gets covered with confetti. I say to Stéphane If you want to get fucked, I can do it. He doesn't seem to believe me. I ask him Is your ass clean? He says Yes. I take out an Olla condom, we don't have any Manix large, but I like the Olla. They're the ones we used in the Quentin days. They're kind of thick, but very bendy and soft. In the bathroom, standing up in front of the toilet, I make him put his head in it and I fuck him from behind. Then I bring him back to the bedroom and I fuck him on the bed from the front, then from behind. It lasts a long time, and it's really pretty good, I pull in and I pull out and his ass goes, flotch, flotch, flotch, really loud, he groans and moans underneath me. I begin to lose my hard-on because he's too loose. I keep going for a moment. Then we have to stop because I've gone too soft. We go and wash our hands. I tell him he can fuck me. He says he wants to piss on me. I jump into the tub and he pisses on me and I don't wash it off, we head back to the room, anyway, the sheet are already pretty soiled. The fucking is great. Deep. Long. I let myself get fucked like never before. I find he's getting better and better. But then it becomes pretty obvious that we're too stoned to come like that. I look around for my watch. It's ten, we've been fucking for four hours. We finish off the lazy way, he licks my balls, I come and then I offer to work over his ass with my left hand because my right hand has got cum all over it. He explodes. We cuddle. I roll one last joint. He falls asleep. I smoke half and then realize I'm fading so I put the joint down and fall asleep.

I wake up pissed because Serge didn't show up last night. We watch TV. I try to resist but I end up giving in and calling Serge around seven p.m. Answering machine. I start to leave a message in case he's screening. He picks up.

—Hello?
—Hi, it's Guillaume.
—Hi, you doing OK?
—No.
—Ahh…I have people over right now. My mom.
—That's nice.
—How was last night?
I'm thinking.
—It was disappointing. I mean I didn't know you weren't going
to come.
—Me neither. I didn't know I wasn't going to come.
Silence.
—Well, I go on, you're with people and I really don't have any-
thing else to tell you. It's up to you.
—I'll call you back.
—OK.

I hang up. This guy makes me sick. I tell Stéphane Do you
realize he stood me up and I'm the one who calls? But that's also
what's great about it. Being impressed. Showing it. Like a slut.
But not too much. I was happy with It was disappointing. I
was hoping he understood that I meant both that he was a dis-
appointment and that I was disappointed. I wanted to upset
him a little. But at the same time I still wanted him to fuck me.
His super soft skin. His perfect muscles, not too big, not too
small. Beautiful.

3. Excess

This weekend the cousin of my friend M. died. She had third-degree burns from an accident last year. Jojo, the guy who helped my mother out with the gardening, shot himself in the head. Terrier is recuperating in the country after a suicide attempt. Everything is going well.

Thursday night I went out on my own again. Stéphane was sleeping, exhausted from a combination of work and the partying I force on him. Me, I was wide awake and in great shape, of course, since I got up around one in the afternoon. I didn't take anything before I went out. I went to the QG. Nobody was there. Then to a *groove party* nearby, it was pretty empty. After that, it was time to go to the Queen. Men's night tonight. Let's say it was only a few more men than usual. I know the faces. I dance. I schmooze. An old guy, a tall Black American, around forty-five, tells me he has coke he brought back from the States. I tell myself this might just be the good stuff. I ask if I can taste it. He says for that we have to go to his place. I end up in a taxi headed towards Avenue de la Grande-Armée.

Four Black guys, younger and cuter, are playing cards in the living room. He directs me straight into his room so that I don't hit on any of them, the old pro. OK. We do way too much coke on a corner of his business card. Normally coke makes you speedy, but when you do a lot more, more than half a gram, say, all at once, it pulls you down instead, kind of like heroin but not as solemn. I don't care. I came here for this, and plus the old guy is getting more and more wasted and that's fine with me because

I don't really want to have sex with him. I roll a joint from the lump of hash I brought with me just in case. We smoke it. We drink a beer. We do some more coke. *I want some head and I want some tail*, he says. I suck his big black semi-hard dick for a long time. He's super wasted, and so am I. In the end, it's cool to fuck like this, super fucked up. He sucks my dick too for a while. I let myself go. I suck his some more. I ask for some coke again. We do more coke. He rims my ass. And then he says he wants to fuck me. Without a condom of course, given the atmosphere and the droop in his cock. I tell myself that even without a condom it isn't very risky and he'll never be able to come anyway. Are you HIV-positive? I ask him, my legs in the air. Yeah, Baloo the bear answers. He has a hard time getting his dick in, but eventually he does. He fucks me for a little. He must have been a really good fuck back then. We stop because he's getting too limp. I ask him for a beer. While he's gone, I steal a black dirty jockstrap by Gazelle, New York, that was laying on the floor.

I came home at six a.m., after I'd stopped by the Transfert where there was no one left. I started in the bathroom with the dildo sitting on the maxi butt plug I have that's twelve inches tall and twelve around the base. I knew very well I wouldn't be able to take the whole thing in, actually I only know one guy who can, it was just that I was lazy and it's the only big toy in my collection that stands up by itself. It wasn't really working, because after a while it starts to hurt the coccyx, but I was still making a lot of noise with my ass. I heard Stéphane moving around in the next room. I said Are you sleeping? He answered No. I kept jerking off. He came into the bathroom. He looked devastated when he saw what I was doing. I said Are you OK? He nodded Yes. I said Would you mind fucking me with a dildo? I'm not getting anywhere by myself. He said No. I said All right then let's go. I grabbed a towel, selected the toys. I didn't roll a joint, I didn't want to overindulge. I decided to start with a big one.

Fucked up as I was, I knew it would go in with a good hit of poppers, so I picked out the replica of Kris Lord's dick (10 x 7 inches) and then the enormous double-header from San Francisco, thicker than an arm. It was great. First, he fucked me really good with the Lord. Then I asked for a change. Not only did the monster go all the way in with no trouble but I was able to get fucked with it for a good ten minutes. I said I was going to come. He pulled it out. I came all over myself, convulsing and twitching. Since it was seven, Stéphane went to work. I slept.

4. Something a Little Sweet

On Friday during the day, I went to work with M., who had her little three-month-old cousin at her place, the son of the dead woman. I took him in my arms. I noticed, when he started to trust me, that he looked at me the way Stéphane looks at me. I liked it. Then I walked home along the quais. Then I fucked Stéphane. It was the first time I fucked him again after a week of abstinence. I had a huge hard-on. I put one finger, then two and then I shoved the head of my dick all the way past his second sphincter on the first try. It was just like with Terrier but better because I've made a lot of progress these past nine months. It was really great.

Then we went out for dinner and then we went out to the Queen. We got there at around three a.m., a little early for getting in without waiting in line, but I have an in with Sandrine who's at the door. So I roll up all cool and confident but it's still chaotic, too many people, guys are getting thrown out, the bouncers stop me. Excuse me sir, no one said you could come in, so wait over there. Fine, I don't really care, I know I'll get in. Then Sandrine gives the OK, the OK that means we get to squeeze by all the assholes in line and don't have to pay a cover, and then we go downstairs. It's super packed, there are lines at the bar, lines at the bathroom, it's mobbed, the music is excellent, I almost feel like dancing the whole time. I'm just a little surprised to be acting the way I am without being high.

Sunday night. Terrier tells me on the phone that now his pharmacist gives him Xanax without a prescription. He also mentions that he hooked up with a super hot Iranian guy who lives near me and who, in this order, fisted him (first time in his life), fucked him with a dildo, then finally fucked him. The guy straight out pissed on him to finish off. I tell him I consider it your duty to give me his number. He tells me that he didn't get it. I tell him that's just like him. He tells me No, you see, it was seven a.m. and we were wasted on beer and hash, the guy invited me to spend the night, I chose to go home. I ask him And you didn't ask for his number? He says No I didn't ask him for his number because he gave it to me without me asking but I threw it out on my way home. I say No way. He says You bet. I say You're really crazy. He says No I am not crazy, I threw it out because I didn't like him that much, that's all. We argue, just for the sake of it, to see if he would have given me the number if he had it.

Terrier is looking good these days. He's cut out the Prozac and some other stuff so he now just takes Xanax because if he doesn't he gets the shakes. He goes out every night. I tell him that I think you have to be brave to go out alone at night, to go do who knows what with who knows who. He tells me he has to go to Dieppe soon to see a fuck buddy of his in his forties who has a chateau. Today, the guy asked him about a two-week trip in October to the Antilles. The guy hadn't fucked him yet, just with a dildo. It was nice, so he says. The guy has all the right toys: clamps, dildos, latex chaps, leather underwear. Terrier says Yeah but he's a little too femme for me and I don't like it, I need a more manly man.

We talk for a little while longer and then I tell myself Stéphane's probably a little tired of hearing me have so much fun with his predecessor so I cut it short. Terrier and I, we're getting along these days. He's gotten used to the idea that we'll never live together again. He doesn't soak my doormat with turpentine anymore, he doesn't cut his face with a razor blade any more (actually he used to do this so carefully that the wounds completely healed within five days). In any case, it's going all right. We'll be able to return to our guided tours of Paris during the day. I prefer not to bring him along anymore to pick out porn at the sex shop for reasons that I should have noticed from the start. In fact, I knew this wasn't a good thing to do, but it turned me on to mess with him a little.

I get close to Stéphane in bed. He snuggles up in my arms. You're like a croissant, I tell him. Butter or plain? He asks. Butter, I tell him. But also a little plain, he replies. That's true, I say, but you're intelligent. So it's cool.

It's midnight. Stéphane is sleeping. Tomorrow is Monday and as usual he has to get up early. I look at him. I think he looks super beautiful tonight. He didn't get a lot of sleep last night. After the Queen we went by the Transfert and brought home a super hot guy with a big dick which means we didn't get to bed until eight. Stéphane got up around eleven to go have lunch with his friend H. He didn't want to blow her off because he hasn't seen her in a year. He came home around five. He told me that she thought he'd changed, for the better. That she asked him how things were going with me. That he told her He brings me to the edge of the abyss, and then we take off on a hang glider. He says that H. told him I must be a good guy. I shuddered. I didn't say anything.

I toss and turn, not able to sleep thinking about Serge. It's like he took Quentin's place. I feel like calling him again. Like telling him I want you. I want your skin. Something that excites him. For him to tell me to come over. I'd lord over his bed with the remote control, facing the big TV. We'd try to find ourselves. Demons.

5. Problems

Stéphane comes back from his opthamologist friend. The black spots he's been seeing for the past two weeks are signs of a detached retina. He might lose an eye. They have to operate immediately. I think That makes sense, he doesn't want to see what's happening with me. He's checking into the hospital the next day, he comes by after work to pick up some things. I'm in bed, wasted. I say You want me to go with you? He says No no, it's not worth the trouble. So I don't go with him. I make myself something to eat. Then around ten, I head out to Le Bar for a change. I bring home a guy, a cute preppy who turns out to be completely lame and antisex but really handsome. As expected, I fuck him. As expected, it's terrible.

The next day around noon, Terrier calls. I tell him what's going on. He says he wants to see me. I say OK since Stéphane isn't around. I never sleep over at someone else's place, that's the rule. Otherwise, I can do whatever I want. So this is OK. He comes over on time, I had offered to take him to a restaurant, but I changed my mind late in the afternoon and without telling him went to Dubernet and bought some things to eat, I got some partridge terrine, foie gras brioches, I made a small salad on the side. We have burgundy to drink. After coffee I start seriously wanting sex. I lean up against the kitchen cupboards and push my hips forward to make him drool over my half-hard dick hidden under my faded 501s. He starts to make a fuss but I end up getting him down on all fours sucking me off, it's truly great, he forgets everything else, it lasts a long time just the way I like it, he drools so much it runs down my balls and down his chin, I bend over to kiss him, I can tell that it drives him crazy, I pull away, I lead him to the bathroom so he can wash out his ass, and then we head to the bedroom and I fuck him deep for a long time, I go in and out, pounding him hard, he pants and breathes heavy making faces, he's sporting a goatee these days and it looks really good on him because he's got such a gorgeous mouth, he's completely bunched up underneath me, this is so much better than with Stéphane but I don't care right now I'm looking straight into his eye while ramming him harder and then he's blowing a huge load as he closes his eyes and screams, without touching his dick, and I pull out and spray him with mine.

The next day, Stéphane's surgery day, I have an enormous amount of work to do and I can't go see Stéphane. I call him when he wakes up to let him know I'll come by the day after. I think about Quentin's operation, last December. After, he got back to fucking pretty quickly. He cruised the Minitel with one hand. He fucked and was fucked with a dildo on his back the first few days to make sure he didn't move his torso. I would undo, wash, and retie this sort of shirt-sling thing he had to wear, everyday. I would feed him. I would dress him. I would bathe him. It was cool. We had quite a few orgies while he was like that. As soon as he didn't need me any more, we grew apart again.

The following day, I still have a bunch of things to do. I am running way too late for the time I said I would be there, but I can't bring himself to call him because I feel so guilty. I arrive at the hospital around seven thirty even though I am supposed to have dinner with my dad at eight thirty. By the time I locate the right wing, then the room whose number I forgot, and there isn't anyone anywhere to ask anymore, it's already eight. Stéphane is asleep. I stare at him for a while. He wakes up. We talk. I caress his hand. I'm surprised that there are flowers in the room, usually they are not allowed because of the risk of infection. His ex came to see him earlier in the day and brought them. Me, I brought him things to eat, foie gras, cookies, and chocolate, since the food is always so bland in hospitals. I talk to him about stuff that ran through my head during my hospital stay a year ago. I tell him I saw Terrier and that I couldn't help myself, I had to fuck him. He says he's not surprised. He asks me about Terrier. The eye that isn't covered in a blood-soaked bandage looks at me sadly when he tells me that he thought I wasn't coming at all.

A few days later Terrier calls me around three in the afternoon. He asks Do you know what time it is? His voice was very hoarse. I say Why, don't you have a watch? No I broke it. I tell him It's three. He says Ah OK and do you know what day it is? I say Friday why? He says Ugh I wanted to know if it's been three days or four days since I've been asleep. I say Not bad! And how did you do that? Simple. After going around to all the pharmacies where no one gave him anything he slit his wrists and then stopped the bleeding and then took some sleeping pills. I say So how do you feel? He says All right, except I'm a little hungry. I say I'll pick up some food and be right over. I bolt out of my apartment, I swing by the supermarket near where he lives and buy Coke, organic apple juice, cheese, saucisson, canned spinach, Nestlé milk, grated carrots, some sourdough bread, endives, smoked salmon, butter, yogurt, little jars of baby food—vegetable-lamb and apple-banana (they have no apple-quince), a newspaper for him to read.

I get there, he lets me in, all in white with the white sweatpants I gave him. On me they're tight, very provocative, on him not so much, but he's still as beautiful. I take a bite of the celery remoulade, then some saucisson, I insist that he eat some of the baby food. I make him pull the sheets back on his bed, we take a quick nap, he shows me pictures of his parents' and grand-parents' weddings and I comment on them. We chitchat, we make out some, we squabble, he tells me that while he was away resting in the countryside, he slept with Frédéric, a friend of my mother, so I find out that Frédéric has a very nice cock, eight inches, thick. Terrier sucked it but then said We should stop, we don't have condoms. In reality, he really wanted Frédéric's friend and Frédéric's friend's boyfriend too. Terrier is such a slut, just like me. Oh yeah, I also brought him a jar of greengage plum jam that I made myself and that I was supposed to give him a month ago, a jar stuffed full of fruits as big as porcini mushrooms, with a red lid. I yell at him about his suicide attempt. Well what do you expect? he says to me, You never come by to see me, you never return my messages. It's only when I am sick that you pay attention to me. A little while later he says I was really touched that you didn't eat my jam or give it to someone else. I tell him that it was for him. Eventually we head out to buy some cigarettes and he walks me back to the métro stop.

6. Diversions

I wake up at four in the afternoon, after going to sleep at seven in the morning after fucking this asshole that I brought home from the QG because he was the first acceptable guy who stuck. The evening was horrible, I wasn't having any luck at all, even though I kept telling myself, it's not a big deal, there's too many hot guys tonight, that's what kills the vibe, I still felt like a piece of shit, like I didn't exist. A guy I knew whom Stéphane and I had already hooked up with was there. I'd been feeling up his ass through his leather pants, I told him I couldn't really feel it. He undid his belt so I could get a better feel, I put my hand in, shoved my index finger between the crack and rubbed his ravaged hole, he dropped his pants, I fingered his ass in front of the whole bar, he was calmly sniffing poppers, that got me hard. I put his hand on my crotch. Proposed we go back to my place. No response. He went down to the backroom. I was furious that he blew me off like that. I followed him, found him opening a condom to pound some guy in the back corner. I stayed to watch, staring intently, concentrating. Ordinarily no one comes up to me in backrooms because I don't look that interested. In fact, I think it's pointless, that kind of groping. At best, it's a quick fuck standing up. Ugh. But there I was staring at him hoping it would bother him. Then the guy next to me started to feel me up. I returned the favor. We kept going. My enemy stopped fucking. That pleased me, I told myself that it was me who threw him off, I felt somewhat avenged.

Stupidly, I continued on with the other guy. And the moment he turned towards the wall and started jerking off faster, I felt so depressed that I said How about we finish up at my place. He asked Where's your place? Just around the corner, I answered. I knew there was no point in bringing him home, but I didn't have the courage to go home alone. Once we got home we fucked of course. When I almost had my whole hand in his ass, he started saying Oh yeah, your hand's up my ass, oh yeah, I like that, almost as if he was dubbing a porn movie. I looked at his dick. He wasn't hard. That grossed me out. On top of it all, he wanted to see me again.

I woke up feeling super gross. I got on the Minitel almost immediately. There was nothing, except a guy I'd chatted with a few times already, he contacted me again, this time about some plan involving ecstasy and women's underwear. I knew he was lame, Quentin told me, they had sex last year, but anyway, there was nothing else and I didn't have enough energy to go out and look for something better, so I told him OK. Later he called me back to suggest the same thing but as a three-way, with a young guy he knew, twenty-seven years old, good-looking, versatile. I said OK, naturally.

They arrived towards late afternoon. The young guy looked good. The one I knew already was as lame as I expected. Totally out of it, apparently on his second or third E of the day, apparently, and plus his stuff was shitty, he tried to charge double the market price, he was actually a shitty drug dealer. He didn't get hard. Éric and I took care of everything ourselves. Then the old troll left. That was cool. It was still early. We had a lot of time before Stéphane came home, he was supposed to return really late from a meeting. I thought it was good for me to fuck someone beautiful my own age. I gave him my leather chaps to put on. It made his tushie really big. Every time he would turn around, I'd stare at it, it was so fleshy, curvy, white and round. Like a mother's breasts.

He didn't know how to do anything but suck, piss and fist. But I have to say he did those very well, eyes wide open, dick hard. First I sucked his dick. After that he wanted to play with my ass. He was very precise, I was hard without touching myself, his hand went up my ass all the way past the wrist, I double-checked how deep in the mirror. I could feel myself starting to come. I asked him to pull out quick. I came. He said I'm so moved. I asked Why? He said Because I was hard without touching myself the whole time I was fisting you. I told him That's normal because you did it right, when I used to fuck my ex with a dildo, I would be hard the whole time. I rolled another joint. Then I turned my attention to him. I used the riding crop on his cock, holding it in one hand, smacking it with small precise strokes harder and harder, on the top, then on the sides, then on the balls more softly, then back to the shaft. His cock was raging hard. I gave him my cock to suck, he suckled it really well. My hard-on was heavy, pliable, full, the one you'd have when you've already been doing stuff for an hour or two. We kept going at it.

He forgot his poppers at my place. He called the next day to tell me. I told him that was a classic move. He said With you, everything's classic. That made me laugh. On second thought, I could have told him that it was simply a matter of statistics. He told me he hasn't done a lot of fucking. In my world, a lot of fucking means like more than three guys a week. That's what I do these days. Quentin had done that a lot before he met me. Even after for that matter. At one time he would have a different regular guy for each night of the week, leaving weekends *open* for new finds. Fucking is always better with regulars. The problem is you have to manage the interpersonal stuff. But Quentin is a little schizophrenic, so that doesn't bother him. When nobody really exists, there's room for everyone. I wonder if I am like him. I don't think so, but I am not sure.

7. It's Starting Again

The next day is Monday. Stéphane and I go out for dinner to Au Diable des Lombards.[14] I love that place. It's the Ritz of the ghetto. Plus, now that I am older, I always run into people I know. Tonight, we run into this tall guy, model-like, but not too bad, to whom we had given our number at the restaurant three months ago. He'd left us a message a week later but we were going on vacation, we called him back and left a message saying we were leaving. When we got back we didn't call him again, it had gone a little cold. I start talking to him again as we are leaving. We'll see. We go for a final drink at the QG. We run into a buddy with whom I had pretty hot hookups two or three times, I call him the Doc because he's a doctor. We bring him home.

It's already been an about an hour since the three of us started fucking when someone rings the doorbell. Shit, I say to myself. It has to be Terrier. We stop. Then nothing. I get back to ramming Stéphane. Stéphane gets back to blowing the Doc. The Doc starts playing with Stéphane's nipples again. The doorbell rings again. It's got to be him. I pull out. I keep the condom on while I go let him in, to show him that dropping by on people at three thirty in the morning is not OK. But that doesn't work at all because when I open up he falls right through the doorway, super drunk. How much have you had? A bottle of whisky. I look down at the dirty carpet in the entrance. He says I want to sleep. I say Hey, you go back home and sleep. He says I want to sleep here. I say You're a pain, you're really a pain. I split. The other two are still in the bedroom. I tell them what's going on. They calm me down. I go back to see Terrier. OK, you can sleep in the guest room. Since he won't move I drag him into the room and I shut the door.

After, it's impossible to get back to fucking because instead of sleeping, he roams the apartment. We joke that we should tie him up to the radiator and fuck in front of him, that would be funny at least. And then I hear the door to the medicine cabinet in the bathroom sliding open. When I get there, he has this happy look. I immediately look for the bottle of Lexomil I just had filled. It's empty. This little fucker has come to my place to kill himself. It's the third fake attempt in two weeks. At least the last time it was at his place. All right. I grab him by the collar and drag him like a kitten to the toilet. What the fuck are you crazy Guillaume? No, no, I'm not, you're the one who's crazy. But when we get to the toilet he refuses to puke. I'm sure if I put two fingers down his throat he'll bite them. I give up. I leave him there, collapsed on the floor. The others are still in the bedroom. I don't know what to do, I say. What did he take? A bottle of whisky and a tube of Lexomil. Well that's not enough to kill him, he'll just sleep for three or four days. But I don't want him sleeping here for three or four days when I'm not here, he did this on purpose, he knows I'm going away tomorrow, I told him today on the phone. I ask the Doc what one normally does in this type of situation. The Doc says that in this type of situation you call the paramedics, you stop washing your dirty laundry in private, when he wakes up in the emergency room, he'll know that this is serious.

I call the paramedics. I'm high, we smoked two stiff joints, did a bunch of poppers, I'm worried they'll hear it. Hello, good evening sir I have someone at my place who's just tried to commit suicide. What did the person use? A tube of Lexomil and a bottle of whisky. They don't want to pick him up, I explain that I don't have a car and can't take him to the Hôtel-Dieu. OK, they're on their way. We start putting his clothes back on. He resists as much as he can. The Doc takes off but wishes us good luck. We look more or less normal when the paramedics arrive, at least I think we do. They don't seem particularly happy to be here. Come on, sir, you've got to get up now, no, no, you can't sleep here, come on, let's get dressed. Stéphane and I finish dressing him. His boots, we don't bother.

Terrier is truly one organized boy. In his métro-card holder, there is his ID, his insurance card and some money. Phew. They wheel him down in a chair. I follow. See you later. In the car next to the stretcher I freak out telling myself they must think we're a bunch of dirty depraved faggots, but then I say to myself Actually they are probably more used to this type of stuff than I am. The streets pass by through the windows of the ambulance.

At the hospital, there are homeless people looking for a place to sleep who are being thrown out and a bunch of cops. I'm still super high. They unload Terrier. Male nurses, female nurses. They bring him in on the stretcher. The head nurse, a solid brunette, gives me an accusing look and sends me to fill out some paperwork for "my friend." I walk through the sleepy hospital. The waiting room is open and empty. The Black guy is nice. I ask him how many attempted suicides they usually get a night. He says Oh we see a lot of misfortune.

I go back to the emergency room to give them the paperwork. I asked what was going to happen. The nurse told me they were going to pump his stomach and I'd have to wait. So I waited. I knew there was nothing to wait for but I couldn't leave. I heard Terrier scream my name really loudly. There was a big metal clang. A nurse rushed off. I went up to the desk. I asked the nurse if there was a problem, but she didn't have the time to answer because the head nurse had arrived. They spoke in whispers.

Then the head nurse turned to me and said You're Guillaume? I didn't dare lie. I nodded my head. She said He's asking for you. He wants to see you. I said I think that it's better not to.

I waited some more, paranoid from the joint I smoked that still hadn't faded, plus every half hour tons of cops kept showing up with guys who were more or less covered in blood. Terrier wheeled by looking whiter than a sheet, finally asleep, with a drip in his arm. I was told that I could call around noon when he would be awake. I walked all the way home. I got undressed in the hallway and then I went into the bedroom and when I sat down on the bed Stéphane woke up and I told him what had happened and then I took him in my arms as usual and we fell asleep.

I saw Terrier again some time later. Stéphane was at his parents' in the country. As always, I tried to fuck him. He didn't want to. I told Stéphane I thought Terrier was right. It wasn't good for him to have sex with me.

8. Party Time

I made some jam for two or three days and then I finally agreed to go away with Stéphane for the weekend of the eleventh because it was with a group of friends and we left for London.

Night people are the most civilized of all. The most difficult. They pay more attention to their behavior than aristocrats in a salon. At night, you don't talk about obvious things. You don't talk about work, or money, or books, or records, or films. You only act. Speech is action. Always on the lookout. Gestures charged with meaning. *Clubland. All over the planet.* Tonight we're in London. I recommend the FF for drugs, it's purely for the connoisseur. They're there by the way. The cream of the crop. The most beautiful, chic, hardcore in the world. The club is full. We each take half an E that I still have from Heaven, but it isn't enough to handle the music here. Too hardcore. I go look around for something else after I've rolled and smoked a joint in the corner of the bar.

> *Look around*
> *Pleasure*
> *Pleasure*
> *Pleasure*
> *Give yourself over to absolute pleasure*
> (OPM, *Pleasure*—Bubble Mix)

In the corner by a pillar there's a guy bent over over a spoon that someone else is holding. I stand next to them, not too close. I wait for them to finish. The one snorting leaves. I ask the other one *Do you sell anything?* He says No. *Do you know anyone who sells anything?* He says *I'm gonna see if I see someone I know. I'll be back in a minute.* He comes back five minutes later with a tall bodybuilder in a body harness. The bodybuilder takes me to the other end of the bar. The dealer is big and black and very sexy. *How much for an E? Fifteen. And for acid? Five.* The E is five pounds more than at Heaven, but it is surely better here. But I only have ten quid on me so I buy two hits of acid. Stéphane and I each get half. I go back to see the dealer to buy two E's for later.

After another joint, I manage to dance even to hardcore techno, still a little frustrated because the beat is too simple for what I love to do. Besides, all the leather guys dance terribly except for the few who are on so much speed that they can follow the beat. I still end up dancing in the near darkness at the back of the club. The floor is wet, way too slippery. It is so hot that I'm drenched in sweat in one minute. It's cool, it warms my dick up. I had almost forgotten about it because of the drugs. Later, I start getting out of breath, I go and chill by the edge of the dance floor. I don't know where Stéphane is. He doesn't dance anyway, he's self-conscious about that too.

I begin to get bored. I go to say thanks to the guy who hooked me up with his dealer, you never know, and it's a good thing to do out of principle. He's still in the same spot. I say, *Thanks for the hint.* He gives me a huge glamorous smile. Me I can't. I find Stéphane. I am full of hate for this place. The music is too shitty. The people are too snobbish. The super butch bodybuilder guy who grabbed my package when I went by him is still staring at me with eyes that are both hungry and devoid of any expression. He pisses me off. I tell Stéphane I can't stand these people any more. I only like people who know that there are more important things out there than themselves. And worst of all, there's nothing here but asses patiently waiting for a dick because they know they're cute enough to get one. That pisses me off.

The bodybuilder walks by again. He's 5'7", one hundred and seventy-five pounds of muscle, at least. Shaved head. Bare-chested. Not a single hair. Enormous nipples, one pierced with a big chrome ring. Bitch, I say. I look at him, not in a nice way, I think. He stops halfway up the stairs. Apparently he liked my expression.

I've had enough. I suggest to Stéphane that we should split. This place closes in half an hour anyway, and we might as well avoid the line at the coat check. I grab my jacket. I put it on. Stéphane waits for his. I chill, leaning against the safety barrier that blocks the entrance. He's there. He comes up to me. His pupils are very dilated. *I want you to fuck me*, he grunts with his awesome Cock-ney accent. I look at him. I say *I'm sure*. He says *Come. With your boyfriend*. I say OK. I go find Stéphane. We head back down-stairs. Now there's a line for the coat check. The men's bathroom is full. We go to the ladies'. A stall opens up. I had already noticed the girl who comes out, a brunette with a white top in black trim. She smiles at us, ultra-stoned like us. We go in. We only take off what we need to, pants down to ankles. The head of his dick is pierced, and he isn't hard. He sucks our dicks. When our dicks become usable, he pulls out some condoms. They use really thick condoms here, but it's all right, I'm hard. I fuck him. He's tense and stiff, his ass is a little too high. I'm still able to penetrate him without any lube, thank you acid. The problem is that it's uncomfortable and I don't feel much of any-thing. I pass him over to Stéphane. Stéphane pounds him. This turns me on. He passes him back to me, so on and so on. We eventually lose what hard-on we have. He wants us to shoot our loads on him. I ask Stéphane You feel like coming on him? Stéphane's like Not really. I say Me neither I don't want to waste it I'd prefer to do something back at the hotel with my regular. So we don't come. I say *I think it's OK like that.* We get dressed. He says *I'm sure to see you around some time guys.* His politeness irritates me. I ask *Where? Do you often come to Paris?* He's like *No.* I say *Then it's not so sure.*

At the exit, the Indian taxi driver who throws himself at us staggers so much on his way to his car that we head back to the entrance to get another one, an apparently sober Black guy. He listens to disco. It's cool. We pass by milk delivery trucks parked on the City's huge deserted streets. The Black guy drives well and fast. *You're a smooth driver,* I tell him, *I like that.* He's like *Oh.*

I want Stéphane to fuck me wearing the latex hood, full face with only holes for nostrils, that I bought at Clone Zone this afternoon. I'm sure it'll be great on acid. He agrees. He fucks me. Two times in a row. The bed makes an infernal racket. And then he fists me. I come three times, he comes once at the end. I take some Lexomil to cut the acid and to sleep. Spliff. The vibe is still kind of rough.

The day after, I want to look hot. I shave and leave a goatee, to accentuate my mouth. I give myself some really long sideburns. Black leather pants. Rocker's belt. Rangers. Super tight bright red t-shirt with silver stars, cropped to the navel, with some hair and my stomach showing. First class. I share an E with Stéphane for the depression. It's not working out between us. I dumped him once already last week. I realize I've been trying for some time now to replace him. Yesterday I asked Sandrine, a friend who lives here, if she had a boyfriend. She told me No, I'm alone. I'm waiting for something good. It's good to be alone, too. I said Yeah I agree. I thought that I should also be alone and wait.

Tonight
It's party time
Tonight
It's party time
Tonight
It's party time
(Alex Party, *Read My Lips/Saturday Night Party*)

At Substation, the evening got off to a pretty dismal start. Not a lot of people. We drop two E's we got at FF. I got progressively higher, very strong, but very good. Started dancing by the pinball machine where Stéphane was playing with tall Christophe. Then to the dance floor. Then I realized that I had just taken the best ecstasy of my life. I danced like I hadn't danced in a long time. Maybe forever, in fact. Less repetitive. Freer. More choreographic. I jumped in the air more times, at the end of the night, spun around ten times in a row. Super DJ. The best set I ever heard, I think, the happiest, and deep house, really massive. At one particularly high moment, I tried to catch his eye, it must have been three already, the place closed at four. I gave him a thumbs up. He did the same. As I was dancing, a tall guy leaned over to me and he said *I like you. I pray God for you to stay alive.* That threw me a little but still I said *Thank you.*

The little skinhead danced really well, in this frenzied way. We were the two best dancers on the floor, once the one or two girls who were there at the beginning of the night had left. We watched each other, appreciating each other. At one point when his back was to me, I grabbed him and pretended like I was fucking him. It felt good to hold his narrow, muscular hips. Then I turned around and it was his turn and he humped my ass tap tap tap tap in the middle of the dance floor. We kissed for a long time. Stéphane had run off somewhere. A little nipple play.

I caressed the small of his back, his waist, I put a finger at the top of his crack, he felt soft. I touched him exactly as if he belonged to me. Stéphane came back. I pulled away a few inches and said *I have a boyfriend.* He said *Where is he? He's here,* I said showing him Stéphane. He grabbed me by the shoulder. He turned me around. He pushed me towards Stéphane. *Don't play around with love if you've got a boyfriend,* he said. *Or you'll get a punch in your face.* And then he left me alone with Stéphane. Stéphane left again. I went and bought myself a beer although as a rule you shouldn't mix E and alcohol.

It was closing. I got in line at the coat check. The little skinhead kept coming and going shouting, *Everybody's counting their money! But I want some flesh! And just nobody will give me a shag! Just because I'm a gay national star!* I asked the Black guy in front of me *Is he really the star he says he is? No, he's just the contrary,* the guy answered. *He's what we call in English a complete asshole.* I feel like he said that because he was jealous.

Stéphane goes to sleep to forget about me as soon as we get in. It's four a.m. We could have been fucking. I jerk off. It's great. This really was the best night out though. *Don't play around with love if you've got a boyfriend.*

When we got back from London I told Stéphane I was leaving him. He told me that it didn't surprise him. He went on a bar crawl. I jerked off. It was great. And then I listened to one of the house compilations I bought while over there. After that I listened to Propaganda's *Duel.*

> *The first cut won't hurt at all*
> *The second only makes you wonder*
> *The third will get you on your knees*
> *You'll start bleeding I'll start screaming*

I thought about Eric P. who knew how to choose music so well and who always felt like jumping when he was going near the window after he'd been smoking.

The first cut won't hurt at all
The second only makes you wonder
The third will get you on your knees
You'll start bleeding I'll start screaming

I wouldn't be surprised if he killed me. If he had a gun, that is.

Selling your soul
Selling your soul
Selling your soul
Never look back
Never look back
(Propaganda, *Dr. Mabuse*)

9. Separation

Stéphane said he'd be out of the apartment at the end of the week. I'm glad he's not leaving right away. Still, it's not too much fun between us. We hardly speak to one another. Sometimes we cry. We sleep together without touching. Finally he leaves for a week to stay with his parents. We call each other. I say that I don't know anymore, that I need to take a step back, that if we continue seeing each other, it has to be under better circumstances, when I would hurt him less, when I'm doing better. When he comes back, he's going to stay with a friend. He moves out while I'm at work. I look for a studio or a one-bedroom for myself. I eventually find something a little out of the way but not too bad. I box things up.

The morning of the moving day, a guy who I hooked up with two months earlier on Minitel called me on the telephone to offer me a free piercing. I asked if we could see each other towards the end of the week. He said he was only free that afternoon, after that he was going away. I said OK, come by. I had been thinking about it for a long time. Lots of guys I had been seeing or knew had it done. Not me. It was one of the only things I hadn't already done. And now I felt like doing something serious. Plus he's the one who brought it up. Interested in a piercing? I replied Yes but of what if not the face not the nipple not the dick? He wrote That leaves your navel your perineum and your sack. My sack? He typed The balls. I wrote Why not? He wrote that he would call me back.

He came over to my empty apartment with his small case, a little late because he'd just repierced a guy he'd pierced last year. He was very tall, broad shoulders, quite ugly and badly dressed. We chatted over a glass of water. He showed me his piercings, both nipples, the one on the right had two rings, he'd added one recently. I asked him if it was healing well. He said Yes, I just have to disinfect it regularly because it's a little swollen. He squeezed it to make the pus come out.

We talked for a long time because I wanted to be sure I could trust him. He showed me his tools. He told me we'd begin only when I felt ready. After a little while I said that I thought we could go on with it. I sat down on the living room couch, the only piece of furniture left in the apartment. He gave me a shot in my scrotum to anesthetize it. We waited. It was still sensitive. I asked him to give me another. We waited. My scrotum was swelling a little. It was still sensitive. I said that I didn't want to feel any pain, that I wanted more anesthesia. He told me he'd never seen that before. I thought that he wouldn't have minded seeing me suffer. I said There's a first time for everything. He gave me a third shot. We waited. I talked to lighten up the mood. I pinched myself. I wasn't feeling anything anymore. I said It's OK, we can go on now. We went into the bathroom because of the blood. I sat on the edge of the tub. He pulled on my balls, placed the surgical clamps on both sides of my sack. I was watching. He began to pierce, with a needle about two and half to three inches long with the ring attached to the end. The needle went through, then the ring. He had a hard time screwing the little closure ball shut because the blood made his latex gloves slippery. He disinfected it. I held the bandage because it was bleeding.

He made a call on his cell. Another piercing. A nipple I think. He left. I waited for Stéphane. He was supposed to come help me move some stuff. The bleeding wasn't stopping. Stéphane arrived late, looking very happy to see me. I told him there was a problem, that I just got my ball sack pierced and it wouldn't stop bleeding. He asked me But that means we won't be able to have sex for how long? I said two, three weeks. He groaned as if I had hit him. He punched the wall. I realized that I had just fucked over our new start.

I stuffed my underwear full of toilet paper. The blood was starting to stain my 501s. We took his car. He drove me to my new place. He carried up the stuff I had with me. I was trying not to move too much so the bleeding would stop. He stayed for a bit and then he left to go to sleep, he had to get up early the next day.

10. Christmas Eve

For Christmas, I was alone in my new apartment. My bank account had been wiped out by the move, I'd had to work hard to bring in the cash. As soon as I had finished I got sick. Stéphane came by and brought me ham and canned soup before he went away to his parents. We were supposed to go see a painting exhibition that was ending, the one time he was free on a week-day afternoon. And then I got sick. Both of us knew it was the end without admitting it. He didn't stay long.

I called my mother to tell her we could still maybe get together as a family, which was a bit phony. Had she offered, I would have refused. I was thinking about Quentin. Our first year, we'd ended up one inside the other on Christmas Eve. He had smiled at me while on top, Merry Christmas my love. We had kissed. For New Year's Eve, the same thing. It's been three years now that we haven't observed the tradition.

I got on the Minitel. I connected with a guy whose screen name was Fuck No Condoms. This little guy asked me what interested me in his profile. I told him Fkn u w/o a condom. I thought he was suspicious of me. I don't specify safe sex in my profile, but it is true that I do have a profile of a guy who does have safe sex. Guys who like to fuck without condoms never go into detail about what kind of fucking they like, hard or soft or raunchy or man-to-man or whatever other nuance, what really interests them is wallowing in poisoned cum, in a dark and romantic fuck, I'm saying this in a condescending way, but it's true, it's very powerful. One time I was in a three-way like that and I stalled, I kept losing my hard-on in their asses, and when they fucked me, I was too freaked out about having unsafe sex, I mean we don't know anything about reinfection but what we do know is that by doing that kind of thing you can catch all kinds of other shit. That said, when that little pervert squirted inside the tall skin-head's ass, no condom, it was breathtaking. The kiss of death, they say.

When he called me he told me he felt like fucking rather than being fucked tonight. I thought to myself, finally one who isn't stupid. I said I think there's going to be a problem then because I don't get fucked without a condom. He said he wasn't going to come over. We didn't have the same despair. I promised myself that when my T4s dropped below two hundred, I'd get back to it.

I took the last E that was in the fridge and jerked off shoving a bunch of stuff up my ass while watching a porn movie that I kept rewinding. I was so stoned that I knocked over the Christmas tree and the CD tower while handling the bag of dildos. I thought that was funny.

11. Merry Christmas!

I woke up around one. I wasn't hungry; I felt good because of the E. I just drank a glass of water and got on the Minitel. I connected with a guy who had a nice plan. Reciprocal fucking and play with Jeff Stryker's dildo. Everything went as planned except after we opened our asses up wide with the two dildos he brought over, we stood up, I offered up my ass to his big glistening condomless dick. He slipped it in me. It felt good. He stopped pretty short after. I turned him around so I could have my turn. Then back to the dildo. I shoved the Stryker deep inside him and fucked him with it while I sat back down on his purplish-blue cock. Then he did the same thing to me. We each came while fucking ourselves deep with the dildo. I told myself that this more or less worked out because there wasn't any semen in either our asses.

That evening I was planning to have dinner in the Marais, at a friend's who for years regularly used to invite Quentin and me to dinner. I'd also been to his place once with Stéphane. I arrived on time. We had an aperitif with his current boyfriend. I said that I'd just left Stéphane. We had dinner. After that I found myself out in the cold streets. It must have been around one a.m. I wondered whether I should go home, sleep to get some rest, or else go out. I decided you have to have faith in life, Christmas day needs it. I walked through the night to Quetzal. I thought there would be an interesting crowd there, the hardcore ones, the ones with no family. There were indeed quite a few. I got a beer, I set up in this spot where you get the best view, near the door to the bathroom. I looked over the merchandise. I was completely detached. If there wasn't anything, OK, I would go home gladly.

There wasn't anything particularly amazing. And then I saw this tall Black guy in a beanie, really tall, around 6'4", two hundred and forty pounds, super beefy, on the chubby side, young, a beautiful face, a reserved look. We smiled at each other. I went over and asked him *Where are you from in America?* He said *I'm not from America, I'm from Africa.* I said Oh OK, *so you must be some sort of African prince.* That made him laugh. We talked, about him, about me, about zen. His hotel was at l'Étoile, Americans are always so scared of shady neighborhoods. We head to my place.

When we got home instead of jumping on him right away I rolled a joint stretched out on the bed. He didn't want to smoke. He asked me if I smoke all the time. I said No, only every evening. He said So you're a drug addict? I denied it. I smoked my joint.

We weren't fucking. He got undressed anyway because the heat was on full blast. He was lying next to me in his t-shirt and briefs. I asked him if he wouldn't mind if I sucked his dick. He said *You can try to, if you really want to.* Five good minutes later there it was, he was sporting a real hard-on. I slipped a condom on him and sat on his big and pointy dick. He wasn't moving. We weren't kissing. I fucked myself. After a while, he turned me around and fucked me really quick and really hard almost without touching me. I had to brainwash myself, repeating that I was a little white whore who was getting fucked by a big Black man so I could manage to stay hard and then come, at the same time as him for that matter, I have to say he took his time, It gave me all the time I needed to take care of myself. I asked him afterwards if he usually didn't use his hands more when he fucked. He said he actually does. I thought about that.

12. Negotiations

Quentin calls me. He tells me things are going bad with him and Nico. I say You don't love him anyway. At least I dumped Stéphane. He says I want to see you. Do you want to come over? I say Are you serious? With your boyfriend showing up on us at any moment? It's out of the question. He says Let's meet up at Quetzal then. Going out seems totally beyond my powers and pointless as well. On top of that, I want him to be the one who comes, makes the effort. He's the one looking to get me back after all. I say No I'm not going out. You can come over here. He says OK, I'll be there in an hour. I know he needs at least an hour and a half, given the cumulative effects of the weed and the Xanax. He told me he had cut back on his dosage. I don't know if that's true. He lies all the time. Two hours pass and I know that there's a problem. I check at his place. Answering machine. I speak in case he's screening. No one picks up. He calls two minutes later. The code isn't working. I say OK I'll come down. I throw on some jeans with no underwear, my bomber jacket with no shirt, and sneakers with no socks. No one's downstairs. The code works fine. I wait five minutes. I think that he must have gotten the wrong street. I run in the rain to the same address on Faubourg Saint-Denis. I remember the four-way we had four years ago, a few doors down, at these two hunky guys's place, tall, ripped, versatile, both with huge cocks. They had a giant ball of great hash. Everybody had fucked me but it was Quentin they obviously preferred, with him there were more things they could do. I wound up with a big dildo in my ass, which I wasn't used to at the time, and then I took off because it was just too much. The next day, Quentin told me that he'd woken up with one of them fucking him.

No one there. I go back home. After what seems like ages, the phone rings. I say You're on the wrong street, it's not Saint-Denis, it's Saint-Martin. I hang up. He arrives totally smashed. He criticizes the apartment that everyone loves except for my sister and me. I tell him I know. It's all I could afford. He rolls a joint that looks too strong to me. We talk about the past. He tells me he's changed. We talk about our possible future. I tell him I think we should fuck now so we'll know where we stand. He says No, he thinks it's too soon, maybe later, like tomorrow at his New Year's party where there'll be coke and no Nico who has to spend it with his parents in the country.

After a while, he asks me to come sit on his lap. I'm not in love with the idea, but I go over anyway. Sitting there, stiff as a marionette, I compare it to how it used to make me feel. We kiss. It's technically perfect but it doesn't get me hard. He ends up leaving. I jump on the Minitel but there isn't anything going on there so I head out to the sex club.

When I got there, there was practically no one. A young well-built guy was lying there waiting, legs spread, ankles in the stirrups of a sling, with a big hard cock, completely naked except for a pair of navy-blue Converse sneakers without socks. I went into a private room all the way in the back. I waited. Two ugly looking men poked their heads in. I made a face. They left. A half hour later, I was still there. Nothing was happening. I left the room. I walked around. The guy was still lying in the sling. I walked up to him. I started to jerk off. I got hard thinking that he was there to be fucked by just anyone. I pushed my dick up against his asshole. I told him, I don't have a condom. He said It's no big deal. I spit on it to lube it up. I had a hard time getting in. And then I did it. I fucked him with finesse. He stayed hard without touching himself. Another guy appeared. He came up to watch. Instinctively, I pressed up against the guy's asshole to keep the other one from seeing we were fucking without a condom. He saw it anyway. He left. I kept going. I felt myself getting close. I asked myself Do I come in him? That's what he wants anyway. And then I pulled out and shot off on the floor. I went back to my private room. I ended up getting fucked, dildoed, and fisted by a really hot little guy who worked me over like a god saying to me That's right man, have a blast, let me see those eyes roll back in your head.

13. And Happy New Year!

I got to Quentin's at ten past midnight. The guests weren't done
kissing yet. I inspected the apartment where nothing that needed
to be done had gotten done since I left. Everybody told me I
looked great. Quentin was fucked up on drugs. Coke, I knew,
but also joint after joint he was extorting from some poor girl
clinging to his coat tails even though I know he has his own
stash. An hour passed and there still wasn't any talk of the coke
he'd told me about the night before. Since I was done waiting
for him to be polite, I went and asked him for it. I said I'd
prefer not to have to do this, but since you're not offering, I have
to ask. Where's the coke? He said How much will you give me
for it? I said Nothing, are you kidding me? I'm not about to pay
you for a line of coke. He said OK, fine. He took off. I waited.
He finally came back and told me to take the yellow straw from
the vase on the mantle in the bedroom and meet him in the
bathroom. Nico was also in the bathroom, he'd just gotten back
into town and talked about how great it was to meet up again
after a year. I wanted to kill him but I kept my mouth shut so I
could get some coke, all I did was move his arms from my shoulder, that was a little too much.

The coke was pretty shitty, hard and weird. Or else it was the
party that was. I still got some surges of energy. Danced a little. Quentin looked over from time to time, stoned but also
enamored. Then Nico would come by for reassurance. Of
course we're going to fuck and sleep together, Quentin said,
cut us half an E, the first wasn't enough. Nico came back to say
he wasn't able, he didn't know how to, that there were too

many people in the kitchen. Quentin yelled at him. I was disgusted. Can't you see he just wants some attention? He didn't
answer. He didn't move.

I danced some more, without conviction. Had a discussion
with some stars of the ghetto whom I didn't like and who didn't
like me either. Around two a.m., a guy arrived, terribly beautiful, a really monstrous beauty, very young, who jumped in
front of me in line for the toilet. When he came out, I couldn't
resist, I had talk to him. I said Are you David? He said No, I'm
Ivan. Ah, I said, Then you're not the dealer everyone's waiting
for. He said No I'm not, David's supposed to drop by though,
I saw him a little while ago at another party. I thought to myself
This guy is really perfect. He said I'm kind of tired tonight. I
said Go lie down or do some drugs. He said I already took some
coke but I don't feel great. I asked him his age to know how old
you have to be to get skin like that. Twenty-one, he said. Quentin
told me later that this guy was kept by a famous designer. He
and his group of beautiful people, they go to the gym every day,
tanning beds every day, drugs every day. They don't do anything, they have sponsors. All of them between eighteen and
twenty-two.

After around two hours, I felt myself fading. I was sitting next
to him, reading some stupid thing he had written and wanted
to show me, the sweet little guy who was playing records all
night leaned over, he said You look sad. I looked up, I thought
he was hitting on me, it bothered me actually because I hadn't
even noticed him before and now I thought he wasn't bad, and
I told myself that I was only thinking that because he was hitting on me, and then I thought, Don't I have the right? It was
dumb. Nico hovered around us dying of jealousy. Just a little
earlier, for the first time since we met, he propositioned me,
probably he sensed that Quentin was after me again and that

scared him to death. It's true I've always wanted his nine inches, but his offer came a little too late.

After three hours when I saw myself in a mirror I looked drained, grey, dead. I asked Quentin How can you just keep going? He said It's hard. I thought That's nonsense. I got my coat and I left. I walked all the way to the quais, Place Stalingrad, there was practically nobody. I hung around anyway, and chatted with a guy dressed up in riot-police gear. I got in bed around six a.m. The next day I woke up with a fever.

Quentin called me two days later. He wanted to ask for a favor, he had to come over to explain it. I greeted him in a bathrobe. He held out a small blue package. A gift. I said Thanks and put it aside without opening it. He lit a cigarette without asking for permission. I pointed out to him that this might bother me. He looked surprised. I began to insult him, for Nico, for me, for his perpetual lack of awareness, his terrible treatment of people. I shoved the package he brought me back into the pocket of his bomber jacket. I threw him out. He called the next day to tell me he was hurt but that it was probably delicious to be tortured by the one you love. I didn't believe him for a second. I thought This time, it's over.

14. Teeth Marks

A few days later I was feeling better. I went back to Quetzal. I saw some friends. We caught up on all the news. Dennis got around to telling me he was worried because he was waiting for his test results and he'd been doing stupid shit. I said What kind of stupid shit? He said, Well, last year I was with a guy for a few months and we were fucking without condoms. I said Ah. He said And I just found out he's sick. I said Yeah that sucks. He said on top of that he was still unemployed, that he didn't get the job he was hoping for. To lighten things up, I asked him which of the guys there that night were a good fuck, even though I don't have much confidence in him for that type of thing, I don't think we have the same criteria, but it's been four years since we've fucked, he might have made some progress.

He pointed out a little guy, our age, maybe slightly younger, shaved head, tight white t-shirt, really nice body, really popular, talking with some girls who were just as popular just a couple feet from us. He said There's him, you'd get along fine with him I'm sure. I said Why? He said He's a really good fuck. I asked Is he a top or bottom? Well-hung? Into S&M or vanilla sex? Dennis answered Yes to everything, but more bottom than top. I looked at him again. I thought Well why not. As if by chance, the guy took off his shirt right at that moment. I thought that was a little much. Of course his body was amazing. Completely shaved. Big nipples. Not a hair on his chest. I said But what's he like to fuck? More cerebral or more physical? Dennis said More cerebral. The last time I fucked him he told me Wait, he went looking for a mirror to put under him so he could see my dick up his ass. Dennis seemed to think that was hot. It turned me off. I didn't find him hot enough to care if he uses me. I asked Was it with or without a condom? Without, said Dennis. I decided not to fuck him. It was getting too tempting.

I went to the bar to get us some cold beers. I ran into some other friends. Marcelo told me that he had gotten his other nipple pierced. He said And you when are you going to get yours done? I said Me? No, I am not into nipple piercings, I don't want to lose my sensitivity. Marcello asked me if I still had his number. I said Yes. He said Then call me sometime, I still haven't forgotten what we did together in Italy. I said No, me neither, and that was the truth. But I didn't want to call him. I found myself alone in the middle of the bar with a beer in my hand. I looked around and saw my dreams destroyed.

Finally I hooked up with a new guy. My height, short brown hair, beautiful face, nice body, black jeans, black t-shirt. Another popular one, but whatever, I was hot for him. I looked at him. He gave me a reasonably interested look. I smiled. He smiled back, his teeth weren't that great, a bit spread out and pointy. I thought this made him sexier. We chatted. I quickly asked the two or three essential questions. Yes, he was versatile. No, he wasn't into rough S&M. I said OK, let's go. He didn't have a car, evidently he was broke. We took a taxi. We groped each other a little in the taxi. It was nice. Then, once we got in my place, he started grabbing my ass in the stairwell, kind of macho, I let him do it, he put his whole fist between my ass cheeks to make me walk up the stairs, it reminded me of Quentin, a little too rough, a little too hard. It made me horny actually that for once a cute guy my age was going to take control and not the other way around.

In the hallway he started biting my neck. I don't like that at all. I backed away immediately so things would be clear. We went in. I poured us two whiskeys, I rolled a joint, we started smoking. Then we got undressed, naked he was really gorgeous, we kissed, embraced, I was really turned on. He started biting me again. I stiffened up. He stopped. We started touching each other again. He bit me again. I backed off. I looked at him. What do you think that will do for me, biting me like that? I said. You think I enjoy it? I haven't stopped trying to show you the opposite. So what's the deal? What are you trying to do? He said I just felt like doing it, that's all. He came back in close so we could start fondling each other again. I said, I think we're going to stop there. I stayed sitting at the top of the bed. He got up, put on his black underwear, black socks, black jeans, black t-shirt, black sneakers, in silence. I walked him to the door without saying a word.

I shut the door. I stayed there without moving. I told myself What's happening to me? How can something like this happen to me? I watched him cross the courtyard from my window. I thought This guy in black was a sign. If I stay here I'm going to die. I'm going to end up putting sperm in everyone's ass and everyone is going to end up doing the same to me. The truth is that's the only thing left that I want to do. In fact, it's already happening. Of course I won't be able to tell anyone about it. I won't be able to meet anyone. I'll wait to get sick. Surely it won't be long. Then I'll be so disgusted with myself that it will finally be the time to kill myself. I told myself that the only thing left to do was to leave.

15. Exit

I got lucky. I was offered a job far away, overseas. I thought, I'm heartbroken, I'm headed for the end of the world, that's what you have to do in this case. I accepted. I spent another month arranging my affairs, seeing people, friends, my grandmother. I wanted to leave things in order.

I called Terrier on the telephone. I hadn't shared any news with him in a long time. He told me he wasn't doing anything. That he was still unemployed. That he just stayed home all the time, except the weekend sometimes, to go see his mother. That he no longer went out. That he was sick and tired of waiting for Prince Charming. I didn't suggest that we see each other, I was afraid that it would be too sad. He didn't suggest it either. He wished me a good trip. Said that he would come see me. I told him that wouldn't be a problem. I wondered if I would pay for his trip someday. Maybe.

Stéphane was my last date. He had told me that he would prefer to see me right before I left because he was too busy before, but I had thought it was for a deeper reason, that he thought it was best that this goodbye would be for good. He was supposed to come by and pick me up to go to lunch. It was a Saturday. Of course, I hadn't been able to get up in time to be ready, I had spent the night out again. I opened the door for him in my half-tied bathrobe. I immediately went back to bed. He sat down on the edge. We talked. About him, about me, about his new boyfriend. And then then we got so emotional that we held each other in our arms. Electric erection. We kissed. It was powerful. I told him, Get undressed. We found ourselves naked on the bed. I was super hard. I told myself that I was going to leave him with a good souvenir. I leaned over towards his dick and I sucked it like I had never sucked it before. With love. He almost came. I stood up. I said Who is fucking who? He said I feel like fucking you, I don't remember what it feels like. I agreed, I found it better than the other way around given the context. It was absolutely amazing. Afterwards I invited him to lunch at a brasserie in Les Halles. We drank like fish. We laughed. He took me back home by car. I watched him leave, the profile of his beautiful little head framed by the car door window. He waved at me before heading down the street. It was night. I know that I should have left him much earlier. When I told myself for the first time that I would never be in love with him. But it felt so good to be loved by him. So good.

I'm Going Out Tonight

A Novel

Introduction by Thomas Clerc

For those who have never read Guillaume Dustan, *I'm Going Out Tonight*, published in 1997, the second volume in this first trilogy, is the best gateway to his work. Two years after the sexual radicalism of *In My Room*, which could potentially have scared away the unsuspecting reader, Dustan explored another world equally as consubstantial as his room—that of the night club. Dustan was one of the first writers to have introduced this modern place of pleasures to French literature, affording him an almost mythological respect. It is surprising that dancing, a favorite activity of young people in general, did not have its own "Balzac" until Dustan, unlike the cinema world which had produced the cult film for a generation, *Saturday Night Fever*,[1] in 1978. The reason is that literature is often written by writers who stop frequenting these kind of places once they hit their forties (that is, if they ever frequented them at all), and instead turn their attention to places where age is not so diriment, places like brothels or casinos, especially in heterosexual culture.[2] We can draw a history of literature through its characters as well as through its spaces, and from this perspective, Dustan is an innovator.[3]

The Pink and the Black

For Dustan, night clubs were not just any other place. Not only were they places the author regularly frequented, but they also corresponded more broadly to a moment in the life of the "thirty-year-old man," when the subject was at the top of his game, despite the disease lingering in the background. The night club was a space where youth appeared to shine, not just Dustan's own youthfulness, but also that of an "eternal youth" before its unavoidable decline. At this age in life, when it is not too early to start writing or too late to head home, the night club encourages an experience of expenditure that recalls Georges Bataille, even in the mystical dimension. Dustan, however, never reached the age of forty, that period during which a writer's work supposedly ripens and achieves a mastered form of expression. His premature death did not allow him to settle or to polish a style that indeed had no need for it. In a certain sense, the night club was his descent into hell[4] and foreshadowed his future disappearance. Beyond the generational difference, the statement by one of his favorite writers, Marguerite Duras, "it's soon too late in life to go to the Tabou," was confirmed in a completely different way: by AIDS. The virus has a discrete but nevertheless firm presence in *I'm Going Out Tonight*, and the dedication of the book, "In memoriam Alain Ferrer," a deceased friend of Dustan's, is reinforced by the mention of his death as early as the second paragraph. To paraphrase a slogan from Act-Up Paris that remains beyond redemption, "Night clubs = AIDS," we could say that for homosexuals at the time the simple pleasures of partying and of life were indissociable from their opposite. For all that, *I'm Going Out Tonight* radiates a certain euphoria that we do not necessarily think of when we evoke Guillaume Dustan. His critics have insisted on the depressing nature of his world, but *I'm Going Out Tonight* proves them wrong. It's a mild, Zen-like book that offers a more nuanced ethos to the reader in which the pink wins out over the black.

The Night Club, a Heterotopia

I'm Going Out Tonight is a novel that elevates the concept of the night club from the ranks of a setting for fiction to that of civility, even civilization. This nocturnal establishment, which unites the novel, is a place where types of relationships other than typical diurnal ones are explored—a locus for alternative experiences. Even though it is located at the heart of the city, or rather, *under* the city, the night club, in this case La Loco, is a place that eludes it in order to offer different, less normal, crazier rules that are constructed in excess by its users themselves. The night club is a "heterotopia," a concept invented by Michel Foucault in a very famous text, another type of space where all that is judged deviant no longer is so.[5] In the upside-down world of the club and of the night, the oppressive values from above are abolished to the benefit of a sociability that the author both theorizes and puts into practice.

Dustan's consistency comes from the fact that he selected key locations that were in no way simple backdrops to a realist narrative but on the contrary places that he assiduously patronized because they seemed to offer the possibility of new experiences. In a certain way, Dustan's political project was born in the night club. The reader who is discovering *I'm Going Out Tonight* does not know it yet, but can feel it, and will confirm it retroactively after reading the entire collection. The body itself, as well as nocturnal conviviality, are at the heart of a new ethical code and of a new esthetic that eventually lead to a political avant-gardism that would be developed in the second trilogy. With the work to come still inchoate, *I'm Going Out Tonight* was content with displaying nightlife and showing the pleasures it could bring on a phenomenological level. The most obvious sign of this claim resides in the very title of the work, where the pronoun "I" rings out like a manifesto: *I'm Going Out Tonight* is simple and magnificent, universally borrowable by any subject, a title-sentence with its verb in the present tense, and its four short words that whip the ears with their repetitive vowel sounds.

Although marked by its homosexual bent, *I'm Going Out Tonight* has the intelligence not limit itself to that. The world of nightlife abolishes differences, and Dustan's "communitarianism," a problematic concept if ever there was one, tends to merge into a generality of pleasure. This accurate description of a minority world is also a snapshot of the sociality of night life taken in the specific chronotope of 1990s France. *I'm Going Out Tonight* is therefore a book that clearly exceeds the micro stakes of the "ghetto," something the entire corpus of Dustan's works will continue to prove. This novel sketches out a community that transcends class and sexual differences: Dustanian universality is born in a mixed, working class night club that is not exclusively gay. Fresh because of its theme and the approach Dustan brings to it, committed beneath a superficial appearance, *I'm Going Out Tonight* is both mundane and serious, Nietzschean and Warholian, superficial and deep at the same time.

The Empty and the Full

Similar to *In My Room*, *I'm Going Out Tonight* is a conceptual book in its form: the respect of three classical unities or place, time, and action is absolute, since Dustan recounts an evening at La Loco in less than a hundred pages. Engrossed in a pure *present* that is both a stylistic characteristic of the time as well as a style of writing unique to Dustan, the reader easily makes their way through the description of a night out at the club up to the final return to "the room," which echoes back to Dustan's previous text, and for which the club constitutes an outside. *I'm Going Out Tonight* maintains the stylistic minimalism of the first novel as it singularizes it. The narrative, composed of various fragments of unequal length, at times single sentences, glorifies the perceptual dimension of the night club. The text stays as close as possible to the physical sensations of the club goers. In this hypogeum of sorts, Dustan advocates for the pleasures forbidden by the world above. From this point of view, *I'm Going Out Tonight* picks up the corporeal theme that we saw in *In My Room* but points it in a much more hedonistic and joyful direction. Dustan the dancer constructs an image of a subject who wishes to let go, and lose the very self-control authoritarian society demands of him.

Narrated by a full subject, this work centers with superb finesse on the seductive quality of emptiness. On the one hand, events are simply described in successive order by a consciousness that is steadily emptying out. The style of the text, as it attempts to adhere to phenomena, reduces the action to the subtle repetition of its operations. The first-person narration constructs autonomous moments that appear to lead to some end, which it then cancels deceptively. In a stimulating article,[6] Bénédicte Boisseron suggested we might compare Dustan's style to Coca-Cola (a parallelism that would undoubtedly have pleased the author), a beverage that embodies the "death of materiality and the self-reference of desire in a tantalizing mise en abyme."[8] Flipping through the pages of I'm Going Out Tonight constitutes a form of light arousal due to the qualities of the drink as well as to its iconic status. We could read the text according to Jean Baudrillard, for whom the contemporary passion for the real has mutated into hyperreality: that is to say, the degree of fascination this text exerts draws perhaps its source in this repetitive and shallow totality, this absolute transparency where the pragmatic dimension wins over everything without hierarchy. This type of reading, however, provides only a partial key to the text, which is not a critique of the modern subject lost in a gaseous version of reality. Describing emptiness is a positive experience of ecstasy.

Indeed, the night club was a locus of dispossession of the self. What a paradox that the intense subjectivity of the "Dustanian subject" was absorbed in an almost Buddhist like quest for de-subjectivation carried out by music, drugs, and the intermingling of bodies. That the vindication of pleasure was also given as a political act was perhaps Dustan's greatest achievement. Dustan, a fanatic individualist, was also an heir, a continuator of the anarchist spirit of the '70s restructured by liberal postmodernism. The context of AIDS reinforced community ties: the heterotopia of the night club was not cut off from the world, it offered a protection against the disease by affirming the preeminence of pleasure over death. Here, more than in the other two novels in this collection, Dustan began with the specificity of homosexuality and moved beyond it into a Dionysian quest.

Dance or Death

Blending his own experience with that of his brothers in the struggle, Dustan embodied the condition of the young gay activist of the 1990s. The world of nightlife and its restitution were inevitable. More than Foucault, Dustan's ultimate reference was Nietzsche, who frequently appeared in Dustan's prose and whose defense of the figure of the dancer seemed the fieriest of commands: "Truth for our feet! Truths upon which we can dance!"[7]

In fact, *I'm Going Out Tonight* is a musical: due to a rhythmic infusion its writing is where the action occurs. For this literalist author, the night club entailed short sentences and a simple repetitive style that imitated the pulsing bass of techno music. In the final third of the novel, large blocks of blank white page mark the progressive loss of consciousness of the narrator-protagonist which grew throughout the night. In a stroke of genius, Dustan inserted multiple series of blank pages that represent the *satori*-like perceptive state, the confusion made possible by that locus of anti-normative behavior that is the night club. *I Dance, Therefore I am* would perhaps be the best subtitle for this synesthetic text. Sight, the most aristocratic of the senses, has a problematic role to play in that the nocturnal settings of the place and the artificial lighting alter the perception of people and things. Sight cuts the viewer off from their object. This cut (and on another level, the cut between private and public, literature and experience, and pleasure and intellect) is something Dustan looked to abolish because it was a down-time in the accomplishment of desire. Sound, conversely, is fundamental in a world saturated with music and where communication is reduced to what is essential—the body.[8] The numerous musical references serve to reinforce the setting of this era, but it is the deafening musicality and direct structure of Dustan's sentences that sets the tone of the story, as shown by the abundant blank verse: "I was unquestionably / at the basement of Palace" or "The music is worse. / I rest on the edge of the dance floor."

Dancing was another way of warding off death, just like sex and exercise, which are other types of self-care. Physical activity or exercise was certainly a direct response to AIDS, a way to ignore it but not deny its existence. The collective quality of the night club united a community. People danced not so much to be seen, but rather to dissolve into a mass that did not prohibit the self, but rather multiplied it. Although he was no doubt a snobby writer, Dustan proclaimed his hatred of snobbism when it excluded others. Dance and the whole of adolescent culture, on the contrary, united people in a common and participatory quest that prefigured a polis based on pleasure and constituted it in action: with dance, heterotopia was a realized utopia.

Pop Literature, Underground Literature

Dustan was not content with creating a representation of the night club, he wanted to share the experience of it. Dustan's modernity lies also in this defiance against reducing literature to a simple *mimesis*—a faulty position, an esthetic. Dustan doesn't have anything to "tell;" rather, it is reality that is important to him. As opposed to the detached qualities of fiction which thrives on its capacity to lull the reader to sleep, autobiography provides direct access to the world of experience. *I'm Going Out Tonight* is more than an analysis of actions at a night club, it's a performative that brings them to life.

There exists a literary Dustanian paradox, for both the underground and pop culture coexist within it. Underground literature, which is made below ground, tramples the established order just as dancers immerse themselves in a world freed from bodily constraints. With its pop culture theme and standard language, *I'm Going Out Tonight* laid the foundation for a literature addressed to the biggest of crowds. There is a pop culture fantasy within Dustan (and in the texts of other writers whom he admired) which links dancing and literature through the notion of mass culture. Literature's only value is to be shared by all, but in reality, it is reserved for the elites. Dustan, who would later go on to outline a surprising panorama of French literature,[9] had a democratic ideal; the values of liberty, equality, and fraternity found a place to express themselves literally within the space of the night club. The contradiction between pop culture and the underground is not truly resolved in Dustan's work, but it is posited with an acuity that is rare in French literature. Autobiography plays a decisive role here: although Dustan speaks from a singular position, he does so in a voice in which many can recognize themselves, a whatever singularity, a collective voice that aims, in the context of the night club, at abolishing the distinction between what is personal and what is anonymous.

This second novel, in comparison to the other two in this volume, is hardly sexual. After the orgy of *In My Room* (which the other orgy in *Stronger Than Me* will answer to), *I'm Going Out Tonight* occupies the middle ground, a form of detumescence if you will. It is therefore not happenstance that it is also the best written, the least harsh, and the most accessible text of the first trilogy in that it offers the reader a possibility of contact. Whereas *In My Room* aimed at metaphorically attacking the reader (which is explained, in part, by the fact that it was the first work published), and *Stronger Than Me* would paint a picture of the sadomasochist scene, *I'm Going Out Tonight* proved to be Dustan's first attempt at constructing a communal space: the night-club-novel. The former, according to Dustan, should be considered not only as the basis for future society but also as a metaphor for literature on the condition that we understand that the night club is a club that is open to everyone and not an exclusionary place ruled by trendiness. From this point of view, the excursions that Dustan allowed himself outside La Loco were a call to go beyond a restricted idea of what the text represented and to reject a literature of milieu, which functioned as a deterrent, the milieu being both the homosexual milieu but also the mainstream standard literature that informs dominant taste. Typically, participation is an antagonistic action to representing; the writer-dancer that Dustan was fervently desired to combine them both. *I'm Going Out Tonight* is an invitation to all of us to answer that call.

in memoriam Alain Ferrer

Lapin, I love you

When Love's last word is said,
And its dreams suddenly broken,
Why weep for days now fled,
Or dreams that charm them dead?

The magic kiss is spent,
The romance sadly broken,
And the bruised heart now spoken
Was the last word love said.

Madly you claim! Oh have pity
Love will be yours for all time
You charming yes, but she so pretty
And spring sings its song sublime

Day follows day,

Love disappears
Like flowers too

In vain you seek,
Your heart throbbing
and your eyes fill with tears

When Love's last word is said,
And its dreams suddenly broken,
Why weep for days now fled,
Or the dreams that charm them dead?

The magic kiss is spent,
The romance sadly broken,
And the bruised heart now spoken
Was the last word love said.

(Octave Crémieux, *Love's Last Word: Quand l'amour meurt*)

There's a certain pleasure in not following the rules. Like going to Gay Tea Dance[1] in a pair of 501s two sizes too big, low top shoes, and a preppy checkered shirt. It wasn't planned. I got dressed this morning for my date with Diane and since it was an important thing for me, I didn't think about what I was doing after, and which could only be, obviously, what I am doing now: heading down rue Lepic, towards Place Blanche to go to GTD which is at La Loco ever since the Palace closed.

But I take a look at myself in the café window halfway down the hill and I decide that this will do. I have a secret weapon under my shirt: an old indigo Marine Nationale t-shirt from Alain Ferrer's brother, snug, elastic, good cut, with these really short sleeves that highlight my biceps, sexy because of the logo and the holes I burnt into it with my joints. It was Alain's lucky t-shirt. I had traded him my own lucky t-shirt, a black t-shirt from the U.S., tight, good cut, a souvenir from a parachuting competition, with the location, the year, and a graphic showing three guys in formation, in free fall, holding hands, that looked like the warning sign for radioactivity, which was a bit frightening but also ultra-cool. We made the trade on rue de Bellefond. I hesitated for a long time before. In my mind, it meant that we were becoming brothers. It was Quentin who told me last week that Alain died. It had already been a couple of months. I hadn't known. I wasn't in France.

The last time I saw him, it was at Le Bar in '94. He was with his man, me with mine. I had told him that I would call them so we could come over for dinner at their place, but I didn't call, it should have been the other way around, we were the older ones and we had more money. I had not seen him ever since he had gotten shacked up. We actually got to know each other during the three years when he was Quentin's regular, then occasional, lover. Mine too, as a result. We went on vacation to his place, in Spain, summer of 1990. I remember how he would dance, like a maniac, in the gay club in Valence, to this house hit we liked best, *Es Imposible, No Puede Ser.*

Alain was special. *Everyone* would stare at him when he walked in. Even though he was really small. Very skinny, but very good-looking. Always dressed like Zorro, his jacket like a cape, his jeans like black tights, and his big shoes. Each of his poses was a perfect picture. I think he did it deliberately. He had to have studied himself for a long time, the way these young proles can, whose studies aren't demanding and who only have their bodies to capitalize on. He was a great fuck. Relentless. Endless. Bottomless. Wrapped up in himself. I didn't know that he was positive. Maybe he didn't know. He was just the type who wouldn't know.

I remember very precisely the shape of his body. I remember his smell, which I criticized. I still can't believe he is dead. At the same time, it doesn't really completely surprise me. It's been a while now since I thought about what he was doing with his life, without work, shacked up with this guy who represented security, OK, really well-built, handsome face, hung, super in love, but not nearly fun enough for him. I think he must have felt his youth fading away, little by little, and with it, the absolute power he had over other people. He didn't know what to replace it with.

I really need to shit. There wasn't any toilet paper earlier in Diane's guest bathroom, and that's not something one talks about, so it had already been a while, but I don't want to break the rhythm, and plus, I'm sure that at the beginning of the night the toilets at La Loco will be clean and well-stocked, so I don't stop at the café rue Lepic, or at Quick[2] on the boulevard, and I drift towards the entrance through the crowd of people hanging around in front of the Moulin Rouge.

It's been forever since I've come here. The bouncers are wearing new uniforms, silver bomber jackets and black 501 jeans. I head towards the music getting louder and louder but the doorman, a sexy dark-haired thirty-five year old, badly shaven, blocks the entrance, and I tell myself, —Shit, what's going on, but the guy kisses me on the cheeks saying something that I didn't get until after that was —Happy Easter, pretty boy! Cool. I fork over ten bucks and head towards the coat check.

I leave my coat. I grab my cigarettes and my credit card. I leave my lighter. This morning I forgot to grab one. I was trashed, I went to bed at six a.m. with Dimitri after getting home from Station. That's when I dumped him. We slept together anyway. Talked. Cried. Him, mostly. We'd only known each other a week so it wasn't that big of a deal. I hadn't wanted to buy one before at Saint-Jean[3] on the way to Diane's because I wanted to stay within my daily budget. And finally I bought one, at the same time as an extra pack of cigarettes, when we were out for a walk, she and I, on rue Lepic.

But I don't take it with me because I know that I can't act casual asking for a light when I have one on me and that it's a good ice-breaker. So it's better to not have one. And plus, that gives me one more thing to do, it's easy to get bored shitless at clubs.

I head back down the stairs at a sustained pace. I strut across the hundred or so feet of the already open bar. The bartender is super cute, small, and hyper-muscular. There's almost no one there. The first time I came here, it was ten years ago. I was twenty. Franck brought me. I was in shock. I had never seen something like that. All these people, hundreds and hundreds of guys dancing, in the back there were dozens, beefy, shirtless or wearing white tank tops, like wallpaper. I thought —This is Dante's *Inferno*, and I rushed in.

It's so early that the staircase that leads to the big dance floor is still closed. I look to my left towards the bathroom. Both stalls are occupied, so I wait concentrating on my sphincter muscles which can barely hold on, and then something settles inside, and I feel OK. One of the doors opens. I go in. I close it behind me. I check the dispenser. Empty. I leave. I wait for the other one. The door ends up opening. I head in and notice right away that there isn't any toilet paper either which is really unbelievable at seven thirty p.m. So I go to the women's bathrooms at the end of the hall, there's no girls here tonight anyway.

This is what I should have done from the start because there are four toilets instead of two, but I didn't know, I've never had to go in there until now. The second stall is open and has toilet paper. I wipe down the seat and sit. Mmmmh. Relief.

I pull my pants up. I double-loop the belt to my jeans, so that it makes it shorter, never mind the bottom, people can see my socks but they're dark, so it's fine. Once I exit, I look at myself. Readjust my shirt. Smooth down the back, the sides. And then I want to wash my hands, but there's no soap in the dispensers, neither here nor in the men's bathroom, bravo La Loco. So I rinse them and head back to the bar.

There are already a few more people. I look around telling myself that it's cool to be here again, amongst my brothers from the neighborhood. Only fags. Only guys I can look at without any risk of getting the shit beaten out of me. Even if it's just in their eyes. Only guys who would theoretically want for me to want them. A place where I don't feel I must have my guard up the whole time. A place where I'm no longer an animal waiting to be attacked. Paradise.

I ask for a light. I smoke a cigarette. I people-watch. I'm not really in a rush to start drinking anyway, I decided that I wouldn't spend more of what I had left on me, plus the cash that I'm going to have to take out anyway later because I only have enough for one drink and I know that won't be enough to get me through the night. But I want to see what it's like when I'm not drunk. Alain never drank alcohol. He would always give us his drink ticket so that we could drink in his place.

I ask for a light. I smoke another cigarette. Then I end up getting bored, so I give myself the green light to have my first drink. I head back upstairs towards the entrance so that I can be served by the bodybuilder. It's marked Corona on the crates next to the Heineken, so I think I could do a tequila-Corona, Christopher taught me about this in the States, a shot of tequila, over there it was Cuervo Gold, to get you going, and then beer, smooth and lemony, to bring you down softly, reviving yourself every time you take a sip. It's the same principle as coke and weed. A must.

But that would be too expensive, so I think I'll just have a beer, a Corona, I love that, but beer makes me feel bloated, I always get a gut, a belly perpendicular to my pecs and not behind them, so I get a vodka. Some strong liquor should get me feeling good. The bodybuilder bartender comes closer, white and tanned. He's so well-built that he could be without question on the cover of *Honcho* or *Mandate*. Then I feel bad, too lean. I say, —Vodka on the rocks please, thinking, —I should have gotten the beer. The drink is a light pour, but there's plenty of ice, at least it will be cold. I take a sip. I feel better.

I leave my drink in hand and head towards the back. People are looking at me. No one's obviously drooling. But I know that I'm a lot more interesting once I've warmed up a bit. So I have to be patient. And also I spent the whole week screwing around with Dimitri (much younger than me, no belly). So it's my turn not to be desperate. Good thing, considering I have no success with the guys I'm attracted to. It should be said that I only look at the hottest and most fashionable guys. Two bodybuilders, thirty-five to forty years old, American type. An Arab, twenty to twenty-five years old, in leather 501s. I still have quite a few gym sessions ahead of me before I reach that level.

Actually, I'm getting bored. I usually don't get here so early. I get here around ten ten-thirty p.m., I stay on the top floor a bit, it depends on the music, and then I join the nightlife aficionados on the bottom floor, here or at Le Palace[4] it works the same way, there's the big dance floor on the top at the start of the night, but it's downstairs where things get serious, where everyone ends up, where we cruise. I almost always leave with someone every time I've come alone. Mostly memorable guys. I can still picture the Doc's pecs, abs and thighs, in a black t-shirt and leather 501s in Le Palace's basement. It was there too that I hooked up with the soccer player's son. The most beautiful man I ever had my hands on. I thought it was genetic but I ran into him at the gym and he works out too.

The basement doesn't open until around nine p.m. I head down to dance on the main floor. There are really too many people with massive bodies. I feel small, not muscular enough. I walk around the dance floor to find the spot where the sound is best, and it's at the end of the walkway, almost under the speakers, but it's a bad spot, too far from everything. The dance floor won't work, there isn't room to move. So I go back to the same spot as where I started, in the enclosure at the beginning of the covered walkway. I always end up here because it's where you get the most action. And also because, nobody knows why, this side parties harder than the other.

Eye contact with a quite good-looking guy, but not sexy enough. The music is better. A guy gets off the low table next to me. I hop on and dance, not bad. I start to sweat. I take off my shirt, then my t-shirt, I throw them down on a sofa. I'm dancing hard but not letting go completely. My thighs hurt, I can't do anything repetitive with my arms for more than two minutes, I'm out of breath, I can't go like I used to, it bums me out. I'm out of prac- tice. Before, I would dance every week for hours, and club dancing is truly a complete sport, and then I practically stopped, and now look what's happened.

A beefy guy comes over to dance right under me. I stumble. I catch myself on the railing so I don't fall. The guy bails. Then I start concentrating on the music which had gotten even better, and I dance, almost all-out, but still a little unenthusiastic throughout. A slightly more average guy comes over to dance at my feet, facing me. He matches his arms gestures with mine. He smiles but I don't feel like returning it.

The music gets boring. I jump off the table, heavily, I'm scared of hurting myself, I don't trust my body. I put my shirt back on so I don't catch a cold leaving it entirely unbuttoned down the front. I roll up the sleeves which are now folded up just above the start of my biceps. I have a new technique for my t-shirt: instead of letting it hang stupidly from behind, I shove the first four inches in, enough to be sure not to lose it, not completely in the middle, a little to the left to signal that I am neither 100% top—

that would be completely to the left—nor 100% bottom—that would be completely to the right—but both. So I put it in the middle, but a little to the left, because if I placed it right in the middle, or in the middle towards the right, that would mean that I am versatile but more of a bottom, so in reality a total bottom, but since I am not muscular enough I pretend to be a top thinking that I'll have more luck.

I ask for a light. I smoke a cigarette. I finished my vodka. I'm starving. It's time to go eat. I was actually already hungry when I passed by Quick but I didn't want to eat, I told myself that I would leave, it would give me one more thing to do. I head towards the exit. I stop to look at two young super cute guys dancing in front of the pinball machine. There's one who did a complete turn, bending backwards. He's bare-chested, the top of his overalls hanging by his thighs, perfectly etched abs, not an ounce of fat, my God, if only I was still like that.

And then I saw the sign—No reentry and I think, —Shit. So I head towards the bouncer from earlier and I lean in and I ask, —If we leave we can't come back, is that right? But he winks his eye, and nods, —Go on, with his head, and at the same time he opens the security gate to let me through, and I leave saying, —Thanks. All of this couldn't have lasted more than five seconds. That's what I love about nightlife: communication reduced to the essential.

There isn't an ATM at Place Blanche and I'm really concerned given that I'm in a t-shirt and shirt and it's not more than fifty degrees out. But I tell myself everything is fine, that the cool air is lovely, that I am strong and that I'm not going to catch a cold, and I take rue Lepic to go to the Société Générale up the hill to the left. Halfway, there's a BNP that I forgot about. I stop. A young German tourist couple in front of me make three or four withdrawals in a row, it takes so long that the people behind me deliberate and decide go to the ATM I wanted to go to, three hundred feet away, but I'm here, I stay, and finally I withdraw two hundred francs and head back down the street, speeding because it's freezing.

I head into Quick. There isn't a big line. The girl at the counter asks what I want and I don't know, so I say, —Whatever is the biggest, what is it? And she says, —The Quick'n Toast, and I say, —OK and she says, —The meal or the sandwich? And I say, —The sandwich, and she says, —Twenty francs and seventy cents, Could you wait a moment please? I'm waiting behind the other fag who must also be from La Loco and who is not bad-looking but he doesn't appeal to me because of his small mouth.

I eat there, not taking my time, at a bad table, behind the people in line, but near the napkin dispenser, and I grab two napkins while eating, arms glued to my sides, I'm not cool tonight, probably because I feel alone, but I don't tell myself that, I'm not detached enough from my emotions to think about it, I just tell myself that I'm bummed that I'm not dressed properly to show off too.

I empty my tray and I leave and I head towards La Loco and the bouncer blocks my way. —Good evening handsome!, he says, kissing me on both cheeks. —Hey, it's me, who asked you if I could leave, don't you remember?, I say. —Of course I do, I'm just taking advantage, he says while letting me in.

I head through the door while looking at him more attentively. He's actually pretty doable: full mouth, pretty earlobes, decent amount of hair in the v-neck of his black shirt. So I slip two fingers from my left hand inside, between two buttons, and there's still plenty of hair, and I tell myself that this would be a pretty exciting confrontation, his and mine. He would most likely fuck me. I wouldn't want to fuck him because he's much heavier than me, and older, and probably not a bottom that often, and I only like tight asses, but that could be fun, so I look him right in the eyes to make a point and then I go in.

There are already two guys at the register. I hesitate. Do I wait in line to explain that I'm coming back in? No, that's stupid. I head directly inside the club, and then I turn around and I see the bouncer giving the OK sign to the cashier.

Now, it's crowded. I go up to the bar. So, this time, beer or vodka? —You already had some vodka earlier when you wanted a beer, I tell myself, plus a beer takes longer to drink, and then you didn't get one at Quick where it's three times less expensive precisely because you were going to get one here, so now, you get one without bitching about less than eleven ounces of fat gain. So I ask the bartender, —A Corona please, but he makes a face, and he says, —A whisky-coke? And I say, —No, a Corona! We had trouble hearing each other because of the music. He brings back a Corona with a wedge of lemon, not lime, but I don't feel like complaining. I hand over fifty francs. I wait a little. He doesn't come back. Apparently beer costs the same as liquor. Fine. I still have a hundred and twenty, which means that potentially I'll be able to buy some ecstasy later.

I take a couple steps and run into Jean-Luc. We kiss. —Hey!, —How are you? —So-so, he says. That's the first time I've heard him say that. Usually he always says, —I'm good!, in the same piercing way, so I instantly think that his, —So-so, can only mean, —Bad results. This freaks me out too much, so I don't ask for details. I tell him about how Quentin wants to interview me, but that I think it's a trap. I ask him what he thinks. He says it's not out of the question. —Yeah, I don't think I am going to do it, I tell him, in any case we've already left two messages each, and we still haven't made an appointment, they must have gone to press already. I ask him about another guy we know from an AIDS group who said at dinner four years ago now that he was having unprotected sex with his boyfriend because he was sick of condoms. He's doing well. I tell Jean-Luc I ran into another guy we were really close to, and who isn't aging well. —Unlike you, I add, to show Jean-Luc that I noticed he doesn't have any pimples on his face anymore.

Right then, Jean-Luc and Stéphane walk by, the eternal couple that I had not seen in ages, and we all say, —Hey!, —How are you?, sincerely happy to see that none of us were dead or visibly sick. I wonder if I should ask more questions, but about what? Their jobs? Tacky. The most memorable fucks they've had recently? Nosy. The recipe for staying together? Now that, that would be interesting but I didn't think to ask at that moment. Anyway, the essential had been said. There was a silence. And then they say, —We're gonna go walk around, see you later!, And they leave.

—I haven't seen them in ages, I tell Jean-Luc. He says, —Yeah, I was telling Jean-Luc that it must have been four years since we've seen each other last, right around when I moved from Sébastopol. Silence. I think back to the life we used to lead there, Quentin, Jean-Luc, and me. To all the things that happened. And then I say, —I'm wearing Alain's brother's t-shirt. I didn't know. It's Quentin who told me. Jean-Luc says, —Yeah. And then he doesn't say anything else, and I don't say anything else, and after thirty seconds I think, —One minute of silence, so I keep quiet.

I look around. There's a really cute guy at the bar. He's talking to the bartender smiling from ear to ear. They're laughing. I think, —He's a natural. Jean-Luc saw that I was watching him. He watches too. I turn around and say, —He's cute. Jean-Luc says,

—Not bad. But you can't say this guy is only not bad, this guy is really cute, the type that isn't easy to get, even totally out of my league, unless I was more muscular. Nine more pounds of muscle and I could fuck him. Maybe less?

Jean-Luc says, —Should we go downstairs? People are annoying here. I look around. He's right, vibe is pretty snooty. We take off towards the back. The basement still isn't open, even though it's a quarter past nine. So we wait while watching the guys.

—Have you seen all the muscle men here, I say to Jean-Luc. Jean-Luc agrees to this almost palpable fact. —It wasn't like this ten years ago, now Paris is like Los Angeles, I add exaggerating just a little. —But what do these guys do for a living?, I ask, you're not like that unless you go to the gym at least five times a week. So must not do anything else. I'm being critical because I feel unsettled. It's only been seven months since I started back at the gym, after three years of almost nothing. It's not easy. Actually, what is easy to tell, it's what I've lost. The exercises that I did with thirty-three-pounds weights when I stopped, I did with seventeen when I started back again. Now I'm up to twenty-seven and a half. I'm catching up, but I'm not there yet.

Jean-Luc quickly reassures me, —Yeah, but you know, since most of them are bottoms, with the competition they'd better be really well-built. When you're a top, you always score, it's not the same. I remember that argument, so I say, —Yeah, that's true.

I check the placement of the tank tops hanging under the naked torsos that pass by. Most of the time it's on the right. The fact is that these guys generally fuck each other, other muscle men, I mean, so Jean-Luc's point isn't really all that true. In my opinion, they just want to be adored. That's why they work so hard. To be under the gaze, between the hands of someone who at every second thinks to himself, —He's so handsome! That's a rush, it's true. Respect for the muscle men.

All of a sudden people start moving downstairs. —Want to go?, I ask Jean-Luc. —Not now, it's going to be too cold, he answers. He's right, it's always freezing at first. So we wait and keep talking about the gym, and then I've had enough and I say, —I'm still going to check it out, and he says, —OK. I take two steps towards the stairs and say to myself, —Shit, it's going to be really too cold, I'm gonna get sick, and I turn around but Jean-Luc has already left, so I head down thinking that I'll have room to dance.

There's one guy on the dance floor. Practically no one at the bar. And it's really super cold. I head back up.

Upstairs it's good, it's warm, but there are so many people that it would probably take me ten minutes to get to the staircase leading to the big dance floor, so I give up, and I place myself at the same spot as before and pull out a cigarette. A guy with a lit cigarette not too far away. I ask him for a light showing him my cigarette and mouthing, —Got a light?, without making a sound because the music is so loud that I would have to scream for him to hear me.

The other night on MTV David Lynch was saying how he always blasts loud music while he films because the actors don't move in the same way. They move more mysteriously.

I take a drag from my cigarette while drinking my beer. And then in a flash I see Dimitri making out with another guy practically under my nose, like a couple feet away on my left. Fuck he didn't take long to replace me, the asshole. And then the two faces detach and return to vertical and the guy shows me his face, and it isn't Dimitri but another cute twenty-five-year-old guy with straight hair. I look straight ahead. I take a sip of my beer.

People begin moving downstairs in a steady flow. It has to be hotter now. I've finished my cigarette. I take my chances.

Downstairs it's still a little cool but it's tolerable. Anwyay, with my t-shirt and shirt, I'll be fine. The dance floor isn't too full yet, it would be great for dancing, but I don't like the pumping New York music, so I stop behind the banister and watch.

And then I realize that I'm a little down and that I should move, and even though the music is only slightly more bearable I head down the three steps and dance. I endure three or four songs without much enthusiasm.

My shoes aren't tight enough. I bought them on sale in London, half a size too big, they were all that was left. They are really pretty, a reddish brown, thick leather, unadorned, with thick soles, but not great for dancing because they're not high enough, so the ankle is loose and it's annoying because it's harder to get the ankle and the leg to move together. For it to work I would pretty much have to wear a second pair of socks. I'm still going to tie my laces again on the platform by the walkway. It's a little better now.

I'm starting to get hot. I feel like shitting again. Anyway the music isn't that great. I head back up.

This time I go directly for the toilets towards the end. My stall is still open. A little dirtier. I finish my beer sitting peacefully. At least if I take some E later, I won't have to rush to the toilets like the other time at Paul's party. I readjust myself. Leave my beer there for decoration. Rinse my hands. Check myself out in the mirror. Not too bad. My shirt hangs straight. I splash my face, I dry my hands on the sides of my jeans and I'm ready to go.

This time downstairs it's super crowded. I head towards the dance floor, but there's so many people that I bail, and stay four rows from the steps.

I check out everyone around me. One of the guys I had an orgy with two weeks ago following Les Bains's[5] after-party is six feet away from me, stuck between two beefy guys. He turns around. We are face to face. —Hey! —How are you? We kiss each other on the cheek. I would have preferred on the mouth, we had sex anyway, so that would make sense, but maybe because it was an orgy he doesn't think it counts.

His face is really ravaged, I remember it being like that but not that bad. Full of big wrinkles when he's what? Thirty-five? And plus you can't see his body at all, even though he's ripped, but this navy blue thing he's got on makes him look tiny, it's ridiculous, he looks like a shrimp even though his body is sublime. Not to mention his nipples (huge), nor his dick which is also really great. Heavy, wide, lots of foreskin.

There's a lull but I feel like talking so I say, —So, do you always just jump up in the air?, alluding to the last time I saw him right before I closed the door to the guy's apartment we were both at. I don't know why, he must have been happy since the four of us heartily fucked without condoms, he showed up naked in the hallway, I was saying goodbye to the guy whose house we were at, he said something that I couldn't hear, and he jumped up and down, like he was punctuating something, and I thought, —Here's someone interesting. But since he had done nothing more but smile, a big glamorous smile, when I had suggested, an hour earlier in the kitchen while peeling an apple that maybe we could do it again both of us another time, I knew I wouldn't find out anything else.

—Ugh, I'm smashed, he says, I've been working nonstop for five days. I don't have the slightest idea of the kind of work he does. But I don't ask. You never know what people do. Who cares. —That's rough, I say. —And now are you done? —No, I start again tomorrow, he says.

I didn't ask him if he had seen the others again. Only if he had gone back to Les Bains since. He said Yes. I said, —It's super cool since it's the Guettas. He agreed. There was a pause. And then he said, —See you later! And I said, OK, batting my eyelids, and he took off towards the dance floor. I saw him kiss someone on the cheeks. They started talking. I thought I did well by not asking him to fuck again, he already rebuffed me once, this time it would have been totally miserable. Yet the sex had been really great when we found ourselves alone, standing in the bathtub. I really liked his style. On the other hand, given his face, if I had not already had sex with him it wouldn't have even crossed my mind to hit on him. So, it's all good. And anyway, it's at least one less occasion to fuck without a condom.

I make my way through the crowd towards the dance floor. There's a free spot next to the first step. Downstairs, it's wild with the pumping New York shit they've been playing for ages, the alphas adore it so there's nothing else to do except wait until it passes.

Everyone moves their extraordinary bodies. And just to my right, a body appears that's even more sublime than all the others. The t-shirt slowly rises to the shoulders revealing a torso whose every muscle is not only huge but perfectly defined. The thing starts to move. I head back upstairs, that'll calm me down, there's more people up there.

Nice surprise. I emerge to some rather good techno instead of the awful disco that I was expecting, given that's what they always play on the big stage. I head down towards the dance floor. There's already a lot less people, you can actually walk around. And there, at the bottom of the stairs, in the middle of the platform, in front of the staircase and the dance floor, I see something that makes my cock shudder. The type of thing that doesn't happen very often. Shaved head. Bare-chested. Black leather vest. Black 501s. Black Rangers. He moves a lot, but well.

I get closer for the details. The keychain is on the left. He's thirty. Beautiful face. Goatee. Considerably more muscled than I am. Black leather wristband at the bottom of his left bicep. He glances at me while continuing to dance. So I decide to show him what I got. I'm weak at the knees at first, I don't like it when I know I'm being watched but the music is good and I settle into the rhythm pretty quickly. Fast and strong. If he looks at me again he'll like it.

After a while I start checking him out again, and pretty soon he looks at me, but in a disinterested way. I dance some more, I let myself go a little more and, and then he stops looking at me, so I decide to take a break to preserve my dignity and I leave to walk around the walkway. Nothing interesting. The go-go boys do their job.

I walk across the dance floor. A little guy stares at me intensely. On the other side, a pretty decent-looking guy, but another arrives and French-kisses him. I stop just before the end of the walkway, with a stunning view of the sexy skinhead, still dancing in the same spot, about sixteen feet away from me. I ask for a light.

And then nothing happens. So I change position. I get closer to him, three feet to his right. But that's still not close enough for something to happen. He keeps dancing. I get closer. And closer. And closer. Now I am right next to him. If he was paying any attention he'd realized that I am hitting on him. I turn my head towards him. And still dancing, he turns his head and looks at me with his blue eyes and he says, —You're hot but I'm not alone. So I say, —Ah…

And then I try to find something else to say but I can't think of anything good fast enough and it's too late, so I move towards the back and then I stop, and I think, —Well, I can unwind, at least I'll be able to dance peacefully, and I start dancing to some good techno.

My dancing gets better and better. I get closer to the front steps to get a better view, and since there's more space right at the bottom by the dance floor, I head down the three steps and dance really hard, pogo-style, over a ten-feet-long and five-feet-wide space, boom, boom, boom boom, until I'm out of breath, and then I go a little easier, but then I get bored so I stop.

He's still there dancing.

I head back up the big staircase to bum around the upstairs bar.

Ten feet of crowd and I stumble upon François the math teacher in the center of a group of friends, super exclusive, very beautiful, very well-dressed. They laugh and dance in a circle and François wiggles his little ass in his black leather chaps, a thick leather bracelet around his left arm that's perfectly offset by a black leather vest and a tight black shirt with very short sleeves that must have cost a fortune. He isn't as ripped as the average alpha male, but he makes up the difference with his hardcore look.

Jean-Luc had brought him back at daybreak at Sébastopol five years ago. We met when they woke up, so I guess you could say we know each other, but even though we always saw each other, before as well as after, in all sorts of S&M and fashionable spots, we had never really spoken until I met him at Les Bains's after-party. He bought me two tequilas on the rocks after I told him that I had stopped working to write the second one.[6] I thought that was cool, and I finally hit on him. We discussed a sex hook-up, he asked questions like, —So what are you into? —Ok, and this?, and I was OK with just about everything, which made us both pretty turned on, but he wanted to do it without taking anything, which turned me off a little. And then he suggested a little foreplay with my tits using his cigarette, a classic, but he brought the butt a little too close. —It feels good when it's warm but not when it burns, I said. On the other hand, the French kisses were pretty hot. But still I found him to be too rough, too domineering. Basically, when he gave me his number telling me to call him in two weeks because he had too much work before, I thought that I probably wasn't going to do it.

Nonetheless he's triumphant tonight, and he's moving really well, a lot more flexible than what I can manage to do. I don't know what's happening, I've lost my enthusiasm, I must have gone out too much these past few weeks.

He does some waves, chest first. If I stay here another second more, I think I'll have to go talk to him, it's been a while since he's seen me, but I don't feel like it, so I head down to the basement, and as I pass by him, I pinch his butt.

I don't look back. I keep going through the crowd. I check out all the guys. With the music it's like a music video. And all of a sudden I freak out, I feel lonely, I almost head home. And then I pull myself together, I tell myself that it's still early, the interesting stuff happens at the end of the night, that I just need to hold on. The problem is that I feel that I am really starting to sulk, and nothing good's going to happen to me with that kind of energy. So I take some deep breaths, a few in a row, to calm down, and

I straighten up, I stretch my chest, I roll my shoulders back and down, and I feel better, I feel a quarter of an almost natural smile creeping across my face, replacing the tense fixed grin from before. I look around. It already looks better.

I go back to the basement. I dance. After about five minutes, I'm already too hot. I take off my shirt. I roll it up. I tie it around my waist. Another five minutes and it's time for my t-shirt. I don't want it to be soaking with cold sweat when I put it back on. I keep dancing, and then I start to get tired, so I decide that it's time for a pick-me-up. I pass through the tight crowd to reach the bar. Paul is there, leaning against a pillar, talking to someone. I don't care, I go right up to him and say, —How've you been? He says, —Good and you? I say, —Yeah, my head says, —No. I keep going., —So, was your party last night? He normally throws one on the last Saturday of each month. —No, I just got back from vacation, so I didn't do it, he says. I reply, —Oh, good, I say, because yesterday I was at Station, and all of a sudden I thought that it must have been the night of your party, but it was too late, it was already five, and I was really pissed that I missed it. — How was Station?, he asks. —Saint Tropez in Paris? I say, —No thanks! he says, in a disgusted tone. Here I'm exaggerating, considering I stayed until five thirty a.m. There was a group of exotic looking women, probably trannies. The one in the middle with an enormous mouth, eyes, black hair returned my gaze. I thought, —She looks like Lapin.[7]

Paul throws his head back. He laughs. He acts all bougie since he started throwing these parties. —And how was your vacation, was it good? I ask, —Awesome!, he says. —Where were you?, I ask. —In Thailand, on the island of Phuket (as if I didn't know that Phuket was an island), then in Sydney for carnival (such a faggy vacation). —Cool, I say. —And yours, was it good?, he asks, —Yeah, I say, I went to Toulon and squatted with a friend while I tried to make progress on my second book, and now I've been here in Paris for about a month, I was supposed to only stay for a week, but I can't bring myself to leave, there's so much to do. He nods his head. And then, instead of buying me a drink like the last few times we ran into each other, he starts talking to his friend again. I can't hear anything, the music is too loud, I'd have to be right up on him to hear but that would be too needy, and plus I hadn't been particularly nice to his friend.

The last time I was in Paris I had sex with Paul. I didn't particularly intend to. I had already done it four years ago at Sébasto's and it hadn't been that great. At the end it mustn't have been for him either, since I'd explained to him in great detail all that wasn't good with the way he fucked. But he wanted me, and he had me. He gave me some super good E, and bought me drinks at all the bars in the Marais, and when I told him I wanted to smoke he found me some sublime hash in no time at all. Then I told him there wasn't any issue with me ending up at his place. I was so fucked up that I barely felt anything when worked my ass after fucking me. Yet I should have been suspicious because the first time I did that I told him that one couldn't possibly imagine touching a guy's hole with fingernails like that. Only that time, I was a lot less fucked up, just high on some hash as usual, so I didn't let him use me.

There's a lull between him and the other guy, so I lean in towards his ear and say, —I have to still tell you that it took me two weeks to heal after the last time, since your nails were too long. That made him laugh. —Oh yeah, you already told me that four years ago, he says. —Yeah, but you haven't cut them despite that, I tell him. Nothing. He starts talking to the other guy again.

I'm a little annoyed. After a blow like that, he could have at least bought me a drink. I look around. Then he's quiet. I say, —Do you have any E for me? —Maybe, he says. So I say, —I can pay if you want. He says, —If you pay, then yes. —Fuck the last time you gave it to me, I say laughing trying to stay nice. —I have long nails, he says. So I say —So it's a hundred, right? He nods. I reach into my jean pocket and pull out a hundred, without hiding it just to fuck with him, and he gives me some E with one hand while taking my money with the other, and I say, —Thanks, and he says, —You'll see, this one is really pleasant, and I say, —I hope (since the one he sold me the last summer cost twice the normal price and was pretty average) and I add, —And that way I even saved myself a drink.

In theory you shouldn't drink alcohol when you're on E. It's not too good for the liver, but most of all it brings you down. If necessary, clear alcohol, pure. Ideally a little bit of acid or speed and some cannabis or also, supposedly, a very small amount of Special K. But I don't have any of that tonight, which isn't so bad, since I don't especially want to get completely wasted. —Later, I say to Paul, and I head into the crowd towards the dance floor. The skinhead from earlier passes by me, followed by what must be his man. We look at each other. He really isn't bad. The other less. I retrieve the E that I had put in my front right pocket and I slip it into the mini pocket just on top to be safe.

The dance floor is a cluster of alpha males getting off on all their muscles. The music is still just as weak. I feel like going back and asking Paul where people are going after, but he wasn't very nice, so I don't. I decide to go take a piss and grab a drink of water. I don't like the bathrooms downstairs because they're small and get dirty quick. I head back upstairs.

I go into the men's room and take a piss at the trough, it's quiet since there's no one around. And then I wash my hands and throw some water on my face and neck, and take a look at myself in the mirror.

An Arab guy in jeans and a jean shirt, thirty-five years old, brawny, comes out of a stall. —Wow, are you hairy!, he says. I turn towards him and I say, —Yeah, staring him straight in the eye and smiling big, I'm an animal. —Hey, there are certainly people who must like that, he adds. —Yeah, I have plenty of fans, I tell him laughing. —But still, that much hair, it smells, he says. —You're tripping, I say, me, I always smell good (that's what Basquiat says in the Schnabel movie I saw three days ago), I smell like honey... He laughs and he says, —So you must be a little bee... I think about it for a moment to see if I agree, and then I say, —Yeah, I say, going flower to flower!, and my smile grows even wider, and I hold it like a precious gem as I walk away, wiping my hands dry on my jeans, going back down the stairs towards the basement.

I run into Tom in the antechamber. The night is starting to take shape.

He's still just as cute as ever. Even more so, since he's been on the triple therapy. As his everlasting friend George told me at the ASMF party in February—It's crazy how it perks them up! It must be said that before he always had a tan because of the drugs he was taking for his Kaposi's sarcoma. His boyfriend, an American who was struggling to find a job in Paris, forget about a residence permit, died three years ago. It was horrible, an entire year of diarrhea in Tom's apartment over on rue Quincampoix, and then he went to die at his mother's house in the U.S. Tom is for me the incarnation of courage.

Tonight he is looking very good. A perfect look, with a little black choker and a '60s-style rayon short-sleeve shirt that shows off his huge biceps and his full, round pecs. I won't mention his nose and his thick wet lips. I've always wanted to have sex with him, but without success. I met him when he was Quentin's regular lover, about five years ago. At that time nothing ever happened because I think he was a little in love with Quentin. Quentin, on the other hand, would spill all the details on how things went in bed, and what he said was totally credible, so it made me drool. Plus, I heard other things. Anyway. And more recently, last summer, while we were smoking a super strong joint in the place where I was squatting in Belleville, which should have helped matters, he told me when I brought up the subject that now he couldn't because we knew each other too well. Well, screw it.

—Hey! How are you? So? You're in Paris? Tom asks, and we kiss each other on the cheek. I confirm and then I start to complain. The music is boring, do you know where we should go next? He doesn't, there's nothing special going on aside from at the Queen, but things will get better here, and it looks like Pascal is going to DJ all night, they're not going to stop at one a.m. like usual. —Oh that's cool, I say (reasonably impressed that he's on a first-name basis with the DJ), I have some E. I'm such a hick, I think. You don't say things like that, unless you're going to offer some, and even still. This one time my friend Todd just stuck his tongue out and there was half a pill on the end of it, he signaled that it was for me, and I took it just like that. Classy. Tom and I catch up and then he takes off. I stay there, I don't feel like going back into the crowd.

—Hey!

This one, it's been ages. I don't even remember his name. Seven years? Eight years? It was when Quentin and I were starting out, we actually met him at Gay Tea Dance to be exact, and we took him home for a threesome at rue Henry-Monnier. Apparently, it was a good memory for all of us because every time we see each other since, we say hello, which isn't always the case with past hookups.

I give him a kiss on both cheeks. Usually I don't do that, but here it's been years since I have seen him, and I feel like being close. I wonder if he was the one who was wearing that sort of mauve leatherette jockstrap with strings, but I don't think he was, it must have been someone else, the same type but bigger, he's also a nice memory. At any rate, he hasn't changed a bit. His face has aged a little maybe, and he's got a goatee now. He also seems trendier, he doesn't have those tight, distressed 501s like before, but beige army pants. I think they make him less sexy.

—How are you? he asks, It's been ages since I've seen you. —Yeah, I say, I left Paris for two years. And you? —Ok, he says. —Still single? (one of my favorite questions). —No, I've been with a guy for five years now, he replies. —Oh yeah but how come I've never seen you with him? I ask. —He's British and lives in London, he says, but it works out, with Eurostar. —Cool, I say, and plus, you don't live together, so it makes it a lot easier under those circum- stances. He agrees. —And do you see each other often? I ask. —It depends, he says, sometimes practically every weekend, sometimes less. —And here you're out all by yourself, I say full of innuendos. —No no, he's here somewhere, he says. Oh look, there he is.

The new guy is my size. Shirtless. A bit of a potbelly. Him at least it's clear he doesn't go to the gym more than three times a week. Real army pants, dark green. Big brown boots (Caterpillar?) Short chestnut hair. Blue eyes. Slightly thin lips.

—Andy…uh, what's your name again?
—Guillaume.
—Andy, this is Guillaume.

He looks me up and down. Actually, I would even say he was checking me out.

—He likes hair, his boyfriend says.

Indeed, mine is visible. My shirt is completely open, the sleeves rolled all the way up. —Oh yeah? I say, and I kiss Andy on the cheeks. But I'm not that into him, I really don't like pale, hairless men. And above all, he doesn't have a big-enough mouth. That said, it's always nice to please.

—What are you guys up to after? I ask. —We don't really know, it seems like things will keep going here, the French guy replies. —Yeah, I say, there's a rumor. —Otherwise there's always the Queen, he says. —Yeaaaah, I say, —It's disco on Sundays, isn't it?, disco night kills me, here it's much better. —Yep, he says. This is where we met, remember? I say. —I remember.

Andy asks him something in English. I don't listen.

I don't think Andy is a queen. He's normal, the other one too. Maybe just a bit more precious. They both must fuck each other. The one I know has to be a bit more of a bottom, Quentin fucked him hard back then. But who knows. Surely he must have evolved since, just like me, like everyone. We all get more butch as we get older. Even Terrier[8] has become macho. The last time I saw him at the ASMF party, he wouldn't stop getting his dick sucked.

—I'm going to go walk around, I say, later! It's crazy at the bar so I head off towards the left, along the walkway. It's beginning to be *cruising time*. Eye contact. It took me a long time to realize that when someone looks at me, it's because he's interested. And yet I don't look at anyone I'm not attracted to. I'm not interested in knowing that I'm attractive to someone who isn't attractive to me. And when I find a guy attractive I'm actually kind of shy. Except when I really like them a lot. Then I can't keep from hitting on them. So it all works out rather well.

I head back to the dance floor. Since I don't want to drink, I'll go dance. The music has gotten slightly better. I find a spot that isn't too asphyxiating near the speakers, it's better in the corner where everyone's shirtless. And I dance. I let the music infuse itself in me, moving very gently at first. And once my ass finds the rhythm I accelerate. The pelvis moves on its own. I shift from one foot to the other. The shoulders start to roll and the arms follow. Faster. I shift back to the pelvis to balance myself. The energy stops at my navel. I contract my abs. Dance above. Chest forward, arms in the hollow of my abdomen. Chest back, arms raised, belly beating the air. The music isn't deep or fast enough for me to do what I really want but still I do it wholeheartedly. Everyone is smiling all around me.

I tie up the sides of my shirt so I feel better about my upper body and it's sexier. It's better to forget the bottom half, I can't feel anything with these fucking big-ass jeans, just my knees, not the ass or thighs like when they're normally tight.

My shoes are really too big, it's annoying.

And plus the music has gotten totally stupid, all HI-NRG with the beat in double time, no echo, no nothing. I look around for a good dancer who I can get in sync with, it's a trick I recently learned, it's motivating, but no one inspires me, well, maybe that guy, but I try, and then no, it doesn't work.

I decide to take another walk around. I go through the dancers, it's a whole art, you have to seize every opportunity not to get smacked or elbowed in the face. The dancers have the right of way. The nighttime crowd is civil, nothing like the daytime. This surprised Delphine and Bettina when I took them to the Queen two months ago. No one pushes or shoves. You feel a hand—or the tips of fingers—on your hip, your shoulder, your arm—two hands when you're too liquored up to pay attention. You're gently rotated to make you understand that you have to give way. You give way. There's also the lit cigarettes that mustn't burn anyone. People hold them up high at first, but once they're half-smoked they flip the lit end around to the inside of the palm. Transporting a full glass is a game of skill in itself. Personally I cover the top with my hand for more security. If it moves too much I'd rather lick my palm than be covered with a gin and tonic. There are never any fights. It's peaceful.

I run into Tom at the same spot as earlier. This time, Georges is with him. It's funny because I know Georges in a completely different way than Tom. We were in the same class senior year. That's fifteen years ago. We didn't really talk to each other a lot back then, he mostly kept to himself and I was one of the superstars. It was about six years later that we ran into each other, back when I started to get engulfed in the ghetto. I saw him a lot at Palace. He was already pretty well-built, maybe a little less than now, I'm not sure. Me, I was strong and proud and I would dance like crazy without getting tired for hours, while everyone watched me, It was cool even though I was very unhappy because of Quentin.

Georges and I have gotten even closer in the last two years. I saw him each time I was back in Paris. I felt good being around him because of all the things we had each lived through in parallel, nightlife, the sex, the drugs, the failed relationships. But this time I didn't contact him. He gives me the impression of having found such strong inner peace that it's annoying me. But he's a really good person.

Anyway Georges is shirtless and I am staring at his nipples, which aren't over-developed but beautifully chiseled, and I kiss him on the cheeks (we've never fucked, that's also probably what's bothering me) and I say, —Hey how are you? —Yeah, real good, he says (I knew it!). —How about you? —Mmmm, I say, in a semi-pathetic tone. I think I'm going to drop the E pretty soon.

Georges asks me how Marcelo is doing (Marcelo is Lapin). He met him last summer when we came to Paris together. I say that I dumped him after it got to be too much, we were hitting each other, but that it's OK. —Do you guys still see each other? —No, he didn't have a visa anymore, he went back to Chile, actually in the beginning he was working, he had a residence permit for nine months, and after we struggled to get him a tourist visa and then had to humiliate ourselves with the cops to get them to extend it, normally he was supposed to come back in September with a student visa but that didn't happen since I broke up with him, and now he's in Santiago, that freaked me out a little because there you can't get access to treatment unless you have money, finally he found a really good job, but a really good job in Chile means like 400 dollars a month, anyway I call him once a week to keep his spirits up and I'm planning on going there next winter to see if we have a future together. How about you? Still single? —Yeah, he answers laughing, I've sort of given up. —Yeah, I say, either way it's a mess.

—Where's your man? I ask Tom. —Gone for the weekend, he says. —That sucks, I would have liked to meet him, I say. I always want to see what other guys' partners are like. The alchemy of couples, that fascinates me. —Is everything still going well between you two? I ask. —So-so, he says. I say, —Oh… —It's fine but I'm not in love, he says. —Yeah that sucks, I say. It's not the same when you don't think it's Real Love, I tell him, emphasizing the capitals.

I don't remember what we say next, and then Tom and Georges say something to each other that I don't hear, and then no one says anything, each dancing in place, and since George dances particularly well, with all the latest arm gestures, which I haven't yet learned since I'm only rarely in the capital, I fuck with him a little by imitating him. After a while he notices and says, —Are you copying me?, in an outraged tone of voice and I say, —Yeah, I'm trying to learn all the latest moves. He doesn't comment, which means I'm really an asshole but that he forgives me.

That's when I should have bought them a drink to repair the vibe, but I didn't think of it. I said, —I'm going to go walk around, and I head over to the walkway.

Heavy traffic around the corner. I leaned up against one of the big black leatherette couches waiting for it to die down. I looked around. I was feeling a bit worn out. A guy was staring at me, a young skinny skinhead, badly shaven, with his head bent forward and mean eyes. I looked away. I moved on.

Just after the turnstile there was a spot on the couch. I sat down. I've been standing for three hours, I thought. To my right was a pretty unremarkable young Chinese guy. I watched all the guys go by. The skinhead came around and stood about six feet away, leaning against the guardrail. Talking to a guy who didn't appear to belong to him. He kept looking at me, I don't know, with the expression of a masochistic hooligan, or rather of a vicious thug, yeah, that must be his trip, vicious thug. A couple years ago, I would have totally fucked him, I thought to myself. After about five minutes, I got up. I took the path by the stage, retracing my steps.

While I walk upstairs I realize I have to shit again. It's really incredible, now ecstasy does the same thing hash does to me: my body knows it's about to relax so much so that it anticipates it.

I find my stall. My empty Corona is still there. I shit and then I wipe myself like crazy and then I get up and I retrieve the E at the bottom of the mini-pocket in my jeans. Since it doesn't have a groove, I break it with my teeth so I don't lose any of it.

The half left in my hand is too big, so I break off another little piece to make it really a half, below a certain threshold there's no effect. On the other hand, I don't feel like being super fucked up in case it's too strong like at the Queen two months ago. Thankfully Todd's British boyfriend was used to this sort of thing, we hugged it out until we both felt OK. That's why I only take half, if it's not enough, I just take the rest later.

I'll never get old.

I button my shirt back up and tuck it back into my underwear, and I zip up my jeans and buckle my belt and I loop my jeans belt back on my leather belt again. They're still not tight but at least they're not baggy. And then I walk out of the stall and I rinse my hands and I drink from the faucet, and I rinse my mouth and I throw some water on my face and my forehead and neck, and I dry my hands on the sides of my jeans and I look at myself in the mirror. I adjust the sides of my shirt. A little smack behind to flatten it. Here we go again.

I'm going downstairs.

I'm going to dance.

I'm waiting for the E to kick in.

It normally takes around a half hour. That's long.

After about fifteen minutes, I think I feel something happening visually, but it passes.

After a half hour still nothing. I go to the bathroom at the end of the passageway, it's too annoying to go back upstairs, and I look in the filthy mirror hoping that my pupils are dilated. No dilation. This fits with the total absence of any effect from the half-E. I guess what Paul really meant by, —really pleasant: — nothing. At any rate it's obvious that it's not the same kind he slipped me when he wanted to fuck me. I leave the bathroom in a huff, even more because there's nowhere to sit down. A guy walks by and looks me right in the eyes. I look at my watch. Eleven twenty. If nothing's happened in ten minutes, I'll take the other half. I'm afraid that one won't do anything either, when the dosage is too weak nothing happens unless you take the whole thing all at once.

I head back to dance. Then, after a couple minutes, I finally feel something kick in. I slow down to better feel what's happening: muscles relaxing, warmth, deeper breathing. My back straightens all by itself. This is cool. Then, all of a sudden it's out of control, and I feel like barfing but I calm down by breathing slowly, without moving, and it passes. I never puke anymore when I take E. I've mastered it.

And then it's the best: I start smiling, a smile I can't help but make, and that I don't feel like stopping, because I am truly happy. I'm feeling really good. I still hold back a little, this isn't London. The last time at the Queen the boys in the bathroom got totally pissed when I went there to drink some water, It's completely ridiculous.

It smells like hash. The musclemen next to me are smoking dope. Things have really changed in ten years. Before you'd never smoke openly like that in a club. It will be legal soon, that's for sure.

Ok, so now I'm hot, I am feeling good, so I take off my shirt and I play with my body. Boom, boom, boom, I roll my arms to the beat. There's still a lot of people, so I can't do what I really want, like jump in the air or walk like a duck, or walk like Linda Evangelista, or shake my ass, or dry hump an imaginary ass, but it's not a big deal I'm still happy.

Right when I start to tell myself I'm really thirsty and that I should go grab a drink, Tom passes by and gives me his Corona, my favorite beer! I'm dreaming… I take a sip and give it back. We dance next to each other a little. Smiles. I think he must have taken some drugs too but I'm too lazy to check his pupils to be sure. Actually I don't give a fuck.

He leaves. I keep dancing, not too bad at shaking my ass, and then I start to tell myself that it wouldn't be a bad idea to take the other half that I still have, wondering if I'm not totally coming down off my high, in any case I'm not peaking that's for sure.

Since it turns out that I still feel like shitting (even though I was really convinced that I was empty, it's the E that does this), it's time to head back up to the upstairs toilet. I try to cut through the dance floor since it's the shortest, but the people are moving so quickly that I should avoid that mess (smile), and head off down the right side peacefully walking down the walkway (relax).

Thrilled by this choice, I cross the few feet that separate me from the walkway on shaky legs and smiling like an idiot at everyone (it's good to be stupid), and that's when I run into Georges leaning against the wall while taking a hit (so cool!). He hands it to me, I take a drag, I give it back with a wink and head off.

After climbing the steps looking divine (with one small hitch on the path, though) I march triumphantly down the darkened hallway. —Guillaume!, I hear behind me, so I turn around (Hey?), and Paul, whom I've already moved past, and who's with a guy, asks, —Everything going OK? —Yeah, super, I reply, —I'm going to take the other half, and feel a smile starting from behind my ears and I take off and he goes, —Have a good night!, and I nod my head, already gone.

The walkway is dark, it's nice, I don't even know how I am walking it's so easy. My God, the skinhead is still standing there from earlier. I head towards the left. A guy smiles and brushes my left nipple as he passes by. He's hot so it's nice. I run into the guy whose name I forgot and his British boyfriend who likes hairy men, and I smile at them as I pass by, and then finally I get to the stairwell, so I head right, and climb the stairs. Calm and serene. The top of the staircase is blocked by some sort of grey security rope. There isn't anyone upstairs anymore, they're cleaning it for the next event. I step over the rope. The empty bathrooms are still filthy. But not revolting.

My beer is still there. Still empty. Oh no, there's still some at the bottom. I drink the last drops, and then I try to get the slice of lemon, but it won't work with my fingers, I'd need something else, so after a while I give up and I piss, and then I sit down to shit. This gives me the idea to rest. I sit back against the wall. I tip my head back. I close my eyes. This is great.

And then I wipe myself (I checked when entering that there was still toilet paper. *No* problem), I get dressed with only my t-shirt, not my shirt, I want to be more *casual*, I roll my shirt up and hang it off my belt (left side). I retrieve the half of ecstasy from my mini-pocket and I put it in my mouth, and then I flush and I leave and I look at myself, it's good I'm not too wrecked, and I rinse my hands, and then I take some water, cold, in my palm, and I drink it. Another guy who wasn't afraid of the security rope arrives. I take a last look at myself and leave the room.

I stop to get a cigarette (I don't have my shirt on anymore, my cigarettes are in my back left pocket). I ponder the dark and empty club. An Indian man is washing the floor some distance away. I go back down the stairs. Ask for a light. Take a big hit to get back that fiery feeling I had last time at the Queen, with those Rothmans Blue cigarettes, but especially with some stronger E. Right now, I'm not hallucinating as much.

It's then that I think about chewing some gum. It'd be a blast to chew some gum while smoking. I'd have to ask someone I know. Like Jean-Luc for example, who is still here dancing right at the bottom of the stairs, and who always has some on him. So I head down to the dance floor and stand right in front of him and say, —Jean-Luc, you wouldn't have any chewing gum? (in a languorous voice). He opens his eyes. —Umm no, bummer, I gave away the last one not too long ago. —Shit, I say,—I really want some gum. —They have some by the coat check, he says. Blow pops. My hope is reborn. —How much?, I ask. —Not expensive, something like two francs, he says. I search my pockets. Perfect, I have like seven left. —Jean-Luc, *you saved my life*, I tell him and I leave.

I walk along the edge of the dance floor to access the small stair-case that leads straight to the exit. I'm walking super slowly because I'm really fucking high. I get to the coat check and think they must be able to tell. There are only two rows of jackets left. The blond girl is talking with a brown-haired guy. No one is paying attention to me. All good.

—Good evening… Are there any lollipops left?, I ask the guy who's sitting on the counter with his legs dangling. —There's two, he says. —One will do, I say. —How much? —Two francs.

I pay, I take my lollipop and I head off passing the first straight couple of the night as I head down the stairs.

This lollipop is incredibly hard to open. It takes at least five minutes, the same amount of time it takes to get back downstairs, find a corner of the walkway, try to open it with my fingers, and when that doesn't work, with my teeth.

After a while I finally manage to tear up a small piece from the wrapper that's sticking to it, and I peel it off, and I put the sucker in my mouth.

It's Coca-Cola flavor.

It's huge.

I try to suck it hard to make it smaller because it's stretching my mouth out, but that doesn't work either, so I settle for folding the white stick in two, it's a little less ridiculous like that I think. And then I head back on the dance floor.

That's why all the young super energetic guys had them yesterday at Station. It makes you salivate and then you aren't so horribly thirsty like you always are on E.

It's also pretty helpful to have the sugar for energy.

It's right then that I recognize Frédéric. He's dancing shirtless in the middle of the crowd just a few feet from me. I head towards him, —Hey, I say. He smiles big. We kiss. —How many years has it been since we've seen each other? Three years, I think, since he worked reception at my gym. We met back when I used to live on Henry-Monnier, he and Donald were neighbors, and we'd run into each other on Saturdays at the laundromat. —How's Donald?, I ask. He nods his head towards him, dancing shirtless on the steps.

It's already been a few years since Donald's metamorphosis. Back when Quentin and I had sex with him, he was super skinny, a twig, his stomach stuck to his spine, skinny legs, and a small hairy ass. The only thing that hasn't changed is his beautiful Latino face. As for the rest, now he's an athlete. I hate him a little bit because back then I didn't do so good, Quentin always took over during threesomes. I would have liked to do it again correctly, but then it was too late. I smile at him from where I'm standing without going over and kissing him hello.

I'm standing in the hallway. Andy comes over. There aren't a lot of people around. I can see his bluish gray eyes staring me down. He says, —I want you, in his amazing English accent. Silence. —Really bad.

I am completely fried, totally peaking again. I roll my shoulders. I say, slowly, —That's nice, but I really don't feel like fucking. Silence. I don't want to be rude. So I explain, —Look, I'm on E and I'm feeling good, I don't feel like fucking right now.

Actually it's his mouth that bothers me. It isn't big enough.

—And plus I don't really like blonds, I add. —But I'm a redhead, he says. *I've got red hair.* —Not really, I say. —Down there, I'm ginger. More than here, he says with a twang. He points to his head.

I stare at him thinking, —He's a freak. I like that. —Do you like this?, he barely sputters in French. I say, —Yeah, I do.

His boyfriend arrives. ——Do you like him?, he asks. —That's your boyfriend, I tell him.

I'm so old-fashioned.

The math teacher is dancing on the dance floor. I'm above him, on the walkway, by a column. He turns his head. *Eye contact.* Straight as an arrow. He breaks first.

I'm in the downstairs bathroom. I take a piss. It relaxes my body. I take the opportunity to check if my balls and cock are a lot or just a little bit shriveled by the E. It's not too bad. I zip up.

I turn on the spot and exit the potty.

I turn right around to exit the squat toilet facing forward.

Down the stairs.

One guy says to another, —Next week, I'm going to Madagascar.

I'm hot. I stop at the bottom of the small stairwell. There's some fresh air.

People are starting to leave.

A tall thin guy leaning against the railing in front of me stares at me with the intensity of someone with nothing to lose.

The guy to my left, beautiful face, young, buff, says to the guy next to him, beautiful face, young, buff, —I work for a newspaper. A business newspaper.

The tall skinny guy is still staring at me.

I head back to the dance floor.

The muscle men are still out there. Calmer. Wearing more. Beer in hand.

Nod hello to Gabriel, who works in porn. We don't get along too well right now. Back when I met him, about five or six years ago, I was very disdainful.

—Do you remember me?

I say, —Yeah, I think so. What's your name again?

—Thierry. We fucked one time at your place and once at mine. You're Guillaume.

I remember. September '93. I was back from Italy. A month of swimming, push-ups and abs. I was unquestionably at the basement of Palace. We had dinner at Diable⁹ with a friend of his who just got back from Goa. And then we had sex at my place. He wanted me to come in his mouth but I couldn't. A few days later we had an orgy at his place, bareback, with a Swiss skinhead we cruised together the first night.

So apparently semen keeps you young. He has more wrinkles than at the time, when he was already pretty rough-looking, but he's still just as fit.

—That was a good memory, he says. I say, —Me too, it stayed with me. I had fucked him pretty good with a dildo to make up for myself. Barebacking used to freak me out back then, I went limp.

He turns in arabesque in his charcoal t-shirt and greenish-gray sirwal pants. Dances with his Black boyfriend who's just as graceful as he is. Very nice.

That was Nicholas.

He's changed. confident. Shoulders. He has a classier look. Shorter hair. Clearer skin.

I head towards him and I put my hand on his tight gray-blue t-shirt that says *Fashion sucks*.

I don't say anything. He looks at me doubtfully. —You don't remember, do you? I tell him, —Uhh, a year, a year and a half ago?, he says. —No, more than that, I tell him.

It's been about four years now. I met him on the Minitel. He came over to rue Bellefond. We fucked (safely) and used dildos while making out hardcore, it was hot, and then when I did him again he was clearly more passive, almost maso. It was actually me who had pushed him down that path by playing the macho dominator, but I ended up feeling alone.

His face lit up. —Ooh! You're in Paris right now?, he asks. —I am back for good, I say. —You're the one who wrote a book, he says. We talked about it with David, the one who you call Doc, we were on vacation together last summer. How did it turn out? — Yeah, I answer, not bad, 3000.[10] —Yeah, that isn't bad, he says. —And you, how are you? I say. —Ok, he says.

Four years ago, he was freaking out about his T4 count.

—You're getting more and more stylish, I tell him. —What? (the music is really loud). I say again, —Stylish! He still didn't hear me. —Stylish! Now he understood. He shrugs and smiles a little.

The music is worse. I rest on the edge of the dance floor.

Nicholas says something in Thierry's ear. They know each other too.

I don't think I'd do most of the guys I've done if I met them today.

I'm withdrawing from sex.

Andy comes towards me, shirtless. I'm dancing, shirtless. He says, —So? You don't like me? No one's ever hit on me like that before, I think. I say, —Pfff… it's not that… it's just that I don't really feel like fucking tonight. Pause. —You coming to London? I don't really understand what he means.

—Do you ever go to London?, his boyfriend translates, and joins us. Here's an open relationship that's working, I say to myself. Actually, I am supposed to go there soon. With some E it would probably be good with Andy. —I'm going there in ten days, I say. —Ok, let me give you my number, Andy says with his thick accent. Do you have any paper? I shake my head, No. —Ask the bartender, I tell him. He leaves.

—If not, we could always have a threesome here, his boyfriend says. I say, —Yeah, that would be nice, but I don't feel like fucking tonight. He doesn't say anything.

We dance.

Andy comes back. He hands me a small piece of blue paper. He says, —Call me? I reply, —Of course. I put his number in my back right pocket.

Cold. Put something back on. People often catch a cold on E because they don't pay attention to freaky stuff.

With Tom and Georges, shirtless on the walkway. —Uh oh! You gotta shave all that!, a little queen tells me while passing by.

I don't say anything. I look at Tom. Then Georges. —It's a young crowd, I say.

They smile.

The lighting is orangey-pink.

I think all three of us must be exactly as fucked up.

Me and this other guy are the only ones who didn't shave our chests.

I don't feel like doing anything anymore.

I decide to go sit down.

All the couches are pretty much empty now.

I put my shirt back on so I don't stick to the leatherette.

I spread out.

I put my feet up on the low table in front of me.

I settle in more comfortably.

I close my eyes.

My mouth half-opens.

Serenity.

When I open my eyes back up the guy who was on the other couch isn't there anymore.

E without hash is different.

I rest.

I don't think.

I don't think about Alain.

I don't think about Terrier.

I don't think about Stéphane.

I don't think about Quentin.

I don't think about Vincent and how the condom broke last year, how there was blood, and how three months later he tested positive.

I don't think about Marcelo. I don't think about how I'm scared that he's sick. I don't think about the fact that I can't bring him here because he isn't a woman.

I don't think about how I've been waiting to die for seven years.

I don't think about how love is impossible.

I breathe.

I'm fine.

I feel the lollipop fall out of my hand.

I open my eyes.

Nothing on the horizon but two couples, lovingly glued to each other.

I close my eyes again.

11

After a while I wake up. The music is better. *Funkier.* So I get up.
walk towards the now empty dance floor. I start to move.

I head down to the arena. I walk to the middle. I dance pure
disco-freak style. Rolling my hips, clapping my hands. It makes
me laugh. I feel light. Balanced. Suffering is unimaginable.

When I look up, I notice an ugly Black man trying to cruise me.
It never fails, when I start dancing extra cool I always get hit on
by Black guys. I ask him for a light. Continue to dance. It's cool
to be able to just throw your ashes on the ground.

Andy and his boyfriend are getting their bomber jackets by the DJ booth. They put them on. Head across the dance floor. Stop by me. We kiss goodbye. The guy whose name I've already forgotten is just behind me. He puts his hands on my hips briefly. I feel his heat. I say, —Bye.

I keep dancing for a little and then I stop to go get a drink and pee and on the way I run into Tom and Georges. —Everyone was there tonight, I say. They agree. Ask me what I'm going to do. Georges would like to go to the Queen, Tom prefers the QG. I tell them that I don't really feel like seeing people, that I'd rather go home and jerk off alone.

It's starting to get cold. They've opened the doors wide to chase us out. Tom and Georges grab their bomber jackets by the DJ booth. They put them on. I walk with them as far as the middle of the dance floor. When they get to the end, they turn around to say, —Goodbye! And then without thinking I say, loud enough to be sure that they hear me, anwyay there's no one there, —I didn't call you because I was a little depressed.

They signal that it's no big deal.

I stay there alone. The DJ plays U2's *Lemon*. It's the *hetero sound* that begins. Girls arrive and start dancing.

So I go back up to the coat check. Grab my bomber jacket. Go back down towards the exit. Realize that I missed the doorman from earlier. In place of the gay team now there's two Black guys big as sumo wrestlers wearing navy blue sweatsuits.

The streetlamps sparkle because of the E.

Take advantage of the light.

I decide to walk home.

Halfway up rue Amsterdam I reach the chewing gum part. I had forgotten. So I light a cigarette with the lighter that I had left in my bomber jacket to have the two different tastes in my mouth at the same time.

At Trinité, a group of Black people are listening to a beatbox under the bus stop. A bum is taking a piss in the bushes in the square. My high's almost gone. How long was that? Two hours? That's the thing, the E was a hundred francs but it was also two times less strong than when it cost two hundred.

An old drunk guy starts talking to me about politics in front of the Gare Saint-Lazare. I cut him off as politely as possible.

The streets are empty.

For me, all alone.

I finally arrive at Madeleine. Key for the entryway. Key for the stairway (on the courtyard). I climb the six floors.

The door opens up to a royal blue carpet, turtle poufs, and packs of candy that are the basis of the décor at Delphine and Tina's.

I go straight to the kitchen stocked with organic Buddhist food. I heat some water for a tea. I open up a pack of muesli waffles they brought back from Belgium. They're really good dunked in tea.

I put on the CD of the *Lost Highway* soundtrack that Tina had the smart idea of buying. Track thirteen, *Insensatez* by Antônio Carlos Jobim on repeat. That's the song you hear during the sequence when Balthazar Getty lays down in his parent's garden in sweatpants and slippers. He's sublimely beautiful, laid out on a deck chair, and then he gets up and looks over the fence into the neighbor's garden where he sees an inflatable ball or maybe it's a duck float, on the surface of the water of the kiddie pool.

My girlfriends are awesome. Plus they're away for the weekend.

I head into the bedroom. I empty my pockets. That's when I find the small piece of blue paper with Andy's number on it. It's folded over on itself eight times, lengthwise.

I read:

Andy

from La Loco

the guy-ginger

hair (redhead)

In London

(his number)

call me

to fucck!

I laugh a little.

I finish undressing.

I slide under the comforter.

It feels good to lie down.

I feel something super soft with the top of my head.

I reach up with my right arm to check it out.

It's the cloth from the guest mattress resting against the wall.

It's crazy how soft it is.

I must be having an E flashback.

So I pretend as if it's someone, as if I were touching his skin.

I caress it as if I were making love to him.

And then I come to my senses and say to myself, —Do you realize what you're doing?, and that makes me laugh, but it's killing my high, so I stop.

I wonder if I'm going to jack off.

I don't feel like it but it would be a shame not to take advantage of the E.

So I jerk off.

And then I fall asleep, and I dream about Ken Siman.

—Paris-Toulon-Paris
March 31st–June 19th, 1997

For their encouragement, suggestions, support, affection, and inspiration, many thanks to: Aaron Travis, Adamski, Adri, Agnès, Aiden Shaw, Aimé S., Al McKenzie, Alain D., Alain Royer, Alain W., Alexandre, Anne-Em, Annette Rosa, Antônio Carlos Jobim, Army of Lovers, Baby Ford, Baz Luhrmann, Benoît L., Maître Bernard, Bomb the Bass, Boy George, Brad, Brett Easton Ellis, Brian Transeau & Vincent Covello, Bruno D., Bruno V., Carrie Lucas, Catherine C., Spatiale Céline, the cats Joséphine (†) et Julie (†), the dogs Batman, Blanqui, Puce (†), Rynx (†), Zéna, Zénita, Christophe Martet, my clone Christophe, Claudio Coccoluto/One love, Clicking the Mouse / I Must Be Dreaming, Club America, Coldcut & Queen Latifah, Constantin Paoustovski, Controlled Fusion/You, Dale Peck, Damien and Marjory, Dani L. et Claude C., Darrell, Darren Emerson, Datura, Carissimo Dave, David Lynch, Dead or Alive, Deele, Dennis Cooper, Depeche Mode, Diable des Lombards, Didier Blau, Dimitri, Dominique, Double Exposure, Edmund White, Elisabeth S., Éric of XXL, Éric Lamien, Éric Moroge, Estherka (†), Eva Osinska, le grand Fabrice, the Face, Fatima, the soccer player's son, Fyodor Dostoevsky, Fire Island & Ricardo da Force, Francis Bacon, Françoise et Danièle Cheinisse (†), Franck de L., Frédéric Moreau, Frédéric Maria, Garbage, George Michael, Georges, Gilles Rivière, Gore Vidal, Grace, Grace Jones, Gus Van Sant, that Halloween TV on the Castro, Harry Matthews, Heller & Farley project, Hervé, Hunter S. Thompson, la fée Isabelle, Jack-Alain Léger, Jacqueline Girard, Jacques L., James Ivory, J. D. Salinger, Jean-Hughes F., Jean-Luc et Stéphane, Jean-Luc F., Jean-Paul Hirsch, Jeanne Moreau, Jelani, my beloved Jessye, Reine Jev, Joey Negro, Joey Stefano (†), Jonathan Demme, Katherine Mansfield, Ken Siman, Kiki C, Kim English, Subliminal Kro, Lars von Trier, LaTour, Laure Adler, L.B., Linda Fiorentino, Lionel and Ludo from Toulon, Loïx, Loleatta Holloway, my friend M., Madonna, my family, Malcolm McLaren, Marguerite Duras, Marina my karmic little sister, Mark Leyner, Marlène Dietrich, Martine F.

(Petit Ours et Lapin t'aiment), MC Lyte, Mel & Kim, Michel G, Milos Forman, Monica DeLuxe / Don't Let this Feeling Stop, Mukka, Muriel Moreno, Nadamo et Rodriiiiiiigo, Nadia and Nedjma L., Nastrovje Potsdam, Nathalie R, Nelson, Nicolas X., Nicole Cz, Nina Hagen, Ntrance, Mégabolg, Jean-Pierre, & my future godchild, Odile Terlez, Paul Oakenfold, Paul Otchakovsky-Laurens, Philippe, Philippe and Philippe, Philippe Sollers, Pierre C., Pierre the pianist of la rue de Bretagne (†); Ramirez, Reefa, Régine, Renaud Camus, René Ehni, Reynita, Roberto, Ronald, Saint-Gabriel, Sandra Bernhardt, Foreverlove Drine and Jean-Christophe N., Serge B., Shalamar, Sharon Brown, Stéphane P., the witch of La Cloche d'or, Sylvie B. and her crazy brothers, Taishen Deshimaru, Thierry Fourreau, Thierry X., Third World, Tim, Tom and Julie H., Tom Stephan, my trainer in Tahiti, Truman Capote, Woody, Woody Allen, Zarah Leander / *Der Wind hat mir ein Lied erzählt.*

Stronger Than Me

A Novel

Introduction by Thomas Clerc

Stronger Than Me, the third and final opus in this first trilogy, is a borderline book. Having already dedicated his first text to sex, Dustan went on to radicalize his gest by orienting it in a clearly sadomasochistic direction. *Stronger Than Me* is a rough book, a very rough book for those who don't really appreciate descriptions of gay S&M sex. There is something strange, however, in this sexual remake, as if *Stronger Than Me* formed a pair with the first novel, but in order to perfect it. Penetrating a zone where the stakes of S&M were desubjectification, Dustan remade *In My Room*, but stronger.

Dear Mr. Masoch

Even in his depiction of homosexual sadomasochism, Dustan continued to innovate. This might seem paradoxical, given that the S&M phenomenon with its endless clichés is a well-known scene. Yet, this is more the case in practice than it is in representation. Quite frequently described from a heterosexual framework, S&M has expressed itself in other disciplines, such as cinema for example, but has had greater visibility in critical theory than in role literature. Foucault, for example, delivered some remarks regarding S&M, although in peripheral interviews.[1] Dustan was therefore able to bring out a literature that existed less than the reality it was based on. The text overflows with explicit scenes that cannot be qualified as *trash* since they contain that oxymoron of *hot coolness* that corresponds so well to S&M. It is thus quite revealing that the cruelest chapter of the text, which occupies its center, opens on an image of the mother.

It is out of the question to attempt an interpretation of sadomasochism in Dustan's work, or to dedicate any time to the morose charm of its etiology. But for all that, we cannot avoid the questions raised by these practices to which our author dedicated an entire book (as well as a few scenes of *In My Room*). The term "novel," which we contested in the preface of this trilogy, should be understood here in the restricted sense as "*Bildungsroman.*"

The Experience of Limits

Not without humor, Dustan ended chapter 27 on both a sincere and theatrical note: "It's not the pleasure that's absorbed me until now, but the apprenticeship," linking sexuality to pedagogy. Because of its artifice, sadomasochism demands a more precise technique than regular sex. In *Stronger Than Me*, Dustan anticipated the didactic nature of his political endeavor; his experimental side encroached on radical literature. Inscribing Dustan in an avant-gardist tradition might seem pointless considering the specific historical connotations associated with the term—the lack of permanence of which has been noted since the 1980s[2]—and Dustan's distance from the literary elite. And yet, stretching the limits of what is acceptable (which the title, living up to its name, exemplifies) geared the book towards an informed public: unless the reader was a jaded adept at S&M, the book's non euphemistic nature spoke for itself. Furthermore, subversion was affirmed in its very form, here, as a remake: *Stronger Than Me* is a hardcore remake of *In My Room*. It is a new take on the same story. Written by a subject dominated by his sexual passion but who looked to dominate said passion by writing about it, *Stronger Than Me* materialized a purposeful will. As a specialist explained, "in the military world, the avant-garde designates a small reconnaissance group that scouted ahead, preparing the path for battle troops and for those who made battle decisions."[3] In this double limit-experience of S&M and writing, Dustan was both master and student at the same time.

S/M

By linking Sade and Masoch, Dustan placed himself under the guardianship of two philosophers. More of a masochist, he wrote, "I am not a sadist," although in one specific porno-graphic passage linking finances with tyranny (pornography understood in its etymological sense), he accepted the role of Chief Sex Officer. A Sadean spark lived within him, due to an extreme taste for direct debauchery, descriptive excess charac-teristic of hypotyposis, and what would come later, his obsession with political systems. But we should also highlight everything that separated Dustan from Sade. In addition to being a concise writer, Dustan separated theoretical sections from descriptive scenes. After this first trilogy, sex would disappear from Dustan's corpus, as if the manifest excess of *Stronger Than Me* had been meant to annihilate it. But most of all, Dustan was diametri-cally opposed to a negative image of mankind. Despite all this, Sade was the subject of an unpublished note by Dustan titled "Sade, critique of indecision"[4] in which he highlighted his artistic debt to the author of *The 120 Days of Sodom* the moralistic style of which Dustan would pastiche in his later works. "Virtue is boring," he wrote, "for it is the daughter of the fear of living; doing wrong does not aim at doing *evil*, it aims at making (*oneself*): reinventing oneself, the poetics of action." It is from this quote that Dustan drew the ethical and esthetic law that governs his oeuvre: intensifying existence by action and therefore proposing a type of literature that is performative and compels to the reader to enjoy (*jouir*). His handwritten note ended with an order: "Live more."

The Watchful Eye

You will not find an interpretation of masochism here, as that lies beyond our expertise. But let us remark that "the masochist always reveals himself."[5] Autobiography, an act of self-revealment, inscribed Dustan within a tradition attested since Rousseau. *Stronger Than Me* deployed a camera-eye technique that did not allow anything to escape, even if it blinded the reader with its clarity. Showing the unshowable is a crazy endeavor, one that is arguably at the heart of so-called realist literature as well as at the origin of what Pascal Quignard called "the sexual night," which associated writing with the invisibility of the two primitive scenes: our death and our conception. Clearly, for Dustan, S&M could not be given a psychoanalytic interpretation. That is not to say that this type of reading is not permitted, inasmuch as the author himself, with a mix of disarming sincerity and textual perversity, slipped in the most conspicuous elements of Freudian hermeneutics, beginning with the dedication, "to my mom." It was quite cheeky to place the rawest, the most violent, and finally the most disturbing text of the trilogy under the gaze of the mother, who was invoked several times. The father, moreover, was not absent, and was subjected to the moral aggression of the narrator who showed up very late to their planned meeting at a museum in Berlin.

Masochistic Humor

For Dustan, S&M was a form of life that was closer to the ideas of Foucault and Deleuze than to psychoanalytic ones. We know that Deleuze opposed masochistic humor to sadist irony: the anticipated subversion of a desire to submit answered the castrating dimension of a dominating spirit, undermining that very domination. Dustan invoked this ludic quality of S&M on the back cover of *Stronger Than Me* in a text that was not integrated in the book itself but constituted a section in its own right. Imitating the comedic structure of a fairgrounds S&M play in which the participants were actors, Dustan parodied himself as a slave in the long central chapter in which he did not hesitate to offer himself as a victim to the reader's voyeurism. In the same stroke, he never forgot to play his role as the sadistic master, demonstrating the reversibility of roles in what was not for him a perversion (according to classical Freudian analytics) but rather a practice of reciprocal pleasure (in the Foucauldian analysis). There was something "humorous" in the absence of concession of the technical description of his verbal abuse, as well as in other small elements distilled here and there, for example when Dustan refused to be "tortured" by the music of Dire Straits, a band he hated—it appeared masochism did have its limits.

Power and No Power

Dustan envisioned S&M as an allegory of the domination hidden by the diurnal order; it didn't have to do with the pathological but rather the political. Bringing to light that there was domination was already to carry out a demystification of the false innocence of the world above. Since Dustan never settled for mere showing, but rather played the game as both master and slave, the autobiographical novel completely took on its virtue of realization. The representation of homosexual S&M was equally political via the juridical, if we consider the homophobic judgement passed by the European Court of Human Rights which held that fully consensual S&M practices were not protected by the European Convention.[6] In fact, Dustan's sadomasochism was ballasted with an implicitly subversive dimension because it did not essentialize the places of domination; Dustan was both dominator and dominated, top and bottom, sadomasochist and masochist all at the same time. This was perhaps the originality of Dustan's contribution to the issue. This exchange of positions pleaded for a democratic quality of sexual activity that did not assign defined places to its subjects—this is very different from Sade who only viewed sex as violence towards someone else. Reversing the essentialist interpretation that would like to paint Dustan as a pure masochist, S&M appears as a process of unlocking paradigms, a strategy to relax identities, and a practice of contesting power.

Political posturing becomes pure in this book, as if Dustan's extreme corporeal engagement legitimized, in advance, the explicit discourse he would later create. This physical gift occurred via a total and quite impressive autobiographical commitment. Any detour through traditional fiction would have been obscene as Dustan did not want to write about sado-masochism as a theme; he experimented with it as a sort of *analogon* of what he thought literature was, an over-exposition of the self that should trouble the reader.

No Words

We can make conflicting arguments about sadomasochism: that it is a complete self-exposure to the other, a violent regression, a polemical image of power, role-playing, etc.... Despite its implicit affinity for Foucauldian-Deleuzian thought on this specific point, *Stronger Than Me* is in no way discursive. This is where it gets its power; it fully belongs to literature in so far as it does not deliver any explanation of sadomasochism. Indeed, no theory of sadomasochism is convincing, because sexual practices must be seized by their actors themselves and not according to the discourses that seek to confine them, whether that be to condemn, glorify, or even analyze them. Literature, again, exceeds all interpretive systems (which are inconveniently contradictory) by neutralizing them. *Stronger Than Me*, without a shadow of speculative allusion, dilutes its sources in the regime of the visible.

We could even go so far as to say that Dustan wasn't a sado-masochist, but that through this experience he formed a non-predicative identity composed of several removable labels. S&M was perhaps the ultimate test of the paradoxical de-subjec-tification that transformed him from homosexual to gay. Proof of this lies in Dustan's abandonment of sexuality in the rest of his work, as if he had to pass through an experience of limits in order to get rid of the assignment to "sex" through his identity. The paradox is quite strong: Dustan refused to desexualize homo-sexuality (as a certain *queer* tendency would have it), but it was through sadomasochism that he would, little by little, free him-self from his identity.

Build It, *He Said*

Stronger Than Me has a legible construction; it is structured around a very specifically dated flashback that is framed by a pro-logue and an epilogue indexed on the year 1998, the date of the composition of the text. Its thirty-six chapters are staggered from 1981—a politically flagship year during which the Left came to power and a large number of discriminatory laws regarding homosexuals were abolished—to 1995, on the eve of his first literary publication (*In My Room* would be published a year later in 1996). We witness a retrospective construction of the author's identity at the very moment when he had already published his two preceding "novels," and when he could, with relative ease, envision how he had become who he was at the time.

This narrative construction introduced, through repetitive sexual scenes that ran the risk of being viewed as static, the dynamism of a book that was *de facto* leaning towards the present. This construction highlighted the processual quality of Guillaume Dustan's identity—from young, cultivated bourgeois man to diligent practitioner of pleasure. The most beautiful pages, those that unveil the initiatory aspect of homosexuality, implicitly refer back to *Practicalities* by Marguerite Duras: "A man's transition from heterosexuality to homosexuality involves a very severe crisis. No change could possibly be greater."[7] But while Duras dramatized the passage from one to the other, Dustan, strengthened by his previous novels, concretely showed the sexual trial of the backroom into which he entered accompanied by a guide.

Sentenced to Death

The constant relation that Dustan forged between sex and death nevertheless made it impossible to separate S&M from its morbid side, which infused the entirety of *Stronger Than Me*: "I was twenty-six. Everything made me want to die" (chapter 17). Let us take another look at the attraction to extreme sexual practices and the opening sentences of this preface. What kind of learning was this if not the Montaigne-like apprenticeship of death? From this angle, when he announced his seropositivity at the beginning of chapter 10, this had less of a bombshell effect—it was something his reader already knew from previous novels—but rather justified the radicalness of his undertaking. The indivisibility of death and life explained the urgency with which Dustan took hold of his destiny between 1995 and 2005, when his final text was published, two years before his death. How could one forget the presence of the disease, since life had become so tenuous? "Statistically, I had about five years left" (chapter 10). Far from being a destiny unique to its narrator, many characters in *Stronger Than Me* were also HIV-positive. Dustan, through the disease, joined a declarable community at the antithesis to secret-keeping. S&M's ambiguous nature was thus complete: a sexual enterprise that considered itself both a vitalist response and a flirt with death: "The risky behavior of men can be explained by the virile need to prove that one is stronger," explained Dustan in a later notebook. We could read this text in a stoic manner, but how could we deny its Christlike aspect, where the masochistic subject's absolute fantasy is to be killed by love.

When all is said and done, what is "stronger than me?" Is it Sex, an ideal that catapults the subject towards self-abandonment? Is it Homosexuality, which is self-evident? Is it AIDS, a disease that destroyed a major portion of the homosexual community between the 1980s and the 1990s? Its form, that is to say its composition, gives us the key to a possible reading of this text. *Stronger Than Me*, the last part of this trilogy, ends a cycle. At the end of the book, Dustan leaves for Tahiti, a sunny paradise, a world before sin, a location that affords him a new space and time. His epilogue circles back to the narrative present. We have moved from the initial "say nothing to be accepted" to this final "say everything to be unaccepted, but free." The ferocious radicality of *Stronger Than Me* does not comprise any other solution than its own overcoming. Its author's great intelligence was to have understood this. After *Stronger Than Me*, a new Dustan would emerge, one entirely oriented towards life.

"My mother always taught me not to talk to strange men.
But I always do."
— TWA, *TWA Theme*

"I was convinced that parties like this prolong people's lives, whirl us
around in the snares of mystery."
— Konstantin Paustovsky, *Story of a Life,
Volume 5: Southern Adventure*

Prologue

(1998)

I don't have enough memories of my childhood. Before I was five, nothing. After that, a couple episodes. Gifts in preschool: I was able to choose first from all the cool things because of my place in the alphabet.[1] Forts made out of chairs and blankets in the living room of the apartment. Boxing matches between my sister and me, refereed by my dad. I'd get wound up like crazy. On vacation in Corsica (I was five), I called the neighbor we used to play with a dog. Mom yelled at me. I'd look at men's swim trunks, even my dad's. My father was the sun. He didn't want that. He turned his back on me. He left me. I was left alone, reduced to ashes, cold, dead. I went to middle school over on Milton Street. People noticed I was nearsighted. I started wearing glasses with thick lenses.

My father was the sun. The strongest. He wanted to be the greatest. Like his own father before him. Like me, after. He was good at painting. He studied medicine. Something conventional, bourgeois, respectable. Like me, after. He married my mother whom he had met when they were seventeen. She was beautiful. Two children were born. In our family photos, one thing is clear: he wants to split. He ended up doing it when I was seven, my sister six. He left for another woman, a rich one. My father was handsome, always perfectly dressed, no flamboyance, no sense of humor, no friends. He thought he was the Law. He exercised his power. He said no. I really wanted him to love me. But that was impossible.

Books gave me shelter. Between the ages of six and sixteen, that's all I did, read, while listening to Bach and Duke Ellington (with Ivie Anderson). The world no longer existed. And then, I knew everything. I was the best, first in my class. But I was afraid of everything. I wanted to be like the Fantastic Four, in *Strange*, to have superpowers, to be a mutant. To build, using only my thoughts, a wall around myself. To be invisible. Or, even better, to be like the Human Torch, blond, beautiful, in flames, flying through the air. Although sometimes it would have really come in handy to be like his friend, the Thing, endowed with super-human strength (but no one wanted to love him because he was covered in scales).

I never rebelled. I obeyed when he forbade me to finish the brown scarf I had started to knit for my mother (I must have been ten or twelve). I gave in when he opposed one after another of the projects that would have allowed me to grow. I never acted otherwise. I couldn't stand that he disapproved of me. I was only allowed to leave the math section for the literature section in senior year when Françoise Cheinisse (we had been friends since sixth grade) and her little sister Danièle were poisoned by their father (a toxicologist at Fernand-Widal, so he knew how to do it) just before the good doctor shot his own mother and left to commit suicide in the woods near Chartres (his wife had died from leukemia a couple years earlier). I was supposed to be with them out in the country that weekend, the first weekend in September. To go horseback riding with Françoise, and then also it was sort of a tradition to close down the local pool at Châteauneuf. I don't remember why I didn't go. I always thought that if I had been there, I would be dead too. A year after, I saw Françoise again. In a dream she told me what was going on with her and Danièle. That went on for years. In my dreams they never died. The only thing I thought was that Françoise didn't die a virgin. She had been with her first guy the year before. Danièle was too young. I was probably afraid I'd end up like them.

Marcelo is looking at me, in the photo I have of him, on the desk where I am writing. He looks like my father. This scares me. And then I tell myself that there's nothing shocking about that. On the contrary even, that's probably what turns me on. But there are big differences. He smiles at me. He's giving. He teaches me not to hate myself. So I'm peaceful. I know that it's not like with my father, or even like with Quentin. With them, I didn't exist. I was only an appendage. They were people for whom no one existed but them. People who don't know what love is.

1

(1981–1988)

I was sixteen years old. My Italian teacher took us to see a play. I got there late. Chaillot was closed. So I wanted to know what sex was like. Sex was stronger. Stronger than fear. Stronger than me. I went down to the gardens.[2] I had read in the *Nouvel Observateur* that people went there to cruise. I hung out in the bushes, feeling slightly afraid. A guy approached me, much older than me, thirty, with a mustache. He asked me what I was doing there. I said I'm cruising. He said Me too. I followed him behind some kind of Greek monument. We kissed. I had already made out with two or three girls, but this was different. Electric. After that we sucked each other off. The taste was awful. I came, I don't remember how. I didn't allow myself to really pay attention to those types of things back then. I was covered in sweat when I got home, I felt like vomiting.

After a year, I had recovered. I went back. This time I walked straight up to a guy, a different one of course, just across the street, at Beaugrenelle. We did the same thing as the first time, only longer. I saw him again. One day he ended up fucking me. We went down to the tower's bowling alley covered in sex sweat to catch a cold drink. I liked the discrepancy. But he was ugly. Things got better when he invited me over for his birthday. I met a small group of preppy boys. I fucked them one after another.

In an interview, Joe Dallessandro explained that he liked big and strong guys who would fuck him and vulnerable girls who he could screw. I followed him to the letter. I didn't want to stop enjoying the wave of approbation that welcomed me when I entered a restaurant with Claire or Laurence or Nathalie, which wasn't there when it was Hervé or Frédéric or Christophe. I didn't want to blow my chances. I was made to succeed. To have a beautiful and intelligent wife, with a good name and a good family. Beautiful and intelligent kids. A prestigious job. A tasteful house. So what if I have to lie. At Sciences-Po I had already learned not to tell people I was Jewish. It kept me from seeing that frown pass over their faces before they distanced themselves. For a fag, it was better to do the same. Say nothing to be accepted.

2

(1988)

It was Emmanuel G. who took me to a sex club for the first
time. I had never been to that type of place, or to a bar for that
matter, or even a gay club (I had stopped cruising in the Tui-
leries years before, ever since the day I brought home an older
blond guy in a red track suit, no underwear, he grabbed my
head, smacked my cheeks with his cock, forced me to suck him
off. I let it happen, hypnotized, telling myself that this wasn't
normal. Then he drove his dick so far inside me that I felt like
throwing up. I asked him to get out). I met guys with friends,
on the street, or at the gym. Anyway there weren't that many. By
twenty-two, I must have had around twenty guys and exactly
seven women.

We had dinner in Les Halles, Emmanuel and I, in a tacky place
with colonial décor that isn't there anymore, near the Niki de
Saint-Phalle fountain. Then we crossed the Seine and headed to
Trap. Trap was this place that was completely anonymous. From
the street there was no way to figure out what was going on
inside. Emmanuel rang the doorbell. The door opened. After we
got checked out head to toe (I didn't know it was our youth that
he was looking at), the dark and handsome doorman (whose
name I learned later) let us in. Red lights. Bar to the left, a lounge
to the right, a staircase that led to a floor that was shrouded in
darkness. There were a lot of people. Twenty to thirty guys. My
age or a bit older and guys who were thirty to thirty-five. Big.
Muscled. Handsome. Confident. Thank God, there were ugly

guys too. At least uglier than me. That calmed me down. We grabbed a drink at the bar right under the TV where big, muscled, well-hung guys were fucking. Then Emmanuel suggested we head upstairs. It was darker on this floor but you could still see the faces of the guys who were waiting to go further back, where it was completely dark and I couldn't see anything anymore.

We headed back farther into the darkness towards an open door. I felt a wave of heat hit me. The stench of poppers. I told Emmanuel that I wanted to go in, but only if he held my hand. He gave me his hand. And then he crossed the threshold. I followed him. I squeezed his hand. I paused for a moment. I couldn't see a thing. I was scared. There was only a tiny red light far away. I was completely incapable of estimating the size of the room, or how many people it held. But I could feel that it was really full, because of all the bodies around me, near me, ready to touch me. I thought about the métro during rush hour. That made me smile. I calmed down. The Hi-NRG music that was playing in the bar downstairs started to run through my head again.

Emmanuel felt my hand relax. He led me forward, through the bodies. Six or seven feet further away (but I had the impression it was a lot more), he stopped. He grabbed me by the shoulder, made me stand in front of him. I followed along. He had the upper hand on me ever since he had aggressively fucked me a couple weeks ago. He had been circling around me for a while in class before, but then I was taken. Then I more or less dumped Christophe in tears in front of everyone in the restaurant in Milan while eating a plate of gnocchi.

He crossed his arms around my stomach. Someone placed their hands on me. I couldn't really make out people's faces and I started to freak out at the idea that the guys were old, gross, covered in sores. Hands were running all over me. My crotch.

My chest. I let it happen. Then I remembered this letter in *Libération* where a guy told about how he used to go into backrooms and cut guys' butts with a razor. I started to freak out but I was already hard. It was too late. A hand undid my belt, unbuttoned my jeans, dug through my underwear. I froze when he grabbed my cock. Emmanuel was holding on to me tight. I calmed down. Let it happen. The guy was jerking me off. It was good. And then suddenly someone's lips pressed against mine. I had no idea whose mouth it was (an old guy!, herpes!). I jerked my head away.

But the mouth came back again. Now I was getting used to the darkness, so I could identify its owner, a super ugly guy in his forties. I turned away again. The mouth slid across my face, around, under my ear, and since at that moment I had a dick in each hand and someone was jerking me off at the same time, I let it happen because it felt too good. His mouth came back up towards my ear and he drove his tongue in. GROSSSSS. I turned away, wiped my ear off with one hand (that was holding a dick a few seconds earlier). Then I felt Emmanuel starting to let go so I did a half turn and I said, not too loud because no one was talking, you could only hear squeaking and breathing, Don't let go, OK? He said Never, and he grabbed me by the waist.

I got back into position. Things started again right away. I was being felt-up from all sides then the guy who was in front of me tried to kiss me and since he was hot I let him do it. Thirty seconds later, I was getting sucked off, I didn't know who was doing it and I didn't care, I almost wasn't afraid of him biting it off with his teeth. And then someone pulled my underwear down, slid his hand between Emmanuel and me down to my ass, started fingering me. Mouth, dick, chest, ass, all of it at the same time, I liked it. I arched back. Someone's hand pressed down on my neck, I knew what that meant and since I was super excited I bent over the cock, I took a whiff, it didn't smell so I started to suck it and that's when Emmanuel let me go.

I stopped sucking but I stayed hunched over, fascinated by what I saw, the dick I was sucking, the hands, the crotch, all the bodies surrounding me that were becoming more and more indistinct. I could be swallowed up by this jumble of hands, dicks, mouths. I could stop caring about knowing who they belonged to, if they were big, old, ugly, diseased. I could easily go off, go crazy, swallow every cock that came my way, become an animal, only to come out hours later, clothes torn, stained, naked, covered in sweat, saliva, sperm. I was already thinking about how the bourgeois guys from Trap would look at me as if I was a slut, a whore. I stood up quickly, tears in my eyes. I stumbled over to the door holding my jeans up with my hands. I got dressed by the exit, my heart racing, without daring to look ahead.

3

(1988)

But I went back. A week later. Alone. I noticed this guy leaning on the ramp. Older than me. Thirty. Cute. Checkered grey-blue shirt, rolled up. Well-built. Dissatisfied look. I walked towards him, relaxed because I had already come in the backroom. I asked him if he liked it here, playing it cool given the face he made earlier when he was looking around. We criticized it. When there was nothing left to say I looked him straight in the eyes. He French-kissed me. He played with my nipples (disappointed to see that there wasn't much there, but he didn't show it. He would tell me about this a couple years later. We went on to see each other after that summer, not often, but regularly). It seemed more prudent to go to his place, since he was a perfect stranger.

His place was OK, clean. He rolled a joint with some Moroccan hash. It was the first time I smoked since it had made me sick five years earlier in the country with my sister's friends. But he didn't need to know that. He played some house records, the best of which was this song that I didn't know, *Bam-Bam*. Actually in that genre I only knew MARRS's *Pump Up the Volume*, which I danced to with these prehistoric moves (I had learned them that winter in New York). I was happy. My knowledge was increasing. We drank some grapefruit tequila and then he fucked me, with poppers, on the living room couch. We finished on the carpet. With the poppers, the hash, the alcohol, the music, fucking was different than what I was used to. It lasted much longer. It was way more intense.

I saw Gilles regularly that summer. We would go tanning on the lawn at Les Halles. Had dinner at Studio, cour du Temple. When I came back from taking a piss (I always have to pee before eating in restaurants, half out of curiosity, half from the stress of having to spend so much time looking into someone else's eyes), he had made himself comfortable, his legs stretched out and spread under the table, you could sort of see the bottom of his ass through his torn 501s. So trashy that it made me shudder, me who was always so clean in my Lacoste.

I got to know the violet light in the middle of my head, eyes closed, when I took a hit of poppers while he was fucking me, from the front, then from the back, the skylight was open, it was August, I looked at Paris thinking of the scene (was it *Our Lady of the Flowers* or *Funeral Rites*?[3]) where the two guys have sex on the rooftop. He ended up fucking me with a dildo that wasn't much bigger than his dick but that seemed enormous. I had a dizzying, cold sensation when he put it inside me, it was the first time in my life that I had been fucked by something other than a dick, I took a big hit of violet light for it to last, it was so good. Hypnotic.

So good that I couldn't get hard to have sex with Nathalie, who by all accounts, was the woman of my dreams, beautiful, elegant, intelligent, aware of my tastes and in love with me, and whom I would have married even without a name and without a good family. I had to choose, so I left her and continued to see Gilles until he dropped me, anyway he had always said that he couldn't love me, he was still hung up on his ex.

So I decided to become a bombshell. At the end of the summer, I shaved my head for the first time in my life. I bought an old green bomber jacket (extra small) off my sister's boyfriend. My mother didn't recognize me when she saw me coming out of the métro. I thought I was off to a great start.

4

(1988)

I still remember Christophe's horrified expression (who I was seeing for the first time since the gnocchi incident) when he sat down, like he was going to burst into flames, on my bed that I had moved from my bedroom to the living room, right in front of the entry door of my one-bedroom apartment. I didn't give a shit about his reaction, I had decided to live out my fantasies. I poured some tea and then sat back down on the armchair facing him. I was wearing a souvenir t-shirt from a parachuting contest. Black. Tight jeans. Studded belt. He said I looked unhealthy dressed like that. He was properly dressed, like always. I didn't say anything. We drank our tea.

Then I went over and sat down next to him and kissed him and we had sex. Even if I didn't love him anymore, I always loved his nose, his mouth, his incredibly soft matte skin, the dark rings around his black eyes, his dick almost identical to mine. Two mirrors rubbing against each other. He always had this extraordinary ability to move smoothly from one position to another, like an animal. He didn't fuck me because he had decided to stop having anal sex with guys. He never liked it that much before, I remember how angry he got back in Milan this one time when I convinced him to try it and I was dirty. As for him, I wasn't allowed to fuck him ever since the first time we made love, I had been too aggressive. He got a fissure that, according to him, would come back if we tried.

I met Quentin shortly after, it was like something out of a novel, at BH[4] where I had dragged this little slut that made me do coke for the first time in my life, off the hood of a car when we were leaving Boy. Quentin fucked both of us, the slut and me. The next day I asked him for his number. I saw him again. I was fascinated by his confidence and his uncommon, even super-human, ability to arrange for his own pleasure. He ate (well). Drank (only the finest wines). Fucked (the best looking guys). He was strong. He was free. He had a motorcycle. Things to teach me. I decided to have him. It was easy seducing someone. Christophe, for example. Franck, Frédéric. I always achieved my goals.

* * *

In the weeks that followed, Quentin got to me with his other lovers. I tried to keep Christophe on the side to show him my inde-pendence, but since I wasn't in love anymore, I no longer wanted Christophe, so it didn't work out. We split for good that fall.

5

(1988)

At Broad.[5] Grapefruit tequila. That's what I've been drinking since I met Gilles. I danced to Comateens' *Get Off My Case*, my favorite song at the time. No one was hot. No one was hitting on me. I walked back home, it was the beginning of fall. I stopped at the Henri-IV square near the end of île Saint-Louis. I jumped over the barrier. There wasn't anything interesting in the gardens. I took advantage of the view it gave over the Seine. I went down the stairs towards the quai (with that feeling of being watched, which I was beginning to like). I walked around. Six guys in total, two of whom were already pretty busy behind a tree. I retraced my steps very slowly. A little mustached guy wearing a plaid shirt stared at me. Not bad. I approached him.

We made out. He used a lot of tongue, in a rather sensual way. Soon after he started playing hard with my nipples, which, along with the kissing that was still going on, got me really excited. I tried to find his so I could do the same to him. They were incredibly big and bulgy compared to mine, which barely stuck out from my flat areolae. This went on for hours and then he ended up pulling my dick out and jacking me off. I did the same to him. It made me laugh because he was wearing these totally preppy plaid wool pants. We sucked each other off taking turns. We came while making out and playing with each others' nipples, it's unfortunate we didn't have three hands each. He was Scottish and worked at the British Embassy. I didn't think that was something you'd tell a stranger. He gave me his number.

I crossed the Seine.

Jussieu.

I liked rue Linné for its crocodile fountain that sat across from the entrance to the Jardin des Plantes. It was right around here that I passed by, walking fast, a young short-haired guy, with a black bomber jacket, tight jeans, big boots. We looked at each other. Ten feet later I turned around. He walked thirty feet and now it was his turn. I stared at him without moving. He kept walking. Fifteen feet later he turned around again. I smiled wide. He started to walk again, towards me. Once he reached me I said Do you want to go to my place? It's close by. He said that he was in a rush. I said that we could go to the entrance of the park, under the carriage gate, about a hundred and fifty feet away. He said OK. We headed towards the spot. Three a.m. No one in the streets. He took me in his arms. He was a lot burlier than me. We kissed. He grinded on me. I liked that. He ended up feeling my ass up. That's always what ended up happening, you just had to wait. I unbuttoned my bomber jacket, pulled the front of my t-shirt over my head to show off my chest, that was another trick I had recently learned. I felt the heat. I saw some thick hair poking out around his collar, that turned me on, I took off his checkered gray-blue shirt and then I felt his naked chest against mine, hairy chest against hairy chest. Like a real pro I took out some poppers. When he wanted to fuck me I also had what was needed, condoms and a little tube of KY. He turned me around and he started to fuck me, from behind. From the other inside pocket in my jacket, I got out the nipple clamps I bought last week (my first). I place them on while he was starting to pound me. Obviously, I knew what I was doing.

Oh! Oh! Oh! Oh! Oh! Oh! Oh! Oh! Oh! Oh! Oh! Oh! Oh! Oh! Oh! Oh! Oh! A-a-a-a-a-a-a-a-a-ah! I gave him my number because he was living with a guy and he couldn't take a call.

Normally I like it the other way around, to have the guy's number and not give out my own. Actually there wasn't any "normally" yet. I still wasn't used to all this stuff. But I digress. He called two days later, around eight. I was cooking for myself, some pasta, or else frying ground meat with canned salsify. He said he could swing by that night. I told him that was perfect, that I was actually free this evening. When I opened the door, he was still just as sexy and virile in his black bomber jacket, grey 501s.

We each had a whiskey and then he rolled a joint (*beginner's luck*: a guy who can roll joints), which we smoked while talking about classical music (he played the cello), before going to the bedroom into which I had moved my bed back because having it in the hallway was a bit over the top.

We started kissing. He took my shirt off, so I took off his, and then we sat down next to each other for the pants and shoes, he kept his underwear on (nerdy), so I kept mine on too, caressing each other on the bed getting really hard, and then I got fed up not seeing him naked so I grabbed his underwear on both sides and pulled them down. His balls weren't shaved (Mine were, ever since Gilles. Before, I had noticed all the hardcore fags at the gym were groomed but I snubbed it), his pubes weren't trimmed short but he had a really big dick (I knew that already), a little pointy (oh well). I sucked it. He smelled like a redhead. Then he pulled me up to kiss me, and then he laid me down on my back, my ankles on his shoulders, it turned me on to see that, the huge torso of a guy who was bigger and stronger than me, above me, ready to penetrate me. He started to enter me, super hard, too big, it got stuck. Ouch. He pulled out, he waited ten seconds, tried again. Ouch.

He pulled out. He used some KY. He fingered me with some lube. Handed me the poppers. I relaxed. He pushed two fingers in, that wasn't too bad, then he replaced them with his dick. It went all the way in, I could feel his pubes and balls against me, I was stuffed, he leaned over on me, we kissed, I let myself go, I was feeling good. He fucked me rhythmically, slow at first, harder and harder, first from the front, then from the side, then from behind (it reminded me of this military guy, thirties, mustached, very good looking, who played footsie with me on the métro. I brought him back home, ditching the friend I was going to meet. He fucked me in every position ever created). I would edge myself to the point of busting, take a hit of poppers, I didn't want it to stop. He came. I asked him to stay in. He continued to fuck me the same way and then started to go limp, so he told me he needed to stop. He pulled out, he took off his condom and asked me where he should put it. I told him In the ashtray. He took a walk to the bathroom. Then he came back to bed where I was waiting for him, more or less jacking off. He sat down between my legs, facing me. He put three fingers inside of me, gently, firmly. I got hard really fast. He pulled them back out. Then he put four in. I couldn't think about anything other than this feeling of fullness that no one had ever talked to me about. I was so hard. Hard, hard, hard, hard. He passed me the poppers and I took a big hit and I felt him push in deeper.

I lifted my head up. His was looking down at what he was doing. I felt his hand get swallowed up by my ass (how could something like that happen to me?). A-a-a-a-a-a-a-a-a-a-a-a-a-h! I came at that same moment. He pulled out slowly, asked me if I was OK, I told him Yes, and then I felt my cheeks stiffening up. I thought Tetany, I knew the symptoms ever since I dated Magali three years earlier, I looked down at my hands and I watched my nails dig into my palms, so I told him that I was having a tetany episode and he said Shit. Do you have any medication? I muttered out no, that I thought it would just pass by itself. I let myself go. My body curled up, my head rested on the hollow of his thigh. He gently caressed me until it passed.

6

(1988)

At Boy. I hit on this older guy, my size, cute, obviously a top, playing pinball by the bar. I wanted us to fuck this younger shaved blond, obviously a bottom, who cruised me on the dance floor. Everything went well. I fucked the blond guy who got fucked by the other guy too. One dick in the ass, one dick in the mouth. I was the ham in this sandwich, on top of the blond kid and under the brunette. The blondie had really short hair, like fuzz. The next day he actually went out to buy us croissants for breakfast. I fucked him again when the other guy left, doing a better job. I wasn't able to come because of the condom. He came first. I finished off by hand. When I opened the door to his building, I found myself in a strange part of the 17th arrondissement. The sun was shining and I felt good in my new skin. Reality offered no resistance. I was the Human Torch. I was The Thing. I was Fantastic.

7

(1988)

At Boy again. No troubles getting in. I'm young. Cute enough. Super short hair. My green bomber jacket comes down just above my ass. My ass is super firm, round, fitting tight but not too tight in my old 501s. I'm wearing a button-down sky-blue oxford shirt to not look like everyone else, sleeves rolled up above the elbows to look manly. Plus a pair of semi-new Nikes, without socks. I copied Quentin, I didn't leave my jacket with the coat check (his was an out-of-style jacket, part leather, part raincoat. I always dressed in style), so that I wouldn't have to wait when I wanted to leave. I pushed open the swinging doors, I dove into the noise and the crowd. The DJ was playing some trashy disco song that I loved, dancing to it was the best. I carved out a small path through the bodies on the floor to a corner and I danced. Dancing was both a pleasure and an asset. After that, the song wasn't as good so I headed to the bar at the back. I cruised along the walkway where people were standing, sitting, dancing, chatting, sleeping, looking at me or not looking at me. Things are easy to read in Paris. People who act like they don't see you don't like you. If not, it's good. The bartender came over right away. I drank leaning against the bar so I could check everyone out. No one really stood out so I headed back to my spot in the middle of the walkway, in front of the stairs that lead down to the dance floor, a strategic place.

One. Dance. Two. Scope out. Three. Look away. Four. Too ugly. Five. Not a chance. Six. Dance. The music is too acid tonight. I decided to go pee. I was making my way through the crowd when he appeared. Big, beefy. Black bomber jacket, black t-shirt, black 501s, black slicked back hair. Beautiful face. Big mouth, badly shaven, glittering eyes. I wanted him so bad that it was like slow-motion. He stared at me. When we finally passed each other, carried away by our desire, all I could do was turn around hoping he would do the same. He turned around. I didn't move. He moved towards me. I took a step forward. His face now was right above mine. He said Hi. I said Hi, do you think you're gonna stay here awhile? He said No, we can leave right now. Wow, he's fast. I asked Should we go to my place? It's nearby (I was squatting at Quentin's while he was traveling). He said OK. We headed towards the exit. I followed him through the crowd.

Doing this at Quentin's bothered me a little, but since he was always going on about freedom... I also found it to be pretty appropriate for my new self. I carefully rolled a joint. He asked me if I had any toys. I got out my dildo, my pair of nipple clamps. I was already wearing my cock ring. After a while I found myself naked, on my back, my feet on his thighs. He was sitting cross-legged, facing me. He fucked me with the dildo. I loved watching his chest, his muscles, his flat stomach, his black hair. He kept his jeans on so I didn't know if he was hard. I was.

He pulled out the dildo, it was dirty, I went to wash my ass in the bathroom, a little stoned, when I came back, he was smoking a cigarette on the bed, I laid back down, I knew what he wanted. Sex. He touched my hole, squirted some lube, he shoved three fingers deep in me. Then four. He added the thumb. I was relaxed, it was never going to pass through, his hands were too big. He told me to take some poppers. I took a hit (back then they were still real amyl nitrate). Then I felt the largest part pass through, his knuckles and his palm. A sharp pain shot right through me, unbearable. Aahhhhh! He pulled out. He waited. It dissipated. I told him he could start again. Now I wanted to feel his hand inside me. He placed his pinched fingers again near my hole, he pushed steadily, until it got stuck again, and then I hit the poppers right away without bracing for any pain and… all of a sudden I felt it go in, I swallowed his hand in a split second. It was incredible. It was good. I looked at him. He was proud (he was young too. twenty-seven, twenty-eight). I told him That's too much, I can't. He said Yes, yes, you can, you'll see, go ahead, take another hit, and since it looked like it wasn't the first time he was doing this I trusted him, and took another hit and the pain turned into something incredibly strong and made me completely hard. Presence. Truth. So he went even deeper and I said No, no, I can't, and I came a-a-a-a-a-a-a-a-a-a-h! Then I had my second-ever tetany episode but I didn't give a shit.

* * *

The next day I felt like making him a really nice breakfast. I saw him again a week later. He asked me to marry him but I said no because I already had Quentin. He took it out on my asshole so hard that after I walked around with my legs spread apart and I could barely sit. When Quentin came back, he noticed. He fucked me even harder than usual.

8

(1989)

An S&M party. Already a good feeling of belonging. I just entered the competition for the most beautiful ass. I came in second, after having incontestably won on the applause meter, but the guys on the jury wanted to vote for one of their friends, a huge slut with a gaping hole. I won a shitty dildo, super hard. It's getting late. Things are starting to loosen up. I walked around. This guy who I thought was even cuter since he had sex with Quentin (who told me in great detail how amazing it was, and that he had a huge cock) is grinding against the thigh of a He-man. I head towards them. Actually, they aren't doing anything, it's lame. I feel avenged from the complete indifference this guy was manifesting towards me. Farther off three guys are standing around another guy, his naked ass in the air. One hand is trying to force its way in. Another slaps the pitiful ass, super hard, the poor guy shakes each time. I give him providence. I place a hand on each of his butt cheeks. I spread them. I run my fingers around his almost satisfied hole. He relaxes. My palm slides in. I continue my walk around the party. No one is left except these old guys who are whipping each other. I go back to the bar. It's a madhouse. A giant circle of people, actually, around two small mustached guys all in leather pressed upright against one another. At first I don't get it. Then the one behind gets on his knees and I see that he has his hand in the ass of the one in front. He is pushing with all his strength to go in deeper. Fisting is very physically demanding. The other guy is completely smashed on poppers. In two minutes that's it, practically up to the elbow. So A (the one in the back) presses with his free hand on B's back (the one in front). B leans forward. A gets B to kneel down only using the strength of the hand that was inside. Not bad… A's arm slowly comes out. Then A covers *both* of his forearms in elbow grease (The jar was at his feet). Yes. He first puts in his eight fingers squeezed together, no thumbs. He spreads his palms out to loosen the ass. A real pro. Then his hands enter. A charitable soul gave B a hit of poppers (now on all fours). Both forearms slowly disappear. Very slowly. They stop right before the elbows. And then they come out, just as slow. A looks at the audience. Everyone applauds. B gets up, his face incredibly red. I tell myself at fifty years old, why not?

9

(1989)

At the end of the year I found myself in Brussels doing an internship. I came back to Paris every weekend. With Quentin every time we had sex was better than the last. I opened myself up even more. He wasn't the biggest but he was incredibly skilled. He was trained in San Francisco and New York, where he had spent a year back in 1980, the golden age of poppers-sniffing sinsemilla-smoking leather clones who danced, danced, danced and fucked, fucked, fucked. He had never stopped since. My experimental side complimented him well. I loved collecting new sensations. I was always buying new toys.

We put in place an extremely efficient routine: we smoked our umpteenth joint for the day. I would go wash my ass. Nipple clamps for both of us. He would start fucking me with a dildo or fisting me to open me up, and then would fuck me (*safe*) for 20 minutes, half an hour, sometimes more, while adding lube all the time and taking hits of poppers, in every position and in every spot possible, at least twice a day.

We would go out, to BH, the trashy night club on rue du Roule. Twenty-four and twenty-seven years old, not an ounce of fat, very short hair, perfectly styled. We were the hottest. We would bring guys back home. When they were tops they would fuck me. If not, I would watch Quentin. I felt like such a bottom with him that I wasn't really able to top others anymore. When he was really going at it, he looked just as in love with them as he was with me. That gave me an intense feeling of weakness.

As I was leaving one Sunday evening I saw Alain, the little guy Quentin would fuck during the week, heading up the street to take my place in a bed that was still warm. I thought that Quentin could have at least asked him to come a little later. In Brussels I was hooking up with Jean-François (now dead), the doorman at Wham, thirty, thirty-five years old who was smooth-talking me. So that way I also had a lover.

He was HIV-positive, even a little sick. That scared me given that I was negative, but I forced myself. One night, I didn't understand why, he was talking down to me. I felt for a brief moment that he hated me but I ignored it like when I thought Quentin was being sadistic: I did nothing. A little while later, Jean-Francois's condom got lost inside me. In December I had retinitis. Every morning I felt like vomiting, dry heaves so powerful I would have to stop in the street.

10

(1990)

I took the test in January, like I did every three months. Positive. My legs crumbled under me when the lab tech told me the results. I was hoping it was a mistake but it wasn't, the western blot test was positive too. I thought Well that's it, now I'm like the others, remembering the massive guilt I felt when Pierre, one of Quentin's exes, had cut his thumb in the kitchen, there was so much blood and I was so scared that I fled. Quentin didn't say anything when I told him the news. That night he jerked off lying on his back as if I didn't exist. Then he cleaned himself up and finished his joint. I asked him for a hit. He handed it to me. I felt like I'd better not touch him if I didn't want him to dump me. It was when Pierre became positive that Quentin dumped him.

I was scared that I would never be able to have sex again. I told myself that it was just like riding a horse, after you get thrown you have to get back up right away. Quentin wasn't really available, so the next day I got on the Minitel. I got fucked. I breathed a sigh of relief. I always had that.

Back then there was no treatment. Statistically, I had about five years left. Sentenced to death. There were a lot of stories of guys who died in a couple months, in a year. I thought about that. Ten times a day. Twenty times a day. Every time I was hungry, every time I was cold, every time I was tired, every time I felt weak. I thought that the virus was winning. Death was the essence of my thoughts. Every thought ceded to it. Death was going to have me. There was nothing I could do. I sat in my cell. I awaited my execution.

Little by little I stopped. I stopped reading. I stopped going to the movies, the theater, even exhibitions. No more parties. I saw my friends, my family less and less. What was there to talk about, anyway? I worked it out so that I wasn't in photos anymore. One day I went to my mother's. I found all my old letters. The ones from Françoise. I threw everything out.

Quentin kept me around. There was still some interest, for my money, for my ass, for my conversation. I should have left. I didn't have the strength. I knew that if I was alone, I would never escape my thoughts. I needed him to forget. To forge ahead. Drunk, high, digesting, in front of the TV, at the gym, dancing, fucking, always with new guys, my mind stopped. More precisely, it limited itself to what I was doing. I was absorbed. I was at peace. That said, when Professor Machin, an old friend of my father's who was taking care of me at the hospital, told me there was something, a drug, no one knew if it worked, it was still too soon to assess, but it was something, it was a gamble, I said yes, I swallowed, three times a day I swallowed.

11

(1990)

Work took me to Greece in the spring. I started off by sleeping in the airport because of a surprise strike. Twenty-hour delay. It wasn't that bad though, it helped me forget about my problems. I had organized all my meetings in Athens around the weekend, so on Saturday I took a bus full of Greeks (the young guys were truly sublime) and went all the way to the gay beach, a giant slab of marble above the sea.

There was pretty much no one. I tanned. But then I got bored so I cruised this guy who seemed German, but tough luck, he was a French guy, moderately sexy but I needed some company, so I took him to dinner out at the port of Piraeus crowded with families, the parents were singing, the kids were screaming, the food was drowning in oil, but it was fun. He wanted to go to bed early and I didn't want to have sex with him so I went out by myself to a disco, on top of a hill, after wandering around the city while I waited for it to open. I got there early, there weren't many people there yet, I danced to *Sweet Dreams.*

> *Some of them want to use you*
> *Some of them want to be used by you-u*
> *Some of them want to abuse you*
> *Some of them want to be a-bu-sed*

* * *

The club closed. The beefy tattooed Marine still wasn't interested in me. I looked around one last time, the little mustached man who was cruising me earlier was right behind me. He started to hit on me in broken English. He actually wasn't that bad, looked thirty, thirty-five. I French-kissed him and then he took my hand and he bluntly placed it on his package which was really *big*. Then it began.

At his place he first showed me his collection of ancient coins. I bent over. He felt my ass. He lowered my pants, and then fucked me (safe), on poppers, holding on the the display case, then in every room in the apartment, for hours (in any case at least one), with an energy that's been unrivalled even eight years later (except for Chad Douglas on video with that little blond guy in a scene well-known by connoisseurs), in every position imaginable, he *never* went soft, we were dripping sweat. Then sperm. I finally went back to my hotel sharing a heaven-sent taxi (Sunday, at six thirty a.m.) with an older couple who didn't speak English but smiled at me. The adventure.

12

(1990)

At Quetzal with Quentin. We have a date with Marc and Éric, two guys that he met at Transfert the previous week. Quentin went to their place to fuck Éric in front of Marc. He proposed that they do it again as a foursome with me. He told me I could abuse the little one and get roughed up by the big one. I said OK. At any rate, why say No? And now we are here. Us and them. Much older than us. Ten years older. Late thirties. The big one is really ugly. He straight out has a gut. But he is wearing a bomber jacket, tight faded 501s, Rangers. Seems very sure of himself. The little one is bald, shaved, wearing a bomber jacket, tight faded 501s, Rangers. They're actually just like us except I'm not bald yet and Quentin isn't ugly yet and he has some Doc Martens on. He doesn't want to be like everyone else. The little one has gray skin. He is very nervous. He's almost twitching. It's true he has a great ass but he arches his back so much that I feel sorry for him.

* * *

I didn't say a word, as usual. We drank some beers. They talked about sex. The little one was laughing nonstop, really hard. Quentin was feeling his ass in front of everyone at the bar. We ended up leaving. At home Quentin continued to caress the little guy's ass while smoking a joint. I thought that it had been ages since he'd done that to me. Marc, a bit unhinged, ordered Eric to get undressed and to suck Quentin off. Consequently, I sucked Marc off. Then Quentin fucked Éric (safe. Quentin always had safe sex. He was still negative). I thought, that's what he wanted. The orgy was only a pretext to fuck Éric again. It's understandable, it was going really well. So well that Marc, jealous, started to whip Quentin's ass. He wasn't too delicate, so Quentin ended up telling him to stop (not right away though, he didn't want to be too rude and he didn't want to stop fucking Eric).

So Marc started to whip Éric and went at it harder and harder since Éric is highly experienced, but after a while Éric, who had already suffered a lot without saying anything, was in so much pain that he arched back with every blow (there will be trouble at home later, I thought, but years later they're still together). That upset Quentin who asked Marc to stop. Marc stopped and sulked since he's usually in charge. I went to drink some whiskey in the kitchen.

Marc followed me. I didn't say anything to him. He kneaded my nipples while I was drinking, pretty rough, like everything else he did, but it was OK, it didn't hurt, on the contrary. Once I got pretty hard he slapped my dick a couple times and then he asked me if I wanted him to work my ass. Quentin must have briefed him. I said Yeah, but only did it really gently, since I wasn't nearly as experienced as Eric. I was lying but it was for a good reason. We went back to the bedroom where Quentin was getting sucked off by Éric. Marc fumbled through his toy box. He pulled out three dildos, a chrome egg and a scrotum pouch. I thought This guy is a connoisseur, because of the last item. It was a leather pouch, with snaps, that you stuff your dick and balls into on top of one or several cock rings, and you fill the whole pouch when you're halfway hard. The sensation of not being able to get totally hard because there isn't enough room in the pouch, getting hotter and hotter and sticky with sweat, could be really cool. I couldn't get it on because I was already too excited. I thought about my mother, that was the only thing that really worked, and I was able to get my balls in, then my dick, and close the snaps.

Since Quentin was already using the bed, I laid out a sleeping bag on the floor with a towel on top and then I rolled a joint while Marc stuffed the egg inside me and charged over it with the first dildo. The dildo pushed the egg deep inside. I could feel its metallic heaviness. I was playing with my nipples while smoking a joint and hitting some poppers. The dildo was a reasonable size. Everything was going swimmingly. And then Quentin and Eric, whom I had heard finish, came over. Quentin was surprised that I still had free hands. This is why I loved him. Quentin was hellish. Quentin was the Devil. I told him that now that he was there to help me smoke my joint and give me poppers, I didn't need them anymore. So Quentin went to get the leather collar and the handcuffs. He put on the collar while Eric placed the handcuffs, then he attached it all with the spring hooks that were designed for that. No hands! My dick was swelling to the max inside the pouch, it almost hurt, but I was also feeling good because Marc changed dildos and started to use a pretty big, black, slightly pointed one that I didn't like that much, but still, he was doing it rather well so I balanced it with a nice oral trip alternating between Eric's dick, a bit soft, and his big swollen balls, he was wearing six metal cock rings at once. But after a while Quentin, inspired by my example, or rather simply tired of servicing me (the joint that he was smoking was finished), dragged Eric near him so he could be fucked with a dildo. Since I didn't have my pacifier and I couldn't jerk off because of the pouch, I became more sensitive to what was happening further down, where Marc was busy pushing the black dildo from earlier in a little too deep. I said that it was starting to hurt. He slowed down but he really didn't know how to use a dildo smoothly, and it was still too deep so I told him I would prefer something less brutal, thinking about the third and last dildo he had selected that was even bigger, so really big, but more supple, that would do quite well for a while before I untie myself and jerk off, and he said OK.

He pulled out the black one and he put four fingers deep inside me. Fine, obviously we weren't going to use the dildo, but fist. I unlocked the handcuffs from the collar (it's something you can do yourself) and I grabbed some poppers. He added in his thumb. Then he pushed his hand. And it went through, I quickly unbuttoned the pouch so I could jerk off, I was afraid that I wouldn't be able to get hard because of the pain. That's the risk with this kind of practice, you're on the edge, the sensations are so intense. But not at all, my dick was perfectly soft, but completely full of blood, and in the span of three seconds, I was able to get a massive erection back. Meanwhile Marc had gotten his hand even deeper. I felt that he was opening it to fetch the chrome egg (from the back of what? my *rectum*?). He pulled his hand out with the egg inside it. But I didn't have time to come so I asked him Could you please put it back? He stuffed the egg deep inside me with two fingers, and then he put his hand back in to retrieve it again. I let him do it again a third time and then I thought that I had reached my limit and that a fourth time would be annoying. As soon as he pulled it out I came, in huge quantity. Then I checked. There was quite a bit of blood on his glove, but obviously it was only from superficial vessels. Good. I looked at him. I said Wow, and then I peeled myself off the lube-covered towel to go wash up. Egg hunting, another thing I had never done.

13

(1991)

Soon after, I met Thomas, at BH one night when I was alone. He had just won a one-week trip for two to a Club Med in Tunisia. He invited me to go with him. I went. Like always when I distanced myself from Quentin, I came back to life. Everything wasn't perfect without him, but at least I was myself. I wandered around the beach under the Easter sun, in the wind, completely high, listening to *Satellite of Love* on repeat on my Walkman. And then I went to get my haircut alone in town, at an Arab barbershop where I was the only foreigner but that's what was cool, and when I left, a guy followed me, walking his bike. I didn't know what to make of it considering his type, a local with no money. I ended up turning around suddenly at a moment when he was really close. I asked him what he wanted. Make love with you, he answered. I looked at him. He actually wasn't that bad looking after all, another little mustached, beefy guy in his mid-thirties, a type I was apparently destined for throughout the world. I asked him when and where, he said Tomorrow, I have a friend who is lending me his house.

The next day I told Thomas that I wanted to go back to the hammam, and just like the first time, he wanted to stay by the resort pool, so I headed out to meet him at this Arab café full of guys who stared bullets at me since I was the only foreigner. My *date* arrived just as I was starting to feel uneasy. He looked at me as if he were in love with me but I didn't smile too much because I didn't want to hurt his feelings. How do we do this, I asked? He said On my bike, so I hopped on behind him and we left. We got totally out of the city, he was pedaling valiantly. Forty-five minutes later we arrived at this small project under construction. His friend's apartment wasn't finished but there was a bed. He threw himself on me and French-kissed me deeply, so energetically that I almost started laughing, then he pulled his dick out which wasn't bad looking at all. I stopped laughing. I got to work.

We got undressed because I asked him to. He kept his undershirt on and his socks, I thought Sexual repression. He wanted to fuck me standing but I insisted that we go on the bed, I figured a little sensuality would be good for him. On the bed I put a condom on him that I brought with me, then I laid down on my back, he started like that and then pretty quickly he turned me around, he fucked me too fast and too hard, while smacking my ass, I was surprised (after I asked him where he learned that, and he answered in American movies, I dreamed about world culture), and then what was supposed to happen happened given his relentless rhythm, I couldn't help coming. I told him that I finished, he pushed on the gas, since I already came it didn't feel too great but whatever, I grit my teeth and thirty seconds later it was over. I turned around and then I saw the condom at the edge of the bed, empty, and I said You took it off? And he said Yes, I don't like them, and I turned pale.

At first I was scared so I didn't say anything. And then halfway back I felt so guilty that I told him I was seropositive, that he has to get tested in three months. He didn't understand so I explained, and then he got it. If you have AIDS you shouldn't make love, he said. I pointed out that One I didn't have AIDS, two he shouldn't have taken off the condom. He said that he didn't like that and that I looked like I was healthy. I asked him if he had sex with a lot of guys and he said no but that there was this teacher from Lyon that would come and see him twice a year and that he was going to live with him in France, I was a bit skeptical but after all you never know.

He asked me to meet up with him tomorrow evening in front of a hotel on the coast to see me again one last time before I left. Since I was feeling guilty I said yes, pretty sure that I was going to get my ass beaten by him and all his friends. On the other hand, I couldn't imagine what he could have told them, so regardless I bullshitted Thomas again and I met up with him and his bike under the palm trees in front of the hotel. He told me that he had done some research on AIDS and that I had to eat a lot of honey because it washed the blood clean. I gave him my number in Paris. He never used it for the two years that I still lived at that address, but I still eat honey today.

14

(1992)

Boyzone. Alone. One of my mom's friends lent me her apartment for the week, that way I wouldn't have to be at home, things suck with Quentin at the moment. I was drinking a beer while watching the porn video. At the same time I checked out the guys who were there. My eyes landed on him. He was the only doable one. He was wearing a red bandana around his neck, which meant he liked fisting, and a cock ring on his Perfecto jacket, on the right shoulder, therefore a bottom. Tight stonewashed 501s, torn above the butt. Frye boots. Smaller than me, rather well-built. He was obviously a big slut. Actually I was a bit repelled by his mug, somewhere between pig and bulldog, but I told myself that my disgust was part of the pleasure. When you want to fuck all the time, you can't be that picky. So, when he glanced at me discreetly for the third time playing the Midnight Cowboy part with my Heineken (which I was drinking straight from the bottle), I concentrated on my beer and then I turned my head in his direction and I stared right in his eyes thinking really hard that I was going to:

destroy his ass.

I felt it was getting him wet. I didn't talk to him. He was hanging around this huge jerk. I waited. The jerk ended up leaving to walk around the back room. The slut didn't waste any time asking me if I came here often, telling me he never had seen me before. I told him that I had come to take a look around because at the moment I didn't live too far away. Mysterious. I put my hand on his ass staring straight into his eyes. I French-kissed him while rubbing his ass. He stretched out his ass. I pushed my tongue and my hand in at the same time. He arched his back even more. That's the advantage of S&M bars: no one gets offended if you have a little sex front of everyone. He was eating my tongue. I stopped as soon as I started to get hard. I just wanted to know if it could work. We agreed on a plan consisting of reciprocal fisting. Right when I proposed that we leave I already didn't want him anymore. We left under the gaze of people who had already slept with me, or with him, or with neither of us and who were drooling without a clue. He followed me down the Avenue Trudaine, glistening under the rain, empty. We passed in front of my high school. I thought about Claire, Hervé, Françoise. We talked about the places we went to, the hardest places. His voice disgusted me. I kept quiet so that I wouldn't end up not having sex.

In the elevator, I turned him around, I pushed his face against the mirror. Since he was smaller than me it was easy to give him the impression that I was in control. I was the only one who didn't believe it. I untied his belt. I looked at his face, pressed, mine behind, normal. I was annoyed because I wasn't getting hard and I wouldn't be able to keep the cowboy act credible for much longer under these conditions. So I decided to stop grinding on him and to pull his jeans down. I had to spread his white, fleshy cheeks, to reach his hole, shaved, gaping. The elevator stopped. It would have been a mistake to exit right away. But I wasn't that dumb. I took advantage of it to pretend I was interested in all this. Pulled my hand from his ass to his mouth. Put in two fingers (to get them wet. He knew the drill). Let him get off by sucking on them for two minutes. But not for too long before I dove back down massaging his hole with my sticky fingers. I still wasn't getting hard. I started to freak and made a mistake. I got out of the elevator first. Then a second mistake. I didn't turn the lights on. Now I was in an all-out panic with keys I didn't recognize, and a lock to find in the dark. I still managed to open the door. I made him go in first (three: see above). I threw my bomber jacket on the bed. Turned on the small lamp. Put on some house. I started to roll a joint. I suggested he go wash his ass. He told me he had already done it (obviously). I said OK (four: dumb, I shouldn't have said anything). I finished rolling my joint. I took a drag (five: you have to take three hits for it to take effect) and I passed it to him.

Without a word, I got up and I went to the bathroom (six: it freaked him out). I stripped half-naked, just the bottom, because I was cold. The hot water wasn't running, it went on for ages, I didn't understand why. In fact it was because I was using the wrong faucet (seven). I douched. I dried off. I should have put on my jeans without underwear to go back to the room. Or even gone in there naked, but at that moment my pecker was too small, all shriveled up by the cold. That would have still been better than coming back with a wet towel around my waist (eight).

He didn't get undressed. I felt even worse. I sat on the bed. I took the joint back (nine: I should have caressed him). My towel opened. He touched my ass. This pissed me off because I was planning to start things off, but I didn't say anything as I didn't want to come off as ridiculous. He wasted no time driving a finger all the way in. As tense as I was, it didn't feel great. He should have gone slower at the start. I let it go. Ten. I even cooperated by lying on my back, legs spread. I took a hit from my joint trying to jerk off with some lube. He slipped in three, then four fingers, too quickly. I wasn't getting hard. Then he tried his hand. It got stuck at the knuckles. I took some poppers but it made me lose what little erection I had, and I was already worrying that he was going to hurt me, but the poppers automatically relaxed me and his hand slid in. That definitely hurt so I asked him to pull out but he said that it was fine, that I should take another hit of poppers. I had no desire to continue this nightmare but I tried to calm down. Eleven.

I took another hit of poppers. It hurt a little less. I tried to jerk off but I couldn't get hard again. He turned his fist a little inside my tight asshole. That was hurting. After five minutes (twelve: I shouldn't have waited), I ended up telling him that I would rather stop, that I didn't really like getting fisted without being hard. He seemed surprised (I didn't know then that it could actually feel quite good under certain conditions. Ones in which you're relaxed. I asked him if he wanted me to work on his ass. He said OK. So I went to clean myself up and I came back. I rolled another joint to start things off again. We smoked. We didn't touch each other. I came towards him. The closer I got, the more I wanted him to go away. He was lying down on his side. I slid one finger in his ass. It went in like a knife through butter. I got hard right away. I started to jerk off. Two fingers went in just as easily as one. So I wanted to fuck him since he was so loose. Not face to face, I did not want to see his mug. I didn't ask him what he thought (even though the little enthusiasm he manifested was enough for me to see he wasn't liking this). I just said I'm going to fuck you. I turned him over. His ass was enormous in that position. I put on a condom, but too late, I had already gone half soft again. I thought I was going to be pathetic. As if that wasn't already the case. I slipped a third finger in to get myself hard again. That worked just enough for me to penetrate him. I didn't feel anything inside. I wasn't hard enough, and he was way too relaxed. I kept going though, I slapped his ass a little so that he would tighten up but that didn't do anything. I pulled my soft cock out. I ripped the condom off so that I could get hard again. Without a word I started fingering him again. Three, four, five fingers. I kept pushing but it wouldn't go in. I could feel how contracted his anus was around my hand. I didn't know what to do. I pulled my hand out slowly. I put it back in. It still didn't go in (which wasn't all that surprising since I hadn't relaxed him). He ended up telling me that it was hurting. I told him that it was probably best to stop. He gave me his phone number so that we could do it again while high on acid, maybe that would help.

Three weeks later I was in front of his building in Les Halles, totally depressed after a workout at the gym. I called him from the café across the street. He told me to come up. I climbed the stairwell covered in crappy carpeting. His place had carpeting too, and dirty. He didn't have anything to smoke. We shared a beer (I hate beer). He showed me some polaroids of people fisting that he took during an orgy the night before. Assholes dripping in grease around dildos or forearms that were coming out of them. Not one hard dick. Then he sold me two hits of acid. Invited me to the next orgy. I didn't go.

15

(1992)

Ever since I've been positive I've seen myself as a loaded gun.
Sperm replaced the bullets. With it I had power, like guys
attacking banks with syringes. The first time was a skinny blond.
I took him from behind. I got soft. Shame. I pulled out. I jerked
off. I couldn't get hard again. I pulled the condom off. I jerked
off thinking about what I could do. I pushed back in, no condom.
I ended up going soft again because I was thinking too much. I
pulled out again. I finished myself off by hand, plenty of guys do
that. He didn't see anything. I was the only one who knew.

The second time it was a little brown-haired boy who welcomed
me bare-assed wearing chaps. I went soft as soon as I put the condom on as usual. He was on his back. It was stupid because that
way I ended up alone, and when I felt alone I only wanted to do
one thing, and that was to die. But it was also true that I wasn't
attracted to him. One way or another I was only having sex with
guys I wasn't attracted to, I had decided that I didn't really give a
damn. I wasn't going to be picky. I'd take what I could get. I
needed even the smallest piece of desire. With ugly guys there
wasn't any competition. I was sure that they wanted me. That
sustained me.

I pulled off the condom and then I jerked off and it made me
hard thinking that I could bareback him, he hadn't noticed anything. So I went in, I was rock hard. I fucked him and it felt
amazing. I pulled out to come, it was so good to have an orgasm

like that, like before when I was alive. I came in my hand. He turned his head. I was sure that he knew. He just said that it had been so long since anyone had fucked him so delicately. I was totally offended. And then I thought that I was going to hell. That I was lost.

16

(1992)

Vacation in London with Quentin. Totally grim. We did so many drugs that we missed our return plane. I went out and bought tickets for two days later and some soup as a bonus since he had caught a cold. Through the dark cobblestone streets, the asphalt glistened in the rain, I was wiped out, it was Monday evening, a family was getting out of their car, I was surprisingly happy.

I had read in the community newspaper that there was a leather S&M party the next day, in a nearby club. I needed some comfort after Quentin's low blow. Needless to say, it didn't work out. First I struggled to even find the place. I went in. I paid. Guys were getting dressed in a communal dressing room, like in gym class when I was fifteen. I followed suit. Inside they were all in leather or in latex. I was wearing a latex body suit that I had just bought (for too much) off the roommate of the guy we spent the day with on Sunday, after the club, getting high on E, acid and joints (with the hash I had brought from Paris because Quentin had left first—he had some free time since he was unemployed— called to tell me that he couldn't find any here, and I almost got caught at customs, they totally made me take off my Rangers *and* my socks, thank God the twelve and a half grams were in my underwear). As usual, Quentin managed to monopolize the guy, at the end I left crying, in the middle of the night in some rough neighborhood where I miraculously found a taxi instead of getting robbed and beaten by a gang of guys loitering at the gas station where I had taken refuge.

Nothing really happened at first. I talked to a fat naked skinhead wearing a harness but he was fat. So I went to the bathroom and took an E, which turned out to be a terrible idea because obviously it made it impossible to get hard. I ended up finding myself on the floor looking for my chrome cock ring that had cost a fortune and that had slid off either while I was blowing someone and/or getting boned, because my balls and dick were so shriveled up. But then, all of a sudden, I saw myself. I felt so humiliated that I froze. I looked up. Twenty feet in front of me, an alpha-male in army pants and harness who was playing video games earlier was getting his nipples sucked and nibbled on by three guys, his big dick perfectly straight. My life wasn't like that.

17

(1992)

I was twenty-six. Everything made me want to die. Getting up in the morning. Taking the car out (a Lancia coupé my father had bought me. Quentin loved to go fast), to go to work. Going down every morning at ten past eight to move the car the mornings I didn't go to work. Grocery shopping. I did it so much that it hurt my hands, I could barely carry the bags up the six flights of stairs to my apartment, thinking that I'd have to move when I got sick (there was still no treatment. I was still taking AZT without knowing). It wasn't even worth killing myself, it was only a matter of time.

That was pretty much it. M. was the only person whom I was still seeing, about once a month. I was alone. At the same time I was surrounded. Quentin, still unemployed, played it cool, stayed at home, hit up guys on the Minitel at least three times a day. I would find them in my bed with him when I came home from work. Sometimes I would ignore him. I would refuse to have sex with him. I knew what that meant: boycott. If I was being infantile or bourgeois, Quentin was capable of ignoring me for days, a week, even more. Which meant that, since I only had him anymore, that I didn't have anybody at all. So most of the time I gave in. Considering what I was used to with him, it was pretty pathetic.

Sex just made me want to die even more. It had been so long that Quentin had been telling me I wasn't good at it ("No, not my nipples, not like that!"). So long since he'd shown me he was happy. I started to go limp. I'd go limp when I fucked which wasn't all that new. I'd go limp when I bottomed. I'd go limp when I jerked off. The result, predictable, but which I didn't foresee, was that, since I was no longer useful, Quentin more or less left. He had a lover. He saw him three times a week. He would tell me in great detail how AMAZING the sex was. I found myself alone for half the week and every other weekend. I knew I had to leave him but I was really afraid of what life would be like without him. I wasn't strong enough. And then when he was nice to me I felt so great. But that didn't happen so much lately, since Quentin didn't like to fuck guys who didn't get hard, the ass doesn't react.

One night we were in bed, completely wasted as usual. He was watching TV. I was on my side of the bed. I was bored. Before, after sex I would cuddle up against him. I felt safe. Not anymore, that also wasn't working anymore. I wondered what still turned me on. There were two things: old guys and S&M. Old guys because they wanted me. S&M because when the guys were tied up and gagged, they couldn't criticize me or turn me down. The following days I looked on the Minitel. I ended up finding a bottom, submissive, in his forties, pretty ugly but super obedient. I tied him up. I gagged him. I whipped him. I fucked him (safely). He didn't complain, quite the contrary. I saw him again (me who never sees anyone again). I was beginning to heal.

18

(1993)

In the beginning of the year we moved into an Haussmann-style apartment in Les Halles, Quentin, me, and his best friend Jean-Luc. Even if he was structurally on his side, I was happy to have a third person around. We all used the Minitel for hookups, a lot. There were really all kinds of people on there. I started a Polaroid collection of my most interesting tricks: the guy who drank his own piss, the guy I tied up to the red office chair with sixty-five feet of rope, the little biker guy that I fucked through a hole in his leather pants, the guy who whipped me all over as if it were a massage (I got hard without touching myself), the lawyer who worked nearby and would come over and get fucked with a dildo during his lunch break, the hairy guy with whom we had hung fish weights on our nipples and a Rangers boot on our balls, the guy from Martinique with a huge dick who would go soft while fucking if you didn't play hard with his nipples, the little slut who told me Sex is my strength, the American who slid his balls inside my ass after penetrating me with his big dick (curiously, I already knew him. I hooked up with someone on the Minitel, Nice Bastille Cock, a swimming trunk hookup, I took a shower with him, also in a bathing suit, and then the guy destroyed my ass (safe) with his huge eight-inch rod, then the American arrived, and the two of them started to play this whole macho-man gang-bang thing, so I kicked the American out so I could breathe a little), the one who had a neck brace and two-inch-long nipples, the one who went to mass nearby. Each had his specialty.

One guy came during the interviews for the houseboy position. Actually it was a mistake, he thought it was a servant hookup. Quentin had another trick going so I stepped up. I liked that guys could see that we played by different rules, in a different world. The guy was really gorgeous, young, shaved head. He looked me straight in the eyes without blinking. I made him get naked, except his Rangers. He was already wearing a cock ring. I just added a black leather collar and a pair of nipple clamps. Simple and tasteful. I was already shirtless, in chaps, a zip-up thong, German boots. My indoor outfit. I only took my riding crop, which I slid under my chaps, down the right leg, for easy access.

I told him On your knees. He knelt down looking at me straight in the eyes. I instantly got hard, just with that. I grabbed his head and pushed it against the bulge in my thong. I rubbed it back and forth, like an object, against my bulge, getting harder and harder. Before my cock started to pop out of the thong I opened the zipper, I took it out and he sucked it, very well, deep-throating it. Too bad he didn't like getting fucked. When I felt that he was beginning to get soft I grabbed him by the collar. I led him to the kitchen. At the doorway I pushed him down. On all fours! I said. I made him crawl in like that, pulling on his collar, to the middle of the tiled floor. To get you used to being on the floor, OK? He nodded yes.

I let go. I pointed to the bottom of the shelf. Do you see that, there's everything you need, I said. I got out some pink Mapa gloves, some floor cleaner, a mop and bucket, and I placed them one by one under his nose. I said, Begin. He got up to get some water. I said No, you're going to do this on all fours, I want to see your ass in the air, that's what excites me, the maid who washes the floor with her ass in the air. He crawled all the way to the sink. It got him hard, the little bastard. In front of the sink he said Now what do I do? I said Now, you get up. He filled up the bucket and then he knelt back down like a good boy. He started to scrub. He was doing it well. Conscientiously, taking his time, arching his back. I put one of my boots on one of his ass cheeks. I pushed down pretty hard. I did the same on the other cheek. I looked at the red footprint my boot left, while rubbing my package.

Then I knelt down behind his ass. I pushed two fingers into his hole. He was pretty tight, but I couldn't believe that he never got fucked. He seemed more like a married guy who lives out his fantasies somewhere else. I caressed his ass. No reaction. So I slapped it and he immediately froze up and then got back in position, arching his back, and scrubbed harder. I thought OK, now you're gonna get it, and I kept going until his ass was deep red and he turned around and said I'm done. I said Good, let's move on. He asked Can I have a glass of water? I said Yes. I went to the sink, I filled up a glass of water that I held to his lips (gorgeous, pink lips). I made him drink all of it. Did you like it? I asked. He said Yes. OK now you're going to clean the bathroom, I said, thinking that it really needed it. I stood in front of him, I grabbed his collar and dragged him like that until we got outside the room, too bad the bathroom was so close, choking him a little and pushing his head down towards the ground, like a dog.

I locked the door, I didn't want Quentin to disturb us. I threw him directly into cleaning the toilet bowl. What could be more humiliating. I looked at him. This gorgeous naked man, in black Rangers, in the air, in a dog collar and nipple clamps, was cleaning my toilets. It was beautiful. I got my riding crop out. I placed the supple leather buckle exactly at the seam between the sole and the uppers of his left boot. Then I dragged the crop up, slowly, across the shoe, the rolled-up sock, the calf, the back of his thigh. At the bottom of his butt, I made a sharp turn towards his crack. I focused on the hole. Then I dragged the whip up his spine, still going as slowly as before. He stopped scrubbing the floor. Nothing existed except for what I was doing to him. His mind grew more and more empty. More and more surrendered. That got me hard. When I got up to his neck I slid the crop under his chin. I grabbed the other end and pulled him like that under his chin with the stem until he was levelled with my cock which I had already pulled out of my thong and he swallowed it while I started to whip him, not too hard, starting with his ass and covering, inch by inch, from the left to the center, and then from the right to the center, and from the center to the left and the center to the right, every available part of his body. Harder and harder. After a while he started to jerk off. After a while I pulled my dick out of his mouth, and while whipping him I jerked off for twenty seconds and I doused his back in come. He came all over the tile. Then he asked me if he could clean it up with the same sponge and I said Yes thinking He really is perfect. I wiped his back off with some toilet paper, and then he picked up where he left off.

19

(1993)

Winter came and went. My dad offered to take me on a weekend trip abroad. We hardly ever saw each other, he wanted to reconnect. I said no to Prague, Venice and Budapest. He agreed on Berlin. The ultimate deal we made was that I would only go out once, Saturday night, and that I would be back in my room ready for some cultural excursions Sunday morning.

* * *

Saturday night came. I polished my black Rangers, the ones I bought off Jean-Hughes one night when were really trashed at his place in Vanves, Quentin, me, him, and his best friend, an angelic little blond, we sang *Precious Little Diamond* in unison, an outrageously otherworldly funk hit from the '80s. I *customized* the boots with some brown laces to great effect. I got my tight pair of white 501s out of the closet that I would never wear when I was with Dad, a white ribbed tank top, a plaid shirt and leather suspenders that I bought for myself the night before when I did some *shopping* on my own.

I smoked a joint and then walked over to the hardcore district. Tom's bar was my first stop. Eleven. There were a ton of people outside and inside, but everyone was over six feet tall, all dressed in leather, I felt a little out of place so I finished my beer while watching the fisting video that was playing above the bar and I crossed the street to go to Connection where the crowd was less leather and a lot younger. I danced to some disco, energized by the atmosphere of the place, this cute little dark-haired boy was a sure thing, and a very handsome little blond was more than a definite maybe. I went down the stairs to the back room, which was huge, a series of crowded caves and hallways, packed. Almost immediately I found myself sizing up this massive cock belonging to a mustached guy in leather chaps and black tights (that's standard, I almost always find super well-hung guys in back rooms. They're probably over-represented in those types of places), the trick with the tights I had never seen that before, it was quite practical, all you had to do was lower the front and lodge it under the cock ring, everything was accessible in a second. I stopped because I didn't want to come right away. I went back upstairs to get a drink and dance. When I went back downstairs, about an hour later, I stumbled just as fast on another mustached guy in leather chaps and black tights, the same caliber, same huge cock, but this one kissed significantly better. So much better that after a while I felt like starting a conversation with him. We went to drink a beer at the bar that was in the back room. I asked if I could go to his place. It was already three a.m., I was going to be out of it tomorrow but I felt like experiencing something.

We walked for a long time through the trees, the sleeping houses. He was walking his bike alongside him. We didn't talk much, but didn't mind the silences. And then we finally arrived at his place, a sort of loft apartment in an old industrial building with free-style paintings all over the walls. I was beginning to be able to see the factory chimneys through the window. He closed the black curtains, we smoked a joint while listening to some techno, then I tried to fuck him (safe), but he didn't have any lube so I grabbed some oil to jerk off and I asked him if he was OK with that and he said yes. The oil makes condoms porous so I might as well take it off, I thought. I pulled it off and showed him what I was doing and since he didn't say anything I fucked him like that, face to face and then from behind and then face to face. We kissed. I liked him.

Afterwards he fell asleep. I couldn't close my eyes. I got up. I looked at his records and his books in German, his things, and then I went and took a piss and I came across his closet. All the hardcore gear was hanging in there: latex suit, leather shirt, leather vest, gas mask. It was already seven, I was supposed to meet my dad at ten, so I got dressed. He woke up, I explained to him that I had to go. He offered me some coffee. His kitchen was incredibly convivial, with wood everywhere, and funny things. I drank his coffee and then I started to ask him questions about his life and he started talking about his man and suddenly his voice cracked and he started to cry, I didn't know why, if his lover died or had just left him, I didn't dare ask any more questions, he kept crying in his chair, facing me, tears running down his face, he looked at me without really seeing me. I wondered if it was because of me, about the unsafe sex, if he was sick. He couldn't stop crying. I tried to comfort him, caressing his head saying Shhhhhh. He ended up calming down. I asked him for his phone number in case I came back. I felt guilty. He gave it to me, I kissed him, I left.

Outside the sun was shining and no taxi would take me, probably because they didn't like guys with shaved heads, black sunglasses, a three-day beard and white jeans covered in stains with a stained tank top tucked under the belt. And then a giant black Mercedes stopped just when I was dreading a métro journey that would last for ages. I understood why when I saw the leather 501s the mustached driver was wearing. He straight-out had an S&M cap on the passenger seat and I got a bit excited at the thought of hooking up with him but I really didn't have the time so I dozed all the way back to Ku'damm only opening my eyes from time to time to see Berlin. The avenue was blocked by a bike race. The Sunday-morning crowd watched as the riders passed by. Delay. It was already half past ten when I got to the hotel. My father who likes drama had left without waiting for me, but he did leave a note saying he was at the contemporary art museum. I had a big German breakfast with cheese and charcuterie so I wouldn't pass out, surrounded by blond tourists, took a quick shower and I left in a hurry, I didn't want to ruin our family reunion, I had already not wanted to go with him to the Jewish cemetery where we didn't have any relatives.

I took the subway, the line passed through old stations not far from the former East Germany, I dozed off, rocked by the sway of the car. I got off at the right stop. I walked through the flea market drenched in sunlight, there were tons of leather pants for sale that weren't expensive, I tried ones on that didn't look good on me. When I got to the museum, I saw my father through the big glass windows. He told me he had already walked around the entire place. Yeah, was it nice? I asked, and I sat on one of the benches in the hallway, facing the big paintings and massive sculptures, without taking off my sunglasses. He asked me how I was doing. I told him that I hadn't slept all night. I asked him if he wouldn't mind telling me what he saw because I could barely move at this point, and instead of causing a scene, he told me about the paintings. My strength came back. After a while I got up. We toured the museum, with the image superimposed in my mind of a crying man sitting in his kitchen.

20

(1993)

It was an afternoon in June and the weather was miserable. Quentin was at his boyfriend's. I looked out at a gray Paris, through the bedroom window. I was using my oven to dry out some grass leaves I had plucked from the flowerbed, a little at the bottom, the weakest, a little above where they were good. I rolled a joint with it adding what little hash I had left, the size of a nail clipping. The result was really average, but it still gave me a little buzz since I had an empty stomach. I got on the Minitel. As usual there was nothing. I had already been with Fuckmedeep, and it was OK but not good enough to do it again. Manlyman was at our house last week for dinner. The others were clearly worthless or totally on other trips. And then I found this funny profile: Sexy stallion in FF, 35, 5'9",185 BF BM, WANT TO GET WRECKED WITH A FIST.

I wrote back: HEY, RD MY PRFL. A minute later he wrote back: RD, INTRST. So I typed back: FREE NOW? UR PLC MN? JNT? He replied back: FREE NOW, WHR U? NO JNT. I wrote back: LES HALLES. He replied: OK. So I asked him: TEL? He gave me his number. I gave him mine too, to make him feel safe. He disconnected. My phone rang (Quentin and I had gotten two lines precisely to not have to disconnect). We came to an agreement. About an hour later he knocked on the door. I opened. As it often is, his profile was far from the truth. In this case thirty-five was more like forty-five, 185 was 200. He was bald not shaved, his face wasn't great. But not repulsive either. The whole thing with the Minitel was that I would often find myself having sex with guys I would have never otherwise done. He seemed clean. He looked at me with an intense neediness. I felt so important that instead of saying Sorry this ain't gonna work, and shut the door, I said Hi, and let him in.

I came on strong. Turn around! I said. Show me your ass! He put down his backpack. He turned around. I grabbed his wrists and I placed his arms up against the wall. With the edge of my boot I kicked his legs apart so that he was spread-eagle. That's when I realized this guy was a huge slut. His jeans were split open in an L-shape along his crack and at the bottom of the right cheek, and when I touched it, the tip of my fingers came in contact directly with his skin and the ring, a good half-inch wide, already greased up, and half-open, of his pussy. One finger would clearly not have been enough, so I immediately jammed in two, which I pushed all the way in with no problems. It's amazing what assholes can become. His was super flexible, puffy, swollen with blood. I pushed in my fingers as if I wanted to lift him up with them. His second sphincter opened up without much fuss. I massaged his prostate. He moaned. I checked to see if he was hard with my other hand. Yes, but small dick.

I said OK, come sit on the bed, I led him over by pulling both on his belt and on his ass where my two fingers were lodged so deep that he had to walk on his tiptoes, which was exactly what I wanted. Too bad you can't keep repeating the same thing in life, this stuff was good. Now it bores me. Anyway maybe I would do it again if the guy were blond, really young, super cute, if… I told him to jump in bed. I put him in position. On all fours! No! Ass in the air! There, that's it, knees forward! Ass higher! Yeah, like that, pushing in a third finger and turning it like a clock left and right, I opened the condom with my teeth (not wearing one was still unusual) that I took from the fuck bowl on the shelf next to the bed, I slid it with one hand onto my cock, and dove in.

I pounded him really hard, it was so loose that I had to go full speed if I wanted to feel something. I was holding onto him by the top of his jeans. We both were still completely dressed. I'll wash my jeans later. For now I was hard, that was all that mattered. I kept pumping, pumping, pumping, he was making a lot of noise, it was not unpleasant, but after about five minutes he was so open that I couldn't feel anything at all so I told myself that he didn't come here for this anyway. I stopped. You can't really say I pulled out since his hole wasn't holding me. I pulled off the condom and jerked off a little while looking at his gaping hole, almost an inch wide. Now that's a slut's hole! I said. He trembled with pride. I said OK, let's get serious. I got out some grease, covered my left hand up to the wrist, with my right I took a big nugget of cream which I jammed right into his hole (he appreciated the attention), I placed my left hand (I kept the right one free to jerk off) pinching my fingers in front of the entry, I pushed softly, firmly, consistently, he asked Can I have some poppers?, I said Yeah, do you have any? trying to save mine if at all possible, after all, I was doing him a favor. He said Yeah, in my bag, I went and got his bag, it was annoying because my hands were sticky, I gave it to him. I got back into position. He opened the bag, unscrewed the poppers, sniffed nonstop while I pushed more and more inside not wasting a second, without making scissors with my fingers to relax the walls, not one contraction of his sphincter, nothing until my hand was lodged inside, his ass closed on my wrist. I made a fist. I started to turn to the right, to the left.

Would you punch my ass? He said it in a completely calm voice. It was the first time I heard that expression (I started using that term, too, in the years that followed. Sometimes), but it was pretty clear. I punched. At first I was afraid that I was going to hurt him, and then I realized that I had to pull on the muscles, towards the back, to relax everything in order to go deeper, just like when Quentin would fuck me, so I brought them towards me, almost opening his anus, and then pushed deeper into his ass that yielded more and more, I squeezed my fist to make it bigger. I started twisting at the same time as I was moving forward and backward, and pulled out, I made a figure eight, a Möbius strip, like the guys who spin cotton candy at the carnival, he was so open that my closed fist could go in and out like that. It was exhausting and he still wasn't coming even though he was making lots of noise, so I went in even harder and he jerked off even harder and finally came screaming. I pulled my hand out dripping in melted cream but there was only a trickle of blood, and I fed him my balls to eat so that I could finish myself off. I jerked off, applying pressure to the head of my penis, thinking to myself that he may have been ugly but he got the job done. I came on him and then I sent him away to wash up. I tossed the sheets and the towel into the washer. Then I washed myself. I made some tea and rolled a joint and he told me about his life which was interesting: he and his partner lived with a slave at their house for one year, something I've always wanted to do.

21

(1993)

I cruised him on the Minitel. He said he was straight, twenty-eight years old, cute, well-built, well-hung and looking to fuck someone with a dildo. I said to myself Why not, since I was smoked out on hash, and today again, I had nothing to do. It had been practically two years since I had stopped having sex with Quentin, I had to take care of things. Between searching for sex, waiting for it, having it, then passing out high, I could fill entire days. I waited for him to arrive.

He was all in black. Cowboy boots (I've always had a weakness for cowboy boots), tight jeans, Lacoste, Perfecto. Cute indeed, actually really cute, really well-built too. We settled in. I had already pulled out what we needed. He stayed dressed. He just took off his boots to climb on the bed. He put on some gloves. As soon as he touched my ass I knew I was in for a treat. This guy was really subtle. He fucked me perfectly with the dildo, working my ass from right to left, forward and backward, as if he was kneading dough or something like that. With the second dildo he pulled out his cock which was magnificent, not huge, just thick and long. He put on a condom and jerked off with his left hand while fucking me hard with the Lord. I was sniffing poppers while jerking off, super hard. That was great.

Then he pulled off his condom and got up and said Come suck me off. I squatted down on the Lord and I went to suck him off but he moved off. Not like that, he said. Lick! I started to lick.

He moved off again. Not like that, he said. Little licks. I touched his balls lightly with my tongue, he said Good. I knew that he was close. He picked my head up to look at the head that was dripping, he was jacking off super slowly, I was totally hypnotized, I knew that he wanted me to fantasize about him coming in my mouth, I opened my mouth, fantasizing was no trouble at all, it had been six years since anyone had done that to me. Without warning he started to come. I closed my mouth immediately but it was too late, I had already taken a jet of come, the bastard, that's exactly what he wanted. I closed my eyes because he was spraying all over my face, and when he finally finished, I came too, super aroused. I headed off to the bathroom with my eyes closed, with that long-forgotten taste in my mouth, cursing him.

22

(1993)

July thirteenth. My mother's birthday. I woke up late. I got on the Minitel. I made some calls. I took a taxi for Beaugrenelle, I had some memories there. Today was a training session, twenty-ninth floor, the guy was supposed to be thirty-five years old. When I got to his door I heard screams. Then smacks. A whip. I recognized the sound. Then more screams. I pushed my ear against the door. It's fine, I'm leaving, said one voice. You don't want to keep going? said another. No, said the first voice angrily. I told myself that was the moment to ring the doorbell.

The guy who opened up had a mustache, was pretty tall, pretty old, pretty out-of-shape, shirtless in leather jeans and boots. Behind him in the lobby of this loft-type apartment, a real tall skinny guy was putting on his socks, standing awkwardly, his face all red. The guy was probably a loser but I didn't feel like leaving. I was here already, and I had nothing else to do except get back on the Minitel. So, I said Hi!, and walked in. The other masochist grabbed his bag and left.

There was a massive desk covered in papers in front of me, a room off to the left with a bay window that looked over the towers, the big digital clock of Beaugrenelle that read three p.m., the sky. The guy grabbed my nipples really hard. He pulled down on them to get me to kneel. I found myself at eye level with his package. He pushed my face against it, really hard. I thought it was the kind of gesture that only proved the stupidity of the person doing it (later he would go on to crush my head with his cowboy boot, and since he did everything too forcefully, this idiot smashed my ear, nothing serious, no blood, but the cartilage blistered so much that I went and showed it to a doctor thinking it was the beginning of the end because I hadn't made the connection, I noticed the thing only months later. It's called cauliflower ear, the doctor told me. I found that funny).

I didn't say anything. As soon as he let up enough so that I could move my head, I started to lick his bulge with long strokes of the tongue, I was trying to steer things towards a sexier mood. He ended up getting hard. He pulled out his cock. I sucked it. He smelled. I told myself that he probably did this on purpose the days when he had these kinds of hookups. Then he pulled up his pants and he went to look for the whip on his desk. He came back, he knelt down (I was still on my knees) and he unbuttoned my 501s, and pulled them down so my ass was bare (I was wearing a jockstrap). He started whipping me, right away it was too much but I was still able to get hard. After a while it was starting to hurt. I took a look at the damage. My ass was already marked up, marks that would go away in two days max if I stopped now, but not if I kept going, so I pulled up my pants without changing position. He started again, I looked at the floor, beige plastic tile, good quality, in winter those tiles must be a nightmare, now it's OK because it's July, my mother's birthday. The strokes were bearable thanks to my jeans but he was whipping the asshole harder and harder, and it started hurting again, and I restrained myself a little, out of politeness, so I didn't ruin his trip, and then I said Stop! He kept going. So, the S&M rules don't apply? I said, Stop! again, in a firmer, almost pissed-off tone. He stopped.

He told me to strip. I did it without getting up, it was sexier, and kept my cock ring on, normal, but also my socks and my jockstrap, and since he had left I allowed myself a bit of insubordination, I put my Converses back on, classic navy blue All Stars, which made me look like a little slut like you wouldn't believe, at twenty-seven I could still play the teenage pervert. He came back with something in his hands. A leather mask, I had that too at my place, which I had bought off this skinhead who was selling it on the Minitel, I had used it with a lot of guys, and often on myself, I mean I was used to it, but it was still pretty special, that kind of thing. I stood up so he could put it on me. He was shaking a little. He tied the top knot very tightly, and then the back straps too, but it was bearable, the leather really, I was familiar with that so I wasn't scared, and then he tied the lace around my neck but that was entirely too tight, I would have suffocated in ten seconds, I told him It's too tight. He untied the knot, I knew I was pissing him off but he still did it, he didn't want me to leave, two in a row would have been too much for his ego. I put my finger between the string and my neck so it wouldn't strangle me, he tied the knot and then one after the other he closed each eye slot.

Needless to say, I was hard. He shoved his thumb in my mouth and I sucked on it avidly, in the dark, feeling my jaw rubbing against the leather of the mask when I tried to open my mouth all the way up to swallow his whole hand, it pulled tight, I was strangling myself with the lace around my neck, that made me get even harder. Then he pulled his hand back out and he aggressively shoved my face back into his package, leather on leather, so hardcore, but OK, I took advantage of the moment to get high on the smell, I had trouble breathing in deeply, the mask was so tight. And then he relaxed the pressure so I did what I had to do, I started licking, it was difficult since I could only open half of my mouth, but I managed rather well.

This whole time I was rubbing my erect cock through my jock-strap. When he noticed he grabbed my wrists and crossed them over each other. He held them like that with one hand while he unbuttoned his pants with the other and fed me his stinky cock to suck. With how turned-on I was now, the smell wasn't really annoying, on the contrary. His dick was pretty big, not too hard or soft. His pubes weren't trimmed. His balls weren't shaved. I swallowed them as much as I could (the hole in the mask was too small and the hair made it hard to suck it efficiently). He made me stop. I heard him walk away. I stayed put obediently, keeping my hands behind my back.

He returned. He grabbed one of my wrists. He placed a metal handcuff on it that was too tight. Then a second. It hurt, but not terribly. Then I felt something rub against my ankles and it was another pair of handcuffs, leather, with a little more give, and it wasn't going to hurt. He zipped closed the mouth opening. That was it. There weren't any other holes in the mask except the small ones under my nostrils, it was going to get hot! He pulled me up quickly, I barely regained my balance, he dragged me to my right pulling me by the lace at the top of the mask, he was walking fast (when I did this I played it rather slow pulling on the neck to choke only slightly), I was stumbling because of the cuffs around my ankles, I banged into something (not hard, it was OK, I thought that I wouldn't have a bruise), a wall, something else, a door (I wasn't able to see anything), and then he pressed me against something that was about the height of my waist and he flipped me backwards, I trusted him hoping only that it wouldn't be covered with razor blades, it's crazy what you do with strangers, up until now, I hadn't had any problems with the five or six hundred guys I had already hooked up with, half of whom were probably one-on-one, either at their place, or mine, without anyone knowing where I was, at the beginning I used to leave the addresses with Quentin and then I ended up telling myself that I didn't care if my murderer was ever punished, so I stopped doing it, maybe now was the time when things would go wrong, but no, I landed on a slightly cold horizontal plane. He grabbed my feet, swung them around. I found myself almost laying down, there wasn't enough room, with the circle of a sink at my back. The faucet was jabbing me in the sides, I freed myself by wriggling. I was able to put my handcuffed hands in the hollow of the sink. I arranged myself properly.

That's when I heard the sound of the clippers. Then I felt them against my chest. This asshole was shaving a circle around my nipples. I thought about screaming but it was a bit late. He had me. There was only one thing to do. Either get pissed and tell him to stop, which would kill the mood and I would split (which he certainly wouldn't have minded, he could have really fucked me up). Or I would try to enjoy it. That's what I decided. All I had to do was use some hair removal cream on the top half of my body to be able to go on vacation with my father as planned. How would I explain it? I did it because I was too hot? He moved on to my stomach. Methodically, strip by strip. I focused on my misfortune. I started to moan like I used to with Quentin. I whimpered, in a sort of slight disassociation that allowed me to enjoy the whimpering without it seeming insincere. He stopped. He said Do you want to see? I find S&M funny sometimes, it's really a childish game. Messing around. I nodded. So he unzipped my eye covers and I turned my head to the left towards the mirror and I saw what he had done.

Each of my nipples was surrounded by a circle of white skin two centimeters wide. My stomach was shaved from the bottom of my ribs to three centimeters below my navel. The rest was the same, hairy. It was pretty classy. I muttered Hon! Hon!, to make him understand that I had something to say to him. He unzipped my mouth. I asked Can I get down?, I'm in pain, now. He said OK. He turned me around again, downwards this time. As soon as I regained my balance I asked Can you untie me, I want to roll a joint. I needed to get excited again. He said You can if you want. Me, I don't smoke. Too bad for your stupid face, I thought to myself. He took the handcuffs off. I took off the mask, somewhat feverishly, I have to say. I took a deep breath. Then I reached down and untied my ankle cuffs and without paying any attention to him I went to find something to roll my joint with in my things in the living room.

He followed me. I could tell he felt uncertain, so I said Would you like to find a third? What I didn't say was that if we didn't find one I was splitting. He must have understood. He said, Yeah why not?, looking mildly enthusiastic. I asked, So should we go on the Minitel? He said OK, so we went into his bedroom, which faced the damned bathroom. I rolled a joint while he looked. There wasn't much of anything. Another bottom, who was claimed to be young and well-built. He asked what I thought. I was like Yeaaaah, not convinced. I took a hit of my joint. And then the phone rang and he went to answer it and I took the opportunity to change his profile while adding myself ("Hey do you mind if I modify your profile? That way it's clearer."). That's when I got cruised by a guy named YVOYEUR. Young, that was nice, voyeur less so, I thought, but he typed BERNARD? BEAUGRENELLE? I typed YES. It was interesting that he already knew the master of the house. He asked me how it was going. I typed NOT BAD U WANT COME WATCH? He answered Y NOT, so I typed TEL? He told me he would call. Two minutes later the phone rang. Bernard answered. He described me ("very submissive"). He asked me what I liked, again. He repeated it back to the other guy. OK, see you soon. He hung up. When does he get here? I asked, hoping that it wouldn't take ages. The time it takes him to get here, he doesn't live far, Bernard replied. I asked him if he knew him well. He said that the guy came over from time to time. I asked if he was as cute as he said. Yeah, he's not bad, Bernard said. I laid down on a pillow at the head of the bed and I smoked, and then I got cold and afraid of giving him any ideas so I said, I'm cold, I'm going to put something on while we wait, and I went to the living room to put on my tank top.

Fail. He joined me holding a pair of pretty hardcore nipple clamps, sheathed at least, with weights. He pulled up my tank top to put them on. I looked at my nipples so that I didn't have to look at his face. First he kept the weights in the palm of his hand and then he let them fall down the small chain, it gave me a little jolt that distracted me from the burning of the clamps. My jockstrap filled up. So he made me get on all fours and he started whipping me with his martinet, this time all over my body, and it definitely felt better now that the sensation was balanced out by that of the clamps. I almost enjoyed it. The doorbell rang.

Bernard went to open the door. I stayed on all fours, my naked and reddened ass facing the door. Young voyeur was going to be pleased. I didn't turn my head to look at him. It was going to be a surprise. The first thing I saw were his stonewashed blue jeans. At the very bottom were beige deerskin moccasins, not too light nor too dark, the very supple kind, with only one seam, no other ornamentation, not the Italian style, but very Native American, *roots*. I found it extremely sexy, it reminded me of Bion, the playboy of my eighth-grade class, a blond pretty-boy who walked on his heels, pelvis forward, and who always had new shoes, each pair sexier than the last, he alternately had the black *and* burgundy Sebagos and then these moccasins in white leather with little colored beads, moccasins were really trendy then.

They made comments, sounding detached, as if I wasn't there. Not bad, blah blah, slut, good sucker, blah blah blah. I looked up. His thighs were thin but well-defined. His pelvis was around my size. I looked up. A black leather belt, thin. I looked up. A white polo shirt that wasn't Lacoste but looked good on him. I looked up. He was handsome. Short, chestnut hair, cut like a straight guy. Twenty-five years old? Olive skin, brown eyes, big mouth, long lashes, well-defined eyebrows. Like in a dream. He looked down at me, from above. He said Not bad… In a very neutral tone. Let's hope he participates.

At first he didn't do anything. He stayed back. He watched. I blew the old guy, doing poppers. He threw me to the ground, whipped my ass, made me smell his cowboy boots, I didn't want to lick them. That's when he crushed my ear. And then Prince Charming slid his foot under my nose. I didn't really know what to do. Do you lick a deerskin moccasin? I didn't know, so I didn't try, only sniffed. I breathed in mouthfuls of white tennis sock, summer-warm. With the toe of one shoe he pulled off the sock from the other foot. I moved toward his clammy toes. Sniffed them hard. I was getting really high. He pushed his big toe across my lips. I sucked hard on his big toe, then the other toes, everything I could get my mouth around. I was getting super hard. You're going to eat his ass now, the old guy said. It surprised me that he would allow himself to decide for the other. Maybe he was submissive. It could have been cool to be abused together. For right now I stared at his jeans as they fell along his white underwear, his tanned, curving, slightly hairy thighs. He pulled his underwear down.

He offered his ass. I placed my nose between his crack. His hole wasn't shaved, wasn't washed, but wasn't dirty. I placed my tongue right in the middle. Contact. I licked. Breathing in slowly at first, to get used to the smell, and then when I realized that it wasn't so strong, I took deeper and deeper breaths to get swept away. I thought of those American porn movies where tops get eaten out to to ensure a good hard-on before fucking. He arched. I licked him with slow strokes of the tongue, from inside his thigh all the way up just above his hole. Skin, hair, hole, hair, skin. Skin, hair, hole, hair, skin. Right when I was able to get him to really relax, he turned around. This bastard knew how to frustrate me just right. We were perfect for each other. He pulled his package closer to my face, grabbed the back of my head. He pressed it. I got drunk on his scent. He shoved his dick into my mouth all the way until it hit the glottis and I had to let everything go to breathe.

He talked to the old guy while I was sucking. After a while he pulled out. Got dressed. The old guy led me to the bathroom. Told me to get in the bathtub. I got in. To open my mouth. I opened up. They took out their cocks. I tried to suck off the young guy but he moved out of my reach. His piss stream landed on my lips. You're going to swallow it, OK? The old guy said. I had to choose, either take it or leave it. It didn't seem too concentrated, the color was pretty clear. I went for it. It went down fine. I put myself at the source and I drank. He was pissing very slowly, controlling the flow. I eyed up the pink head of his penis and his silky white cock. It turned me on. He stopped.

Now the other one wanted his share of the fun. His piss was disgusting, stinking, deep yellow. I let it fall out the sides of my mouth. He got angry. I spit it out and said it was too concentrated, that if he wanted me to swallow, he needed to drink, sorry. OK, very well, he said. He wound himself up to take his revenge, he didn't want to lose face in front of the young guy, I closed my eyelids really tight so they wouldn't get burned. Open your mouth! He said. I kept my eyes closed shut, I opened my mouth, I could feel two streams of piss entering inside, I was clearly in for it. They left telling me to clean up and then come meet them. I felt around for the water, and then I rinsed myself, first the eyes, then the mouth, then the rest. I dried off with a towel that was lying around.

I met them in the living room. They were drinking a beer. The old guy told me to kneel. I knelt. He went into the kitchen. Came back with a candle. He lit it. I said Not the hair. Shouldn't you gag him?, the young guy said. That immediately got me twice as hard. I didn't move. The old guy came back with a ball gag. I had the same one. He fastened it at the back of my neck. The latex ball held my mouth open. In two minutes I was going to start drooling, or else it would be a total ordeal to swallow my saliva. He handcuffed me again. My dick was so hard that my cock ring was hurting me.

The young one pulled my package out from the jockstrap. The first drop missed my dick. But not the second. I didn't go soft, actually the opposite. The suspense was killing me. I was completely focused on my sensations. Waiting. Burning, like a well-placed blow. At times I stayed back because it got too hot, and then the pain would fade away so I would stick my cock back out and… Aaaahhh! The wax trickled drop by drop. It was an endurance game. They encouraged me. I watched my cock getting slowly covered in white. Like in a dream. The old guy moved down progressively until he was pouring wax just on the head of my penis. He ended by pouring it directly into my urethra. Once it was all covered, he pushed me forward, I rolled, my shoulders on the ground. He wanted to do my asshole next, that was serious. I shook. I looked over my shoulder thinking this fucker must have started four inches away from my ass, but no, he was standing up, his arm held high, it's just that I wasn't used to this on my ass. I still grumbled. He pulled his hand higher. Second drop of wax on the hole, Ahhhhhhh!

He had already come down a lot when I turned around again. The drops were falling closer and closer together. Now that my hole was completely covered they rolled onto my balls. I was like a ball. And then I felt someone pulling the wax out of my hole (luckily it was shaved) and then putting something in and I reopened my eyes, turned my head to see. The two of them were crouching behind me. The candle planted in my ass. The pretty boy grabbed my dick. He pulled it from behind to let the wax drip down on it. Ahhhhhhh!

I couldn't feel a thing anymore. It stopped. A dull sound to my right. That's for you, it's a souvenir, said the young one. The milky-white shell was the exact mold of the head of my penis.

* * *

They take me to the bathroom to clean up. I lift off the pieces of wax stuck to my skin, to my hair. I rinse. They put me down on all fours in the bathtub. The old guy unscrews the shower head off the handle, lets the water run, shoves the hose up my ass, tells me to hold it all in, let it flow. I let myself fill up, I can feel it pass the second sphincter, it's filling my belly, it's OK, it's warm. He massages my belly so that I take even more in, it's starting to hurt, I tell him, he says Just a little more. I take more, I feel it starting to get heavy (on my diaphragm?). He tells me to hold it in as long as possible. They leave me.

I'm alone in the bathtub, on all fours, my head down, ass exposed. Pretty quickly I feel like I am going to explode if I don't let a little out. I let it run. And then I tell myself let's see what happens if I stick with it for a while, so I squeeze my ass tight, lift it high, my head against the bottom of the tub. It's harder and harder to hold on. After about fifteen, twenty minutes, I can't anymore, I start to get cold, to shiver, I tell myself enough already so I let go. It takes me ten minutes to empty myself out. It hurts. The old guy comes to check, then he leaves.

* * *

When I get back to the living room I see them looking at me and talking. Talking about what they're going to do to me. They agree on something. The old guy handcuffs my wrists behind my back with the leather cuffs. Puts the ball gag back into my mouth. Takes me to the kitchen. The younger guy follows with his bottle of Evian. He drinks. Looks at me without saying a word. The old guy opens up a cupboard, pulls out the trash can, pulls out an empty quart of milk, then grabs the bag, comes close to me, and puts the bag over my head. Very funny. Then he ties a knot around my neck with the handles. The plastic sticks to my face. I panic. I grumble really loudly shaking my head. The old guy pulls off the bag. I'm covered in carrot shavings, tears in my eyes. That didn't make him laugh, the young guy says.

* * *

The old guy makes me get on all fours and shoves four anal beads (size small) up my ass. Then he puts the nipple clamps back on me and works me over while the young one drinks his water sitting in one of the chairs. I moan a little to make them understand that I have something to say. He pulls the gag off with trails of spit attached to it, I say I would like to roll another joint. I take advantage of the moment to go shit out the beads. When I get back, he replaces them with a black butt plug.

* * *

The shitty music stops. I ask if he has anything else and he tells me what he has but it's all shit. Dire Straits is the least nauseating but I can't see myself doing this kind of thing to Dire Straits, so I suggest radio FG.[6]

* * *

They lead me to the bathroom, make me sit on the toilet, piss on me at the same time, the piss flows from my chest to my stomach, along my package, into the toilet. They take turns pissing in my face, the old guy's piss isn't as strong as earlier, I swallow a little of his, the young one's piss is almost clear now, just a little salty, I drink as much of it as I can from the pink tip of his dick until I sense the other one is starting to get angry. They aim higher again, have some fun doing my nose, my eyes, I close my eyelids really tight. They aim lower, I wipe my eyes, they piss on my cock, I watch, I spread my legs to see the image of it, the ribbons of piss flowing on my throbbing cock, they tell me to turn around. Stand up! They piss on my ass. On all fours! Head in the toilet, they piss on my head. They end up needing to stop. Tell me to clean up. I dry with toilet paper and then I use a sponge and some Cif to wash the basin, the ground, the black lacquer walls, all drenched.

The digital clock of Beaugrenelle showed it was nine. I asked Are you hungry? Would you like me to make something to eat? They agreed. I put my shoes back on so that I didn't have to walk on the cold and rather dirty kitchen floor. I did with what was there: pasta with vegetables (zucchini and carrots that I sliced thin, blanched, then sautéed), pasta, and frozen ground meat. After a while, since I was bored all alone, I asked the old guy to put the clamps back on. As a bonus, he also shoved a butt plug in.

I plated the food and served it, theirs first obviously, then mine. They watched me cross the living room, stomach and nipples shaved, weighted nipple clamps, jockstrap and blue Converse shoes, butt plug in my ass. Like in a dream. I sat at the bottom of the couch, at their feet. I said Bon appétit. They said, Thanks.

* * *

I rolled a joint. I smoked half of it with the young one whose name I finally learned, Pierre, then I cleared everything away. I did the dishes. Night fell. When I got back to the living room, the old guy explained to me that I was going to put on a little show for them to end the night. Four dildos, two buttplugs and two strips of anal beads were all laid out on the table. My bomber jacket was covering the seat of one of the leather chairs. He made me sit down and put each leg on the armrest. My ass was completely exposed that way. Now show us what you can do, he said, as he walked over to sit with Pierre on the couch facing me. They watched me while touching themselves. I played a little with my plug, pulling it out, pushing it back in, it was pretty easy considering how long I had been wearing it. The old guy pulled out his cock. He started to jack off. The young one stood up. He directed the halogen lamp right on my ass. He sat back down.

I pulled out my plug, I bent over backwards to grab the lube and a dildo from the table. I got back into position and started to work it in. Since I wasn't that hard it was painful. I tried to jack off without much success. Actually it bothered me to do that in front of them without them participating. After a while the young one got up. He came towards me, dick in his hand. I wrapped my lips around it. He let me do it. I hadn't sucked him off since the beginning, so this got me hard fast. He gave me some poppers. I switched dildos, I grabbed one that was bigger and more supple. After a while he sat down again.

I continued my show with the anal beads. Now that I was hard, it was exciting to watch them. I took my time. I hit the poppers that were on the armrest. Grabbed another dildo, even bigger. This is the last one, I announced. I settled myself backward so that I could ride the dildo vertically. I pushed it in and pulled it out completely. They were playing with each other's nipples and touching each other's balls. They both started coming. I came too. I stood up, totally stiff. My bomber jacket was drenched in bloody ass juices. I took a closer look, actually it wasn't that bad, only the bottom of the inside lining was stained. I walked off towards the bathroom to get some toilet paper. I came back to clean up and that's when I realized I still hadn't taken off the nipple clamps. Because I was upset I pulled them off too fast. The blood came rushing back in and it hurt so bad that I had to bite my lips not to scream.

Bathroom. I washed myself while contracting my sphincters to try and help them recover. Then I went back to the living room. I got dressed, without the jock that was too gross and that I put in my pocket. Socks, jeans, shoes, shirts. My dick hurt. The young one gave me his number telling me that his friend's birthday is in September and he wanted to give him me as a present. He left. The old one wanted me to give him my cock ring as a souvenir. Asshole. I refused, explaining to him that I never gave anything to anyone. On the doorstep, he said You have my number, right? I said Yes. OK, ciao! And I took the elevator.

* * *

It was past midnight. You could still hear firecrackers from the [Bastille Day] celebrations. Of course, I couldn't get a taxi. I started walking with my bomber jacket sticking to my hand and then I got fed up so I rolled it up and tied it around my waist. I passed some groups of drunk guys coming out from the festival, I was hoping they wouldn't notice the anal juice stain that had finally formed on the back of my jeans and that I was trying to cover up with my jacket. At first I was stoned, and then I ended up coming back down, the night was rather cold. I warmed myself up by walking faster. The quais. Concorde. Les Halles. About an hour and fifteen minutes later I was home. I rolled a joint. I jerked off.

23

(1993)

I left for vacation. The burns on my urethra healed by themselves in four or five days. Being completely shaved was a bit hard to take with my family, but aside from that, it wasn't too bad: between swimming laps and doing push-ups, I could see my muscles getting bigger every day. It was my first real vacation without Quentin since I had met him. I took a trip to Italy to visit Alessandro. Dr. Alban was singing *It's My Life*. We sang together speeding around in my rental, a Clio. It was cool. I was only thinking about dying once a day now. Average life expectancy after contamination had grown to seven years. Less than three and a half years since mine, another three and a half years left. Subtracting a year and a half of being sick, I projected another two and a half years of things running smoothly. I could go to the Leather Party in Hamburg next year. This year I didn't have the money, so I missed it.

And then Quentin called from Paris and was smooth-talking me on the phone. He promised me that he was going to be perfect, that we would start all over again. When I got back, I went back with him, boulevard Sébastopol. After two weeks I already felt like dying. But not bad enough to call Pierre.

24

(1993)

I've always had more of a thing for bouncers than for bartenders. Bouncers are more virile. Eric for example, the bouncer at Gold Coast, had a gorgeous face with permanent bags under his eyes, a broken nose and a very large mouth. He was small, stocky, really well-built, and I knew just like everyone else in the ghetto that he had one of the biggest cocks in Paris. It was rumored that he couldn't always get hard. But that's normal with guys who have really big dicks, the rush of blood that's necessary isn't always easy to get. There's also the fact that in the majority of cases nothing great is going to happen for them, that most guys will limit themselves to sucking the head and not want to get fucked, so what good is getting hard. That said Quentin had sex with him and obviously, Eric had gotten hard and fucked Quentin who told me that it was AMAZING! The snag was that I found out through a friend that Eric didn't like hairy guys.

And then I went by Gold Coast one day and he was there, at the bar. I asked him So you're a bartender now, blah, blah, blah. I still liked him just as much, like crazy. I also felt that something new was happening compared to the other times I had approached him, and this something was that he might actually want to sleep with me. I must say that it was during a period when I was in really good shape, toned, appealing. He told me to come by and visit him later if I wanted, in a boutique that he was remodeling. I stopped by. He was absolutely sublime as a painter, shirtless, in overalls stained all over. I was totally crushing and he continued to respond and finally I threw myself at him with my usual subtlety. So, do you want to have sex with me? I asked. He was like Yeah. So I said What are you doing later? He said I don't have any plans. So I told him OK, well why don't you come over for some tea. He said, OK., around six. I gave him the entry code and I left.

I headed back to my place (our place, since I was still with Quentin, we were living together), super stressed-out. I rolled a joint, and then I washed my ass for hours to make sure that there wouldn't be any problems even if he went deep. I didn't know what else to do to kill time, I didn't want to jerk off for obvious reasons, so I went to sleep. He arrived, showered and changed, into skin-tight jeans. Amazing thighs. His package didn't look especially huge from the outside. I made some tea making a superhuman effort to act casual. Since he was, I ended up calming down. We talked about people, about the gym. I kissed him in the kitchen. With tongue, taking each other in our arms. It was amazing. He was warm, not rushed, present. I told myself that in a certain way he reminded me of Quentin, just more human.

I suggested that we have our tea in my room. We brought what we needed. I put on some house music. He lay down on the bed. I sat in a chair, super uptight. I poured some tea. Rolled a joint. We smoked it. I was still in the fucking chair. He smiled at me. He said Come here. I joined him on the bed. We kissed again, sitting cross-legged. Played a little with each other's nipples. I was getting hard, he wasn't. So I pulled his t-shirt off, and then I took mine off, and then I sat on the edge of the bed, I pulled his feet up on my knees, I untied his laces, I took off his boots, big hiking boots with red laces, all the rage that year. I pulled his tube socks off. He had small feet, wide, muscly, hairless. Thick toe-nails, well-trimmed. I put his feet back on the bed and I went to unbuckle his belt. I unbuttoned his 501s, grabbed his jeans by the side, he lifted his pelvis, I pulled them down. He had on tight briefs, the lycra kind, dark grey, beautiful thighs, toned but not super hard, the legs of a thirty-year-old man who took care of himself. I threw his jeans on the chair behind me and turned my attention back to him and what was left. I slipped off his dark grey underwear. Then I found the oversized treasure but kept my mouth shut, I didn't want to tip my hand.

I just leaned in, and I swallowed all of his soft cock, which was already large enough to fill my mouth. It even took a couple of extra mouthfuls to get down to his base. I reached up looking for his (well-developed) nipples and just like that, under the soft and total absence of pressure I was exerting with my mouth, he started getting hard. I took my time so that he knew there wasn't any rush. While sucking him off I slid off my shoes and my jeans. Once he got hard he started stroking my head. I started sucking harder, meaning another half-inch past the head. I put my hand around the rest of his cock so that he'd feel something. He started playing with my nipples. That motivated me. I concentrated on taking it to the back of my throat while breathing through my nose. I started to drool a lot, I smashed my glottis with the tip.

He started stroking my cock with one hand while caressing my head with the other. He lifted his head from the pillow. He sat up straight. He placed his hand on my shaved hole, he caressed it, I handed him some lube, he squeezed out a good amount, he knew what he was doing, he pressed two fingers in, progressively, as you should. I figured that made sense, given what I had to swallow later, that excited me, I jerked off hard and I was able to take his cock in my throat even deeper, I could tell that excited him, quickly I took a third finger and then a fourth and then he laid me down on my back and gave me a two-by-four: four fingers from both hands interlaced in my ass. I took some poppers,

I looked at him, he was hard without touching himself, on my side I was getting really relaxed, so I decided that it was time to get serious and since I wanted to be in control at the start, given the size of his tool, I told him to lie down on his back, that I was going to sit on his cock.

I sucked him a little more until he was hard enough for the condom, which wasn't easy given that he was now nine and a half (ten?) inches long and three inches wide. It totally took me a full minute to unroll it and even then it didn't reach the bottom, but the mood was hot and he wasn't going soft. I covered it all with a ton of lube while jerking him off. I took the thing in my left hand and held it up straight to sit on it taking my time, while jerking off with the lube and sniffing some poppers. I took in maybe the first eight inches, and then it got stuck. Exactly like with a big dildo, it was nothing too surprising. I pressed on but there was nothing to do.

A little annoyed, I started to fuck myself like that, it wasn't that good because I couldn't sit and relax. He pulled me towards him. He told me, actually he whispered: Some poppers. Not simply Poppers, which would have been an order, or, Could you please pass me the poppers which would have been lame, no, just Some poppers, and I gave him a sniff, one nostril, then the other, and he started to kiss me, and I put down the poppers so I could take him in my arms, and I took a drag on the endless joint that we had rolled while he started to fuck me with the first eight inches (by three wide).

Rhythmically. Softly, but growing deeper each time. We kissed each other as if we were hopelessly in love with one another, and in a way that was the truth. And when the passion started to flag, I sat back up and I took the final couple of inches that were left without trying. He really knew what he was doing. With a raging hard-on, I rested my legs in a V on his muscled stomach. I looked at his belly button. I caressed his torso. He looked at me. I thought he was beautiful. It was so powerful that if it kept going like that I was going to come, so I took some poppers and I relaxed a bit more, opened up a bit more.

I started to fuck myself seriously with his cock while we were playing with each other's nipples. Then he got up and tilted me backwards, one arm around my back to hold on to me, I clung to him, he fucked me from the front, my ankles on his shoulders. He went in and out even deeper, it didn't hurt at all, I caressed him, the small of his back, his butt, his hips. Poppers. He sat up straight, held me by the ankles, and went at it horizontally. Then he held my legs together and held them straight against his stomach and his chest. Relaxation. Still deeper, more open. He wedged his palms in the hollow of my knees, leaned in with all his weight, I was painfully hard, he slowed down the rhythm. Poppers.

After a while, I was ready for him to fuck me from behind. He started on all fours, then he had me stretch out completely, pull my legs together, he lay on top of me, I moaned, it was *love*. He slid us onto the side and he fucked me like that from behind in the laziest position, he played with my nipples while screwing me gently, I turned my head to kiss him. Then he brought me to all fours for the home stretch, this time I was really open, he started to go for it deep, as deep as Quentin, and there's nothing more to say, he held me by the hips, I was cupping his balls in one hand while jerking myself off with the other, he was pile-driving me deeper and deeper, faster, harder, I could feel that he was close, and I followed. When he started to come while shouting I let go almost at the same time as him. I told him not to pull out. He made a couple more strokes. Then I felt him go soft and I said OK, that's good, even the best things must come to an end.

He pulled out, removed the full condom, tied a knot, let it drop to the floor into the ashtray. We were entwined. It must have been four years since I had felt that. Trust in someone.

* * *

I saw him again at Gold Coast a couple months later. He wanted to go at it again but I didn't. Several months later it was me who wanted to but not him, he had met a guy and when he was with someone he was faithful. I was jealous.

25

(1994)

Over the course of the fall Quentin had started to move his new lover into the house. I thought that I couldn't end my life in such a sordid way. So I made an appointment with the nearest shrink. The day I went, it was funny, I almost didn't have the strength to walk. I spent almost the entire first session sobbing. It had been years since I'd shed a tear. A month later I left Quentin. I had been training for five years and the world championship was cancelled. I met a guy, the one I called Terrier[7] when I wrote this story, then another, the one whom I called Stéphane. Stéphane was cute. Modest. Very well-hung. It wasn't working anymore with him and his man. He left him for me. He wanted to make me happy. I gave him a makeover: green bomber jacket, short hair, tight jeans, Rangers. Like almost all well-hung guys, he was really into sex when I met him. I did what Quentin never did. I trained him. I taught him everything I knew. Safe, necessarily, since he was negative. It bothered me a little that he wasn't a good dancer. I was such a perfectionist.

26

(1994)

It was a night when I knew that he was getting home late. I got on the Minitel. I got cruised by two guys who were putting on a scat party in Saint-Paul, not far from my place. I wasn't really into it but since they replied NO, COKE, to my U HV JNT? I told myself Why not. I had never really tried to explore this darker side of my personality. When I arrived at Saint-Paul, there were two of them, mustached, fifty years old, not very fit, looking like '70s clones. A homemade commode with a real toilet seat lid was enthroned in the living room, just high enough to slide your head underneath. I fondled them a little to qualify for the coke. I concentrated on the one that was slightly less ugly than the other (and who was hard), but not too much, so I wouldn't upset his friend. I wanted to be sure that my lines were thick enough. They were. The coke was really cut like it almost always is in Paris, but OK it did a little something. Enough to send me to the bedroom, after having declined the honor of christening the living room toilet.

The one I thought was OK started fisting the other one while I spun around doing little things, like playing with nipples. Of course his bowels were full. After ten minutes it smelled so bad I started to retch. Then again. I almost barfed by the bedroom door, I barely held on. I'll be back! I told them, always full of fun when I'm high. It smelled better in the living room. I grabbed my clothes that were all over the couch. I got dressed. I went back into the bedroom to tell them I was taking off, holding my nose.

OK, you have our number, right? they asked, hard at work. Now the white plastic drop cloth was totally covered with it. I went to walk around Quetzal. Nothing was going on. I went home, too awake, but I didn't want to drag myself to Transfert.

27

(1994)

I'm a seduction machine. I wash and moisturize my body daily. I wear contacts. Lotion. A facial scrub once a week. I shave every third day. I trim my nose hair and ear hair, I trim my eyebrows, I shave my balls and my ass every two weeks, on the same schedule as my haircut. I trim the other areas of my body: pubes (1/8"), armpits (1/4 "), back, shoulders, chest (1/16" to accentuate my muscles), sometimes the legs too. I brush my teeth three times a day, I have my teeth cleaned every three months, I wear unscented deodorant, I eat enough protein to make the gym pay off in muscle. Aside from work, I only wear sexy clothes. I'm always in tight jeans, tight t-shirts, or tight tank tops, sometimes a butch plaid shirt, sometimes a bomber jacket with a jean jacket underneath (that was the style back then), or a classy new fad, the butch, waterproof outdoors jacket from the U.S. in a yellow-beige. Or else all of that before but with leather 501s. Those were perfect for shopping in the Marais.

Technically speaking, I'm at the top of my game. I am a pleasure machine. I receive people at home wearing leather chaps, leather thongs, Rangers. I have music, toys, drugs. I have an immaculately clean ass. I can do everything. I kiss. I lick. I suck. I pinch. I twist. I breathe in. I pull. I push. I stroke. I smack. I hold. I open. I spread. I go. I come. I delve. I piss. I drool. I spit. The only thing I still don't know how to do is come in a condom. I'm still able to have an effect. Now guys almost systematically want to go at it again. Everything is perfectly worked out. That's probably why it's not working anymore. It's not the pleasure that's absorbed me until now, but the apprenticeship.

28

(1994)

Finally I decided that I couldn't stay with Stéphane. I was sick of being like Quentin, staying with someone simply to take advantage. I was sick of watching him suffer. I left him.

29

(1994)

Les Docks. I could walk there from my new, grim apartment near Gare de l'Est. It was good because I didn't have the strength anymore to take the métro to go into the city spots in the center of town. Too long. My desire for sex couldn't withstand the four métro stops to Étienne-Marcel. As usual, I found the biggest dick in the backroom. I sucked it. After a while the guy asked me to go into one of the private rooms. He was young and handsome, and very well-built, in a tank top, baseball cap, tight jeans and boots. I accepted.

We finally found an empty one. We went in. We closed the door behind us. We kissed. How many guys have I made out with in my life? At least a thousand. I wasn't getting hard so I went down on his cock that was fat but especially long, hard but a little soft like I like it, outside of his jeans. I pumped it deep while choking on it, crouching so I wouldn't soil my 501s, while jerking off. He let me do it, he liked it, and then he grabbed my head with two hands and face-fucked me, that turned me on, I knelt on his boots and I sucked deeper, harder. He pulled me up and he kissed me, I ate his face, we were locked together, then he went down on my cock and he sucked me off, not well, it's terrible how most guys are bad at sucking, with the tips of their lips, with their teeth, not at the back of the throat, avoiding the balls. Too afraid of seeming like they really like it. Too afraid of coming off as sluts. I started to go soft. I stopped him. I went down on him again. That way at least I was sure that something intense would happen.

When I started to feel him getting close, I stopped. I got back up. I asked him You wouldn't want to fuck me? He said Yes. My ass isn't clean though, I said, we could go to my place, it's just nearby. He said No I can't get hard if I'm not in a sex club. I thought to myself Hardcore. I felt like I was close. I said OK. I went back down on him again, he was a little soft. I got busy. He got hard again, but slowly. I ended up coming before him because I couldn't wait anymore, on the floor between his boots. I kept going a bit. He still wouldn't come. I was starting to get fed up blowing him now that I had come, so I stood up and I started nibbling on his nipple, he had the big nipples of a sex pro. I cupped his balls while he jerked off, and then I moved over to the other nipple and then I could feel that he was really getting close so I kissed him, really hard, as if I wanted him for the rest of my life, my arm around his waist, really tight, my left hand still on his nipple, and he came and I came closer and I took him in my arms. We stayed there a moment cheek to cheek until it started to fade. We got dressed. I asked him his first name. We vacated the private room.

30

(1995)

I wasn't going to the gym anymore.

* * *

One exceptional night I went to Keller. The place where I had met Stéphane a year and several months before. I got hit on by this beautiful leather pussycat, dirty blond (like Terrier), with a goatee (like half of Paris). I was drunk (as usual), I took him home with me, in the comfort of the music, the joints, the lube at hand, and the best selection of dildos.

We kissed. He worked up a ton of saliva. I told myself Ah! He's into drool play. Two minutes later, bingo, he was drooling on the tip of my lips. I swallowed to give him the green light. He spit on my face and then licked it back up. We traded off spitting on each other and licking it off in the sensitive spots, while drinking some beer and pissing on each other (spitting implies pissing as a general rule). He fucked me (safe), for five minutes, and then he came.

31

(1995)

I was alone. I didn't go out to nightclubs or bars anymore. I was a star who no longer wanted to play. A faun who no longer wanted to dance. All that was left was what I had made my life about for so long: joints, the Minitel.

* * *

Forty years old, beginner S&M, looking to get dominated… I told him I wasn't interested. To begin with I never do beginners. Too much work. And certainly not beginners who were forty years old. No guy who was in relatively good shape would admit to being forty years old on the Minitel. They'd say thirty-six and then I would do them.

He hit me up again that same night, I logged on again (our phone bill was pretty high in those days). U WANNA MAKE $$? I laughed since, in the end, all these tricks knew the magic word. I wrote back, YES, CC?, A way to profit off my toys. He offered 1500 francs. I had already done this two or three times with Quentin so I knew how much a long session cost, it was around 2000. I said, OK 1500 1ST, BUT 2000 AFTER. I waited. YOU HAVE A MESSAGE PRESS *SENT, I saw on the screen. NOR-MALLY ITS CHEAPER AFTER, my future client mentioned. I replied, NO AFTER ITS MORE MONEY BECAUSE YOU WON'T BE ABLE TO DO WITHOUT ME.

We spent hours on the Minitel. He said that he didn't dare talk to me on the phone just yet, that he would give me another 200 francs to pay for the chat. He wasn't stupid. He asked all the smart questions. DO YOU HAVE SOME HASH? ALCOHOL? HOW DO YOU FUCK? DO YOU ALTERNATE WITH CARESSES? WHAT KIND OF MUSIC? I said DANCE, HOUSE, TRANCE. He said that he liked trance for sex, but that he preferred techno. I was surprised he knew so much. Apparently, he was really well-versed in my field of work. He asked me what he should call me. He didn't like "master" too much. I agreed that it was actually a bit ridiculous. And anyway, he wasn't into boot-licking.

I asked him what he liked. Getting his dick worked over, his balls, especially his balls. To be bound. He wanted to be bound quickly. And to wear a mask so he couldn't see me. He said I could take it off later, pull him by his hair, slap him, that he already had done that and he liked it. He said that he had just discovered sex, that he had always worked too hard, that it didn't leave him any time, and then that he had just begun recently, that he had realized that he liked to be dominated, that he had accepted it because it was good for him, that he felt better mentally, even at work, that it gave him confidence, he said It's like when they say a woman is well-fucked. He asked me what I thought. I said that I thought that to really experience his sexuality with other men he had to be both a top and a bottom. But that it was already a good thing that he had accepted being passive.

The next day he called. He wanted to role-play. In his movie he wanted to be Jim, the eighteen-year-old virgin kid on the school's soccer team who'd come to be trained by me, the team's coach, a total womanizer who was infamous in our small town. It was going to be hard to pull off the super athlete part, I hadn't been eating these days ever since I became single. I told myself that I was still manly enough to be credible. I was already annoyed but

I said, OK. We planned for a weeknight, around eight p.m. I warned him that at midnight, I would kick him out.

The day of our meeting I came home early. I had everything ready. For everything to go off without a hitch. I took out everything we could use. Handcuffs and footcuffs. Dog collar. Ball parachute and clothespins (when you're really horny, you don't feel the pain. Up to a certain point). Cock sleeve, nipple clamps, inflatable gag, martinet, riding crop. Ice cubes in a Tupperware, some whisky, glasses, three joints, two towels, a butt plug, a child-sized butt plug, he said he was pretty much a virgin, a tube of xylocaine. Everything was in arm's reach by a small table near the bed. I hooked up some nylon ropes to the mattress' handles. Laid out the black plastic shower curtain over the bed. I put on a trance compilation album on the laser player. It was ten to eight. Shit, where is the leather mask? I put my cock ring on, my leather thong, with a zipper, my Rangers, my chaps. A t-shirt so I wouldn't catch a cold. The heater was turned all the way up but it wasn't super warm. He was late. I lit a joint. I drank some whisky with ice. He called to say he was sorry, he had been held up by his boss, and yes, at eight p.m. on a weeknight, that's the way it was at his job. I didn't say anything. He said he was on his way. I waited.

He buzzed. I opened the door of the apartment. He was supposed to walk in alone, walk down the hallway, turn towards the door on his right. I was supposed to come up behind him from the living room where I was waiting for him, throw his mask on and blindfold him (my mask didn't have a zipper). Everything went as planned. He was really short, very bulky, pretty dorky, bowl haircut. His undershirt was soaked in sweat. Gross. I put the mask on him, I blindfolded him. I grabbed the bottle of whisky that he had brought and that I wouldn't ever drink because it was J&B. Oh well.

I grabbed him by the strings of the mask, on top of the head, and I pulled him towards the bedroom. The situation excited me. I threw him to his knees, I made him smell my package, I pulled his pants and his underwear down around his thighs, I smacked his ugly fat ass. So Jimmy boy, you like to be used, you filthy little whore! He had huge balls and the tiniest dick. I grabbed his balls, pulled them backwards, that made him squirm, I pulled harder, until he had to take a step backwards, I said Well, yeah, you're going to have to move if you want to keep them! I made him walk around the room two or three times, pulling him like that. He was out of his mind.

I stopped. He was pretty knocked out, out of breath. I decided I would start to get him drunk. I poured him a first glass of whisky on ice, directly in his mouth. I made sure he drank it all. That's why he was here, to no longer be in control. Come on! A bit more! Yeaaah! And now you're going to smoke a little, then you'll be wasted for what's next. I shoved a joint into his mouth. He took a hit. It made him cough. I made him take another. It felt good to be a little mean. He looked up at me with his watery eyes and said I've never felt so good. I made him shut up by shoving his face back into my package. You want my cock, eh, you little bitch, etc. I pulled it out. I've never had my dick sucked so terribly. Teeth, not much further than the tip, yes sure, he had a mask on, that wasn't really practical, but still. People don't understand the value of hard work.

Thirty minutes had already gone by since he arrived, everything was going OK so far and I didn't want the voltage to drop. I decided that now was a good time to tie him up. I put the leather handcuffs on him, his hands at the front. Now get undressed. Yes you can, come on, go for it! I whipped him a little so he wouldn't lose himself in the depressing monotony of undressing. I tied his hands and feet spread-eagle, onto the black shower curtain that was just thick enough for it to feel sexual. I got to work. I pulled on his nipples (he had little tufts of hair around them, it had been years since I had seen that. Everyone is shaved in my world). I pulled on his balls, I put clothespins on them, Jimmy was going to have to suffer a bit if he wanted to stay on the team. The music was grinding all around us. All of a sudden, I remembered the ice cubes. They hadn't completely melted yet, that way I didn't have to go back to the kitchen, which was good because I was feeling lazy, and pretty tipsy from the joints and the whisky I was knocking back between the abuse. I rubbed the ice cubes over his balls, his cock, his nipples, pushing them down, waiting for them to burn. He moaned a little. A little harder if I stayed in the same spot for a while.

I whipped him for a long time, symmetrically, over his whole body, over his balls, his tiny hard dick that I held in my hand, with little lashes, smack, smack, smack, smack, I went up, I went down, on his stomach, on his chest, on his mask, it was good because I could make it last awhile without getting tired. I had to keep going for another two and a half hours, until midnight. I unhooked him. I brought him to the bathroom. Threw him in the tub. I showered him, hot water, cold water. I concentrated especially on his package. I pissed on him. He said he had never felt so good in a bathtub. I told him I was sure of that. I felt sorry for him, ugly and alone as he was. In a certain sense I could have even said that I loved him.

I ended up blowing him. I had tried to fuck him with the dildo. Strictly impossible since he was nervously clenching his ass. Then my little plug that only went in halfway. That annoyed me. I whipped him again, fairly mechanically, that made him seriously hard, so I leaned over and started to suck his tiny dick again, It tasted pretty bad, not dirty, just old. But for 1500 francs, I thought that this was the least I could do. After two minutes I stopped. I played with his nipples. He came. I pulled off the mask. He told me I was beautiful.

He told me that he wouldn't call right away, that he was OK for a while, let's say two weeks from now. Two days later he was hitting me up. I told him So, eating makes you hungrier, huh? But he wasn't calling to make an appointment, he was calling just to talk. That annoyed me. He told me he couldn't stop jerking off thinking about what had happened. He said Usually what gets me excited is in my head but with you it was also my body, it seemed like the mind served the body. I told him Yeah that sounds right. Then he asked me if I thought he was slutty enough. I told him that there was still a lot of work to do. He called the following week. This time it was serious.

It didn't go so well. I positioned the mattress against the wall to form a Saint Andrew's cross with straps. He couldn't handle the position. Clearly, it must have been twenty years since he had last exercised. I got frustrated with his ass, it was impossible to get my index finger in, after three whiskeys, two joints, and two hours of fucking around. He asked me again if he was a real slut yet. I said, Yeah, it was encouraging, thinking about the 2000 francs I'd be making this time. He never stopped talking, spinning his stupid scenario, soccer, the team, blah, blah, blah, and I saw you in the locker room showers, blah, blah, blah. I answered, I had to answer. After a while I got too grossed out, I shoved his underwear in his mouth for some peace and quiet.

In the end I didn't have a clue how I was going to be able to get him to come. I remembered he liked getting smacked. I did that, I pulled on his hair, I bitch-slapped him. That invigorated him a bit. I untied one of his hands so he could jerk off. He still wasn't coming. Then an idea came to me: I grabbed him by the hand he wasn't using and I lifted him up in the air, my arms outstretched, so that he could feel my strength. He jerked off in a frenzy. He ended up coming like that. Then he left. I felt really tired.

I found him on the Minitel two days later. He asked me what I thought. I told him what I thought, that it was a start. BUT YOU HAD ME HUNG 4 HRS!, he protested. I told him that to realize his dreams he had to start by going to the gym three times a week for a while. He never contacted me again.

32

(1995)

The choice was clear: I needed to buy a sling and suspend it permanently over my bed (like Patrice Collivot, who had a photo of his cock by Mapplethorpe, and who was dead. When I met him, years earlier, he teased me with the promise of an orgy, I'd get fucked by a group of his friends: an Asian who would open up my ass, a hairy macho lumberjack who would fuck me, another well-hung guy who would fuck me with dildos, and him. It never happened. I jerked off for years thinking about it). Or stop everything. Leave. Leave Quentin. Leave my father. Leave Paris.

I was offered a job in the tropics, on the other side of the world. I was going to write my book there, the result of the few sessions I had with a shrink. Dying under the palm trees was out of the question. I told myself that I still had three years, the length of my contract. Here my journey was over. My journey to the end of sex. Now I knew everything. Everything except the impossible. Torturing kids, sperm orgies. I had reached the impossible.

33

(1995)

And then one night there was a mouth to be filled just a ten-minute walk away, on Paradise Street. I went. The guy was really young, twenty-four or twenty-five years old. Pretty shy. I was surprised by the apartment, white with only a few objects, not stuck-up, souvenirs from Africa where he was an aid worker.

Me standing up, him on the sofa, I quickly realized that he was really enjoying it. So I took my time. A long time. When I was ready I asked him if he wanted to swallow it. He said he really liked it in the face. So I pulled out and I jerked off two seconds while talking to him. I exploded. He squirted three feet in the air.

34

(1995)

I still did some dumb shit before disappearing. I hooked up on the Minitel with a young guy, twenty-three years old. We had an orgy without condoms with a third, a pale blond guy around my age. The younger kid was getting fucked doggy-style by the blond. I stood on top of the bed, the blond was blowing me. I turned around so he could eat my ass while he screwed. I watched all of it in the mirror in front of me. And then I got down and I shoved my dick inside the little boy's ass alongside the blond's. It was an amazing sensation, my dick smashed up against his inside this guys ass, in only ten seconds I was about to bust, I had to pull out fast to keep myself from coming.

We went on for hours, we didn't stop fucking, using dildos. We didn't even go soft when we stopped to drink or smoke. The blond guy left, I think he was a little overwhelmed. I kept fucking the little one. He wanted me to finish inside him. I started driving harder and harder, I would pull on the belt I threw around his waist so I could hold on tighter, I was getting closer and closer. Go for it! Fill me up! He said. At the last moment I stopped.

I finished inside another guy, an old ugly guy. He had asked me to do it but it still freaked me out. I saw the nurse again. He showed up carrying a Balzac novel, Pléiade edition. That surprised me. I wondered why he bothered reading if all he really liked was getting guys to cum inside him. Me, I hadn't read anything in the past seven years, except for *Less Than Zero* and

Sandra Bernhard's book that some guy had given to Quentin. There were also some books on zen right before leaving Quentin. And now *The Tibetan Book of the Dead* that a friend had given me for my trip.

35

(1995)

Sitting on the plane I already knew that by leaving I had made the best decision of my life. What was going to happen could be average, super, or even a catastrophe, it didn't matter. I had left. I had done something for myself.

I didn't know anyone at the start of my stay. I went grocery shopping almost every day just to put my mind at ease. But I hadn't made a mistake. Between the birds chirping, the trees growing green, the flowers in bloom, the hens, the black roosters, the cats, the dogs, the mountain, the lagoon, the fish, the slow-moving people, the heat, reality was having an impact on me. The Parisian despondency dissipated. I forgot about death. Nothing was rushed. I would go get my mail once a week from the post office. I would swim. I thought about Stéphane. Why didn't he ever hold me in his arms? Maybe he was scared I would leave. But why did he think I wouldn't be interested in his day? "Oh I'm not good at telling stories." Or even, "You're such a good cook." I couldn't help but lament that attitude.

I looked for a house. I had already seen a few with my real estate agent Ginette who had seven cats because she wanted one in each color. The last one, the farthest from the city, was white, big and open, bordering a lagoon with a big garden that opened up on the beach, the sea, the sky. It was available in three weeks, and only for six months. Take it, even for only six months, Ginette said. Then you'll have lived six months by the sea.

My HIV status. That was another reason why I left Stéphane. The results of the test he never wanted to take came back negative. That was the last straw for me. With Quentin it was different, I was already with him before. I thought that I could only love someone who was positive. Unless I fell in love with a foreigner. I thought about all the sources of love in my life, about Catherine C., about M., about Terrier, about…

* * *

After a month, I decided to start having sex. I waited until eleven thirty to go out. Drove into town. I went into the club where all the local trannies went. I ordered a gin-get. Dolly, the beautiful barmaid, threw back her long hair. She asked me my first name. I said Guillaume. She asked Are you military? I replied Not exactly. She let it go, discreet. I went to dance. A remix of *Sweet Dreams* was playing. I went back to the bar. Dolly said I want you to meet someone. She introduced me to Richard, a tall blond guy, a little stooped, a little soft. I had sex with Richard. It wasn't that great, but it relaxed me.

36

(1995)

I had a few local contacts through people I knew in Paris. I ended up calling them. I grabbed a drink with Rosine L. in town. I don't know how we got started talking about Buddhism. We agreed to meet up a couple of days later to hear a Tibetan monk who had come to give some teachings. I picked her up. I remember my arrival perfectly. I rang the buzzer outside the gate. No one answered. Yet I could hear voices farther away in the garden. I slid the latch, pushed the wood door open. A dog came up, quickly, barking. Someone yelled for him to be quiet.

We're back here! Rosine called out. I followed the stone path back to the patio overlooking the ocean, the dog at my feet. Rosine was back there with four young people. She introduced me to her daughter Tina, a cute twenty-something blond in shorts and a t-shirt. Another small blond, Delphine. Finally, two guys who seemed a little older, sitting at the table: André, Marcelo. Their boyfriends, I thought. Maybe even their husbands, people tend to get married young over here. André, a very handsome-looking, surfer type, said Hi without getting up, but with a big smile. The other guy, dark-haired, brooding, intense, looked at me without saying a word. I felt vulnerable. Later he told me that as soon as he saw me he wanted to fuck me because of the way I was petting the dog, as if my life depended on it.

I found myself immersed in a Tibetan session surrounded by banana trees. It was good but I knew all about it already. When we got back, Rosine invited me to have a drink. Tina had left a note on the counter in the kitchen. She was inviting us to a barbecue at her father's. Rosine asked me if I wanted to go. I said Yes, of course. Night had already fallen. I went back home to change.

I met up with Rosine near the path, as we had agreed. I drove her car, ill at ease with the abrupt rise towards the interior. Another dog welcomed us. There were only about five or six other guests. After dinner the girls went for a swim, topless, giggling with the brooding guy. I didn't really hesitate joining them. It was really hot. I thought L.A., but smaller. Tina was hitting on me. Then I felt a little drunk. The brooding guy was walking back with a cigarette in the corner of his mouth. I found him handsome. Virile. Since I was drunk, I let myself ask him which one was his girlfriend. None of them, he said, I don't like girls. Oh? Me neither, I added. Silence.

Rosine went back home. The girls wanted to go out to the club. I followed along. Tina drove us in her car, an emerald-green Polo, speeding down the hill. I put my hand on her thigh. I decided I wanted to be straight now. It was too hard being a fag. I felt that Delphine and the brooding guy in the back noticed what I was doing. After a while I pulled my hand away.

At the nightclub, my three new friends went crazy on the lame dance music. The brooding guy moved well, I thought. It was very hot. I was a little drunk again. He sat down next to me. I asked him, Would you want to have sex with me one of these days? Not one of these days, he said. Tonight. Tonight or never? I said. He replied Yes. I was a little annoyed. I said OK.

We caught up with the girls as we were exiting the club. They had gone nearby to Paradise for a while, where there were fewer sailors and whores and more preppy locals. I told Tina, I'm gonna go do Marcelo. Oh really, you like him?, she said, completely drunk. I told her You don't get it, I don't *want* to do him, I am *going* to do him now. We're going to his place. No problem, I'll drop you off, she said. I thought she was really cool. On the way back I was in the back seat, my hand on Marcelo's thigh, Marcelo's hand on mine. The girls were screaming and laughing in the front seat, the music, better than at the club, was blaring loud.

Marcelo lived in a room in a former police barracks that was converted into student lodging. He wanted me to put on a condom when we blew each other. That surprised me. Then I sat on him. He fucked me. He started off too fast, like some macho man. Slowly, slowly, I said. My sweat dripping onto his skin. Then the bedroom filled with our cigarette smoke. The rest is another story. I will tell it later.[8]

Epilogue

(1998)

I was finishing up the latest revisions, in the country. I changed the order of certain chapters to clarify the development of the story. I tightened some sentences. I had finally decided not to put quotes at the start of every chapter, I would keep only one as an epigraph, one that I had gotten from a Soviet writer whom I had discovered by chance but whose work I became familiar with (I ended up adding another, from a great track by Trannies with Attitude that I had wanted to use in *I'm Going Out Tonight*, but didn't fit).

I went to sleep without any joints or Lexomil. It was nice to just drift off from fatigue. When I got up to pee, it was cold, I decided to go back to sleep for a little while. I started to dream. In my dream, at first I had some problems on the métro, I had to change lines, stations. It's actually something that happens a lot to me. Then I went back up into the fresh air and I studied a map to go somewhere, a map where Belleville was above Neuilly. There weren't a lot of métro stations where I could get off. I had to go to the Left Bank, it seemed like I was living at rue Duméril, where I used to live when I was at Sciences-Po, between 1986 and 1988. I got off in the 16th arrondissement. I wanted to cross over the Seine. I walked along the streets. Very soon I was at the intersection of the Champ de Mars gardens. It wasn't the right way, so I turned left. Here the avenue Richepin started, where, I remember, Séverine L. used to live, an old acquaintance.

At the spot where the avenue split in two stood a luxurious building, a sort of department store, pierced with bay windows, through which you could see a colossal bronze statue rising, with a red backdrop, under sparkling ceiling lights. The front steps that led up to the building were engraved, Girls on one side, Boys on the other, like in primary school. On the other side of the building was a street lined with houses with protruding *bow windows* and overhanging second floors. The architecture of wealthy neighborhoods. I often dream of cities these days. I thought that I should have brought Marcelo to visit that place, he's such a fan of the Poste du Louvre.

In front of me was this building with an exterior that looked like a church or a Spanish palace, intimidating, nearly free of any openings. I pushed open the door, and entered into a large, bare room, where a miniscule sign told of an exhibition. I decided to leave. When I went to pull on the door, a door that was covered in leather like church doors, it flew open. I just barely avoided it, letting pass a biker in a full body suit, followed by his wife, also in a motorcycle jumpsuit. The biker, instead of an apology, muttered "Huh." Sorry would be better than Huh, I said. He kept going without answering. I left. I looked at the map in a bus shelter. The maps designated uncrossable marshlands, no bridge. It was apparently impossible to cross the Seine. A little boy who was there with his class knocked into my legs. He seemed like an adult in miniature, I wanted to fight with him but he was so little that I just told him to watch where he was going.

Then I noticed that the entrance to the métro was there, only several meters away, on the other side of the avenue. I took a few steps but then changed my mind, I felt like going to see what was at the end of this other street on my right, a paved road at the end of which was another building, like a palace from the seventeenth century with ornamentation repeated in the same pattern.

I walked up close to it to study the faded stone. Palm trees lined the street that ran across in front of it. There was this kind of giant cloakroom that looked like a construction shed down the alley and from far away I could see that it contained the coats of the postal workers who worked there. Soon it was the end of the work day. As I got closer to the palace, I realized that the awning that surrounded it was completely occupied by animals. Dozens and dozens of animals with pinky beige fur, whom at first I couldn't distinguish from each other, started moving. There were monkeys, as big as bears, who were sleeping on top of each other. A crocodile, its mouth open, was perched not far from them at the top of a slide, but he was tethered with a chain around his neck and couldn't do them any harm.

The monkeys started to wake up. I decided to retrace my steps before they pestered me, but one of them sat up on its bottom, stretched out, yawned and jumped down to the bottom of the awning. I heard it behind me: Hey! My name is Junior Wood-chuck. Give me something. I turned around. He was right there, almost as big as I was, his fur was all black now. I looked for something to give him. I didn't have anything on me, just a couple of coins. I was scared he would be offended if I gave him money, but I told myself I would give him the prettiest coin I had. I picked out a two-franc coin for the hexagonal border around it. I placed the coin in his hand. He smiled and told me that he was actually collecting coins. So I thought that for the trouble I could touch him. I placed two fingers on his back. His coat was soft and thick, the flesh muscular underneath. I pulled out my coins to give him something even better. I chose a very small Dutch coin, ten centimes. He was going to be happy with something so rare. He was. He told me I was kind. Not like the other guys who came to fuck him at night in his cage. He liked sex, but the men who came around hurt him, they went too fast, too hard. And why couldn't they wear condoms, isn't there some kind of disease going around?

I opened my eyes. Outside the sun was shining. I thought that this dream was perfect for the book. I started to tell it to myself so I wouldn't forget.

Totally fucked up, that dream.

Trash 2000.

Thank you to Christine B., my mom, Jean-Xavier D., P.O.L., T.F., F.M., Hugo M., Jacky F., Christophe Vix.

Notes

Introduction

1. Christine Angot, Renaud Camus, Virginie Despentes, Annie Ernaux, Michel Houellebecq, Camille Laurens, Catherine Millet, and Marc-Édouard Nabe have all had to grapple with society and had problems with literary legitimacy.

2. David Vrydaghs, "Personne n'a dit que Guillaume Dustan était un intellectuel, ou les raisons d'un échec," *@nalyses* 1, no. 1 (Winter 2006): 207–21.

3. Pierre Bourdieu, "Quelques questions sur la question gay et lesbienne," in *Les études gay et lesbiennes*, ed. Didier Éribon (Paris: Editions du centre Pompidou, 1997).

4. This issue will be examined in the second volume of *Works*.

5. Michel Foucault, "Conversation avec Werner Schroeter," in *Dits et écrits: 1954–1988*, vol. 4, 1980–1988, ed. Daniel Defert, François Ewald, and Jacques Lagrange (Paris: Gallimard, 1994), 1074.

6. See *Dictionnaire de l'homophobie*, ed. Louis-Georges Tin (Paris: Presses Universitaires de France, 2003).

7. Guillaume Dustan, editorial, *e.m@le*, no. 66, December 1999.

8. In French, the word *genre* refers to both gender and genre.—Trans.

9. The fact that Dustan used a pseudonym and substituted characters' names (to be revealed in subsequent books) in no way invalidates these works' basic autobiographical perspective. This was simply a form of protection that, in fact, *confirms* the referential anchoring of the texts.

10. The term *autofiction*, which Dustan rarely uses, is poorly suited to his work.

11. Philippe Gasparini, *Autofiction: Une aventure du langage* (Paris: Seuil, 2008), 304. Dustan's work is associated with the notion of "obscenity."

12. Pascal de Duve, *Cargo Vie* (Paris: JC Lattès, 1993); and Alain-Emmanuel Dreuilhe, *Corps à corps* (Paris: Gallimard, 1987).

13. Harold Brodkey, *This Wild Darkness: The Story of My Death* (New York: Henry Holt, 1996); and Cyril Collard, *Savage Nights*, trans. William Rodarmor (Woodstock, NY: Overlook, 1994).

14. See Gilles Barbedette, *L'Invitation au mensonge* (Paris: Gallimard, 1989).

15. François Cusset's *Queer critics: La littérature française déshabillée par ses homolecteurs* (Paris: Presses Universitaires de France, 2002) does not mention Dustan.

16. See *Les spirales du sens chez Renaud Camus*, ed. Ralph Sarkonak (Amsterdam and New York: Rodopi, 2009).

17. Frederic Martel, *Le Rose et le Noir: Les homosexuels en France depuis 1968* (Paris: Seuil, 1996), 514.

18. "Back then there was no treatment. Statistically, I had about five years left." Dustan, *Stronger Than Me*, in this volume, 286.

19. This issue will be examined in the second volume of *Works*.

20. Michel Foucault, *The History of Sexuality*, vol. 1, *An Introduction*, trans. Robert Hurley (New York: Vintage Books, 1990), 59.

21. Ibid., 21.

22. For another point of view, see Philippe Artières, "Michel Foucault et l'autobiographie," in *Michel Foucault: La littérature et les arts*, ed. Philippe Artières (Paris: Éditions Kimé, 2004).

23. Michel Foucault, "The Lives of Infamous Men," in *Essential Works of Foucault, 1954–1984*, vol. 3, *Power*, ed. James D. Faubion, trans. Robert Hurley (New York: New Press, 2000), 166.

24. See Pierre Rivière, *I, Pierre Rivière, Having Slaughtered My Mother, My Sister, and My Brother…: A Case of Parricide in the 19th Century*, ed. Michel Foucault, trans. Frank Jellinek (Lincoln: University of Nebraska Press, 1982); and Michel Foucault, "L'écriture de soi," in *Dits et écrits: 1954–1988*, vol. 4, *1980–1988*, 415–430.

25. Frédéric Gros, *Michel Foucault* (Paris: Presses Universitaires de France, 2004), 91.

26. See Roland Barthes, *Roland Barthes by Roland Barthes*, trans. Richard Howard (New York: Farrar, Straus and Giroux, 1977); and Michael Foucault, *The Hermeneutics of the Subject: Lectures at the Collège de France 1981–1982*, ed. Frédéric Gros, trans. Graham Burchell (New York: Palgrave Macmillan, 2005).

27. The expression comes from Albert Thibaudet's 1922 monograph, *Gustave Flaubert* (Paris: Gallimard, 1992).

28. This subheading alludes to an interview of Michel Foucault by Bernard-Henri Lévy, originally published in *Le Nouvelle Observateur*, March 12, 1977. See "Power and Sex: An Interview with Michel Foucault," trans. David J. Parent, *Telos*, no. 32 (Summer 1977): 152–61.

29. Michel Foucault, "Friendship as a Way of Life," interview by R. de Ceccaty, J. Danet, and J. Le Bitoux, in *Essential Works of Foucault, 1954–1984*, vol. 1, *Ethics: Subjectivity and Truth*, ed. Paul Rabinow, trans. Robert Hurley (New York: New Press, 1997), 136.

30. Éric Marty, *Pourquoi le XXe siècle a-t-il pris Sade au sérieux?* (Paris: Seuil, 2011).

31. Foucault, "Friendship as a Way of Life," 136.

32. Monique Wittig, preface to *The Straight Mind and Other Essays* (Boston: Beacon, 2002), xiii.

33. "Sex is no longer the biggest secret to life," Foucault claims in *Dits et écrits*, vol. 2, *1976–1988*, ed. Daniel Defert, François Ewald, and Jacques Lagrange (Paris: Gallimard, 1994).

34. According to Dustan, the French Socialist Party is an example of this.

35. Michel de Certeau, *The Capture of Speech and Other Political Writings*, ed. Luce Giard, trans. Tom Conley (Minneapolis: University of Minnesota Press, 1997).

36. On Dustan as pornographer, see my introduction to *In My Room*, in this volume, 38–41.

37. This essential point will be developed in the second volume of *Works*.

38. *La Rabbia*, a documentary film directed partly by Pier Paolo Pasolini, 1963.—Trans.

IN MY ROOM

Introduction

1. A drawing by James Jarvis entitled *In My Room* illustrated another such column, published in the February 18, 1999, issue of *e.m@le*.

2. See Eve Kosofsky Sedgwick, *Epistemology of the Closet* (Berkeley: University of California Press, 1992).

3. Bénédicte Boisseron, "Post-coca et post-coïtum: La jouissance du logo chez Guillaume Dustan et 'Seinfeld,'" *L'Esprit créateur* 43, no. 2 (Summer 2003).

4. See Virginia Woolf, *A Room of One's Own* (New York: Harcourt, 1989).

5. Guillaume Dustan, *In My Room*, in this volume, 93.

6. In *Subjectivity and the Ageing Process in Twentieth-Century French Writing*, a doctoral dissertation defended at the University of Wadham in 2003, Oliver Davis opposes Hervé Guibert to Dustan and his supposed ageism.

7. See my introduction to this volume.

8. Marguerite Duras, "Retake," in *Le monde extérieur: Outside 2* (Paris: P.O.L., 1993), 12.

9. See, for example, Ruwen Ogien, *Penser la pornographie* (Paris: Presses Universitaires de France, 2003).

10. Georges Molinié, *De la pornographie* (Paris: Éditions Mix, 2007).

11. Laurent de Sutter, *Contre l'érotisme* (Paris: La Musardine, 2010).

12. Clerc uses a play on words in the original French, "Neutre Intense," which is also the title of an art exhibition that he cocurated in London, 2008.—Trans.

13. Pascal Quignard, *Sex and Terror*, trans. Chris Turner (London: Seagull Books, 2011).

14. Dustan, *In My Room*, 92.

15. Ibid., 73.

In My Room

1. Le Keller, a gay nightclub located on a street of the same name, in the Paris neighborhood of Bastille. [Words that appear in English in the original text have been italicized.—Trans.]

2. The Queen, a gay nightclub located on the Champs-Elysées, a shrine to nocturnal gay life. Bataclan, a concert hall located on Boulevard Voltaire.

3. Le Transfert, a gay nightclub in the first arrondissement of Paris.

4. Yanko, a Parisian sex shop.

5. Quetzal Bar, a gay bar in the Marais district.

6. SOS Médecins offers house-call emergency services.

7. Le Bon Pêcheur, a large café in Les Halles shopping center.

8. The QG, a gay bar in the Marais district.

9. Modern Mesclun, a character from *Agrippine*, a well-known comic, named after its teenage heroine, by French comic-book artist Claire Brétecher.

10. La Loco, a Parisian nightclub located on Boulevard de Clichy in the eighteenth arrondissement, just a few steps from Moulin Rouge.

11. ASMF, the Association of Sado-Masochist Fetishists.

12. The Minitel, a French ancestor to the Internet, frequently used in the gay world for meeting people, retired in 2012.

13. Folies Pigalle, a nightclub for both straights and gays.

14. Au Diable des Lombards, a hip café-restaurant in Les Halles, trendy in the 1980s.

I'M GOING OUT TONIGHT

Introduction

1. *Saturday Night Fever*, American film directed by John Badham, 1978, starring John Travolta.

2. Consider, for example, Dostoyevsky's *The Gambler*, or Robbe-Grillet's *The House of Assignation*.

3. It should be noted that Anne Garréta preceded Dustan in this regard, with her 1986 novel *Sphinx*, which gave the nightclub its pedigree. Another predecessor was Renaud Camus (see my introduction to *In My Room*, in this volume, 40).

4. Dustan's reference to Dante appears very quickly in the text; see p. 168, in this volume. For Duras's statement, see "The Pleasures of the 6th Arrondissement," in *Practicalities: Marguerite Duras Speaks to Jérôme Beaujour*, trans. Barbara Bray (New York: Grove Press, 2000), 20.

5. Michel Foucault, "Of Other Spaces: Utopias and Heterotopias," in *Rethinking Architecture: A Reader in Cultural Theory*, ed. Neil Leach (New York: Routledge, 1997), 330–36.

6. Bénédicte Boisseron, "Post-coca et post-coïtum: La jouissance du logo chez Guillaume Dustan et 'Seinfeld,'" *L'Esprit créateur* 43, no. 2 (Summer 2003): 82.

7. Friedrich Nietzsche, *The Peacock and the Buffalo: The Poetry of Nietzsche*, trans. James Luchte (London: Continuum, 2010), 325.

8. See *I'm Going Out Tonight*, in this volume, 172.

9. For Dustan's panorama of French literature, see his novels *Nicolas Pages* and *Génie Divin*, forthcoming in the second volume of *Works*.

I'm Going Out Tonight

1. Gay Tea Dance (GTD), a dance party initially organized at Le Palace (see note 4, below) on Sunday afternoons.

2. Quick, Europe's first hamburger chain, with around four hundred restaurants.

3. Saint Jean, a café-tabac on Rue Lepic, in the eighteenth arrondissement of Paris. *I'm Going Out Tonight* is set in a Paris of nocturnal pleasures whose topography and traditions date back to the nineteenth century. Since the 1930s, the city's Quartier Pigalle has also earned a reputation as "the first Parisian homosexual islet." Frederic Martel, *Le Rose et le Noir: Les homosexuels en France depuis 1968* (Paris: Seuil, 1996), 121.

4. Le Palace, a nightclub located on the Rue du Faubourg-Montmartre, in the ninth arrondissement of Paris. In 1978, Roland Barthes devoted a text to the club; see "At Le Palace Tonight…" in *Incidents* (Berkeley: University of California Press, 1992), trans. Richard Howard, 45–48.

5. Les Bains, a straight nightclub located on Rue du Bourg-l'Abbé, in the third arrondissement of Paris.

6. *The second one* refers to *I'm Going Out Tonight* itself, Dustan's second novel, partly written in the prefecture of Var.

7. Lapin, we learn later, is the person to whom *I'm Going Out Tonight* is dedicated, Dustan's Chilean lover Marcelo.

8. Terrier, a character from Dustan's *In My Room*.

9. Au Diable des Lombards, a hip café-restaurant in Les Halles, trendy in the 1980s.

10. *3,000* refers to book sales for *In My Room*.

11. The many consecutive blank pages which follow are faithful to Dustan's vision for a revised edition of *I'm Going Out Tonight*; the first edition had fewer blanks.

STRONGER THAN ME

Introduction

1. See Michel Foucault, *Dits et écrits*, vol. 2, *1976–1988*, ed. Daniel Defert, François Ewald, and Jacques Lagrange (Paris: Gallimard, 1994), 1150 and 1556–1562. These interviews were initially published in English-language journals.

2. See Jean-François Lyotard, *The Postmodern Condition: A Report on Knowledge*, trans. Geoff Bennington and Brian Massumi (Minneapolis: University of Minnesota Press, 1984).

3. Germaine Bazin, *The Avant-Garde in Painting: An Interpretive History of the Great Innovators—from Giotto to Warhol*, trans. Simon Watson Taylor (New York: Simon & Schuster, 1969).

4. This text is extant in the Fonds Dustan at the l'Institut Mémoires de L'édition Contemporaine (Institute for Contemporary Publishing Archives), Abbey d'Ardenne, Calvados, Normandy.

5. Paul-Laurent Assoun, *Leçons psychanalytiques sur le masochisme* (Paris: Economica, 2003).

6. For discussions of this ruling, delivered in the 1997 case of Laskey, Jaggard, and Brown v. the United Kingdom, see *La liberté sexuelle*, ed. Daniel Borrillo and Danièle Lochak (Paris: Presses Universitaires de France, 2005).

7. Marguerite Duras, *Practicalities: Marguerite Duras Speaks to Jérôme Beaujour*, trans. Barbara Bray (New York: Grove Press, 2000), 40.

8. Fonds Dustan, l'Institut Mémoires de L'édition Contemporaine.

Stronger Than Me

1. Recall that Dustan's real surname was Baranès.

2. The Gardens of Trocadéro, a place of homosexual cruising, mentioned by Julien Green in *Journal*.

3. It is in Jean Genet's novel *Funeral Rites*, published in 1948, that one can find this scene between Riton, a militiaman, and Erik, a German soldier.

4. BH and Boy, gay nightclubs near Les Halles.

5. Broad, a gay nightclub near Les Halles.

6. FG, Fréquence Gaie, a radio station founded in support of the gay community, which began broadcasting in 1978 from the kitchen of the Argentine writer Copi. In 1991, the station distanced itself from social activism and redefined itself as a dedicated electronic-music station.

7. Terrier and Stéphane, characters from Dustan's *In My Room*.

8. Marcelo, also known as Lapin, is Dustan's Chilean lover, to whom *I'm Going Out Tonight* is dedicated. Dustan would later describe their relationship in *Nicolas Pages*, forthcoming in the second volume of *Works*.

ABOUT THE AUTHOR

Guillaume Dustan (1965–2005) worked as an administrative judge in France before turning to writing full-time. He is the author of eight books, including the award-winning novel *Nicholas Pages*. He was posthumously awarded the Prix Sade in 2013.